*'Beautifully written and gripping.
Worthy of a film on the big screen.'*
Chris Rogers, BBC

Also by Sarah de Carvalho

The Street Children of Brazil

Solomon's Song

Sarah de Carvalho

HODDER

First published in Great Britain in 2011 by Hodder & Stoughton
An Hachette UK company

1

Copyright © Sarah de Carvalho, 2011

The right of Sarah de Carvalho to be identified as the Author
of the Work has been asserted by her in accordance with the
Copyright, Designs and Patents Act 1988.

A CIP catalogue record for this title is available from the British
Library

ISBN 978 1 444 70188 3

Typeset in Simoncini Garamond by Palimpsest Book Production Ltd
Falkirk, Stirlingshire

Printed and bound in the UK by CPI Mackays, Chatham ME5 8TD

Hodder & Stoughton policy is to use papers that are natural,
renewable and recyclable products and made from wood grown
in sustainable forests. The logging and manufacturing processes
are expected to conform to the environmental
regulations of the country of origin.

Hodder & Stoughton Ltd
338 Euston Road
London NW1 3BH
www.hodder.co.uk

For John Roach

Set me as a seal upon thine heart,
as a seal upon thine arm:
for love is strong as death;
jealousy is cruel as the grave.

PART I

Chapter 1

Belonging

Serra dos Órgãos, Brazil, New Year's Eve 1987

'*S*olomon!' hissed his *Papai* without taking his sharp eyes from the moving fish, now lit suddenly into view under some rocks by a spear of sunlight. '*Vem, vem!*'

Solomon stood up, and with perfect balance picked his way over the small grey blocks of stone protruding above the level of the surging water that separated father and son. He waited in taut silence. The sound of waterfalls cascading into the river above and below them filled the air with a dull roar; above the roar could be heard the shrieks of the parrots, *maracanãs*, *maritaca*s and parakeets, as they flew in all directions overhead, clinging periodically onto tall trees in bright, noisy clusters.

'Duke!' breathed Solomon to his dog. 'Stay put!'

The large motley-coloured mongrel dropped to the ground, obeying his master, his eyes and tail betraying excitement.

Solomon watched as his father crouched even lower, his head down between his protruding knees, his dark face almost touching the surface of the cool glistening water, his straight black hair hanging forward, his athletic body quite motionless. When it came to fishing with bare hands, no one equalled the awesome skill of Ezio Itaborahy. Their Indian ancestors would have been proud of him, Solomon was sure. Suddenly, as fast as the tongue of a snake, his *Papai*'s fingers whipped forward into the cool mountain water and grabbed hold of his unsuspecting prey. In one fluid movement he jumped to his feet and threw the stunned *dourado* high into the air towards his son. Solomon's mouth opened in surprise as he watched the fish flying through the air. Time seemed to shut down into slow-moving frames with each swing of the head and tail as the fish sent hundreds and thousands of droplets of water like stars into the atmosphere. Solomon was balanced on a small rock, his toes clenched firmly on the warm grey stone, the knuckles showing through his olive skin as he watched the fish begin its descent. He lunged forward into the river, stretching his arms full length as the fish spun downwards and fell heavily but squarely into the net.

Ezio punched the air in triumph, laughing. 'Happy fourteenth birthday, my son!'

Solomon closed his eyes and exhaled. Duke, unable to contain himself any longer, splashed out into the river after his master, barking joyously.

'*E grande demais*! It must weigh three kilos!'

'It's the catch of the year!' bellowed Pedro, Solomon's ten-year-old brother, through cupped hands. Pedro had been watching them from a huge black rock that hung about four metres above the river.

'*Papai*! Solomon!' cried another voice. '*Mamae*'s calling you back home for lunch!'

It was Talita, Pedro's twin. She stood at the edge of the river, her shiny black hair blowing across her face. Pedro climbed down and jumped into the river to help his brother. Getting hold of the tail, Solomon smashed the fish's head quickly and efficiently against a rock. It fell still.

As they set off together down the familiar path which meandered over the mountainside and into the valley below, Ezio swung Talita onto his broad shoulders, her little feet neatly tucked under his armpits. Pedro followed close behind with Solomon bringing up the rear, the prized fish lying in the net over his shoulder and Duke padding faithfully beside him, watching carefully that the fish did not escape. The Paraiso river ran beside them all the way with sporadic waterfalls forming deep pools ideal for swimming. The tropical midday summer sun sent shafts of brilliant light through the tops of the tall, leafy trees. At this high altitude the temperature never rose much above twenty degrees centigrade.

'I could walk this path blindfolded!' declared Pedro confidently.

'Well, what are you waiting for?' Talita laughed, her almond-shaped eyes glinting.

'No, really I can! I've counted my steps from each mark.'

'OK, do it! Do it!' interrupted Solomon, who was impatient to get back. 'Here, I'll tie my t-shirt round your eyes. Turn around.'

Solomon put the net down on the damp earth. He removed his old black t-shirt, revealing a maturing, agile body, lean but muscular.

Duke was sniffing and whining with excitement at the lifeless *dourado*.

'Duke, *sai*! Leave the fish alone. *Sai*!' demanded Solomon.

He tied the shirt as tightly as possible around Pedro's small head.

'Ouch!' cried Pedro.

'He can see! Look, he's holding his head up so he can see underneath!' shouted Talita, pointing with her finger.

'No I can't!' replied Pedro indignantly.

'Let's get started, Pedro, or we'll never get to Solomon's party,' said their father firmly.

'Wait!' exclaimed Pedro, struggling to establish his balance. 'I've got to be near one of my marks, otherwise I can't start my counting, can I?'

'The small stone bridge is just ahead,' replied *Papai*. 'Solomon, lead him there!'

Solomon picked up the fish from under Duke's gaze and led Pedro on down the path to the small stone bridge. Pedro started counting out loud, 'One, two, three, four . . .' with his thin arms stretched out in front of him like sticks, his legs marching like a wooden soldier.

They all followed, slowly. Solomon looked around at the world he loved. Nothing could be more beautiful than this, he was sure. Tall trees loomed above them, some as high as nine metres. Long and endless twisted vines poured themselves over the uppermost branches and fell all around the tropical forest like elegant drapes. Trails of giant ants followed each other across the narrow path in perfectly choreographed lines and disappeared under the shadow of elephantine leaves. The forest was ringing with birdsong.

'. . . twenty-one, twenty-two, twenty-three . . .' chanted Pedro with Talita's help.

The surrounding flora gradually changed as their path descended. Lofty bamboo replaced the towering trees. Sunlight poured over the landscape and a breeze wafted towards them from the river, making the myriad leaves of the bamboo shiver.

The narrow path ended suddenly as they came to the lower ridge of the mountain slope. Solomon ran on ahead, overtaking the blinded Pedro, and climbed the wooden gate. His five favourite mountains sat like vast curtains in a petrified circle around their valley. Brilliant shades of changing greens spread themselves as far and as wide as he could see. Solomon was conscious once again of a deep sense of belonging, a belonging he believed he could never find elsewhere.

'It is heaven on earth!' his *Mamae* would say.

Solomon turned to look at his *Papai*. He knew what he would see – a lined face whose expression reflected his own innermost thoughts and feelings. Neither man nor boy could articulate these emotions to one another through the spoken word. Solomon jumped down onto the other side of the gate and Duke rushed up and rubbed himself against his master's bare legs. The boy crouched down and drew his beloved dog into his arms. 'You know how I feel when I stand here, don't you, Dukey?'

Pedro removed the t-shirt from his hurting eyes, barely able to contain a grin that smiled 'Victory!'

'Well done, son!' *Papai* placed a firm hand on his small shoulder. 'I'm impressed.'

Talita applauded her twin and her father lowered her to the ground. They all climbed over the padlocked gate.

Solomon's family came from a line of Indian farmers who had intermarried with Portuguese settlers. The Tupi-guarani tribe had lived on the land for endless generations; understanding the cycles of the earth, the celestial signals and the bottomless wealth of nature's bounty around them, they had lived in harmony with their land. In the early 1900s a wealthy Portuguese banker called Oliveira acquired the entire area. He built a mansion for his family in the cool mountain air to escape Rio's sweltering summer months, and he indulged his passion for collecting African animals. A small private zoo was con-structed for the entertainment of high-ranking guests, including the president, Getulio Vargas, who used the beautifully appointed house as a retreat.

The land was too hilly for sugar cane, and too cold to cultivate coffee, so huge herds of cattle were brought in to graze the land. When the meat proved too tough from walking the hilly gorges, they were gradually replaced by milking herds. The indigenous Indian families were used as labour on this large ranch and Solomon's great-great-grandfather ran the dairy farming with his hard-working wife.

By 1938 the Oliveira family had fallen on hard times; the bank had been sold to settle debts and the family businesses were in liquidation. The zoo had been abandoned for many years and slowly the cattle were sold. With nowhere else to go, the workers remained in the valley, dividing up the newly abandoned land between themselves. Solomon's great-great-grandfather marked out twenty hectares for himself and his family, starting from the gate over the broad hill leading to the highest point in the valley. It continued running down past two of the looming black mountains and ending in the deep, wide gorge where the mansion now lay, decaying back into the earth from which it had risen. The estate workers soon discovered that the cool conditions and fertile soil were perfect for vegetables and flowers. They devised a simple irrigation system from the Paraiso river and soon produce was flowing to the local markets as quickly as they could harvest it. By the early 1970s Solomon's grandfather was ready to retire, his body tired from the pain of arthritis. He gave his two sons equal shares, the lower ten hectares to Mauricio and the upper ten to Ezio, Solomon's father.

Ezio had built their homestead. Painted white with dark green shutters, it was simple and modest. His young bride had planted bougainvillea by the veranda's overhanging porch and it now rambled with abandon over the tin roof. Row upon row of lettuces, *couve*, spinach, broccoli, *mandioca*, mint and *kiabo* lined the neat fields that surrounded the house. In the evenings and early mornings hundreds of sprinklers filled the air with arcs of cool, clean river water. It was a valley of rainbows.

The children and Ezio ran past a field of golden sunflowers followed by a froth of white gypsophila. The neat path led them towards the large rectangular greenhouses where long wooden benches loaded with seed trays stood with the next season's sprouting produce.

Gabriel and Angelo, Ezio's gardeners, were busy potting up seedlings as the small band passed by. He called over to them, 'Come and join us for lunch! It's Solomon's birthday!'

'We've already had lunch, but we'll come for the cake!' shouted Gabriel, the shorter and stockier of the two.

'Happy birthday, King Solomon!' teased Angelo. His shining ebony skin set off the whites of his curved eyes and gleaming teeth.

Solomon laughed and gave a thumbs-up to the two men he had known all his life.

Duke ran on ahead, stopping every now and again to make sure that Solomon was not far behind.

As they reached the veranda, *Papai* strode up the wooden steps holding Talita by the hand. He stopped and glanced back at the boys before flinging open the mosquito-netted door, which creaked loudly on rusty hinges. Solomon was suddenly aware of a room full of people and a great sense of excitement. He paused at the bottom of the steps.

'Go on!' insisted Pedro, pushing him forward and taking the net with its fish from his hand.

As Solomon crossed the veranda, the dog ventured no further than the front door, where he sat down. Someone from inside cried out and voices burst into song: 'Happy birthday to you, happy birthday to you, happy birthday dear Solomon, happy birthday to you!'

Solomon looked around the small room and saw it was packed with all the people he loved most. This was his world.

His mother, *Mamae* Isabella, was standing near the kitchen door. He noticed that her fair hair had been carefully piled up on top of her head and fixed with her favourite tortoiseshell comb. She was wearing her only party dress, short, sleeveless and red, which showed off her slight frame. On her hip clung Solomon's baby brother, Daniel, who took in the scene with enormous round brown eyes as he clapped his small hands together. Next to his mother was Uncle Mauricio. Solomon had learned long ago to keep a safe distance from his *Tio*, whose temper was as short as his haircut. *Tia* Ana, Mauricio's long-suffering wife, sang loudly next to him, her rotund bosom bursting out of her tight white lacy shirt. Felipe and Joao Carlos, Solomon's cousins, were already sitting at the lunch table. Felipe had dreamed of moving to the big city, as far away from his father as possible, for as long as Solomon could remember – unlike Joao Carlos, who craved the simplicity of routine and loved to work on the land, relating better to the archaic pulse of nature than to the upbeat tempo of the world. Solomon looked around the room once again and noticed that their youngest brother, Ze, was missing. Ze was Solomon's best friend.

At the head of the table sat the patriarch of the family, *Vovo* Geraldo, his grandfather. Solomon observed that the very way in which the family were grouped around *Vovo* in this simple room proclaimed his status of respect among them. His upright bearing and thick head of white hair set off a strong, square jaw and a face that reflected long, arduous years of working in tune with the land of his ancestors. Solomon knew he was *Vovo*'s favourite grandchild. It was a truth his grandfather did not hide.

Behind *Vovo's* chair Solomon watched his father, his hero, as the birthday chorus ended. He loved his father with a subtle pain. Every birthday since he could remember, Ezio had taken him fishing, just the two of them, in the pools formed by the Paraiso river in the upper regions of the mountain ranges. Man and boy, son and hero, alone in a place where their souls belonged. These were the days which Solomon cherished above all others.

The atmosphere was full of excitement as everyone took it in turns to compliment the birthday boy with the traditional embraces and kisses. *Tia* Ana got carried away and for a few seconds Solomon thought he would die, suffocated in her bosom. He was rescued by Ze, who appeared through the door behind him, just in time.

'M-M-Mamae! Let g-g-go of Solomon!' he stammered.

Ze grabbed his reeling friend.

'*Amigo*! I have a special present for you. I m-m-ade it!' he was short of breath, having run up the hill clutching his gift.

Solomon looked at the clumsily wrapped matchbox that had been thrust into his hands.

'Open it, th-th-then!' stammered Ze impatiently, his wild wavy hair framing large brown eyes and falling long over his shoulders. Talita and Pedro gathered round.

Isabella was calling to the family to serve themselves from the many steaming dishes she and *Tia* Ana were assembling on the table. There was not enough space for everyone to sit around the table, so she encouraged her guests to find seats where they could.

Solomon tore off the paper, watched by his brother and sister with eager interest, and by Ze with shy anticipation, and pushed open the little box. Inside was something encased in crumpled toilet paper.

'You went to a lot of trouble with your wrapping, friend!' teased Solomon.

Ze grinned awkwardly, but his eyes were shining.

'Hope the toilet paper's not used!' cried Pedro.

'Yuck!' Talita screwed up her face.

Ze punched Pedro lightly, and he ducked.

Solomon carefully peeled off the paper to reveal a carved wooden fish.

'It's a f-f-fish,' confirmed Ze, just in case.

The medallion was beautifully made. Ze had taken hours shaping the piece of eucalyptus wood with his penknife and had finally threaded it on a leather string.

Solomon tied it around his neck at once. 'It's great! *Really* great,' he said emotionally. '*Obrigado, amigo*. Thank you, friend. I'll never take it off.'

Everyone admired the little wooden fish around Solomon's neck and Ze felt three metres tall. He had never bothered much about giving presents before, but a week earlier he had been seized by a strong desire to mark his best friend's fourteenth birthday with a token of their friendship. It was as if the boy sensed that this particular birthday might presage the end of something, and it needed to be marked.

The *feijoada* was delicious and everyone told Isabella so, helping themselves eagerly to more. Solomon put some food out for Duke on the veranda.

'Solomon!' cried *Vovo* over the voices. 'Play something for us!'

Solomon walked back in through the mosquito door.

'I can't, sir. The piano's in your house,' answered Solomon, surprised by the request. 'We're in my house, remember?'

'Yes, yes, yes,' answered his grandfather, as everyone fell silent. 'Of course I remember. Play for us!'

Solomon stood by the door, suddenly confused.

Tia Ana, who had drunk too much beer, let out a little squeal.

'Shush!' said *Tio* Mauricio sharply to his wife, trying to act sober himself.

Something heavy was being pushed on wheels in need of oiling from the direction of his parents' bedroom. There was no sign of Felipe, Joao Carlos or *Papai*. Solomon's mother came over and put her slim arm around his waist, Daniel still sucking his dummy on her hip. Pedro quietly took the baby from his *Mamae*.

The bedroom door opened, and a fine old piano was brought into view. They manoeuvred the magnificent instrument into the living room and pushed it gently against the wall in the small area behind the table. No one else moved. All eyes were on Solomon.

'Solomon,' croaked *Vovo*, clearing his throat as *Tia* Ana helped him rise to his feet, 'your grandmother played the piano well and your *Papai* also has a great musical talent. In fact, in all my seventy-eight years I am yet to meet someone who plays the *cavaquinho* like he does.' He paused to clear his throat and glanced over at Ezio. As usual everyone listened with full attention. 'But you, Solomon, have a gift that I believe can only have been God-given. We are poor, but no riches, no great wealth could buy the gift that you were given at birth. When you play, when you sing, the angels in heaven are stirred, I am sure.' He looked at Solomon. 'Your *Papai* has invested all his savings into this extraordinary talent.' Solomon flushed with pleasure at his grandfather's words.

Vovo leaned forward with his hands on the table and looked intently at his grandson. 'But Solomon, whatever the future holds, whatever it brings you, promise me that you will never neglect this gift you have been given, because a gift such as yours carries with it a responsibility. This piano will remind you of what I have said to you today.'

Murmurs of assent greeted his words.

Solomon wiped his cheeks with the back of his hand and walked over to his grandfather. They were almost the same height.

'*Obrigado*,' whispered Solomon.

'I'm proud of you,' said *Vovo* softly as they embraced.

Then the old man stood back and gestured to the stool by the piano.

It seemed to Talita that Solomon looked down at the familiar black-and-white keys for a very long time. She went over and stood in front of her *Papai* so as not to miss anything. Pedro passed the sleeping Daniel back to his *Mamae* and stood beside her. *Vovo* sat down in his place of honour. The older cousins found the only other unoccupied chairs in the sitting area. Ze stood by the window next to the front door and noticed that Duke was asleep outside.

Bowing his head close to the keys, Solomon put one bare foot on the right pedal. He raised his hands, spreading his long, slim fingers over the narrow ivory bars, and closed his eyes. Tiny sounds, as of rippling water, filled the room and those closest to the piano were transfixed by the music produced by this fourteen-year-old mountain boy. Once again, his audience was transported into another world. Isabella had always known that her eldest son was different. His uncommonly good looks – pale green eyes set above high cheekbones, straight nose and beautifully formed mouth – never failed to attract admiring glances. Now, as he played the beautiful instrument, those sitting behind him watched his head, with its thick dark hair loosely tied, arch towards the piano and away again to the rhythm and flow of the music. It was a moment of magic. Then all at once his sweet voice, as yet unbroken, sang out along with the music. *Tia* Ana rubbed her arms as goosebumps pricked her skin. For Ze, when Solomon played and sang this way, his best friend became someone else, someone he did not know. It always filled him with awe. The music ceased, and Solomon's small audience erupted into applause.

Solomon had smelled her strong rosy perfume long before he had finished playing. During his six years of tuition with her, she had never come to the valley. As he turned a delighted face, *Senhora* Francisca Gonzaga appeared like a vision from the veranda and stood framed by the door.

Senhora Francisca was his piano teacher. Her exuberant style of dress was a dramatic contrast to the simplicity of her surroundings. As she entered the room with a proper sense of her own presence and glided towards the pianist, her spangled jacket glittered and her several strings of beads and gold chains jangled and sparkled. Duke stood behind her wagging his long tail and sniffing her shapely ankles. Everyone who was seated automatically stood, *Tia* Ana even tried a curtsy and knocked over her half-emptied glass of beer, which crashed noisily to the hard concrete floor, much to her husband's irritation.

Senhora Francisca ignored the clatter with dignity and kissed Solomon loudly on both cheeks. 'Happy birthday, my dear. That was perfect, *perfeito*! I arrived at the right time, yes?'

The *Senhora* loved her prize pupil. He was a child prodigy, of that she had no doubt. She had been instrumental in securing him the scholarship at the Santa Cecilia School of Music without which he could not have continued his studies.

Solomon noticed that her face was, as ever, generously covered in make-up and her nails were flawlessly scarlet. She had never told him her age nor confessed her birthday, but he had been told by pupils at Santa Cecilia that she was well into her sixties. He did not believe them. Although she was often harsh and intolerant as a music teacher, *Senhora* Francisca had opened up a whole new world to the young Solomon. Over the years he had discovered a soft heart hidden behind her colourful bravado. Under the make-up her lively and commanding grey eyes, which gave an impression of invincible energy, sometimes betrayed to Solomon a hidden pain. She masked well the devastation brought about by the sudden desertion of her husband fifteen years earlier for a younger woman. *Senhora* Francisca was a devout Roman Catholic and her religion, she had once told Solomon, had provided the strength she had needed to live through great heartache. That, and her five Angora cats.

The little house was suddenly alive with a rush of movement as everyone took it in turns to greet their regal guest. *Vovo*, ever the gentleman, offered the *Senhora* his seat at the head of the table, which she accepted elegantly. *Tia* Ana cleaned up the broken glass and Isabella hurried off to her small kitchen.

'Can I get you something to drink?' Ezio offered.

'Nothing strong, just iced water, *por favor*, it is so hot outside,' she replied, fanning herself with a napkin. She never consumed alcohol in public.

'My *Papai* doesn't drink alcohol either, do you, *Papai*?' commented Talita, who was now standing as close as possible to *Senhora* Francisca. She wanted to imbibe the aura of this figure of culture. She and Pedro had once been allowed to visit the smart townhouse where Solomon took extra piano and singing lessons on Saturday afternoons. These were in addition to his Thursday afternoons at the Santa Cecilia School, situated in the city of Petropolis, twenty-five kilometres below the valley.

'*Nao*, it doesn't suit me,' replied Ezio, handing the *Senhora* a tall glass of cool water. She took a long drink and Pedro ran to fetch her some more.

'Did you have a problem finding us?' asked Solomon, still recovering from the fact that the *Senhora* was in his humble home.

'Your little map was perfect, *querido*!' she responded, receiving the second glass from Pedro and now sipping more slowly before the staring faces. 'What a beautiful piano, *lindo, lindo*.'

'It belonged to my wife's family, *Senhora*.' *Vovo* spoke up, seating himself close to her in *Tia* Ana's chair. 'But as from today it belongs to Solomon!'

'You are very loved, *querido*,' said the *Senhora*, smiling up at Solomon.

Isabella appeared from the kitchen with more *feijoada*. 'Please will you have some, *Senhora*? We are honoured that you have come to our modest house today.' She smiled shyly.

'I am charmed, my dear. It is my pleasure after all this time,' replied *Senhora* Francisca, placing a spoonful of the food on

17

her plate. Although she was not hungry, she knew only too well the disappointment it would cause if she refused.

'Tell me, *Senhor* Geraldo, how was it that your family came to live in this valley?'

Senhora Francisca had suspected this was *Vovo*'s favourite subject, and his grandchildren hastily ran outside to play football behind the house, where they had put up makeshift goalposts. The adults sat down politely at the table to listen to the story they had heard a hundred times before.

Senhora Francisca listened intently and only after several minutes did she feel the need to interrupt. 'So do you own this land? I mean, after all this hard work over the years, is it yours to sell?'

This was a touchy subject amongst themselves and the other farmers in the valley. *Tio* Mauricio could not contain his anger and he answered her sharply. 'We don't! In 1980 the descendants of the Oliveira family, who had deserted our great-grandparents, took us all to court to try to get us off the land! But they bloody well didn't succeed! We've all just been here too long.' He took another sip of his beer and looked at his feet, breathing heavily. *Tia* Ana put her hand on his leg in an effort to calm him down.

'Is there anything a lawyer could do to help you?' the *Senhora* ventured, unfazed.

'All of us farmers in the valley are members of the Association of Agriculture,' replied Ezio evenly, 'but despite this and the fact that we and our ancestors have been living here for so many years working the land, we have not been able to find a legal solution.'

'Our ancestors go back more than one hundred years!' declared *Vovo* indignantly, shaking his head.

18

'This is fascinating,' exclaimed *Senhora* Francisca, looking with a new interest and respect at the patriarch by her side. 'Tell me more!'

Their moment alone, though, was soon interrupted when Isabella emerged from the kitchen to call the footballers in for the ritual of the birthday cake.

Senhora Francisca looked at her watch for the first time. 'It is four o'clock already! I must eat some cake and go, *queridos*. I have overstayed my welcome and my cats are waiting for their supper. But you must come and visit me one Saturday with young Solomon.' She stood and held out her hand to the old man. *Vovo* got to his feet, suddenly feeling tired. 'That would be my pleasure, *Senhora*.'

The table was now laid out with homemade chocolate and coconut *brigadeiras*, each sweet carefully placed in a pretty white doily fringed with lace. Once the young footballers had gathered back inside the house, sweating but exhilarated from their game, Talita proudly carried in the chocolate cake with fourteen white flickering candles.

Solomon blew out the tiny flames with one breath.

Chapter 2

Goodnight

Ovando, Montana, USA, New Year's Eve 1987

'Cut the cake and make a wish!' shouted someone from behind her.

Keira picked up the antique silver cake knife and sliced it through the smooth white icing. She closed her eyes and made a wish, then looked up. Her face lit up as across the room she saw Cass Henderson. He stood propped against the vast fireplace, his blond hair flopping across his face. His eyes did not return Keira's gaze, however, but rested on his pretty, curvaceous girlfriend Alana, who was enjoying his undivided attention.

'What'ya wish for?' hissed Keira's younger brother, appearing by her side.

Keira turned to face him, her thick auburn hair falling forward across her slight shoulders. For a moment he thought she was going to confide in him as she bent close to his ear.

'Callum,' she whispered, and then stood up with an impish smile, 'it's a secret!'

At that moment her father's deep drawl could be heard from the hallway as the door from the veranda banged shut.

'Where's my birthday girl?'

Liam Kavanagh had been out since dawn with six of his cowboys. The ranch was covered in a fresh blanket of snow and the temperature had dropped below freezing. Fifteen hundred prize Black Angus cattle had to be fed at this time of the year, a gruelling job made worse by the cruel and relentless winter elements of Montana. Her father's robust figure erupted into the room and, regardless of the stares of her guests and her teenage status, Keira walked into his strong arms, pressing her face up against a cold unshaven cheek.

'Let me look at you!' Liam held her back at arms' length and studied his daughter. She was tall for her fourteen years and her new black boots raised her almost to the height of her mother, he reflected. Her tight-fitting dress showed off the figure of a girl becoming a woman. She grimaced.

'This is the first and the last time you'll see me in this dress, Papa!' she assured him.

He smiled and as her eyes looked into his, Keira caught her breath. She had never noticed that look in her father's eyes before. It exuded a pride and tenderness for his daughter that touched her.

'You look beautiful, K,' he said gently. 'Just like your mother.' Liam looked around the room searching for his wife. Instead his gaze fell on Cass Henderson. Keira watched his expression darken and instinctively she grasped his arm.

'Please don't, Papa! Please don't ruin my birthday!'

Removing her hand from his arm, Liam strode through the dining room nodding awkwardly at some of her friends and disappeared into the hall. Keira directed a desperate look across the quietened room at her best friend Mary, who at once responded to the appeal in the blue eyes.

'OK!' cried Mary in a loud voice. 'Let's get some music going!'

'What's he doing here?' demanded Liam as he closed the heavy kitchen door behind him and glared at his wife.

Katherine was stacking dishes. Her deep blue eyes met his steadily. She knew exactly who he was referring to. 'Keira invited him.'

Faye, their long-standing housekeeper, quietly left the room.

'I want him out of my home and off my land, Katherine! No Henderson comes near Goodnight, and certainly not near my daughter. Is that understood?'

Liam Kavanagh rarely raised his voice. As well as his reputation as a man of integrity and determination, he was also renowned for his calm and measured nature. He was highly respected. There was nothing that Liam Kavanagh did not know about both land and livestock. It was in his blood. There was logic and harmony in the way he went about things, born of an instinct for the land inherited from the Irish farmers who were his ancestors. Today he owned one of the biggest cattle ranches in the state, with an operating budget of over a million dollars a year.

'Liam,' Katherine said in her soft voice, 'Cass is only a boy. He seems very polite.'

'Cass is not "only a boy", Katherine, he must be all of nineteen and he's Jim Henderson's son. He's got his father's genes, his father's arrogance and worst of all that look in his eyes.' Liam breathed heavily. 'I can't believe he had the nerve to come here today!'

'Oh, come on, pet, he looks nothing like his father. He's got Patty's looks. Anyway, Cass isn't eighteen yet. I know that for a fact, and he's not interested in Keira anyway. He's here with his girlfriend who happens to be Mary's older sister.'

Although Katherine had lived for almost fifteen years in Montana, she still retained her English accent with its slight north-country lilt. She had been working as an airline stewardess when she first met Liam Kavanagh, and there had been an initial sense of loss for her mother and sister when she left her home in Sunderland to marry him and moved to America. However, they had the comfort of knowing that Katherine had become as passionate about her life in Montana as she was about her own roots in the north of England. Liam made sure that the family visited Sunderland most summers, allowing Keira and Callum to form a close relationship with Molly Cartwright, their maternal grandmother.

Liam walked over to his wife, taking her face with its beautiful clear skin in his big rough hands. He kissed her and his anger melted.

'Katherine,' he said more calmly, looking down at her, 'you know perfectly well that Jim Henderson is one of the most dangerous men I know. He nearly ruined me, and he's ruined many other people who've gotten in his way. You have to trust me. Cass is his father's son and I don't want him near my land or my family. I thought I'd made that clear?'

Katherine sighed resignedly as she watched her husband's broad back exit the kitchen into the hall. She knew she could not stop him.

* * *

'I'm not forgiving him, ever!' sulked Keira as she flung the saddle over the back of her quarter horse, Jackson, who was munching hay in his stall in the barn. It was New Year's Day and the early morning sun shone down weakly from the vast clear blue sky. She had refused to go to church with her family, preferring the company of her horse.

'You gonna ride out alone?' asked Ed, trying not to grin as he remembered Cass Henderson's hasty departure from the birthday party the day before. He did not like Cass, not only because he was the attorney general's son, but also because he knew that Keira had a crush on him. Keira grabbed Jackson's bridle from the wall and glanced back at the young cowboy dressed in his great-grandfather's bat-wing chaps of studded old leather, a large buckled belt and a rain slicker. Ed blew hot breath into his cold hands and tied a worn red bandanna around his neck.

'Why, Ed?' she snapped, slipping the bit into the horse's mouth. 'Do you think I need protecting from the snow?'

A year ago her provocative comments would have hurt his sensitive heart, but he was seventeen now and believed he was old enough to ignore them. 'There's a lot of snow out there, Keira,' he warned.

'You worry about me too much, Ed Whitely! Perhaps you shouldn't love me so much!' She tested the girth, glanced sideways at the young man, and led Jackson towards the barn door.

'I love you like a sister, Keira,' he lied. 'There ain't nothing wrong with that now, is there?'

She stopped and looked back at him, sighing. 'I'm sorry, Ed. You're far too nice, always have been. Why don't you saddle up and come out with me? I'd like that. It's just that I'm mad at Papa for telling Cass Henderson to leave the house like that yesterday. It ruined my birthday.' Keira put her boot into the stirrup and pulled herself lightly up into the saddle. 'I guess his feud with Jim Henderson is more important than me!' She knew she didn't mean this, but she was seething and had to take it out on someone.

As they left the relative warmth of the barn with its scent of hay and horse-feed and braced the shock of the freezing temperature outside, Keira looked towards the magnificent homestead that was set on rising ground further down the shores of the huge black lake. Smoke was already billowing out of every chimney from fires that blazed in all the downstairs rooms from October to April. She knew that in the kitchen Faye would be at the huge range, busy preparing the traditional New Year's Day lunch.

The house had been built in 1936 by Keira's grandfather, Patrick Kavanagh, on two levels. A long veranda ran the width and breadth of the ground floor. The roof overlapped it, protecting it from the heavy falls of snow in the winter, which at worst could reach a depth of three metres. Across the veranda every room had spectacular views through large glass doors towards the lake and the mountains beyond. In the summer months the lake was home to loons, mallard and wood ducks, as well as Canada geese, cinnamon teal and beavers. In the upper rooms, generous dormer windows allowed light to flood in and offered an even wider panorama. Beyond the lake the pastures and meadows stretched away towards the Bob Marshall Wilderness, an area of more than one and a half million acres stretching mile upon mile below the contour of the mountains. Everything flourished there; Douglas firs, cotton trees, ponderosa and tamarak pines were home to grizzly and black bears, coyotes, mountain lions, racoons, skunks, badgers, elk and deer. Many of these would now be in hibernation until spring. Of all the mountains which circled the Goodnight ranch, Morrell Mountain stood proudest and tallest to the north-east, snow-capped even during the height of summer when cow and calf grazed in their hundreds under the balmy expanse of Montana's bluest skies.

Ed lived in the old cottage by the lake, near the barns, with his elderly parents Bill and Joanna Whitely. The other five bachelor cowboys bunked down above one of the barns behind the corral. Traditionally they gave each other nicknames: Pinnacle Jake, Buckskin Joe, Wyoming Pete, Rodeo Tom and Bronco Jim. Mesquite Bill, Ed's father, had worked at the Goodnight ranch for thirty-five years and was the farm manager. He was in charge of the men and reported directly to Liam. Joanna cooked for them, cleaned for them and generally mothered them all, which suited everybody fine.

'You planning to take the road out towards Ovando and head for the Blackfoot river, Keira?' asked Ed, straightening out his hat. 'I reckon the snow's too deep to cut across the meadows, but the snow ploughs will have cleared the roads.' He pulled the bandanna up to protect his mouth from the cold.

'Sounds good to me,' answered Keira, staring up at the cloudless sky. 'We'll probably pass my family coming back from church, but they knew I didn't have a headache anyways.'

'Why'd you lie?' asked Ed.

Keira swung round and shot a look that told him not to push the subject.

'Anyhow,' she said nonchalantly, 'why do I need to go to church?' She opened wide her arms. 'I mean, look at all this!'

'Yup. You can't beat this anywhere,' agreed Ed. 'River not coming out with us?'

'Oh, he'll be lying by one of the fires like any sensible dog.'

'You gonna call him?'

'Nope, not if we're taking the main road to Ovando.'

'We could cut across the Monture creek,' pursued Ed, who loved the dog.

As they rounded the side of the homestead and headed on down the drive, leaving the lake and Morrell Mountain behind them, Keira turned in her saddle and whistled. Before long a stocky black Labrador bounded towards them, his hot breath forming small clouds around his mouth in the cold air.

The Goodnight ranch had been named by Grandfather Patrick in honour of Charles Goodnight, one of the great American cattle barons. In 1866, with his partner Oliver Loving and eighteen young cowboys, Goodnight had driven two thousand cattle across seven hundred miles from Texas to the Indian reservation at Bosque Redondo, where some eight thousand Navajo were on the verge of starvation. Continuing northward, they came to the mining camps of Colorado and Denver and eventually reached the timber and gold-mining territory of Montana. One of those eighteen cowboys had been Patrick Kavanagh's father, Finbar.

Finbar Kavanagh had been born in 1850 on a ship sailing from Cork to New York. His parents, Frank and Kay Kavanagh, were originally from small neighbouring sheep and cattle farms in Dunganstown, County Wicklow. Driven by desperation, as neighbours and family members alike died of starvation before their very eyes, they set out to break the law and stole two sheep. Immediately they were arrested and thrown into Wicklow gaol. Nineteen months later, a random group of four hundred miserable convicts were selected for transport to America and Australia. Their perilous gamble had paid off and they were on their way to the New World.

Passionate about land, Finbar Kavanagh fell in love with the stark beauty of Montana the first time he saw it, and by 1889 he was able to buy eight thousand acres of fertile land in the Bitterroot Valley, and two hundred head of fine Angus cattle, with the $24,000 he had saved through his years of toil. This land would become the foundation of the great Goodnight ranch. By now his ageing mother Kay was a widow and Finbar persuaded her to travel the long and arduous distance from the warm, humid climate of Texas to the cooler, dryer one of Montana to share a new life in the cottage he built by the large lake. In spite of her frailty and the years of lonely widowhood, Kay found perfect happiness in this beautiful place with her beloved son, until the winter when she fell victim to the freezing temperatures of the northern plains.

Finbar buried her on the opposite side of the lake to the cottage, under a clump of aspen trees, where today the tomb-stones of three generations of Kavanaghs and their dogs can be found.

As the two horse-riders and the dog reached the end of the mile-long driveway, Ed was starting to feel the cold. 'You gonna stay at a slow walk, or step up?'

In reply Keira kicked her horse into a steady trot as they crossed the highway and headed on towards the small hump-back bridge which spanned the Monture creek. They turned west after the bridge and followed a trail along the bank of the creek itself, but as the path narrowed they slowed down again to a walk, hot breath from both man and beast sending steamy mist into the fresh, icy air. The dog ran confidently ahead, his pink tongue lolling. He knew this country well.

'Did you hear they're gonna manage the river as a wild trout fishery, which means that the trout will all be able to multiply freely at last?' Ed asked, looking down through the clear running water to the river bottom where pink and grey sand-stones laid down millions of years ago by the glaciers glistened like semi-precious gems. Ed was a fine fly fisherman.

'Well, they had to do something. The fishing was scarcely

even worth lying about the last few years, what with the mining and the logging,' replied Keira indifferently.

They rode on, listening to the Blackfoot as it ran fast, straight and furious up ahead. Ed was not used to Keira's silences. She was the one who usually kept the conversation going. He knew she was sad and he knew why, and it was eating him up. Finally he could hold himself back no longer.

'Hell, Keira!' he blurted out loudly above the sound of the river. 'Why don't you fall in love with me? Don't let that Cass Henderson steal your heart! He ain't the guy you think he is. He may be pretty and rich, but he sure don't know how to handle a horse, or cast a long line across the surface of a river. Hell, he don't even know what a heifer is!'

Keira rounded on him furiously. 'You don't even know him!'

'Oh, I hear enough in the bars about his daddy, Jim Henderson, and they say he's out of the same mould. Anyhows, if you don't trust me, trust your Papa.'

'Ha! Papa doesn't like him because he can't stand Jim Henderson.'

'You can't blame him for that.'

'Well, I can't go with you, Teddy Blue – you're like a brother to me, like you said yourself. Brothers and sisters don't go marrying each other now, do they?' Keira was smiling.

They both ducked under a long thick branch draped in powdered snow.

'There's one thing you've got to remember, Keira. You were born here. The land, the open sky, the cattle, the horses, the water, they're part of you. When I'm out with a foal or a little colt in the round corral behind the barn, I look at myself and I see that I'm the richest man on earth. Ain't all the money in the world, or the glamour, or the fame that matters, it's that peaceful feeling when you wake up in the morning and go to bed at night and know that you're truly where you belong. It's a true feeling inside yourself.'

She turned and looked into the face of the boy she had grown up with, attractive in a familar sort of way with two pronounced dimples on either side of his mouth which deepened when he broke into a broad smile. His eyes were kind and they were shining now as he spoke from his heart. She envied him his contentment, and sighed. 'I don't think I've ever found that true feeling inside.'

'Sure you have, Keira, just look around you. Ain't nothing that will take the place of this.' He paused. 'I don't like to see you so sad, is all,' he continued.

'Well, why don't you tell me one of those rodeo stories of yours? They always make me laugh.' She shrugged her shoulders, ridding herself of her melancholic mood.

'Sure, but we better turn back now. They'll be waiting for us back at the Big House.'

It was a long-standing tradition that on New Year's Day, Bill, Joanna, Ed and the other hands were invited to lunch with the Kavanaghs. Ed was not about to miss it.

The old oak table was laden with silver cutlery and pink and white bone china. A gigantic crystal chandelier glistened above it. Two elaborate silver and gold candlesticks stood in the centre of the table, each holding six flickering red candles. A set of antique chairs were positioned round the fine dining table. Christmas cards were arranged on the surfaces of all four sideboards, together with silver picture frames displaying family portraits and photographs of Katherine's mother and younger sister taken on past family holidays in England. Two large pink

Sunderland lustre-ware jugs also stood on the long sideboards, with other porcelain figures and awards from the Cattle Association. Paintings of western scenes set in gilt frames lined the magnolia-painted walls, and opposite the fireplace with its huge burning logs two tall French windows let in light that reflected the snow outside. In the centre of one wall hung a brass plaque with the following inscription:

All in all, my years on the trail were the happiest I ever lived. There were hardships and dangers, of course, that called on all a man had of endurance and bravery; but when all went well there was no other life so pleasant. Most of the time we were solitary adventurers in a great land as fresh and new as a spring morning, and we were free and full of the zest of darers.

These were words written to Finbar Kavanagh in 1890 by Charles Goodnight.

There was a sense of well-being as hosts and guests walked into lunch from the adjacent sitting room. The beautiful room and the warm atmosphere, coupled with the aromas from the delicious food, were almost overwhelming. Silver serving dishes were heaped with crisp roast potatoes, caramelised carrots and haricot beans stood ready on the table. Katherine came in carrying a tray of dishes containing creamy horseradish sauce, hot steaming gravy and her speciality, puffy golden Yorkshire puddings made following the recipe she had learned as a child growing up in the north of England. As she set her tray on a serving table, Faye entered the room, her wide hips swaying from side to side under a long red wool skirt, a proud smile on her face, bearing the traditional New Year's Day crown roast of prime Goodnight beef. They all burst into a spontaneous round of applause.

Keira was invited to sit on Liam's left. She was still ignoring her father since returning from her ride, and in spite of himself Liam was hurt. He loved his wife and his two children and hated any conflict between them. A flushed Joanna Whitely took the place of honour on his right. Sitting next to Liam Kavanagh on New Year's Day in his grand old house was the highlight of Joanna's year, and she always made herself a new dress for the occasion. Aware of this, Liam never failed to comment on it.

'What a pretty dress this year, Joanna. It sure does suit you!'

As usual her full cheeks turned a deeper shade of pink and little beads of sweat broke out above her top lip.

Bill Whitely sat on Katherine's right opposite young Callum, who today more than ever looked like a young version of his father.

'How old are ya now, Callum?' Bill asked the same question every year.

'Why, I'm eleven years old now, Bill.'

'You sure are growing up fast! Pretty soon you'll be the height of your Daddy.'

Callum glanced down the table at his father. Being compared to his Papa was the biggest compliment anyone could give him.

Ed took the chair next to his mother so that he could look across at Keira as much as he wanted. After the ride she had changed into a pair of jeans which showed off her long legs, and a fluffy white mohair jumper which clung to the contours of her developing body. Her auburn hair framed the most beautiful face Ed had ever seen, and he noticed that her usually pale cheeks were still flushed from the ride. Joe, Pete, Jim, Tom and Jake sat gingerly down on the remaining five chairs.

'Right, shall we say grace?' asked Liam genially, and as they all bowed their heads he spoke the ancient blessing. 'For what we are about to receive, may the Lord make us truly thankful.' Everyone said 'Amen'.

Liam carved and soon all twelve plates were piled high with Faye's banquet.

'So,' said Keira with a wicked glint as she turned towards the five bachelor cowboys, 'when is one of you going to get married then? You're all getting on a bit now!'

They grinned down at their plates, feeling self-conscious at her teasing, and said nothing.

'There are plenty of dances with lots of pretty eligible ladies in Ovando,' persisted Keira, enjoying herself.

'We're too shy, Miss Keira,' answered Tom plaintively. His tongue was loosening by the minute with the help of Liam's expensive wine.

'What? Good-looking men like yourselves?' exclaimed Keira. 'You cannot be serious!'

'*That's enough, Keira!*' mouthed Katherine, frowning from the other end of the table. She offered Bill some hot gravy.

'Well, I'm married to my job,' said Jake, the smallest of the five. 'Goin' to have to be one special lady to take first place.'

'Joe and Pete are dating two sisters!' blurted out Jim, sipping from his wineglass and raising his eyebrows at his two blushing colleagues across the table. 'Daughters of the postman, I believe.'

'Oh well, that's exciting!' said Keira, wanting to hear more. 'That must be Beryl and Linda, am I right?'

They both nodded without meeting her eyes, and clearly longed for a change of subject. Katherine stared meaningfully at her daughter. But at this point Callum joined in.

'What about you, Ed? My friends at school tell me that their older sisters fancy you like crazy!'

All eyes turned to Ed, who gave a big broad smile.

'Well!' said Keira teasingly. 'What do you know?'

'He's the best-looking cowboy *I've* ever seen!' declared Joanna roundly. She was only too aware of the effect Keira had on her precious son, and she feared for his sensitive heart. But as she saw his smile, she felt reassured. Joanna and Bill had married each other very late in life. They had been friends for thirty years, both resigned to singlehood, when suddenly a light went on and they decided to get married. By this time they were both in their late forties. Ed had been adopted by them a year later, when he was five years old.

Now Liam decided it was time to change the subject, and he launched into his repertoire of jokes. 'Did you hear the one about the horse that was tied up at a hitching post?'

All eyes switched to their host and Ed sighed with relief. Katherine smiled lovingly at her husband. As far as she was concerned, *he* was the best-looking cowboy she had ever seen, and at forty-four he was as attractive as he had been sixteen years earlier. She had been the stewardess on his flight from London to Paris.

Liam continued, 'A little dog comes along and starts playing around the horse. The horse gets annoyed and starts pawing the ground. The dog looks up and asks, "What are you doing that for?" The horse looks down and says, "Well I'll be darned, a talking dog!"'

They all roared with laughter, and by the time coffee was

served with small glasses of liquor, the jokes were still rolling and Faye had joined them from the kitchen.

'Ed!' cried Keira over the mirth, 'tell us about your rodeo in Alberta last year.'

'Go on, Ed!' repeated the others, 'tell us about your rodeo in Alberta.'

Liam stood and refilled the glasses once again. They had all lost count, but no one cared. They did not have to walk far and it only happened once a year, so they would make the most of it.

'I was in the shoot sitting on a bull called Miss-taker My-jaker . . . and boy, was he a mistake! Had my two feet up on the rails either side of the bull. Had the bull rope around his shoulders, put my hand in the rope loop and made a wrap. Suddenly he clamped right down on the ground. Third try I said, 'Open the gate!' I was ready to ride that beast. All of a sudden he clamped down again, rolled from side to side in that shoot, crashing both my feet on either side against them wooden bars. I swear I felt my bones break into tiny pieces. My two feet were dangling around. Out he shot, and I managed to ride 'im for the full eight seconds.' Ed was now astride the antique chair, rocking backwards and forwards, giving his audience the full show. 'He was bucking and a-blowing into a right spin when I heard that whistle. I let go of that bull rope and the rodeo clowns came a-running. When I tried to stand up, Lordy ole me, the pain in my feet ran straight up my shins to my spine. Everyone was shouting, "Run, Ed! Run, boy!" I crawled faster than they'd ever seen a cowboy go with spurs and chaps in all their lives. The judge said to me later, "Pretty good spurring, Ed!" They put casts on my two feet. But after two weeks I couldn't bear it no longer and cut them off myself!'

Callum was on the floor, bent double. Keira was holding her side, pained with a stitch, and others wiped tears from their eyes.

Faye heard the telephone first and went into the hall to answer it. She returned and whispered into Liam's ear, 'It's your sister Gloria, Mr Kavanagh.'

Liam stood and left the room. He had been waiting for her call. Gloria was a criminal defence lawyer who lived in Helena eighty-two miles away with her husband, journalist Jack Durrant. She was calling to tell him that she and Jack had discovered some vital evidence for a case the three of them were working on. This might be his chance to put an end to Attorney General Jim Henderson's candidacy in the upcoming elections for US senator for the state of Montana. Someone had to stop him. Liam Kavanagh had made it his mission.

Chapter 3

An Angel at the Piano

'Let's go, children! Your father's got an appointment with a lawyer and you're late for school!' cried Isabella from the veranda.

Ezio sounded the horn again and Duke jumped into the back of the old Chevy, barking and wagging his long hairy tail.

Baby Daniel was pulling himself up on one of the old pine chairs around the table and chewing a biscuit at the same time. Talita and Pedro ran out of the bedroom, kissed the baby on each of his chubby cheeks and stood on tiptoes to kiss *Mamae* as they continued out of the door. It was a quarter to seven in the morning. The drive to their school in Correas took twenty minutes and the gates closed at five minutes past seven.

'Solomon, where are you?' Isabella called louder as she started to clear the things from the breakfast table. Daniel was singing to himself and banging the chair with his free hand. Solomon appeared from the bedroom at last with his music bag and rucksack and grabbed his bread roll from the table as he hurried by.

'Please don't be late back from Petropolis this afternoon, Solomon!' she warned as she put his packed lunch into the rucksack.

37

'But Ze is meeting me today after my lesson!' Solomon spoke through a mouth full of bread.

Ezio sounded the horn more impatiently.

'I love you!' Solomon called back over his shoulder, before his mother could object.

He threw his music bag into the back of the truck and climbed in next to Duke. Talita and Pedro sat in the front cabin, Pedro nearest the open window so he could call out to anyone he knew. Ezio revved the engine and turned on the radio. Frank Sinatra was singing as well as he could through the crackling reception, 'I've got you under my skin, I've got you deep in the heart of me . . .' Ezio turned the volume up. It had been their song when they were young lovers.

'Hey Bella! Where's my kiss?' he shouted out in the direction of the veranda.

Isabella had heard the music too. She ran down the steps laughing, and went to his side of the truck. 'You're going to be late, Ezio Itaborahy!'

Their kiss lingered.

'Not in front of the children *p-l-e-a-s-e*!' moaned Pedro, raising his eyebrows and looking away.

'. . . so deep in my heart, you're only a part of me, I've got you under my skin . . .' It had never mattered that the words were not wholly understood; the mood of the melody alone had always stirred them. The three children cat-whistled as the Chevy drove off, leaving Isabella to her dreams.

The early sun slanted across the valley where the morning dew still covered the endless rows of green vegetation. For as far as the eye could see the earth glistened. Duke stood panting next to Solomon, balancing perfectly on all fours as the old truck bounced and lurched down the dirt track. They clanked over the narrow planked bridge at a good speed and Solomon looked over the side of the truck at the fast-moving river below which formed rapids against resisting rocks, crevices and fallen branches. The air smelled gloriously fresh. Sinatra accompanied them all the way.

Their cousins, Felipe and Joao Carlos, were already bent over long beds of lettuces. Within the next two days these would be cut and boxed up thirty at a time, filling sixty wooden crates, and driven off to markets in the state of Rio. The teenagers, without relaxing their concentration, waved as they drove past. School for them would start at six-thirty that evening after the long, arduous day's work in the fields.

The truck swayed over to the left and crunched to a stop, dust flying. *Tia* Ana appeared from her pale pink house in a short crimson dress that was too tight. Small yellow birds sang out from two large birdcages hanging over the patio amongst plants growing out of old margarine containers. Ze ran out from behind her and jumped into the back of the truck next to his friend.

'Good morning!' she said in a husky voice, rubbing her hands together nervously. '*Tio* Mauricio has agreed that Ze can meet you in Petropolis this afternoon, Solomon, on condition that you are back before six!' The smile on *Tia* Ana's round face gave way to a grave look as she directed her gaze into Solomon's narrowing green eyes.

Ezio drove off before his son could answer her back.

Frank Sinatra sang the chorus for the final time.

Tia Ana watched the dust engulf the back of the old Chevy.

After two kilometres the primitive pot-holed dirt road, which meandered alongside the descending river, suddenly widened at a sharp left bend after the tiny village of Bonfims, and with it the surface thankfully became cobbled. Their school was situated in the grounds of the large white colonial house with blue shutters that had belonged to the late Padre Correa. Standing ancient and proud, the house was now surrounded by portable classrooms, school playgrounds and a sports court. However, splashes of brilliantly coloured bougainvillea still flourished, clambering wherever they could, while tall palm trees offered dense shade. Next to the house stood an old white chapel with a bronze bell, which rang out periodically throughout the day.

Five hundred children were educated at the school daily, in two shifts. The house that had once entertained the imperial family in its upper rooms, and had been home to their great-great grandfather in its servants' quarters, was now home to an order of nine elderly nuns who ran the school. Although the school was subsidised both by the Catholic Church and the local state government, each pupil had to pay a small monthly contribution. Grants were given to poorer families with more than two children attending, as in Ezio's case; but they still had to find the money for school books and stationery as well as the uniform with its pale blue t-shirt carrying the words *Escola Catolica Padre Correa*.

As the Chevy drew up outside, the sound of the chapel bell was warning latecomers and the formidable headteacher, Sister Marilyn, was about to shut the gates.

'You are just in time!' snapped the nun in her sharp voice. Sister Marilyn was dressed as usual in beige, with brown tights and white buckled sandals. A small wimple covered her grey wispy bun. She bolted the gate firmly.

'*Bom dia*, Sister Marilyn,' responded the children dutifully, passing her quickly and heading for their respective classrooms. But Sister Marilyn had not finished.

'Solomon!' she barked.

He stopped reluctantly and turned to face the nun.

'You have your music lesson today in Petropolis, don't you, Solomon?' she asked briskly, approaching the boy.

'Yes,' he answered, wondering what was coming next.

She came as close to him as a nun had ever stood. 'I will give you a lift. I will be driving to Petropolis myself.' It was not an invitation; it was a statement.

Sister Marilyn was a secret admirer of Solomon's prodigious musical talents. She rarely missed a performance at the Santa Cecilia Theatre if he was playing, basking in the knowledge that people knew he was a student at her school.

Solomon hesitated, desperately trying to think of an excuse. The thought of spending half an hour in close company with this sharp-tongued, intimidating woman terrified him.

'Solomon! Did you hear what I said?' Her dark eyes bored into his.

'Thank you, Sister, but that is not possible. You see, Ze's coming with me.'

As he had expected, her eyes narrowed into small slits and her mouth tightened. 'Ah. Then that is different.' She turned on her heel and walked away, her head held high.

Solomon gave a sigh of relief. His cousin's dismal reputation at school had saved him.

The receptionist of the Santa Cecilia Music School bustled out from under the counter and greeted Solomon with a kiss on each cheek. It was his first day back after the holidays, and he had been missed. 'You performed beautifully in the concert before Christmas, *querido*. Your talent is miraculous!' Sonja was as loud and as theatrical as her outfits. Solomon stared at her absurdly high heels which gave her walk a sexy swing. '*Professora* Francisca has already arrived. She went straight upstairs!'

Solomon pressed the button next to the antique iron lift. It arrived with a jolt, and the white-haired gentleman in horn-rimmed spectacles who arrived with it pulled back the folding metal door.

'My dear Solomon! How are you?' It was Wolney Aguair, president of the school, who opened wide his arms to welcome his prodigy.

'I'm well, thank you, sir,' replied the modest mountain boy.

As was customary, *Senhora* Francisca sat at the piano playing one of her favourite jazz pieces. Today Solomon recognised Ella Fitzgerald's 'How High The Moon'. She did not look up as Solomon entered. Someone on the other side of the corridor was practising scales with a loud operatic flourish, which floated in and out of the room as he opened and closed the door. Putting his bags down next to a small round table, the only piece of furniture in the sun-filled room, Solomon sat down next to his teacher on a long leather stool and waited. She kept on playing, but in a little while the expected questioning began.

'Name four famous composers who were born this month.'

'Chopin, Mendelssohn, Rossini and Mozart,' replied Solomon without a second thought.

'All correct except Mozart! He was born on 26 January, not February.'

Her perfume was overwhelming today.

'What is the capital of the USSR?

'Moscow,' answered Solomon.

'What is the capital of South Africa?'

'Pretoria?' he hazarded.

'Correct. On 3 February P. W. Botha quit as leader of the National Party, due to poor health, and he was replaced by *Senhor* F. W. de Klerk.'

'de who?'

'de K-l-e-r-k,' she remonstrated.

'Do they finally have a black leader?' he asked.

'No.'

Senhora Francisca always made it her business to find out as much as possible about world events. Newspapers, magazines and encyclopaedias were devoured for information at a time when most of her neighbours did not even know what was happening in the next state. She prided herself on her eclectic knowledge and liked to pass it on to her students. She also prided herself on teaching her students to sing songs in English as well as Portuguese.

Her fingers, adorned with semi-precious stones, continued to play. In time with the melody, her head moved backwards and forwards. Solomon noticed that one of her false eyelashes was becoming looser with every movement and it mesmerised him so that he became distracted. Visions of the spidery contraption falling off completely preoccupied his mind.

'*Finalemente*! What is the capital of Jamaica?'

'Um, ummm . . . *Senhora*, excuse me. Your eyelash . . .'

'Kingston, of course! On 10 February they elected a *Senhor* Michael Manley as prime minister.' She prided herself on pronouncing those English names with as little an accent as possible. She also prided herself on those dates, and as Solomon had no way of checking them out, he never knew whether she made them up or not.

The eyelash finally dropped off and landed on the piano with perfect timing as the last chord was struck. A brief feeling of nausea swept over Solomon as, without the slightest hesitation, she picked it up, ran saliva over it with a pink tongue and stuck it back on again.

'Right! Let's practise that new Tom Jobim song, then,' she said, turning to Solomon with a wide smile. 'In English!' She picked up the music sheet from the top of the piano. 'And then, so he doesn't feel left out, I want to teach you another of my favourite Villa Lobos pieces. I think you are ready for a greater challenge, my dear!'

Although Villa Lobos had been dead for some years, *Senhora* Francisca could never refer to Tom Jobim without quickly referring to Villa Lobos. It was out of respect for both of them, Solomon had long ago decided. They were, after all, considered Brazil's two greatest composers and songwriters.

Ze was waiting, as he had said he would be, next to Dom Pedro II in the centre of Petropolis. He was leaning against the vast statue and looked as pensive as the imperial bronze figure.

'What's up?' asked Solomon as he approached.

'Nothing,' answered Ze, straightening his drooping shoulders and forcing a smile. 'Just Sister Marilyn again. My father will kill me if she manages to kick me out.'

'Come on, let's go and visit the Santos Dumont museum!' said Solomon brightly, wanting to change the subject. He walked off briskly towards one of their favourite places in the city.

Ze ran after him and put an arm around his shoulder. 'He was a good m-m-man, you know,' he said.

'Who was?'

'Dom Pedro II. He helped ab-ab-abolish slavery here a hundred years ago.'

'Yup, but he had to flee the country as a result!'

'Perhaps that's what I sh-sh-should do! Flee the country!' There was silence. 'I was thinking,' Ze continued, '*Papai* could do with my help during the day in the fields. I could suggest it to him before that nun gets me expelled. I could go to night school, and work with my brothers during the day.'

Solomon had been dreading it would all lead to this. 'We'll never see each other if that happens!' he exclaimed.

Ze shrugged and looked away.

At the end of their afternoon together, they walked back to the bus station in silence, each deep in thought. On the corner of the *Rodoviario* they passed a group of ragged children they had not seen before in the city. They were crouching together in a circle on the pavement, counting money. Solomon noticed a girl amongst them who looked older than the boys and she was obviously in charge. The dirty, baggy t-shirts they all wore were printed with the letters I LUV NY. A gift from a tourist, Solomon thought. Their bare feet were filthy and their faces were gaunt. All at once one of the boys, no older than Pedro, jumped to his feet and ran towards them both with his hand out.

'Give me some money!' His eyes were dark with hostility. His hair had been bleached blond with peroxide and stuck to his small head. His skinny limbs were peppered with sores. Wiping snot from his nose, he repeated the demand.

'What's your name?' asked Solomon. There was a sense of menace around these children which he had never encountered before.

'Antonio!' the boy answered defiantly, jutting his open hand towards Ze.

'Wh-wh-where are you from?'

'Rio!'

Another boy joined Antonio from the circle. The left side of his face and neck had been hideously deformed by what looked like a severe burn. Solomon and Ze could hardly hide their horror.

'Hey, rich boys,' he whined. 'What are you waiting for? Give him what he wants!' His voice had also been affected by his injury and came out like a harsh hiss. Inhaling on a cigarette, he squinted at them through drug-dulled eyes.

'We're not rich!' exclaimed Solomon, trying to compose himself. 'All we've got is our bus ticket home.' He was glad he was tall for his age on this particular occasion.

'Home!' hissed the boy with the burn. 'Home! Well, you're lucky you've got one.'

'I-I-I don't want to go home as it ha-ha-happens,' stammered Ze.

'Why don't you stay on the streets with us, then?' The boy gave a chilling laugh and offered Ze a drag on his cigarette.

Suddenly, the girl in the circle stood up yelling to her gang, '*Policia!* Let's get out of here!' Like lightning the gang sped across the busy street, weaving in and out of the moving cars with practised precision, and disappeared up a side alley.

Solomon turned to Ze. 'It couldn't get worse than that, *amigo.*'

*   *   *

Dinner that night in the mountains was rice, black beans and chicken with *kiabo*.

'How was your meeting this morning with the lawyer?' Isabella asked her husband, spooning food into baby Daniel's mouth.

'Good!' exclaimed Ezio with his mouth full.

'What lawyer?' Solomon was curious.

'His name is *Senhor* Dauro Vasconcellos.' Ezio took out a small business card from his shirt pocket and looked at it.

'What does he want?' pursued Solomon, feeling a strange unease.

'He was up here last Saturday morning talking to some of the farmers. He says he has the documents that would legally register the land in my name. The lawyer believes, like me, that our situation is urgent. He said the authorities could claim it anytime, or the Oliveira family could try again, so the sooner we act the better. I've tried talking sense into Mauricio, but he won't listen.'

'Do you trust this lawyer?' asked Isabella, lifting the baby out of his chair.

There was a pause. 'Sure. He showed me a list of his previous cases, all successful. *Senhor* Dauro hates injustice. He says that after all these years of working this land, it should legally be ours by right. He's speaking my language.'

'What do they want from us in return?' insisted Isabella, sitting down and facing her husband. All the children had stopped eating and were listening with uncharacteristic attention.

'He'll charge me his standard fee for taking on the case,' said Ezio nonchalantly.

'How much is their charge?'

'A thousand dollars,' replied Ezio. His eyes did not meet hers.

Isabella's jaw dropped. 'And where are we going to get a thousand dollars from, Ezio?' she gasped.

'We'll talk about that later.' Ezio stood up and changed the subject abruptly. 'Solomon! Would you like to play with the band down at the club tomorrow night?'

'What's happened to Newton?' asked Solomon, getting up to help his mother stack the plates.

'He's gone away for the weekend,' responded Ezio, propping the lawyer's business card carefully on the shelf behind him. 'Besides, you're the better pianist, son.'

Solomon smiled. 'You don't need to flatter me to get me to say yes, *Papai*. You know I love playing with you and the other guys!'

'Thanks, son. And as for you, young Talita and Pedro,' Ezio bent and kissed his daughter, who leaned back in her chair and wrapped her skinny arms around his neck, 'I'll be needing your help tomorrow afternoon boxing up all those vegetables for Saturday's markets.' Pedro leaped from his chair and grabbed one of Ezio's legs and Talita scrambled from hers and grabbed the other. Ezio started to walk slowly and heavily around the room with both the twins shrieking with laughter, each clinging to their father's legs.

There was the sudden sound of a truck approaching at high speed. The vehicle screeched to a halt outside. The children's laughter died and Duke starting barking loudly as if to warn them. Two doors slammed shut and footsteps were heard approaching the veranda. The mosquito door was wrenched open and *Tio* Mauricio exploded into the room. 'Ezio! You arsehole! What the hell are you up to?' His eyes swept the room and alighted on his brother. Mauricio was drunk.

Solomon ran in from the kitchen, and his heart sank as he saw his uncle's livid face. The mesh door swung shut with a violent whine, and the happy, playful atmosphere of a few moments ago was cut dead as the room became charged with fury.

'What the hell are you doing behind my back?' Mauricio repeated.

At this moment, the door opened again and *Vovo* walked in, his lined face drawn with anxiety as his sons confronted each other. 'Calm down, Mauricio!' ordered *Vovo*, breathing heavily. 'Don't let this get out of hand, for God's sake.'

The baby, who had been playing on the floor, started to cry and Pedro finally let go of his *Papai*'s leg and ran to his little brother. Isabella came in from the kitchen and quickly ushered her children into her bedroom. Solomon, however, would not go with her. He was overwhelmed with a sudden compulsion to be his *Papai*'s protector.

'So! I hear you're speaking to fancy lawyers from Rio de Janeiro, eh, Ezio?' snarled Mauricio, jabbing a gnarled index finger at his younger brother. 'How dare you speak to lawyers about *our* land? *I'm* the eldest!' He staggered. The veins in his neck were protruding. His breath stank of alcohol. 'And what about *Vovo*? Have you no respect? Have you gone mad, Ezio?'

'Calm down, Mauricio!' interrupted *Vovo* again, steadying himself by holding on to the back of a chair. Solomon moved across the room and stood beside his grandfather. He could feel his heart pounding.

'I want the best for all of us!' Ezio shouted back, trying

desperately to compose himself. '*Vovo* gave me half the land, and I want it legally registered in my name. The lawyer believes it's urgent too.'

Mauricio was not listening.

Outside on the veranda, Duke's barking became frantic. He pawed desperately at the netted door.

'This lawyer is on our side. He can get us all the documents we need.'

'You sign any documents from that big-shot lawyer and you've lost me as your brother!' Mauricio spat back.

Solomon could bear it no longer. 'Leave my *Papai* alone!' he shouted. 'He's always right!'

Mauricio swung round to confront his nephew. Solomon froze.

'That's enough, Mauricio!' *Vovo*'s firm voice broke in as he took hold of his elder son by the arm. 'Leave the boy alone. It's time to leave. You're in no state to talk about this any more. Let's leave!'

As he propelled Mauricio through the netted door, *Vovo* turned back to Ezio. 'Son, do what you think is right. I trust your judgement.'

Solomon put his arms around his father.

The following morning, *Tia* Ana did not appear at the door of her pink cottage. Instead she called out from behind the netted window that Ze was not feeling well and would not be going to school. Solomon jumped out of the truck and walked towards the veranda. He wanted to know the truth.

As he neared the house she pulled the curtain shut in front of her, but not before Solomon caught a glimpse of a large purple bruise on his aunt's cheek.

'You shouldn't put up with it, *Tia*!' he exclaimed. 'Call the police!'

'Get going, Solomon, or you'll be late for school!' she urged from behind the curtain.

'Is Ze all right?' implored Solomon.

'He will be,' she whimpered.

'Call the police, *Tia*! Don't let *Tio* get away with it every time!'

Ezio sounded the horn, and Solomon ran back to the Chevy.

At four o'clock the following afternoon, a dusty black estate car pulled up in front of the white cottage. From where they were packing vegetable boxes, Solomon, Pedro and Talita looked down the hill across the rows of *mandioca* and watched their *Papai* shaking hands with a suited gentleman.

'What's up with Duke, Solomon?' Pedro turned questioningly towards his brother.

Solomon squinted in the sunlight at the distant figure of his dog. Duke's growls could clearly be heard as he circled the visitor like a prowling lion.

'He doesn't like him!' stated Talita uneasily.

'They're going to sign the documents, aren't they?' said Pedro quietly.

Solomon shrugged. 'We have to trust *Papai*.'

They went back to packing their boxes.

An hour later, Solomon entered the kitchen from the side door to fetch a jug of freshly squeezed lemonade for his brother and sister. He hoped he would not be seen, but his father called over to him from the living room.

'Solomon! Come and meet my new friend, the lawyer!'

Solomon reluctantly put down the tray of jug and glasses

and walked into the meeting, wiping his dirty hands on his shorts. Duke started growling. '*Quieta*!' ordered Solomon. '*Fique*, stay put!'

Ezio stood up. 'Son, meet *Senhor* Dauro Vasconcellos.'

'*Ei* Solomon.' The man's voice was high pitched with a strong Rio accent. 'Pleasure to meet you. I see you're working hard today!'

Solomon took the extended hand with sudden disdain and noticed the diamond ring. It dug into his flesh as the suited stranger gripped his hand tightly. Their eyes met and for a fleeting moment something uncomfortable passed between them, a faint sense of some common destiny. The lawyer's narrow eyes, set under a heavy brow, dropped for a moment as though unwilling to meet the gaze of this tall, straight young boy, then quickly recovered as he gave a loud laugh, showing gold-capped teeth framed by a dark moustache. It was a face that would haunt Solomon for many years.

'Fine boy you've got here, Ezio!' the lawyer said loudly through another false laugh, and he ruffled Solomon's hair with his ringed hand. Intensely irritated and feeling confused, Solomon jerked his head free.

The farmer and his wife, the boy and his dog all watched in silence as the lawyer's black estate car wound back down the dusty track to the green valley below.

'Tonight's a night for celebration!' shouted Ezio to the evening sky through the open window of his truck. 'As from today my land is officially registered in my name!' he proclaimed to the billions of tiny stars, which appeared so close they gave the impression that he could reach out and touch them.

His little family cheered and clapped from the back seat and Ezio pulled Isabella towards him with his free arm. He felt invincible. He had everything he had ever dreamed of – a beautiful wife, four healthy children and, finally, his land.

They were heading for the club in Correas. The voice of Roberto Carlos, Brazil's answer to Julio Iglesias, was crackling on the radio.

'You're looking good tonight, *querido*.' Isabella kissed her husband's neck, breathing in his familiar smell.

The club was situated over the top of a rundown super-market in the main square of the small town. During the day old men would meet regularly in the centre of this *Praca* to play endless games of chess or skittles under the shade of the four tall palm trees which stood at each corner.

'Ezio!' bellowed Julio, the drummer, from the entrance to the club. 'Good evening, *familia* Itaborahy!'

Ezio laughed, grabbing his old friend and giving him a firm embrace.

'Let's play some samba!' Ezio took his *cavaquinho* from Pedro. He was going to allow himself a drink tonight.

They all jumped out of the parked truck and ran up the stairs into the dim light of the club. Solomon went over to the bar and greeted Rogerio, the barman. He was wearing his customary white apron and baseball cap. The cap camouflaged his bald head.

'Hey! We have the honour of your presence tonight, I see!' laughed Rogerio, taking the teenager's hand and arm in a fierce grip.

'Slow down, Rogerio, or I'll only have one hand to play with!' cried Solomon, wincing.

The rest of the band members were setting up on a small

raised stage in the corner opposite the bar. There was plenty of room for dancing between this point and the tables. The dance champions of the club, Carlos and Hortensia, had already arrived. Carlos wore tight black breeches with high black leather boots. Isabella swore that he stuffed his crutch, but Hortensia indignantly denied this allegation. His white silk shirt had full sleeves that flapped like wings as he thrust his pelvis against his partner, who thrust hers back. Over the shirt was a small red waistcoat on which Hortensia had laboriously sewn hundreds of sequins that sparkled under the spotlights. As for Hortensia, she was squeezed into a black off-the-shoulder tube dress that just covered her red lacy knickers. This minimal garment always threatened to slip below her bosom, but to Rogerio's disappointment it had never yet done so.

By midnight baby Daniel was asleep in his pushchair behind the bar. Pedro and Talita were still on the dance floor trying, with some success, to emulate the energetic routines of the dance champions. Isabella was trying to escape the attentions of an elderly customer and Ezio was on his fourth beer. Solomon had stopped trying to ignore Hortensia's frequent alluring glances.

'Ladies and gentlemen!' boomed Ezio down the microphone. 'Tonight I'm the happiest man in Correas!' He took another gulp of beer. 'But I would not be where I am today without my Bella. Where is she?' He squinted through the smoke. The mob of dancers cat-whistled and drew back, revealing a surprised Isabella and the old man, sitting at the only remaining table by the bar. Everyone cheered and stamped their feet. Ezio gestured for the crowd to quieten. 'There is a song I wrote for her some years ago. It's called "*Meu Amor*".'

Isabella hid a self-conscious smile behind her hands. 'And tonight,' continued Ezio, 'I would like to ask your permission to sing it to her again.'

More cat-whistles and applause.

Ezio's left hand moved quickly up and down the strings on his small guitar, while his right hand struck the chords, producing the *cavaquinho*'s unique high-pitched tone. The tune he sang was a traditional one in the style of the *choro* music, the original carnival music that was the precursor to samba which had begun in the *favelas* of Rio.

Ezio's rich, mellow voice blended with the *cavaquinho* as he sang.

> My lover,
> Above all and in the name of love
> I will be what your heart asks me to be,
> Everything that makes you happy.
> My love is all yours,
> My affection is directed towards you.
>
> However, not I alone,
> But us together.

Isabella walked over and stood next to him. Taking the microphone, she looked down into the eyes of the man she loved and sang her response.

> My lover,
> Above all and in the name of love
> I will be what you are, in thoughts and desires.
> You are precious to me.

I will suffer in your pain too,
I will walk together with you throughout life.

However, not I alone,
But us together.

Ezio sang the final verse.

My lover,
Above all and in the name of love
I will never leave you, never forsake you.
You are everything to me,
My darling, my blessing,
I will walk together with you for ever.

However, not I alone,
But us together.

The emotional crowd erupted into applause. Hortensia wiped away tears and lamented that Carlos could not sing as well as he could dance. Ezio stood and held Isabella in his arms. Solomon, still sitting at the piano, picked out the tune of the *choro* and played it all over again by ear.

As the cheers died down, the band prepared to take a break and Rogerio was kept busy dispensing a rush of new orders at the bar. In the relative quiet of the smoke-filled club, loud shouts and heavy footsteps could be heard from the stairway that led up from the square. The doors swung open. A voice exploded into the room.

'Ezio Itaborahy! Ezio Itaborahy! Where are you? You bloody idiot!'

All sound ceased abruptly as *Tio* Mauricio staggered blindly into the club. 'You didn't listen to me, did you? You went and signed that document, damn you!' He raised his arm aggressively and blundered towards his brother.

Isabella froze. Pedro and Talita instinctively moved across to where Daniel was asleep behind the bar. Solomon jumped from the piano stool and rushed over to stand in front of his parents.

'If you want to fight my *Papai*,' Solomon cried out to his uncle, 'you'll have to strike me first!' Indignation flashed in his green eyes.

Mauricio stopped in his tracks for a few seconds, swaying, then put his head down and charged like a raging bull at his young nephew. Isabella pulled Solomon towards her just in time and Ezio took the full blow, crashing back into the African drums.

Rogerio sprang out from behind his bar and leapt onto the back of Mauricio, who instantly began to spin round and round, trying to break the barman's grip. The stunned crowd formed a circle around them and started cheering, 'Go Rogerio! Go! Go! Go!'

Someone else appeared from nowhere and with surprising force rammed his head and shoulders into Mauricio's large backside. It was Carlos. Hortensia screamed as all three men crashed to the ground. Ezio, who had been helped up by Julio from the scattered drum set, dived in on top of them all, followed by Julio and the rest of the band.

Solomon grabbed a large empty beer bottle and stood over the scrum, holding it high in the air. It did not matter to him that his uncle had been somehow wronged by the actions of his *Papai*. 'That's for what you did to Ze, *Tia* Ana and my father!' he shouted as he brought the bottle down onto the back of his *Tio*'s skull. Mauricio slumped forward, blood trickling out onto the abandoned dance floor.

The following morning, the usual piano lesson in Petropolis started an hour late. Solomon overslept, much to his *Vovo*'s agitation, as he paced the veranda impatiently waiting for his grandson to appear. He wore his only suit, a brown check, and had a yellow flower in his buttonhole. His hair was smartly greased back and he had not spared the aftershave.

Much to Solomon's relief, *Senhora* Francisca had been remarkably composed as she flung open her stained-glass front door to the latecomers, wearing a white silk caftan with a matching turban. Unlike most of her compatriots, *Senhora* Francisca abhorred a lack of punctuality, and Solomon was normally very careful to be at his lesson on time. But she said nothing about the lateness of the hour as she graciously ushered *Vovo* and Solomon indoors, out of the sunshine and into the music room.

'Practise a little alone, *querido*, while I give your *Vovo* some coffee,' she said firmly, picking up some sheets of music and handing them to her pupil. 'Mozart's *Rondo alla Turca* in particular needs a lot of work. Don't forget, there aren't many weeks left before you perform at Petropolis Cathedral!'

The invitation to give a concert at the great cathedral had been made to Solomon through the *Senhora*, who was a devout and respected member of the congregation. This was an honour indeed.

The *Senhora*'s townhouse stood in a row of similar houses grouped around a popular square, with a garden full of leafy acacia trees, a bandstand and a dried-up pond. It was conveniently near to the Santa Cecilia Music School. *Senhora* Francisca had remained in the house when her husband deserted her, taking half their furniture and pictures with him. She had never bothered replacing them. Behind the house was a little backyard used primarily by her beloved Angora cats.

Solomon sat down at the piano, his body aching in the aftermath of the previous night at the club. He could not forget the image of his *Tio* being carried out of the club on a stretcher, shouting that he would never speak to Ezio again.

Solomon's eyes felt suddenly heavy and he rested his head on the keys for a few moments.

A piercing scream roused him with a violent jerk. Raising his head, he turned sleepy eyes towards the doorway to see *Senhora* Francisca standing there ashen faced, her hands with their bright red fingernails covering her open mouth. She was staring at Solomon with an expression of shock, and before he could make sense of what had frightened her, she sank to the ground and lay motionless.

'Get some water!' gasped *Vovo*, entering the room. Taking a crimson cushion from the sofa, he knelt to place it under the *Senhora*'s head. The cats seemed unperturbed by their mistress's distress and lounged on in the sunlight.

Solomon pulled himself together and ran to the kitchen to get a glass of water. Returning, he held it out to *Vovo*. Then he retrieved a second pillow from under a nonplussed cat and started to fan the unconscious woman vigorously. This seemed to be effective.

'Help me get her up!' cried *Vovo*.

They managed to raise the *Senhora* and ease her into a chair. Solomon was amazed at his grandfather's sudden agility.

Solomon knelt down beside her. 'Are you all right, *Senhora*?'

Unexpectedly she started to cry. He watched, concerned, as the tears brought black mascara trickling down her powdered cheeks.

At last she spoke in a whisper. 'I saw something.'

'Saw what, *querida*?' asked *Vovo* tenderly.

'When I walked into the room, Solomon was asleep at the piano with his head in his arms.' She straightened herself and dabbed at her eyes with a lacy handkerchief. 'There was some-body standing over him. It was leaning over you, Solomon, its arms were around yours, and its fingers were on the keyboard.'

Solomon felt suddenly overawed.

Vovo was silent, but in answer to his unspoken thoughts the *Senhora* continued to describe what she had seen. 'It was an angel! I tell you, it was an angel! It had wings that were vast, majestic, and . . . it was all white, just like Fra Angelico's paint-ings.' She burst into tears again.

Solomon glanced at his grandfather.

'I saw it!' she insisted. 'You must believe me. I saw an angel!' She turned to the boy, her lips trembling. He had never seen her like this before. 'When an angel appears, *querido*, God is speaking. Perhaps there is trouble ahead for you, Solomon. Perhaps life will sometimes be hard, but today you have been given a sign of his protection. Believe this, and you will see through the trials that are to come and not give up.'

She took Solomon's hand in her own and smiled at him

through her tears. Then, exhausted, she leaned against *Vovo*, who put his arm around her. After a few minutes, they led her upstairs where she lay down on her bed.

Solomon and his grandfather caught a bus home to the mountains. They said very little, but the boy kept looking behind him to see if his guardian angel had returned.

Chapter 4

The Key to the Song of Life

The limousine pulled up in front of the Millionaire's Club on 24 West 6th Street in downtown Helena. The attorney general, Jim Henderson, nodded at his chauffeur as the doors were opened for him, his wife and his two sons.

'Pick us up at three o'clock, Bill!' he said curtly to his driver, before leading the way into the warmth of the lobby in the tall brick building. There was no conversation as the family rode the elevator. Never one for small talk, the attorney general's mind was preoccupied with a phone call he had received the night before from one of his reliable sources in Missoula.

All four Hendersons checked their reflections in one of the mirrors that lined the elevator before it jolted to a halt on the fourth floor.

'Good afternoon Attorney General, Mrs Henderson, James, Cass,' said an elderly butler, dressed traditionally in a bow tie. He quickly turned his thinning grey head towards Mrs Henderson, who was taking off her fur coat. 'May I take your hat and gloves too, ma'am?'

Patty Henderson smiled through her pink lipstick and handed him her furry accessories. Jim was being fussed over by a young waitress they had not seen before and by the head waiter, Robert Montour, who said smoothly, 'We have your usual table, sir.'

'Yup,' said Jim, puffing out his broad chest. The maître d' led the way across the dark oak-panelled dining room and once again Cass took pleasure in the brilliant stained-glass windows that shone out from two sides of the room. Each depicted a scene embodying all that he loved about Montana. He saw elk, wagons, mountains, buffalos, Indians, fishermen, timber-men, ploughing and herding; everything that meant home.

The waitress held out a chair for Patty and Jim turned and hissed under his breath to the head waiter, 'Reserve a meeting room for me at two o'clock, Robert! That's one hour from now. When a Mr Dwight arrives, take him right up and offer him a whisky. Put it on my tab.'

'Of course, sir. I'll let you know as soon as he arrives.'

With a discretion born of frequent practice, Jim slipped a $100 bill into Robert Montour's hand. 'This meeting's confidential, Robert. It never happened.' He winked at the head waiter, who nodded and with dexterity transferred the money to his pocket.

Meanwhile, Patty had made the most of her entrance, complimenting people she knew as she passed through the restaurant to the Henderson table in the far right-hand corner. In Helena, she believed herself to be the nearest thing to royalty after the senator's wife. She was of a tiny build and ate like a bird, terrified of putting on weight. Her naturally thick greying hair was dyed a honey blonde and trained into an immaculate style by her personal coiffeuse. She adored jewellery, and her husband was willing to indulge her in this and in her extravagant taste for couture clothes. To Jim Henderson, a wife who looked expensive was paramount for the image he was determined to present. But to Patty, all this lavish spending on herself was only a small compensation for the pain she suffered every time her husband betrayed her yet again with another woman. Her life, which often seemed futile to her, could be briefly lifted from a slide into depression by yet another spending spree.

Patty's elder son, James, sat down next to her on one side of the table, while Jim and their younger son, Cass, sat opposite. Robert Montour flicked open four crisp white napkins and laid them deferentially on each lap.

A wine waiter approached. 'May I get you some drinks, sir?'

Jim spoke for the whole family. 'We'll have the same as usual, Jay.' To the head waiter he added, 'And the chef's choice for lunch, whatever that might be!'

He flashed one of his bleak smiles at Jay who, caught off guard by the attorney general's familiarity, left briskly, scribbling something on his pad. Jim Henderson made a point of memorising people's names, whatever their social ranking, and he prided himself on rarely forgetting a face. After all, he needed their votes.

Jim had been born William James Henderson Junior on 15 August 1945 in Helena, the capital city of the state. His great-grandfather, William Frederick Henderson, originally from Cornwall in south-west England, had found gold during the 1870s and with admirable foresight had invested his fortune in real estate and hardware tools for miners. The exclusive Millionaire's Club, built in 1885 by affluent stockmen and the mining elite, boasted over two hundred members in its prime, of which Jim's great-grandfather was one.

Jim's father had eventually inherited the amassed fortune of his forefathers, but tragedy struck when at the age of forty-five he had choked to death on a fish bone in front of his wife during dinner at their vast mansion on Gilbert Street in the Mansion District. For the rest of her life Harriet remained a widow, dedicating herself to bringing up their one and only son and the heir to the Henderson millions, and Jim grew up believing that the world was his for the taking. By the age of sixteen he was quite sure that whatever he wanted in life he could get. Nothing or no one could stop him, and his money was there to make sure of it. What he wanted, in 1961, was to go into politics and become the youngest ever senator of Montana.

Jim Henderson downed his draught beer, while Patty and James sipped their aperitifs. 'You need to get some beer inside of ya, James!' he said to his eldest son, contempt written all over his fleshy face. 'If you did, it might make a man of you after all!'

James smiled back sourly. He hated his father and it annoyed him that these jibes still had the power to hurt him. Finishing his sherry, James stubbornly ordered another one. Patty sent one of her warning looks across the table at her husband. Jim disliked the way his wife had always sided with James. As far as he was concerned, it was her fault that his heir had become a ballet dancer. James had been encouraged by his mother to attend the Blanche Judge School of Dance from an early age, and had become its star pupil. Patty had herself been a promising ballet student, and it was one of the resentments she held against her husband that her marriage to him had put an end to her own promising career. A ballet-dancing wife was not Jim Henderson's idea of what he needed.

Patty now channelled her frustrated ambitions into the career of her artistic elder son, and she was overjoyed when he won a place at the National Ballet School of Chicago. It was the happiest day of James's life when he left his father and the Mansion District behind him for good. He had seen enough in his young life to know that the intrigue of politics was not for him, although he felt sure his younger brother was destined for that path. After moving to Chicago, he only returned to Helena occasionally to visit his devoted mother, who begged him to do so in her frequent letters.

'James, did you hear that Cass has every possibility of being offered a sports scholarship by the University of Montana?' Jim boasted, looking diagonally across the table at James as the waitress placed some appetisers on the table. 'After he was voted all-state quarterback player at high school, the Grizzlies' coach told me he wants Cass in their team come hell or high.' Jim turned and punched Cass lightly on the arm. James looked across at his handsome younger brother, who smiled smugly.

'Congratulations, Cass,' said James, meaning it. He continued to look quizzically across the table at Cass, then added, 'But if I were you, I wouldn't get too puffed up. Could be that you get given that scholarship on your own merit, but could also be 'cos the attorney general here has friends in the right places.' James rubbed his thumb against his fingers, signalling 'money'.

Jim Henderson stopped eating and looked angrily at his elder son. 'You watch your tongue—'

'Why don't we try and be nice to each other?' interrupted Patty, conscious that their voices were raised and that people at the next table were looking their way. She fiddled nervously with the string of pearls around her thin neck as the three men chose to ignore her.

'You suggesting that I won't get offered it on my own merit, James?' Cass retorted.

'I'm sure you will, Cass,' said James dryly. In truth he did not want to argue, but he was irritated. All his life he had fallen way short of Cass in his father's approval rating.

'Is that what you're thinking as you prance around the stage in Chicago in your tights and leotard, James? That I arranged for Cass to win the Mount Helena run, that I fixed for Cass to break the mile run at Helena High School, that I paid for him to be voted the all-state quarterback player?' Jim Henderson's lips tightened to a thin line. 'Is that what you think, James? Your brother just happens to have the talent and the determination that's needed to get to the top. People are born with that, James, no money can buy that!'

The waitress returned and removed the empty plates. She could not take her eyes off Cass. His white-blond hair flopped over his wide-set, intensely blue eyes. But there was something else – he had an aura, a charisma, which drew her eyes to him. Some of her girlfriends who had already met him told her that every month there was a different girl in his red sports car. He could take his pick. And seeing him in person like this, she could see why. He was even better looking than in the local newspaper cuttings she secretly kept in her bedroom. With looks like that, she reflected, no longer able to delay carrying the empty plates into the kitchen, he could become a movie star, like Gary Cooper, who had been born on Raleigh Street not far from the club.

As coffee was served, the attorney general lit up a thick cigar and sipped some cognac.

Cass chose this moment to put in a request. 'I was thinking about driving some friends out to Greenacre next weekend, Dad. Will you be using the ranch?' he asked.

'Nope.'

'What's her name this time?' inquired James cynically, as he removed the green foil from his mint chocolate.

'This time?' Cass repeated in the same tone, leaning back in his chair.

'Well, don't tell me you haven't moved on since Christmas!' James teased.

'As a matter of fact I haven't, if that's of interest to you, brother.'

'So what does she have that the others don't?'

'Well, that's probably something you wouldn't understand, James,' sneered Cass, smiling sweetly.

'I can try.'

Cass looked at his brother doubtfully.

Robert Montour approached the table and bent over Jim's chair to speak quietly into his ear.

'Patty darlin',' said Jim, rising and moving over to assist his wife from her chair, 'Bill's waiting for you downstairs. I'm going to have to do some business upstairs, and Cass, I'd like you to join me.'

Cass looked surprised. James did not. He had always assumed that sooner or later Cass would be drawn into his father's web. His younger brother was a chip off the old block, thought James, despite his far better looks.

'Ask Bill to come pick us up in an hour.'

Patty's eyes revealed her indignation at being dismissed in this way.

'I'll make it up to you, darlin'!' Jim winked suggestively.

James stood immediately and put his arm protectively through his mother's. They both turned, and without a word of thanks headed for the lift.

Jim and Cass remained by their table and watched as the slight figures of Patty and James disappeared from the dining room.

'Follow me, son.'

The small meeting room was oval in shape with a mural on both arched walls depicting an English fox-hunting scene painted in sober colours except for the bright red jackets of the huntsmen, which matched the red carpet. As they entered, a man sitting at the far end of the long shiny conference table stood and walked towards them. He wore an ill-fitting suit and extended a knobbly hand. Robert Montour closed the doors behind them and returned to his restaurant.

'This better be good, Dwight! I don't like having meetings on a Sunday afternoon.' Jim took the bearded man's hand.

'You can call me Oscar, sir!' said Dwight, pumping Jim's arm.

'You're Dwight to me, until I decide otherwise.'

Dwight flushed and glanced across at Cass with sunken, bloodshot eyes.

'This is my son, Cass Henderson.'

'It's a privilege to meet you, Cass. I recognise you from your pictures in the paper.'

'Cass, this is Mr Dwight. He's a picture editor on the *Missoulian* newspaper.'

Cass shook the damp hand and they all sat down. Jim poured himself a cognac.

'Everything that's talked about in this room is confidential.' Jim looked directly at Oscar Dwight and then turned and looked meaningfully at his son. Cass had seen that look in his father's dark grey eyes before and it always unnerved him. The attorney general blew a puff of cigar smoke before continuing. 'If others get to hear about this meeting there will be consequences for everyone in this room.' Jim placed a heavy hand on Cass's thigh as if to balance the threat with fatherly reassurance.

Cass shuddered slightly at the touch, and focused on the mural on the opposite wall; a pack of beagles was chasing its prey. He wondered what Dwight was about to divulge.

'Dwight, if this tip-off is fabricated or full of holes, you'll want to leave Montana within forty-eight hours and never return!'

Dwight rubbed his bony hands together nervously and licked his lips. 'No sir, there ain't no holes. Like I says to you on the phone, I overheard a conversation on Thursday night between two of our journalists, Grant Breaux and Hank Jefferson. I'd gone back to my office to get something and they thought everyone had gone home. It was real late, see.' He paused, warming up for the details. 'Hank Jefferson's first wife, Gloria, is a lawyer, they split some years back and she later married another journalist, Jack Durrant, who writes for the *Independent Record* here in Helena. Hank and Gloria share custody of their two sons and remain friends.'

Jim looked bored.

'Hank was saying that one of his sons had been visiting over the weekend, and mentioned something about a case his mother was working on. I heard your name mentioned, sir, as well as some other information, so I reckoned you'd be interested.'

Jim drained his cognac and placed a small tape recorder on the table. He knew that Gloria Jefferson was one of the top criminal lawyers in the state. She rarely lost a case and he was aware that for years she had been investigating aspects of his career.

'Keep talking!' barked the attorney general, pressing the red record button.

Dwight cleared his throat. He never really enjoyed splitting, but he needed the money. There were just too many debts from too many lost poker games.

'Well, it goes back to 1972.' His sharp features reflected his discomfort at the revolving tape. 'And the year of the elections. You were still working for the judge that year, I believe, sir. Judge Conrad Kilabrew, your wife's daddy?' He eyed the two Hendersons and licked his lips.

'Yeah, yeah, yeah, Dwight, get on with it, for Christ's sake!' Jim interrupted impatiently.

Cass noticed it was snowing again outside. He felt a shiver run up his spine. Why had his father dragged him into this?

'As you remember, sir, Attorney General Bill Bridger ran as a candidate for a second term that year and won. But what I heard about him on Thursday night concerned a girl called Maureen. I think it was Maureen Jacobs or Maureen Jacobsen, or something like that.'

Jim Henderson slowly stubbed out his cigar. Cass suddenly saw that his father had been knocked off balance. The big man's face had paled and his hand shook suddenly. Dwight noticed it too and savoured the moment; the long drive through the snow had been worth his while.

The attorney general quickly pulled himself together. 'What about her? What is she to me?' he growled.

'I don't think I can remember nothing more, sir,' Dwight said slyly, and took a swig of his whisky.

Jim's mouth tightened and he spoke through clenched teeth. 'You better try harder than that, Dwight!'

Cass noticed that the colour in his father's cheeks now matched the jackets of the hunters on the wall. He watched as his father took a wad of notes from his inside pocket and threw it on the table.

Jim loosened his tie and undid his top button. He had waited twenty-seven years to run as candidate for US senator for the state of Montana and nothing was going to stand in his way now. He had dreamed about it, longed for it, planned for it, could already taste the power that would be his. There was no way he was going to be baulked now.

Dwight eyed the money, but did not pick it up.

Cass shifted in his chair.

Jim looked at his watch. 'Get talking, Dwight. You've got five minutes!'

Dwight eyed the wad of notes and thought of his debts. 'What I heard Hank Jefferson say was that this Maureen's now enrolled in law school in Texas. Seems she got herself into a mess some years back with people in high places, and now she's planning a career in law, she's realised she's got to come clean about it before it comes back to haunt her.' He paused and glanced at the attorney general to see the reaction to this information.

Sure enough, Jim flinched.

'Anyhows,' Dwight continued, 'about this Maureen. Seems she came from another Mansion District family, but they'd fallen on hard times. I guess they were putting on airs with a soft underbelly of poverty.' He coughed. 'Well, she was just a teenager, a pretty girl, they said, and old Attorney General Bill Bridger went and had an affair with her. That was, until he discovered her real age. Then all hell broke loose, as he had to come clean to the Justice Department before the media got hold of it. They called in Judge Kilabrew, your father-in-law, to sort it out and stamp out the fire before it exploded. It sure was a sticky situation.'

Jim stared at Dwight with loathing in his eyes. He knew what was coming.

Dwight pushed on confidently. 'Judge Kilabrew turned to his son-in-law to handle it. That was you, sir. Apparently, sir, you knew the family of the girl. Seems this Maureen has told everything to her professor at law school. She says that you, Mr Henderson, paid off her family big time, to make sure they shut the girl up. They had to move out of the state as part of the agreement. I expect you knew they were belly up, Mr Henderson, sir?' Dwight glanced furtively at Jim. 'It seems that in return for your generosity you got a top position in Bill Bridger's office after the '72 elections. Bridger was naturally extremely grateful to you and gave you your break. It was part of the deal.'

Jim leapt to his feet. 'What a load of bull!' he roared. He was angry and humiliated that his son was now privy to incriminating events from his past, which he believed had been securely and irreversibly dealt with. In involving young Cass in this meeting he had intended to give him a lesson in the art of handling informers. Instead Cass had witnessed his father being dealt what could be the biggest blow of his career.

Dwight inched his hand forward and grabbed the wad of notes. 'I'm sure it is, sir. But I thought you'd want to know that the press has got hold of the story. And by the way, it seems that this professor from Maureen's law school is a very good friend of Gloria Jefferson's brother.'

The attorney general sank back into his chair. 'Liam Kavanagh! That son-of-a-bitch! I might've known he had a hand in this.' Memories of past encounters with the rancher flooded into his mind. He remembered the time at university when Kavanagh had accused him of bribery and coercion. That was when he had beaten Liam for the presidency of the Association of Students. Ever since then the rancher and his friends had tried their best to scupper his career.

Dwight rose to his feet. 'I should be going, sir. But there is one more thing you need to know.' His words hung in the air like a black cloud.

'Well?' Jim waited.

'It's big. What's it worth?' Dwight felt supremely confident now.

'You sly bastard,' Jim seethed. 'This is all you're gettin'!' He slammed another $200 down onto the polished mahogany table.

'Thank you, sir,' smiled Dwight, quickly taking the money and moving towards the door as he spoke. 'Hank Jefferson said that eight years later you decided you wanted to run for attorney general in the 1980 elections yourself. So you told Bill Bridger that his time was up as attorney general and if he didn't leave his office you'd make trouble for him over the Maureen incident. Judge Kilabrew, who owed you for handling it all, fixed Bridger up with a nice little job in Washington. That left the coast clear for you, sir, to become attorney general yourself.'

Jim exploded, jumping from his chair once again. 'I'd like to see them all prove that! Get the hell out of here, Dwight, before I kill you!'

Dwight slipped hastily out of the oval hunting room.

For a few moments there was a stunned silence.

'Dad, is all this true?' breathed Cass, gazing up at his father.

'Of course it isn't!' retorted his father, pacing the red carpet. 'That son-of-a-bitch Liam Kavanagh! I happen to know he's one of the biggest financial backers of Ken Colter.'

Cass knew that Colter was his father's Democratic opponent in the upcoming elections for senator.

'As a matter of fact, I was out at his ranch in Ovando on New Year's Eve,' offered Cass.

Jim swung round. 'What the hell were you doing out there?' he shouted.

Cass reeled. 'Let me explain, Dad! There's nothing to it! My girlfriend's younger sister is best friends with Keira, Liam's daughter. Keira had a birthday party that day and we were invited.'

'Shit, Cass! Why the hell did you go to Goodnight and why didn't you tell me about this before?'

'I've always wanted to see the Goodnight ranch. Everyone talks about it. But when Liam Kavanagh saw me, he asked me to leave. He said, "No Henderson sets foot on my land, ever!" I had no idea you two were enemies. Why, Dad?'

'It's a long story.' Jim had no intention of going into detail.

75

He continued to pace the carpet, muttering under his breath. 'That bastard! If he pulls this off and gets me out of the race, I swear I'll get him. I'll think of a way.'

The attorney general stopped abruptly and looked across the table at his son. His eyes narrowed.

'How old is his daughter now?' he asked slowly.

'Fourteen.'

Jim went back to his seat, a little smile playing around his mouth. He sat down, lit another cigar and drew on it deeply. Finally he spoke. 'Keira Kavanagh,' he mused, watching smoke evaporate against the backdrop of the hunting scene. 'Cass, my boy, I need you to do something for me.'

Liam Kavanagh put down the telephone. He smiled to himself before picking up the receiver and calling his good friend Professor John Donahue at the law school in Dallas, Texas. After a few rings John answered in person and they exchanged a few preliminaries before turning the conversation to the subject that currently preoccupied them both.

'I've just spoken to Hank in Missoula. The story about Maureen Jacobsen will be on the front page of the *Missoulian* as well as the *Independent* tomorrow morning.'

'Have you spoken to Ken?'

'Sure have, he's blown away! Jim Henderson's out of the race for the US senator for the state of Montana before it even started.'

'Well, the way I look at it, you've done your state and perhaps our country a favour, Liam.'

'I believe we have, John. Oh, and John . . .'

'Yeah?'

'Do me a favour, make sure Maureen's kept safe over the next few weeks.'

'You really think he'd try something?'

'Nothing would surprise me with Jim Henderson. Let me tell you something. A few years ago, Gloria was working on a homicide case involving a young local woman who was found dead in a ditch off the Interstate 15 highway near the turn-off into Wolfcreek. She was so badly beaten they took a while to identify her. The case was never solved because there wasn't enough evidence. But Gloria knows enough to be pretty certain that it had something to do with Jim Henderson. The body was found not far from his ranch, Greenacre. And this woman used to work at Big Dorothy's in Helena before it was closed down. According to a reliable source, Henderson had been a regular client of hers. Perhaps she knew more than was good for her. Either way, John, it's better to play safe than be sorry.'

'Well, my wife and I could let Maureen stay at our place for a while until things quieten down.'

'That would be a good idea. We'll keep in touch.'

'Bye for now. And Liam, take care of yourself.'

There was a knock at his study door.

'It's me, honey.' Katherine walked in wearing her silk dressing gown, her long auburn hair falling over her shoulders. Liam looked up at her and remembered how he had felt the first time he had ever seen her. He pushed back his chair and swivelled it to face her.

She moved towards him across the thick Persian rugs. 'It's late, Liam. I was tired of waiting for you to come to bed.'

Liam looked at his watch. It said eleven thirty. Katherine slid onto his knee and wrapped her arms around his neck. They kissed. 'You look happy. Received good news?'

He kissed her again. 'The best news I've received in years.'

'Anything you want to share with me?' She ran her hands through his thick brown hair.

'Not now.' Liam's pale green eyes gleamed as he took her face in his hands. 'Did I ever tell you that you have the softest skin?' He smiled and kissed her neck.

She looked intently at him. 'Did I ever tell you that you're the best-looking rancher in Montana?'

Lifting her in his arms, he carried her over to the fireplace, where the embers still glowed, and laid her on the rug before it. 'Let me think,' he answered. 'You may have told me that once before, but I'd love to hear you say it again.'

The knock on the study door startled them both.

'It's me, Keira.'

'Come in,' her mother said.

'What are you doing up so late?' asked Liam, looking over his shoulder as his daughter came into the room.

Dressed and presentable, he was sitting on the floor leaning up against one of the three sofas grouped around the hearth, his arm around Katherine beside him. They were both watching the burning logs and drinking hot tea.

'I couldn't sleep.' Keira walked towards them. The light from the rekindled fire threw moving shadows onto the walls and ceiling in the otherwise darkened room.

'Am I disturbing you?' she asked, flopping full length onto the sofa behind them. Her long legs dangled off the side.

'You came at the perfect time,' answered her father.

She looked down at them both sitting on the rug. 'You look like two college kids.'

Her parents laughed and their eyes met. Liam bent and kissed his wife on the forehead.

Keira sighed. 'If I ever find the love that you two have, I'll be the happiest girl in the world.' She thought of Cass.

Her mother smiled. 'Grandma once said to me, "Katherine, you have to search for the key to the song of your life, and when you find it, don't let it go."'

'So is Dad the key to the song of your life?' responded Keira.

Katherine smiled at her daughter, her deep blue eyes crinkling at the corners.

'Do you believe that there is one person in the world we were each born to love for ever?' Keira persisted.

'I do, but many don't,' replied her mother, her own sense of absolute contentment reflected in the serenity of her face as she looked at her daughter.

'But suppose I never find him, or worse, he never finds me? Or perhaps I'll find him and he won't like me, then I'll be left living my life craving the song but never finding the key.'

'There are many keys to life's song, Keira.' Her father spoke now, staring into the fire whose glow flickered gold across his strong face. His wife and daughter both turned to look at him.

'For some people it's finding that perfect love, a soulmate, when the desire to give everything you can to that other person is more necessary than anything else.' Liam smiled down at his wife.

All that could be heard now was the crackling of the fire, as Keira reflected on her parents' words. She felt that something extraordinary had been revealed to her.

'Well, I think I know what my key is,' breathed Keira dreamily as she watched the moving shadows on the ceiling above where she lay. 'But until I know I've found that soul-mate, I won't trust anyone.' Even Cass, she added to herself.

'It's late,' yawned Katherine, 'you've got school tomorrow.'

They stood and Keira went over and wrapped her long, thin arms around them both.

'I love you guys. If anything ever happened to either one of you, I'd want to die myself.'

'No you wouldn't,' said Liam, embracing her with his free arm. 'You're a survivor, Keira, you're a Kavanagh.'

Chapter 5

Leaving the Valley

*T*here was a crash as Solomon hurled his music case across the veranda. 'I knew it!' he shouted, pacing up and down. 'What has that terrible lawyer done to us?' He stopped and turned to his mother. 'We can't let him do this!' A tone of hope crept into his voice. 'Maybe the papers are false? Surely *Papai* wouldn't sign anything he hadn't read properly?'

'*Papai* signed papers that have registered the land in the name of Dauro Vasconcellos,' answered his mother. 'Some men who work for him showed up today with legal documents to prove it and they threatened your father. The land is up for sale and they said we had to leave immediately. Your father did not fully understand what he was signing.' Overwhelmed by a sense of despair, Isabella leaned back in her chair and closed her eyes.

That night the black rock loomed above them as Ezio and Isabella sat on the veranda, venting their frustration and shock through heated voices. Many ideas were put forward, some legal and some not. By eleven o'clock they were ready to kill Dauro Vasconcellos. By midnight reality had set in. They decided that their best plan of action was to approach the local forum of lawyers in Petropolis whose job was to represent the poor. They intended to start a legal process against the man who had taken everything from them.

Throughout the discussion, Daniel slept soundly in his cot. The other children did not.

'I'm scared,' said Talita, who had the only single bed. 'What's going to happen? I don't want to leave the valley, ever. This is our home.'

'Would we be able to take Duke with us?' asked Pedro, already preparing himself for the worst.

At last Solomon spoke. 'Of course we'll take him!' Nothing was going to separate him from his dog.

'You know that guardian angel you told us about a few weeks ago, that *Senhora* Francisca saw?' said Talita suddenly. 'Couldn't you ask it to get that Dauro Vasconcellos and bring him back here to the valley? *Tio* Mauricio would soon sort him out!'

The boys laughed, breaking the tension.

When they finally slept, Solomon dreamed. It was a dream that was so real, it felt as though he were living it. And yet although he knew he was dreaming, he could not wake himself up. He was in a cave on his own and everything was dark. He could hear the sound of wolves howling and a wind was blowing from the direction of the eerie sound that echoed on and on. Paralysis gripped him and when he opened his mouth to cry out, no sound came. He knew he had to run away, but as he tried to move his legs, he could feel he was not going forward. The sound of menacing growls grew nearer and the wind grew fiercer. He started to cry out for his *Papai*. How could his *Papai* have left him alone? The pointed heads of the murderous wolves appeared at the mouth of the cave, the leader howled again and Solomon felt the very breath of life was being sucked out of his soul.

He opened his mouth again, crying, crying, crying from inside and suddenly something seemed to burst in his throat and he screamed out the words, '*Papai, Mamae, socorro! Papai, Papai*, help me! Where are you? *Papai*, can you hear me?'

From out of the darkness a vast ball of light surrounded him and he felt as though he were flying through time. Across the wind he thought he caught the sound of a whisper, '*Come to me, Solomon. Come to me . . .*'

He felt a cool, slim hand touch his arm. He took the hand and sensed himself lifted upwards. He looked down and saw the wolves far, far below. He turned to see who was holding his hand and his eyes were stung by a brilliant light so intense and so awesome that he had to turn away. But in that split second he had seen who it was. Majestic golden wings like an eagle, a face smooth and gentle, a smile so comforting, so warm, and the most beautiful eyes he had ever seen. He knew this was his angel and he never wanted to let go of that hand.

Then another whisper came through the wind: '*Come to me, Solomon, come to me . . .*'

Solomon awoke with a jerk and sat upright, breathless, his heart beating furiously. It was still night, but the light from the full moon poured in through the shutters. Pedro, Talita and Daniel lay still and he could hear the sweet short breaths of those asleep. The voices from outside had ceased and the crickets had reclaimed centre stage. He lay back on his pillow and waited for the morning.

As light dawned and the birds began to sing, a note was pushed through the shutters next to his bed. Lost in the drowsiness that follows wild dreams and fitful sleep, the paper startled him as it plopped onto the floor. His brothers and sister slept on as Solomon picked up the note and read it:

Solomon,
Let's go fishing. Usual place.
Ze

Solomon pulled on some clothes, grabbed a piece of bread from the kitchen and left the sleeping household.

'Come on, boy!' he hissed at Duke on the veranda as he tried to close the mosquito door as quietly as possible.

Papai faced his family as they sat around the table. Daniel, now walking, toddled around the room oblivious to the fundamental change about to take place in his little life.

'I am so sorry, children,' began *Papai*, looking down at his calloused hands clasped together on the table in front of him. Pedro, Talita and Solomon said nothing. *Mamae* gazed through the window at the mountains she had come to love.

'We have to leave our home while the local forum of lawyers in Petropolis try to find Dauro Vasconcellos. It is not safe for us to stay here while this is being sorted out.' *Papai* paused and looked at his wife. The threat of violence from Dauro's men if they did not leave was too frightening for Isabella to bear. Ezio knew he had to protect her and the children. The pain was unbearable. 'I'm a simple man, not educated at all, but always in the past I have been able to rely on my strong intuition. This time I didn't listen to it. I didn't want to believe I was being deceived.' His voice broke and he put his hands to his mouth, trying desperately to control himself.

'But *Papai*, didn't Dauro Vasconcellos charge you a thousand dollars for bringing off the deal?' asked Solomon, his throat tightening.

'He did, son, but I will get it back when the lawyers in Petropolis find him . . .' The unshed tears gleamed in Ezio's eyes. Solomon averted his gaze.

Isabella spoke softly. 'We cannot stay in the valley. *Tio* Mauricio does not want to see your father again. *Vovo* is very sad, but as you know he lives with *Tio* and can do nothing for us. I've written to my brother Marcos, who you won't remember, because you were babies when he was last here in the valley. He's a builder and he lives with his wife *Tia* Bete and their children in the centre of Rio de Janiero. I received a letter back from him yesterday saying that he will be able to get work for *Papai*.' Isabella tried to smile. 'And what is more, he has offered us some rooms at the back of their house, where *Tia* Bete's mother used to live. She died last month.' Isabella crossed herself hastily. 'He says we are welcome to use them until we find somewhere better.'

Pedro felt his usual happy spirits desert him at that precise moment. The prospect of being wrenched from his security in this Garden of Eden, where they had all been so content despite their lack of means, and placed in the centre of a huge city with no trees or river or wide open spaces was too much for his sunny soul to bear. Putting his head in his arms, he started to cry. Talita, mortified more with her twin's distress than with the dreadful news, embraced him with her skinny arms and wept too, burrowing her face into his shaking shoulders.

In contrast, Solomon remained hard-faced and dry-eyed. Inside himself, a storm of emotions raged and screamed, but the need to mourn was trapped and restrained by a developing armour of guilt and anger. From this guilt and anger a new strength and rigid self-control began to build, and with it a hatred of the man who had brought their world crashing down around them. He would never give *Senhor* Dauro Vasconcellos the satisfaction of shedding a tear, ever.

Instead he said coldly, 'When do we have to leave?' Not a muscle on his handsome young face betrayed his agony of spirit.

Ezio observed Solomon's cool stare and Pedro's over-wrought misery. He knew then that he had lost more than his land.

'Next Saturday,' he answered listlessly. He took hold of Isabella's hand as if to gain strength. 'I have spoken to Sister Marilyn and she will give you each a transfer document which will enable you to finish the semester at a school in Rio.'

There was a pause as Solomon looked over at his piano. Following his son's gaze, Ezio said, '*Vovo* will look after the piano for you, until we can come back and get it.'

Solomon nodded, then turned his head towards the veranda where Duke lay as close to the mosquito door as possible.

'Yes, I wanted to ask you your opinion about Duke,' Ezio continued.

Solomon did not look at his *Papai*.

'Do you think, son, he would be happier here in the valley with *Vovo* until we return, or with us in the city? It's your choice completely.'

Duke, oh God, not Dukey, not my dog, don't take my dog from me too, not my dog! His heart screamed, but his eyes remained cold and dry. 'Duke will stay here in the valley,' he answered without a trace of emotion.

Then Solomon scraped back his chair. He stood and tied

his hair away from his face. 'Well, if you'll excuse me, I had better practise on my piano before it's taken away. In case you've all forgotten, I'm performing at the cathedral this evening at seven.'

'I haven't forgotten, *filho*, but if you feel unable to perform—'

'No!' interrupted Solomon, not able to look his father in the eye. 'I've made a commitment and I'll play.'

He walked over to the piano, and soon the atmosphere of the tension-filled room was soothed by the most beautiful sounds.

Petropolis Cathedral with its magnificent stained-glass windows and soaring ancient stone walls was packed with more than a thousand people for the concert that evening. Solomon, dressed in his white tuxedo, played and sang as never before to an enthralled congregation, among the tombs and monuments of Brazil's imperial family.

Senhora Francisca was sure that his remarkable perform-ance was due to that angel. Indeed, the *padres* thought they were looking at an angel, as they sat enthroned in their richly embroidered vestments. They were unusually moved by the sublime voice of the boy from the mountains as it filled the vast house of God. When the congregation rose to their feet as one, in a standing ovation, Solomon stood and bowed three times. Then he gestured to *Senhora* Francisca, who came to stand beside him and, with her usual theatrical grace, shared the rapturous applause.

'I'm leaving the valley, *Senhora*,' said Solomon loudly while the clapping went on. 'We're moving to Rio next Saturday.'

The *Senhora* continued to acknowledge her pupil's success

with smiles and gestures, as the devastating news struck her to the core. But within seconds she was making a plan.

After the concert, the whole family was invited back to the teacher's townhouse for supper. *Senhora* Francisca cornered Ezio as soon as she could, in order to discover the cause of the dramatic new development in the lives of the Itaborahy family. She had sensed for some time that *Vovo* was not sharing with her some problems which had arisen in his family situation. Now Ezio explained as well as he could the details that surrounded the loss of their home and their land.

'But naturally, Ezio, you don't expect Solomon to give up all this for a life without music? Let me make you a proposal, which I'm sure you will agree makes a lot of sense.' She took another sip of her drink. Ezio stiffened, anticipating her plan.

'Solomon can come and live with me,' she said triumphantly, without the slightest thought that her words would not be well received. 'I'll pay for everything and he can continue to attend the Santa Cecilia School and develop his extraordinary talent without interruption. He can go to school in Petropolis and see *Vovo* and his dog every weekend. Naturally he will want to visit you also in Rio from time to time, until you are able to return to live in the valley.' *Senhora* Francisca beamed the confident smile of someone who has made a generous proposal. To her astonishment, she saw that Ezio was looking indignant.

'I thank you, *Senhora*, but I couldn't allow that. I can't accept what you propose. My family is my responsibility and mine alone. It is my responsibility to make amends to them, and no one else's. Thank you for your kind offer, *Senhora* Francisca, but I cannot accept it. Excuse me, please.'

Ezio turned and walked off in the direction of his wife, leaving the *Senhora* open mouthed and deeply offended.

The following Saturday the family drove in convoy from Petropolis to Rio de Janeiro. Ezio's Chevy was laden with beds, cupboards, the table and chairs and plastic bags stuffed with clothes. Neither he nor his two passengers, Pedro and Solomon, spoke much. He could not forget the pained look on *Vovo*'s lined face that morning. They had embraced, father and son, and Ezio had repeated over and over again the words, 'I'm sorry, *Pai*.'

Ze and Solomon had managed to smuggle notes to each other confirming their continuing loyalty and friendship. But as they drove past the pink cottage for the last time, there was no sign of *Tio* Mauricio or *Tia* Ana. Solomon was tormented by the image of Duke, confused and whining at *Vovo*'s side as they drove away. But despite his excruciating misery, Solomon's eyes remained dry.

In front of them drove *Tio* Marcos in his small white van. He had come from Rio de Janeiro two days earlier and had not drawn breath since arriving. An incessant talker at the best of times, the eight years since he had seen his sister called for a torrent of stories and anecdotes to make up for the lost time. His old van was now groaning and puffing black smoke through its exhaust under the weight of their fridge, cooking utensils, two armchairs and numerous potted plants. Isabella's heart was breaking as the distance from the mountains increased. She was grateful to Talita for entertaining Daniel with his favourite toys as the sixty-three kilometres passed slowly by.

They would all remember for the rest of their lives the image of the hand-painted banner that Ezio's band had strung up between two of the tall palm trees in the square in Correas. It read:

TO THE BEST *CAVAQUINHO* PLAYER THIS SIDE OF THE EQUATOR – WE'LL MISS YOU *AMIGO!*'

In Rio, the *favela* sprawled its poverty over one side of a mountain which towered above high-rise apartment blocks patrolled by security guards. Hundreds of colourful box-like houses stole every patch of land over what had once been a beautiful landscape.

'They say it's home to forty thousand people,' said *Tio* Marcos to Isabella and Talita. The faces of his passengers, staring at the scene through the small windows of the van, reflected their sadness. The noise of the congested traffic, the smell of pollution and the overwhelming heat numbed all their senses as they turned off the main road and started the climb up the twisting road through this beehive-like colony of massed human occupation. Goats and chickens ran free, as did small children with large bellies and runny noses. They crossed a concrete bridge over a filthy river, an open sewer fed by small exposed drains that descended from all directions through the overcrowded shanty town above. The stench was overpowering. As they swung to the left, the traffic came to a standstill. Crowds of people swarmed through the narrow alleyways, shopping from open market stalls set up next to huts made of card and pasteboard. *Tio* Marcos sounded his horn.

'*Vamos*! Let's go!' he shouted, waving his arm out of the window at the bevy of people.

'Oi, Marcos, *amigo*! *Tudo bem?*' cried a very large and overweight man in a bloodied apron to their left. His butcher shop was a wretched-looking establishment without doors or windows. Slabs of fatty meat hung on large hooks from the ceiling, each encased in a swarm of flies.

'Don't forget you owe me money!' bellowed the butcher with a cheerful smile.

Tio Marcos beckoned him over. 'Luciano! Meet my sister from Petropolis! Her family are coming to live here for a while.'

Luciano approached the van and stuck a large bloodied hand in Isabella's direction. 'Welcome!' She took the hand gingerly and nodded with a nervous smile.

'And who's this flower?' boomed the butcher, smiling past Isabella at Talita. The little girl smiled back. This man was ugly and fat, but she could not help responding to his warmth in the midst of her present dejection.

'I'm Talita.'

Luciano winked at the pretty little girl before him, rubbed the top of Daniel's curls and turned back to his shop.

'He's a good man,' said Marcos, who was still sounding the horn spasmodically. 'His heart is as big as his body. Every week he goes into the centre of the city taking soup for the children who live on the streets.'

Isabella was shocked. 'How could anyone let their children go to the streets in the first place?' she exclaimed.

'Ah, in desperation people send their children to the streets to beg for money for food,' answered her brother matter-of-factly, 'and many of them find that living on the streets with a gang is better than returning to a *favela* every night where they're either beaten or starved.'

'Whatever happens to us,' vowed Isabella, 'I will never, ever, let one of my children beg for a living.' She wiped the perspiration from her upper lip.

The crowd eventually cleared an opening for *Tio* Marcos, who forced the loaded van up the steep slope that immediately swung to the right. A crowded minibus careering down the road in the opposite direction barely missed them and more horns sounded.

'*Meu Deus!*' cried Isabella in despair. 'That teenager over there on the corner is holding a machine gun!' She looked back in horror, as a strong smell of marijuana wafted in through the open windows of the van. 'Do you know him, Marcos?'

Her brother had expected this. However, he had hoped to welcome her into his home first before having to explain to her about their resident armed gang.

'Don't worry, sister, they give us protection,' he blustered, making things worse.

'Protection! Protection from what?' Isabella grabbed her baby from Talita.

'Calm down. Calm down, sister. They're—'

'Don't tell me to calm down!' she interrupted. 'You haven't been through what I've been through this last month, and now you've brought us and our children to live in a hell-hole where teenagers walk around with loaded machine guns!'

The journey, the stifling heat, the loss, the unknown, had all become too much for Isabella. She knew she should be grateful to her brother, but it was not going to be easy.

Marcos preferred to ignore the reality of the situation that was his daily life, and decided to change the subject.

'You must be hungry, all of you? How about some lunch, a cold beer perhaps? I know *Tia* Bete will have it all ready for us.' He forced a smile at Isabella and Talita, who both sat looking dumbfounded. Despite the similar colour of the eyes, Talita could see no resemblance between her beautiful, slender mother and this infuriating *Tio* with his rounded face, fleshy nose and ballooning belly.

The van roared on up through the heart of the *favela* to find *Tia* Bete, her lunch and her cold beers.

Isabella felt too exasperated to cry, so she closed her eyes, excluding reality for a few blessed seconds, as she remembered her mountains, her lovely little home, her paradise above Petropolis. Nothing, no one, would steal her memories from her.

In the truck behind them, Solomon did the same.

Chapter 6

Bitterroot

May was the busiest month of the year on the Goodnight ranch, and it was the time of year Keira loved best. With spring came bluer skies and warmer days to which the earth responded, and so did she. Long rich grasses swayed in the meadows and high pastures, wild flowers grew freely under the leafy aspen trees around the lake, migrant ducks and other wild birds returned to build their nests near the water's edge and the cry of the loons pierced the air as they dived after fish beneath the surface. Above, the vast wilderness and mountains still peaked with snow, eagles soared, locking their wingspan, picking the thermals and riding the air currents in the big Montana sky. She often wished she could be up there with them.

During the months of March and April fourteen calves were born on average every day, and by May it was time for branding and vaccinating against tetanus, black leg and red water disease. As he did every year, Liam Kavanagh sent out invitations to friends and family for the first weekend of the month.

'Many hands make light work!' he said to Callum as they drove to the post office in Ovando three weeks before the event. Few refused the opportunity of a weekend at one of the most famous ranches in Montana, especially as on the Sunday night Liam always threw the best country-and-western party in the Bitterroot valley, with live music, dancing and as much beer and barbecued meat as a man could stomach.

Liam's sister Gloria, her husband Jack and her two sons Max and Fin would usually drive up from Helena for the occasion. This year, however, Liam had employed his two nephews for the full three months of their summer break. They fitted in well with the other men and knew how to handle a horse; many a vacation had been spent at Goodnight during their childhood. Max, the elder of the two boys, was in his final year reading agricultural studies at Missoula University and, unlike his mother, had inherited his forefathers' feeling for the land. He was the quieter of the two boys and dark-haired like his father, Hank, Gloria's first husband. Everything about him suggested a gentle confidence; his movements were precise, his gaze intense. The dream to run his own ranch one day drove him steadily forward. Fin, on the other hand, intended to pursue journalism as a career like his father and his stepfather. This amused Liam and Katherine because, with his red hair and freckles, he was the spitting image of his grandfather, Finbar Kavanagh, after whom he was named.

Liam's foreman Bill Whitely was in his element. Following the branding and vaccinating came the repetitive but crucial checking and maintenance of over twelve hundred acres of fencing around the ranch, where prime bulls would be put back into the pastures for a further sixty days of breeding. Somewhere in between came the sowing of barley, alfalfa and brome, orchard and timothy grass over acres of freshly ploughed fertile land. Bill organised and delegated tasks to his cowboys with a confidence and skill that only experience and love for the work could bring. Liam trusted him and gave him full responsibility as foreman, but Bill was getting older, and the previous year his wife Joanna had spoken to him, concerned that he was becoming too easily tired. Sometimes her husband complained of shooting pains down his left arm. Liam had since watched him closely. He suggested that his foreman take a week off to rest, but this had been stubbornly rejected. Nevertheless, Liam had given firm instructions that he was not to overstretch himself, and the two extra hands throughout the summer would be a big help. Joanna was thrilled at the prospect of having Max and Fin in her roost as well, and felt eternally grateful to Liam Kavanagh for his sensitive foresight on Bill's behalf.

With forty extra mouths to feed that first weekend in May, Katherine always welcomed Jack's and Gloria's congenial company and assistance in the kitchen. This year she was more than ever grateful, as she had not been feeling well herself for a few weeks. Jack was a keen cook, when he had the time, and he certainly preferred the tools of the kitchen to hot branding irons, needles and bridles. The anticipation of Jack's delicious meals kept the riders riding and the branders branding with a deeper sense of well-being.

On these weekends Liam co-ordinated the herders. Four teams, each consisting of six riders, were assigned to a particular herd at different points of the eight thousand acres. Each team was appointed a leader, and they were responsible for driving their herd down from the pastures and into the corrals around the barns by the lake. Bill and his team of twenty then took over the back-breaking mission of branding and vaccinating, before the animals were driven back to a new meadow. His son Ed was in charge of the horses. Every rider was assigned a horse for the weekend, unless they lived locally and had brought their own. Appaloosas, mustangs, quarter horses, bays, paint and palominos pranced and whinnied in an excitement and anticipation of the weekend which equalled that of their riders.

'These next two days, you're goin' to treat your horse as if it were your best friend! That means feedin' him, brushin' him, bittin' him up, cleanin' his tack and rewardin' him!' Ed instructed the team as they assembled early on the Saturday morning. 'And anyone mistreating his horse won't be invited back next year!' Ed's dimples deepened as he broke into one of his big broad smiles. Placing his hat on his head, he mounted his palomino, which flicked its tail and cavorted sideways, snorting.

'OK folks! Listen up!' shouted Liam. He was sitting on top of the fence around the first corral in his jeans, chaps, boots and spurs. 'We've gotta get going! So Pinnacle Jake, let's recap on your team: Teddy Blue Ed, Callum, Max, Fin, Mary and Keira. I want you all to take the high pastures just below the timber plantation up by those three ponds and bring down the herds we have grazing way out there. Could be more than four hundred including all the calves. It's going to take you close on two hours to ride up there, so remember, don't tire your horses as it's all uphill and they'll need their strength for the work when they get there. I reckon at a slow dairy walk you'll get those piggies back here by early afternoon. My team will bring in the herd pasturing over by the creek, followed by Buckskin Joe and his team who will drive in the second herd from the meadow close to the divide below Burn Mountain. That's if he's able to keep his mind on the cattle and off Beryl!' Everyone whistled and Joe pulled his cowboy hat down over his head to hide his burning cheeks. 'My hope is that by the time Pinnacle Jake arrives back from the timber pasture, old Mesquite Bill here and his mighty team will already have branded and vaccinated well over four hundred cows and calves. Wyoming Pete and his team can give a hand here 'til this afternoon, when you'll take some of the cattle back out to graze on new pastures.'

Liam jumped off the rail. 'Right! What are you waitin' for?' He gave Bill a high five and mounted his chestnut mustang. The shouts of 'yee haa!', 'giddy on!' and 'step up!' were matched by snorts and squeals from the horses keen to be off.

Keira could not think of anywhere in the world she would rather be at that moment. The elation of working in such a team, herding her father's cattle under the Montana sky she loved, brought a surge of adrenaline. As she looked over to the horizon the morning sun seemed to promise a new beginning. Ed met her gaze, and they smiled at each other, sharing the moment in thought and feeling.

Back in the kitchen, Jack was already beginning his preparations for the banquet that evening. He needed to be ready for fifty ravenous people.

'I need some volunteers!' shouted Jack, looking very much the chef in his blue-and-white-striped apron, as he set to work at the chopping table. The radio was blaring in the background.

'We're willing,' responded Beryl and Linda in unison, glad of an excuse to leave the mountains of dirty breakfast dishes to Faye and Joanna.

'Great! You'll find a stack of rindless bacon in the refrigerator and some string in that drawer next to the range.'

The sisters settled themselves to the tasks he set them.

'How you doing, Gloria?' he called over to his wife, as she and Barbara Colter gossiped over their vegetables.

'Fine, darling,' smiled Gloria briefly over her shoulder before continuing her conversation with her old sorority friend.

Ken and Barbara Colter had driven up the night before and were staying in relative luxury in the homestead, in contrast to most of the working guests that weekend who had sleeping bags in the barn. Ken was, after all, Montana's prospective candidate for senator in the upcoming elections, now that Jim Henderson's campaign had been discredited. While Barbara gave a hand in the kitchen, Ken rode out confidently with Liam, his friend and biggest financial backer.

Amidst the noise and activity of the early morning, Katherine had managed to slip away unnoticed to the refuge of her bedroom. As she sank onto her bed, the telephone rang on the small table beside her. It was her mother calling from Sunderland.

'Katherine, pet lamb, are you any better? I've been worried.'

If she was honest, the pain was getting worse. But all she said was, 'I'm OK, Mum, just tired.'

'Have you told Liam yet?'

'I don't want to worry him. He's got enough on at the moment with the herding.'

Her mother sighed. 'Promise me, Katherine, that you will get yourself to a doctor?'

Katherine promised. She replaced the receiver and got off the bed.

Behind the locked door of her bathroom, she retched again and again and only wished there were something in her stomach that could be ejected, but she had eaten nothing. Steadying herself with one hand on the marble washbasin, she bent down and splashed water from the cold tap on her face with the other.

'Oh God, what's happening to me?' she asked the grim reflection in the mirror through panting breaths. She opened her medicine cupboard and took out some painkillers. 'Why aren't you working?' she demanded of the small brown bottle. Slowly lowering herself onto the carpet, she leaned against the wall and closed her eyes.

Faye's voice from the bedroom startled her.

'Katherine, are you here? Katherine?'

'I'm in here, Faye.'

She unlocked the door and the housekeeper gasped at the sight of her.

'What is it, Katherine? Have you eaten something?'

'I'm OK. I'll be fine. I don't want a word of this mentioned to anyone. Do you hear me, Faye?' Katherine winced.

Faye stared at her, a question mark in her eyes. 'What's the matter? What are you feeling?'

'Pain in my left side. I've had it for a few weeks and it's getting worse.'

'Why haven't you been to the doctor?'

'You know I can't stand ill health, Faye. Waiting rooms, doctors, hospitals – you know all that.'

Faye took her arm and led her through the door, across the bedroom to the four-poster bed where Katherine eased herself down.

'I think you should sleep for a while,' suggested Faye, her eyes reflecting her concern.

'No, I'll be all right. Can you get me some water, please?'

Faye disappeared into the bathroom and quickly returned. Katherine took the glass and swallowed three painkillers. They tasted bitter and she had trouble swallowing them. She rubbed her face and took a deep breath.

'Help me up, Faye, they'll be wondering where we are downstairs.'

For the first hour Keira rode at the back of the trail, taking in the surrounding beauty and reliving the developments in her relationship with Cass. Her weekend with him at Greenacre Ranch now seemed surreal. The shock invitation had come out of the blue through Mary, who had telephoned one Monday night, ecstatic with the news that Cass and Alana were going to his ranch with some friends the following weekend and that he had actually asked whether she and Keira would like to join them. Keira had been incredulous, having convinced herself that Cass's dismal departure from Goodnight on her birthday had ruined any possibility of meeting amicably again. She had danced with joy around the house for three days until the rest of the household became suspicious, but had mentioned nothing to her parents other than saying that she was going to spend the weekend with Mary. On the Thursday night the heavens opened and dumped four feet of snow over the valley, closing off all road access to the highways. In utter distress Keira had to let go of her invitation, and was certain that there would never be another. To her amazement, a second invitation came only two weeks later, and this time the unpredictable elements were kind; at last her dream was going to become a reality. She was to spend a whole weekend in Cass's company.

The Henderson ranch was small in comparison to Goodnight, with only a few hundred acres pasturing a herd of Black Angus cattle on the edge of the Lower Holter Lake. They had all left their cars at the Upper Holter Lake, from where the Henderson speedboat was waiting to whisk the party to the mooring by the ranch. Keira had found to her astonishment that Cass was going out of his way to give her attention. But to her mortification, this had left her feeling hot, flushed and confused and quite unable to handle the situation. It felt far safer just admiring him from a distance. To make matters worse, Alana had noticed what Cass was doing and had responded angrily by directing barbed comments at Keira at every opportunity. Mary had felt uncomfortable as well, both for her friend and for her sister. She told Keira that she wished they had both stayed at home instead.

Keira involuntarily kicked her horse on as she remembered that Saturday evening of her stay. Even now, after all these weeks, the memory of it made her feel angry.

Alana had taken offence at something Cass had said during dinner and flounced off to bed in a bad mood. She and Mary had escaped into the cosy Mexican-style study to play a board game together, away from the rest of the party. But Cass had found them and insisted on joining in the game. To Keira's alarm, Mary had soon excused herself, saying she needed to get to bed. This left Keira alone with Cass in the warm but dark oak-panelled room. She had immediately jumped up, feeling awkward, but Cass had insisted she sit down again and finish the game with him.

'It's my turn!' he said firmly. 'And I've got the perfect word just for us.' His penetrating eyes bore through hers as he slowly laid the small plastic letters down one by one on the board.

He watched her face, waiting for her reaction.

The letters spelt L-O-V-E-R-S.

Keira's heart lurched wildly and to her embarrassment she

felt herself blushing furiously. All the breath seemed to be knocked out of her at once.

Cass stood up and held out his hand to her.

Keira looked up at him and thought she had never seen him look so handsome. As he loomed over her in his sky-blue sweat-shirt and faded jeans which clung to his muscular frame, her feelings almost overwhelmed her. She allowed him to pull her up and lead her over to the fireplace, where he knelt down with her at the low oak table. Every dream she had ever had about him was suddenly a reality. Here she was, sitting close to the most wonderful boy her eyes had ever beheld, just the two of them alone in a darkened room.

Cass felt supremely confident about what he intended to do. It was going to be so easy to accomplish this small request of his father's. This little girl was his for the taking; she just could not wait, he could tell.

She would never forget this moment for the rest of her life, she thought, as she took in his beautiful face glowing in the firelight. She was struck with an overwhelming longing to be close to him, yet at the same time felt a strange fear that she was entering a forbidden garden from which there was no return.

Cass continued to smile lazily at her. His face was only a few inches from hers. Edging closer to her, he put a hand under her chin and raised her face to his. He felt her tremble. Slowly, he bent to kiss her and as he watched her close her eyes, he knew she was his.

Keira was ready to surrender to him body and soul. He had made it so clear to her this weekend that he was interested in her, and she just knew they would be together for the rest of their lives. She felt his lips on hers and waited for the bliss to come. But suddenly everything changed. He was forcing her down, forcing himself on top of her until she was pinned under his weight and he was pulling roughly at her top, grappling at her breasts and nearly suffocating her with his mouth. She heard herself calling out to him, pleading for him to stop. He was hurting her! She could not breathe! But he ignored her cries. He was towering over her now, undoing his jeans. As he began pulling roughly at the zip of her trousers, she felt a terrifying sensation of claustrophobia and fear. This was not how it was in her dreams. Where was the gentleness? Where was the tenderness? Where was love? An image of her parents flashed into her mind, and her mother's words about finding the key to life's song. She had to get away! Forgetting that this was the boy she had longed to be with, Keira began beating at him with her fists and twisting her body in a desperate effort to escape from under him. She was sobbing loudly by this time, and it was only because he feared attracting the attention of the rest of the party in other parts of the house that Cass allowed her to scramble free.

Keira backed breathlessly towards the door, and saw that Cass was looking dishevelled and angry.

'What the hell do you think you're doing? You've been leading me on all weekend! I was only giving you what you were asking for!' Cass was not used to being rejected.

Keira leaned against the closed door, incredulous. She could not believe what he had just said.

'But you were being so nice to me, Cass! I thought you really liked me. I don't want it to be like this! You were hurting me. I thought it would be different. I thought *you* would be different. Don't you understand?' She tried to make sense of the storm of emotions tearing through her.

Cass got to his feet and buttoned his jeans. 'Don't I understand? What do you mean, don't I understand?' He ran his fingers angrily through his hair and put his hands on his hips. 'You're a little flirt, Keira Kavanagh, and you've disappointed me.'

Keira forced back the tears. 'Please, Cass, I want to try and explain something to you. Please listen to me!'

He sat down impatiently on the low fireside table and glared across at her.

'I just know it's not supposed to be like this!' She began pacing the space between the door and the sofa, her hands twisting nervously together. 'You see, I have a dream about how it should be, and nothing's going to ruin that for me. You could say my dream is like a . . . like a song, you know how songs are all different, some with high notes and some with low notes, every melody is different. I believe each one of us has our own song in life; something quite beautiful.' She was looking down as she spoke, but here she glanced at his face and saw an expression of incomprehension on it. She made herself continue. 'But we have to discover the key to unlock that song and it's only when we find it that we can feel complete, and our song can be played out. I'm searching for that key Cass . . .'

Keira fell silent. She had said too much. She felt deeply exposed in revealing her private thoughts, but she had to go on now. She took a deep breath. 'I believe that the key to my song is the person I was born to love for ever.' Feeling stronger now, she looked steadily at him. 'I thought you were that person, Cass. But maybe you're not, and if you're not, then I don't want to betray the one who is. Someone in the future, someone I don't know yet.'

Looking across at Keira as she spoke from her heart, Cass felt his anger evaporate. He was suddenly struck by her vulnerability, and for the first time he saw her beauty. Despite her young age, there was a depth about her, a strength he had not noticed before in a girl. What had he nearly done? What had his father asked him to do?

Again, Keira forced herself to look at Cass as he got up and walked over to her. She saw to her surprise that his face had softened.

'I'm sorry, Keira. You're only a kid. It's late and it's time you went to your room.' He gently took her hand and reached to open the door. In silence he led her up the wide staircase to her bedroom door, where he uttered a faint 'goodnight' and left her alone.

But later, as she slipped in and out of sleep in that strange bed, she sensed him return to her room. Or had it been a dream? Like a moving shadow, he entered the room and stood quietly over her. She felt his touch on her face and wanted to turn and draw him close to her, but she could not move and the tall shadow left as quietly as it had entered.

She remembered now, to her dismay, how Cass had ignored her the next day, although their eyes had met fleetingly over breakfast. Later the party had sped back in the boat to the Upper Holter Lake and their waiting cars earlier than planned. In the silence of her bedroom that night, back at Goodnight, Keira had wished with all her heart, as she did today, that she had not shared her innermost thoughts with Cass. Why had she said all that to him? He must have thought she was completely juvenile. What had he said to her? 'I'm sorry, Keira, you're only a kid.' She could only blame herself if he never looked at her again.

Keira was brought abruptly back to the present by Ed's voice up ahead of her on the trail.

'Hey, Keira!' He pulled lightly on the reins of his palomino and waited for her to catch him up.

'Montanans have room to live, to breathe, and above all, to think. You OK?'

Keira looked across at her friend, startled by his perception. 'I'm OK.'

'You know what my mom always says, 'This too will pass.'

Keira smiled. 'You're going to make some lucky girl very happy one of these days, Eddie Blue!'

He smiled. 'If you play your cards right, it could be you!'

'You won't give up, will you?'

'Nope.'

The Bitterroot Valley stretched out endlessly below them. Clumps of pines and cotton trees lined the passes which were laid out with a natural geometry, the creeks meandered off like ribbons heading for the Blackfoot river now hidden somewhere behind the folds of the mountains. The wind carried the pungent, clean odour of sage. Some whitetail does and three fawns pricked their ears and vaulted away, as a cold breeze stirred the long grass laced with wild flowers. The sweating horses snorted and neighed, responding to the wind in their tails. Callum led the trail under the arching sky, now filled with swift-moving clouds whose shadows gave the land motion. Pinnacle Jake and Max rode close behind, each allowing the feel of the country to settle in them, the great emptiness and age of it, the feel of the westward mountains and plains stretching on for ever. It was here that their souls belonged.

Mary rode close to Fin, laughing at his jokes and stories.

Despite her aching thighs, she was relishing his lively company, and he her sweet spirit.

'Watch out for the gopher holes and rocks,' shouted Jake, 'they're worse up here and the last thing we need is a horse with a broken leg!'

They had ridden for almost two hours and were nearing the timber pastures below the Bob Marshall Wilderness. As they rode to the ridge of the last hill, Jake turned in his saddle. 'We'll stop by the first water hole over there and let the horses drink. The first herd should be grazing behind that thick line of pines to our right.'

Mary dismounted her bay slowly and cried out as her boots hit the ground. She was so stiff she could hardly walk, and she sat down quickly, stretching out her legs and flopping back into the long grass with a sigh of relief. Fin laughed and removed the saddlebag containing his lunch.

Keira and Ed allowed their horses to take a drink in the cool water, and then joined them.

'I'm starving!' said Keira as she tucked into a sandwich. Mary sat up and looked across at her greatest friend. While she could have felt intimidated by Keira's natural beauty, model physique and passionate personality, Mary's generous nature and positive attitude did not allow her to. They had never spoken about their time at Greenacre Ranch. Keira had not wanted to, and Mary loved her too much to push the subject.

Jake led his horse towards the picnic. 'Ed!' He smoothed out his golden moustache and crouched down on his spindly, bowed legs. 'We're not hungry, so Max, Callum and I will ride on ahead, check on the herds, and report back.'

'Sure.'

The boy and the two men rode off at a slow trot in the direction of the trees.

'He's a good guy, that Pinnacle Jake,' said Fin, leaning on his elbow and stretching out his long legs. 'You can tell in his eyes that he's in tune with the rhythm of things up here.'

'Jake?' cried Ed. 'He loves the land so much he'll get planted in it!'

They all laughed with him.

'Dad says he's one of the best workers he's ever had,' said Keira, opening a can of Coke.

'Jake's my mentor. Watching him break in a yearling is something else.' Ed turned to check on the horses, cropping grass close by. 'One thing he taught me is that you never go against the grain, you go with it. Otherwise the yearling will end up rebellious like children with their parents. If he backs off in that round corral, you let him go and start again. You wait until the horse is ready.'

'Talking of being good with horses, how's the rodeo going, Ed?' Fin grinned, and put a blade of grass between his teeth.

'Go on, Ed, tell us your latest!' Mary urged, and her brown eyes glistened.

Ed wiped his mouth with the back of his hand. 'Well, if Keira don't mind hearing the story for the twentieth time?'

'No, don't mind me, go right on ahead.'

'I was in Cody, Wyoming, with Jake as it happens. There was this bull called C4. He was sucking all the air out of the earth, scooping up, boy, he blew like an atom bomb. I was out of that shoot and suddenly I got my hand stuck in the rope loop. I looked like a helicopter, he was turning round so fast. I managed to loosen my hand and I slipped underneath the bull. He was stomping and blowing snot all over me, giving me a new hairdo and a new look to my shirt and my pants.'

Mary shrieked.

'Then I got free, and took two steps away and that C4 came thundering towards me and rammed its head against my knee. I flew over his back in a perfect somersault and landed on the ground. Those rodeo clowns were doing what they could to control the bull too. Someone shouted out, "Ed, I think your left leg's pointing north!" They managed to pull me out of there somehow.'

There was a sudden sound of hoofbeats. Keira looked up and knew there was something wrong as soon as she saw the riders returning at speed. She stood and the others followed her.

'What's up?' cried Ed.

'Someone's cut the fences along the top of both pastures, the herds have gone up into the timber towards the Bob Marshall!' shouted Jake.

'Who the hell would do something like that?' yelled Ed, getting to his feet.

'Don't know, but whoever it was, they did a good job. There are clean cuts through the wire in several places along the top of the pastures!' cried Jake.

'Must've been done over the last twenty-four hours, 'cos the tracks and the droppings are fresh,' added Max.

Jake looked back in the direction of the trees as the others hurriedly tidied up the picnic things and mounted their horses.

'Here's what we're going to do.' Jake ran his hand through his thinning hair and replaced his hat. 'We'll have to split up into two teams and spread ourselves out. Max, Fin, Callum and Mary, you'll take the first pasture to the left, riding straight up into the middle of the woods. Keep looking for tracks or new droppings, they're herd animals, as ya'll know, so if you find one there'll be a whole lot others. Ed, Keira and I will take the other pasture, riding up on the right-hand side of the timber. When the first team finds those doggies, drive them out in drag. Max is your trail boss and he'll ride up at the point of the horseshoe. Once you're out of the timber, fire your rifle three times to let me knows you're on your way. We'll round up the rest on the other side and follow ya'll home.'

Keira surveyed the vandalised fencing and a shiver ran up her spine. Who had done this? The tall trees closed in around them and the smell of damp wood filled the air. Loose twigs cracked under the horse's hoofs. The sky appeared and disappeared intermittently through the dark foliage above them. After fifteen minutes Jake saw the first elk carcass laid out before them, shot in the head between the giant antlers. Its stomach had been cut open, and the guts and innards spilled out over the earth.

'What the hell is this?' Ed screwed up his face.

Jake jumped off his horse and, removing a leather glove, touched the blood in the belly of the slain animal. 'This hasn't been here that long. Must be close to four hundred pounds.'

Keira felt sick.

'We're going to have to fork off in different directions,' said Jake, getting back on his horse. His voice reflected his growing concern. 'The herd can't be far away, but the tracks divide here and there's so much land we could miss them by staying together. Keira, you ride with Ed over in that direction and I'll go this way. If you find the cattle fire one shot, wait twenty seconds and fire again. I'll do the same.'

Ed led the way, whistling a tune to calm their nerves. Keira did not recognise it. Nothing had been heard from the others and she was beginning to wonder how long this would all take.

'There's fresh droppings over there, let's head west.' Ed turned his horse and picked up the tune again.

Keira's thoughts drifted back to the homestead as she pictured Uncle Jack and his team preparing for their evening meal. The tracks petered out and soon their path was blocked by a jack pine thicket.

'We'd better tie up the horses and try to find a passable trail on foot.' Ed jumped off his horse.

They had not walked for more than a few minutes when Ed stopped in his tracks and put out his hand. Startled, Keira stood still. Over to their right, through the undergrowth, she saw an eye staring in their direction.

The bear had seen them first.

'Oh my God!' whispered Keira under her breath. Ed's first thought was that the Winchester saddle gun he was carrying would never be powerful enough to deal with a big bear, even a black. But he knew that he had to do something. As he brought the rifle up, the bear reared up with a deafening roar. They knew immediately that they were not dealing with a black. They had walked into a grizzly. Everyone knew that you never disturbed a feeding grizzly. All of a sudden the little saddle gun became scarcely more adequate than a water pistol.

Ed and the bear looked at each other for maybe ten seconds, although it seemed more like ten minutes. Even in the dim light under the trees, the bear's silver-tipped coat gleamed. Ed held the gun steady and waited for the bear to make the next move. He prayed it would not be in their direction. From a distance behind them they heard their horses, terrified by the scent of bear, pulling themselves free and galloping away.

'Damn!' breathed Ed.

The grizzly did not move.

'Start backing up slowly,' Ed hissed at Keira.

They both took a cautious step back, and then another. Soon there was a reasonable distance between them and the bear. It had stayed put, its bulk slumped over the carcass of a second elk left in a similar condition to the one they had already encountered.

'Get behind that spruce thicket over there!' whispered Ed.

They crouched down behind it and waited for the grizzly to get interested again in the elk. Ed strained to see what it was doing through the thicket, when all at once there was another almighty roar and this time it was behind them. They spun round in shock and there was the bear up on its hind feet like a giant man, eyes blazing, lips curled back, the hackles on its neck and shoulders standing upright.

It was only a few yards from them and Ed knew that despite its size it could cover the ground like lightning if it wanted to. There was one tree between them and the grizzly, and he realised then and there that there would not be time for them both to climb it. If they were ten feet from the tree, the grizzly was eight. They were standing in the shadow of death.

Ed's deep affection for Keira struck him through his heart like a dagger as in that split second he saw clearly that now he would never hold her, make love to her and marry her one day as he had so longed to do. But perhaps the ultimate way he could show his love was here before him: he would give his life to save hers.

'I love you, Keira,' he whispered, and she turned and looked into his kind, familiar face.

'Trust me. When I say "go", run towards that tree and climb up it!' He gave her no chance to argue. 'Go!'

As Keira ran for the tree, the bear charged. Reaching the base of the tree, she scrambled frantically for the lower branches. She could hear Ed yelling at the top of his voice. Pulling herself up as high above the ground as she could, she turned and screamed with horror.

'Oh God! No! No! Ed! No! You beast, come and get me!' she cried, shaking the branches of her tree hysterically.

The bear ignored her as it crushed the oxygen out of Ed's lungs with the weight of its body. Ed looked up. Seeing Keira was safe, he closed his eyes, and released his spirit to the Creator of all the beauty he had known in his short life.

As the grizzly grabbed Ed by the neck and began to pull his limp body into the undergrowth, Keira, numb with despair, heard three shots over to her left in the far distance. The first team must be on their way home.

'Max!' she screamed into the sky, convulsed with sobs. 'Mary! Oh God, Mary! Help! Don't go without me!' She swung her head back, looking for the bear. 'You bastard! You murderer! Come and get me! Get me!'

Immediately the bear reappeared, bounding towards the base of the tree, grunting and raging, clawing angrily at the bark. A single shot rang out from a new direction, and closer. It must be Jake. He had found the second herd. The noise of the rifle scared the bear and he pulled back off the tree. Jake's second shot fired and the grizzly turned and lumbered off up the hill, stopping every few seconds to throw a warning growl back. When it reached its elk carcass, it lay down as if on guard, keeping its head turned towards Keira.

Her only hope was Jake. He would soon wonder why they had not reappeared, surely? On the other hand, he would be loath to leave the cattle he had found, and it would never enter his head that they needed help. If he did come looking for them, he would run into the bear himself and she wanted to prevent that. There was no option. She had to try to escape by herself.

Keira watched the grizzly until she saw it had lost interest in her and was feeding again. She started to inch her way down the tree, in agony in case she made a sound that would attract the bear's attention. When she was almost down, it suddenly lurched to its feet and came lumbering down the hill. She scrambled up through the branches again as fast as she could. The beast tore at the ground with its paws, and prowled around under the tree for a while until it seemed to lose interest once again and set off back towards the carcass. Twice more Keira tried to leave the tree, and twice more the bear returned. Finally she abandoned all hope. Putting her head into her hands, she wept uncontrollably.

The crack of a rifle shot startled her, this time much closer than before. It seemed to be coming from behind her. She started to scream. 'Jake! Jake! Jake! I'm over here! There's a bear, a grizzly. I think it's killed Ed! Jake! Jake! Help!'

A second shot rang out, and the bear started to drag the half-eaten carcass up the hill and out of sight. Keira waited breathlessly, only half believing that the grizzly would not return for her. But she had to take a chance. A sharp branch caught the side of her forehead as she lowered herself to the ground. She cried out in pain as blood started trickling steadily down her face.

Keira tried with all her might to get hold of herself. There was no sign of the bear, but she did not trust it. She was sure it was lurking somewhere around her. Tensing herself, she sprinted in the direction of the jack pine thicket, forcing her legs to obey her. Then something moved behind her, and as she turned to face what she was sure would be the grizzly, her weakened limbs gave way under her and she fell heavily to the ground. Something touched her. Keira screamed and looked up, terror-stricken, then squeezed her eyes tight shut with relief. It was Jake.

Back at the homestead, Jack was hurtling round the edge of the sunlit lake in one of the ranch trucks, heading for the corrals where the branding was still in full swing. He screeched to a halt and jumped out.

'Liam!' he shouted.

Liam turned, sweat pouring off his face, a hot branding iron in his hand.

'What is it, Jack?' he yelled back. He was surprised to see his brother-in-law.

'It's Katherine! She's collapsed in the house and she seems to be unconscious. We've called the doctor!'

Liam stood still, incredulous.

Twenty-four hours later, Cass was watching a replay of a football game in the TV room of the Henderson mansion, stretched out on a black leather sofa, when the phone rang at his side. It was Alana, and he listened carefully to what she was saying before hanging up. He sat for some time staring blankly at the flashing screen. Eventually he stood up, turned off the TV set and walked down the long corridor to the other end of the house. He entered his father's study without knocking. Jim Henderson looked up from his reading.

'Dad, Katherine Kavanagh is dying of cancer. It's already in her liver and she's been given a few weeks to live,' said Cass evenly.

Jim straightened in his large desk chair and tried to assume a sympathetic expression.

'And there's more, Dad. The foreman's son was killed out in Ovando yesterday on the Goodnight ranch. They were herding in the upper pastures. Apparently someone had cut the fences, releasing the cattle into the timber just below the Bob Marshall. There were elk carcasses left as bait for the bears. At least five carcasses were found by the herders, but the sixth was found by a grizzly. It attacked some of the group. The foreman's son died saving Keira. He was my age. It will be all over the local news tonight.'

Jim removed his glasses.

Cass stared his father square in the face. 'During the past fifteen minutes, Dad, I've been trying to convince myself of something. I've been trying to convince myself that this had nothing to do with you.' His tall frame stood firm. 'Ambition I have, and push I will to reach my goals, but I draw the line at premeditated murder!'

Jim's eyes narrowed.

Cass continued, 'I also draw the line at raping fourteen-year-old girls!'

Jim raised his eyebrows.

'Tell me, Dad, that what happened in Ovando had nothing to do with you?'

Jim reached out slowly and took a cigar from a silver-plated box in front of him. 'I'm very disappointed at you, Cass.' He took the silver trimmers and cut both ends of the cigar. 'For many reasons, not least that you would presume such a thing. But what most concerns me is that I detect a softening in you. Worse, I discern a softening towards this girl Keira.'

This was not what Cass expected. He turned abruptly and left his father's study, slamming the mahogany door behind him.

Jim Henderson leaned back in his chair and closed his eyes for a few seconds before reaching for the phone.

Chapter 7

Kites in the Wind

The Itaborahys' new living quarters in the *favela* were confined, dark and unbearably hot due to the virtually windowless brick walls and the corrugated iron roof which mercilessly drew down the stifling heat of the burning sun. However, they had their own side entrance, so it was possible to go in and out without having to bother *Tio* Marcos and *Tia* Bete. This door opened onto the back end of a restricted concrete passageway that was permanently wet because it was the only place the women of the house could do their washing. Shaded overhead by a zigzag of pegged-out clothes, this roof-less passage ran along the length of the simple dwelling up to an old rusty gate on weak hinges which led out into an alleyway.

Their side entrance accessed the three rooms which were now their home. To the right, the kitchen area was dimly lit during daylight hours by a grated window with a view of a concrete wall. The other two rooms became their bedrooms, although both only had space for one large bed, and neither had a window. What little ventilation there was came through the bricks punctured with round holes that *Tio* had laid in two slanting lines just beneath the corrugated iron roof. On the other side of the concrete wall was the shabby but popular hair-dressing salon presided over by *Dona* Maria, the loud and domineering wife of Joao Batista, who lived above it with their five children, two sons-in-law and three grandchildren.

During their second week in the shanty town, Ezio made a desperate effort to brighten their dismal new quarters. While his family slept, he took some tins of paint and tried his very best to reproduce on the cold, drab concrete wall the magnificent mountain panorama that had been so much part of their lives at the cottage in the valley. The following morning, as the family gathered for bread and sweet *cafezinho* in the kitchen, there was a joyous time of laughter and tears when Pedro spotted the captivating new vista which, although it was just a façade, opened up a whole new world for the children to nourish their imaginations in that otherwise desolate place, starved of nature's breath.

With determination and persistence, Isabella had managed to squeeze into the kitchen area her pine table and six chairs, clothes cupboard, rug, two armchairs, plants in chamberpots, refrigerator, gas cooker, small worktop and two cardboard boxes filled with crockery, utensils and pots and pans. At night this gloomy abode was lit up by their latest commodity, electricity, but this novelty soon wore off when a tirade of gunshots between the rival drug gangs of the three surrounding shanty towns rang out suddenly through the warm, starlit sky. Then the Itaborahys were glad, for the first time, of the lack of windows and their restricted, although claustrophobic, situation.

Tio Marcos, *Tia* Bete and their two children, four-year-old Vivianne and baby Tiago, occupied the front part of this rambling dwelling. Their cramped living room had an outlook onto the alleyway which ran down at right angles to the main square situated half-way up the shanty town. The view was almost worse than the Itaborahys', because the open sewer ran down before them, and they also looked onto a rubbish dump scavenged daily by mange-riddled dogs, as well as the rear of *Dona* Cecilia's seedy bar and other rickety and dilapidated homes which perched along the perimeter of the *Praca*. Only the small Pentecostal church next to the bar offered a sense of hope, with a fresh coat of white paint gleaming in the bright sun.

Tia Bete was pear-shaped with thick black frizzy hair, which was straightened every week at *Dona* Maria's hair salon. She had smooth ebony skin and a sweet smile, and was highly efficient and organised, despite her family's lack of means. It was obvious to Isabella straight away that her brother depended on Bete for everything. She prided herself on her cooking and was always making a variety of tasty savoury pastries, which were sold in the Pentecostal church every Sunday for a small profit. Her tiny kitchen was immaculate and boasted a brand-new refrigerator with freezer, a gas cooker and the shiniest pots and pans Isabella had ever seen. Her bedroom, next to the kitchen, had a double mattress on the floor surrounded by old cardboard boxes filled to the brim with neatly pressed and folded clothes. The baby slept with them in an odd carved oak drawer that *Tia* Bete had discovered quite by chance amongst bags of rubbish in front of the high metal security gate of an elegant building near Copacabana Beach. A few postcards, showing her favourite sights of the city, were stuck on the wall. Vivianne slept on a mattress in a tiny cubbyhole next to the only bathroom, which was shared by both families. The bathroom was blessed with a flushing toilet and a pipe through which gushed a cold-water shower. The washbasin had only one tap which swivelled uncontrollably when it was turned. A cracked mirror the size of an adult's hand was nailed to the wall above it, but was positioned too high to benefit either of the women. This communal bathroom was entered by two doors, one leading from Vivianne's little room and the other from Ezio's and Isabella's bedroom. When using the bathroom, an occupant had to remember to lock both doors first from the inside, or run the risk of being found naked or on the toilet by a member of the other family.

The building job that *Tio* Marcos had arranged for Ezio in Tijuca was by no means what he had optimistically imagined it to be. It was hard, monotonous labour that entailed humping bricks from giant delivery trucks to the building site, where they were loaded onto makeshift hoists and hauled up through the scaffolding to the construction area. Although Ezio was used to long hours and early starts, the pay of less than $90 a month was a pittance, and at the end of the first four weeks he started to look for something else, driven by the urgent desire to get his family out of the shanty town as quickly as possible. Their henpecked neighbour, Joao Batista, husband of *Dona* Maria, a small plump man with too many wrinkles in his dark face for his forty-five years, worked for Souza Cruz, the tobacco company. The vast factory was situated opposite the shanty town. Joao Batista drank too much and would lure *Tio* Marcos away most Friday nights for drinking bouts in city bars, from which they would often only reappear on Saturday morning, reeling home still under the influence of alcohol. This drove their respective wives crazy; each blamed the other's husband for being the worse influence. One Thursday evening, however, Joao Batista made his presence known outside the Itaborahys' quarters with loud handclaps. The family were eating dinner in silence, each contemplating the view through the high grated window. Nevertheless, Isabella ushered him in and politely offered him a *cafezinho*. Joao Batista explained the purpose of his visit without preamble, hopeful of avoiding being heard by *Tia* Bete. There was a job going at Souza Cruz, he said. 'They pay well,' he added, accepting a refill from Isabella, 'starting at $190 a month. The hours are long and there is only one day off a week. But if you're interested, Ezio, you could come and meet the boss tomorrow, first thing.'

Ezio started work at Souza Cruz the following Monday. Memories of farming his land in the valley tormented him more than ever, and he found himself fighting back tears as the confines of the noisy, smelly factory bombarded his senses. How could he have lost everything so suddenly? He felt a failure as a man, a husband and a father.

Solomon, Pedro and Talita attended a local state school in the mornings, and at 6.40 a.m. they all set off together, *Papai*, *Tio* Marcos, Joao Batista and his fourteen-year-old son Jonas, joining the steady flow of other residents of the *favela* who descended the steep hill like tiny ants weaving their way down to the chaotic streets below. Here they either caught buses into other parts of the city or continued on to work or school on foot. Isabella soon joined forces with her energetic sister-in-law, who every day ironed basketloads of clothes impeccably for other hard-working mothers in the community who would drop them off at the rusty gate from time to time. It paid little, but every bit helped.

One evening after supper, during the first month in their new surroundings, Ezio and Isabella told the children that they would not be returning to their home in the valley. The lawyers

in Petropolis could not find Dauro Vasconcellos. He was a
bogus lawyer; his name was not on record. They had gone to
the address of his office in Rio de Janeiro, but it had been
vacated. Their land had been sold and he had run off with the
money from the sale as well as all their savings.

Solomon's deep anguish intensified. His hatred for
Vasconcellos, who was the cause of all this misery, became
an obsession. He could see in his *Papai*'s face that he had
lost all hope. Solomon's heart ached for the green mountains, the river, the sounds of the birds, the smell of the earth
and the rich tropical foliage. But worse still, not a day went
by when he was not hit by a wave of longing for his dog. It
tore him apart. Ze was his best friend, but Duke had been
his constant companion. Each morning when he awoke the
pain inside was sharper than ever and his head would start
to spin in an endless turmoil. But he had quickly discovered
a routine that became a ritual, which fortified his resolve to
triumph over his circumstances. By training his subconscious
mind to wake up at 5.00 a.m., he was guaranteed to be first
in the bathroom by a good fifteen minutes. Taking great care
that both doors were locked from the inside, Solomon stood
on the lavatory seat and removed the small cracked mirror
from the brick wall. Then he would sit down and stare at
himself. What he saw was always a shock to him, because
somehow this person he looked at was not the same person
he felt he had become through the agony of mind and body
he was enduring.

'Solomon,' he would whisper to his reflection, 'don't give
up. You *will* get out of here and you *will* win. You will track
down that bastard and make him pay for this. And one day
you will take your family back to the valley.' Finally he would

say, 'Duke, I miss you so much. But you would die in this place! Believe me, you are happier with *Vovo*.'

Then he would put the mirror back on its nail, and remembering the guardian angel *Senhora* Francisca had seen standing over him all those months ago, he would search the room with his eyes and say, 'Where are you? Who are you? If you do exist, then help me, please.'

Jonas was the youngest of *Dona* Maria's and Joao Batista's five children and he had inherited his mother's strength of character and his father's short, stocky frame. Jonas's face had smooth skin, free from adolescent acne, a fine nose and dark brown eyes set under thick, curly lashes. Born and raised in the shanty town, he knew everyone and everything that happened in it. He had long ago decided that he would not end up like his father. Although the pull of alcohol, sex and the underworld of drug-trafficking was almost overwhelming to a young teenager in that place, Jonas was determined to withstand it. He liked Solomon the moment he met him. He was different from the other kids Jonas knew and he wanted to be his friend.

His mother, *Dona* Maria, was a 'voice' in the shanty town revered even by the gang members who all liked her and respected her friendship. Although she had no official training or certificate as a nurse, she kept a complete box of first aid materials and medicines in her home, and would attend to bullet wounds almost daily in the back of her salon after hours. As she did this, she would tell the young drug-runners in no uncertain terms to get out fast from the drug-trafficking world. She had been to too many young men's funerals, she said, lives devastated before they had even reached adulthood. But while openly disapproving of what they did, she empathised with the pitiful and empty childhoods that had driven them into the fatal web of drug-trafficking in the first place. The quick money was as tempting as a piece of cheese on a mousetrap is to a starving rodent.

There were certain parts of the shanty town that were out of bounds to the prudent residents of that community. These were the frontiers and boundaries where the three neighbouring shanty towns merged and met with each other. No one ventured beyond them if they wanted to stay alive. In particular, the highest point of the mountain was extremely dangerous, as it was watched over night and day by the armed gang members who shot to kill at any suspicious trespasser.

Jonas's best friend, Felipe, lived near this boundary, at the crossing point with the neighbouring favela. His house was a skeleton of sticks filled in with dried mud and a roof formed of plastic bags. Felipe's mother, *Dona* Rosemarie, rotund and strong as an ox, with black velvet skin and only one tooth left in her head, had built this tiny abode to shelter her four children, who had each been conceived by a different father. Jonas had heard his mother say that she had thrown her last partner out when she had found him abusing their six-year-old daughter.

On Solomon's first visit there with Jonas, one sweltering Saturday afternoon, he was horror-struck by the degradation of the dwelling. But the squalor was somehow subdued by the lushness of the green foliage that surrounded the hovel. *Dona* Rosemarie had successfully planted trees which were now laden with luscious ripe fruit: avocados, papaya, passionfruit, lemons and bananas. But, in spite of this abundant oasis, the stench from their decrepit pigpen rendered the air in the vicinity suffocating, and litter was strewn everywhere.

Felipe, who was as black as his mother but endowed with a perfect set of white teeth, was pushing his younger sister Rosanna on a swing he had made for her out of a rubber tyre and an old rope strung from a tree. They had spent the morning together on the streets below, selling sweets from small boxes at traffic lights so that their mother could buy food for that day. Felipe knew the city streets well and had missed school on many occasions, initially in order to beg for money for food, but more recently to act as a courier for his elder brother, who was a drug-trafficker.

'Hi Felipe!' shouted Jonas, slapping him on the palm of his hand. 'I've finally brought Solomon to meet you.'

'Hey, how ya doing, *amigo*?' Felipe shouted back, flashing a wide smile. 'If you're a friend of Jonas's you're a friend of mine.' Felipe was tall for his fourteen years, and lanky. His right ear boasted a gold earring and he wore a yellow chain around his neck.

At this point a young man naked to the waist appeared from the hovel, drawing on a joint. His muscular chest was covered in fuzzy black hair and adorned by several silver chains. He had a hand down his trousers.

'Who's this?' he growled, eyeing Solomon coldly.

Solomon instantly took a dislike to him.

'He's a friend of Jonas's,' responded Felipe, quite unperturbed. 'Solomon, this is my brother Fernando.'

Fernando was unimpressed by this introduction and disappeared back inside. They followed him in.

'He's part of the drug gang here,' hissed Jonas. That did not surprise Solomon.

Solomon ducked under some low-hanging electricity wires as he entered the mud-and-stick abode. It was larger than it appeared from the outside. Each darkened room seemed to lead into yet another. Immediately inside the main entrance stood a lavatory that Solomon noticed was full of excrement. The next room had a king-sized bed, where *Dona* Rosemarie and all her children slept side by side like tinned sardines.

Fernando, who had sprawled himself diagonally over the bed, grunted as they passed him. Racks of clothes hung behind large pieces of old grey sheet lining the mud walls. From the bedroom another door led to an even darker corridor, which suddenly swung to the left and into a narrow area which was part kitchen, part sitting room. *Dona* Rosemarie stood at the stove which was fuelled by scraps of wood.

'*Mae!*' called Felipe. 'Jonas is here with his friend Solomon.'

The enormous lady before them turned and smiled her toothless grin. She was sweating profusely.

'Jonas, how you doing, *querido*?' she said in her deep, husky voice.

'Good, and you, *Senhora*?' replied Jonas easily. 'This is Solomon.'

Solomon, who had never seen such filth and disarray in a home before, checked himself. 'Pleasure to meet you, *Dona* Rosemarie.'

'You're a good-looking boy, aren't you!' *Dona* Rosemarie looked directly into Solomon's eyes. Solomon turned away, embarrassed more with this large woman's intrusive, intuitive gaze than with her compliment.

A sink that looked as though it had never seen water and certainly not soap stood to the left of the stove. It was jammed with pots and pans, plates and cutlery that were soiled and stuck with bits of dried food. The pile was visibly heaving with flies.

'Come and sit down,' said the deep, commanding voice of *Dona* Rosemarie, 'and I'll give you some homemade lemonade.'

The three boys sat at a table. Solomon noticed that its fourth leg had been replaced by a length of wood which was precariously fixed into the mud floor, leaving the table with a dangerous wobble. *Dona* Rosemarie disappeared outside, rolling her bulk from side to side. She reappeared with some fresh lemons picked from her tree.

'Get some water for me will you, Felipe?'

Four large buckets of water stood between the table and the largest, whitest fridge Solomon had ever seen.

'Fernando bought it for me last month!' croaked *Dona* Rosemarie proudly, reading Solomon's expression. 'Now we can have ice in our drinks!' She gave a loud, rasping laugh as her strong hands squeezed the acidic fruit into a jug.

At the far end of the dark, narrow room stood a sunken sofa, a television and, surprisingly, an old record player. Its casing was blackened, suggesting it had been recovered from a fire.

'What happened to your record player?' inquired Solomon, suddenly aware of how much he missed his music.

'Well, thanks to Fernando, we all nearly got burned alive last month,' exclaimed *Dona* Rosemarie hoarsely, 'but the record player still works!'

'Do you have any records?' asked Solomon, his eyes hopeful.

'You like music then?' *Dona* Rosemarie handed them each her lemonade in an assortment of chipped cups and glasses.

'He's a pianist! He plays in theatres and cathedrals in Petropolis!' Jonas slapped his new neighbour on the back.

'Is this true?' cried *Dona* Rosemarie incredulously, giving another loud laugh. She opened one side of a broken cupboard door under what remained of the record player and rummaged through the chaos, emerging triumphant with a black disc still in its sleeve. 'Here we go! Put it on, Felipe, for our cultured visitor!'

All at once, the strains of the London Philharmonic Orchestra erupted into the humid atmosphere, so completely out of context in that pitiful place. Solomon's mind and emotions were immediately transported back to *Senhora* Francisca's music room, and quite unexpectedly he felt tears spring into his eyes. Angry with himself, he stood abruptly, went over to the record player and lifted the needle off the revolving LP.

'Don't you like it?' bellowed *Dona* Rosemarie, offended. 'I've plenty of samba!'

Solomon could not look round. A force of feelings was churning him up and he needed to get control of himself fast.

'*Mae*!' drawled Fernando suddenly from the room next door. 'Madeleine's sent you a basket of food.' Mercifully the focus swung away from Solomon.

'God bless that woman!' shouted *Dona* Rosemarie to the air above her.

Fernando, his feet dragging, carried in the heavy basket and dumped it down on the mud floor. Rosanna skipped in behind him, clapping her hands.

'Who's Madeleine?' asked Solomon, thankful for the distraction and intrigued by this generosity.

'She's a saint!' answered *Dona* Rosemarie, falling to her knees and rummaging through the gifts. 'A saint! There's a month's supply of rice, beans, flour, sugar, coffee, salt, chocolate and pulses!'

'Madeleine's a nun,' explained Jonas, refilling his cup with lemonade.

'I don't have any good memories of nuns.' Solomon sat down again, remembering Sister Marilyn.

'Madeleine is my friend!' Little Rosanna spoke for the first time.

'Haven't you met her yet, Solomon?' asked Felipe, surprised. 'She lives in a house with two other nuns just above here at the very top of the mountain. You have to have God on your side to live there, and survive!'

'She's from France,' croaked *Dona* Rosemarie, clearing her throat. 'The nuns run a Sunday school for the children, and Madeleine works here the rest of the week.' She examined a bag of black beans.

'She's musical like you, Solomon,' Felipe added. 'She plays the piano, the violin and the organ.'

'I've never met anyone from Europe,' said Solomon quietly. 'But I've met enough nuns to last me a lifetime; I'm in no hurry to meet another one.' He stood up, ready to leave.

'Felipe, go and call Stephano down from the ridge!' ordered *Dona* Rosemarie. 'He's been flying his kite up there long enough under this hot sun.' She added the used glasses to the pile in the groaning sink.

The three teenagers walked in single file along the narrow path which cut through the rock up to a ridge underneath the uppermost part of the mountain. Little Rosanna ran to catch up with them and took Felipe's hand. From up here, children had a perfect site for flying their homemade kites, which could easily be persuaded to catch and ride the wind pockets and soon be hundreds of feet above their heads for hours on end.

Stephano was a year older than his brother Felipe, and amongst his peers he was a master at kite-flying. He had won competitions five years running. Twenty or thirty children stood or sat along the length of the ridge, each holding an empty can or bottle wrapped with string, moving their arms backwards and forwards as they manipulated their kites made from used plastic supermarket bags.

'Stephano!' yelled Felipe, looking into the blue expanse of the afternoon sky at the colourful array. 'Meet my new friend Solomon!'

'*Ola!*' replied a boy seated on the ground ahead of them. Solomon noticed that his back was twisted and his useless legs were folded beneath him. But despite this disability, he saw that Stephano's arms and shoulders were highly developed, muscular and strong, probably due to years of dragging his paralysed body around all day long. His kite, made out of a large red plastic bag, flew higher than any of the others.

'Here,' said Stephano, passing up to Solomon the plastic bottle which held the string of the kite. 'Have a go!'

Solomon shook his head. 'I don't feel like it,' he mumbled.

'You know, my friend,' Stephano continued, 'God never promised to take the hard road from us, he just promised to walk side by side with us through every unexpected turn.'

'Where is God in all this mess, then?' Solomon surveyed the sprawling poverty below them through the shimmering air.

'I believe he's up there weeping,' replied Stephano, reeling in his dancing kite. His hazel eyes looked up at Solomon. 'Don't stop dreaming, Solomon. I have three wishes: to get a wheel-chair, to go to university, and to move my family into a house made of brick.'

'Madeleine!' cried Rosanna, jumping up and running towards the fairest-skinned woman Solomon had ever seen, who was walking towards them.

He stared down at his feet.

'Don't worry,' said Stephano, sensing Solomon stiffen. 'You'll like her. Trust me.'

Solomon did not trust many people any more and he was certainly not going to make friends with a nun.

That night Ezio went out drinking with Joao Batista and *Tio* Marcos. They still had not returned home by breakfast the following morning.

'*Mamae*,' said Talita, putting her arms around her mother, 'don't worry, he'll be back soon.'

Solomon did not like to see his mother upset. He could tell that she had been crying, and her hand trembled as she sipped her hot, strong *cafezinho*.

Pedro arrived back from the bakery, situated on the oppos-ite side of the *Praca* to *Dona* Cecilia's bar.

'They're really hot, just out of the oven.' He threw the white plastic bag of fresh-smelling bread rolls onto the table and went into the bathroom.

Tia Bete appeared at the side entrance, dragging her feet. 'I'm sorry, Isabella, I'll make Marcos's life a misery for this.'

Isabella said nothing.

'Does he know?' *Tia* Bete insisted.

'Know what, *Mae*?' asked Talita, buttering some bread for Daniel.

Isabella looked up for the first time. 'I'm pregnant.'

Tia Bete dragged her feet back along the passageway, shaking her head. Solomon felt his appetite fade.

'Eat, son!' ordered Isabella. 'I'll be fine.' She got up and went into her bedroom as Pedro came back.

'*Mamae* is going to have a baby!' exclaimed Talita to her twin. 'That's why she's so upset with *Papai* not coming home last night.'

'Does he know?' asked Pedro, sitting down at the table and taking his roll from the bag.

Talita shrugged her shoulders. Daniel sucked happily on a piece of bread in his familiar high chair.

'I know why she's upset,' said Solomon.

They both looked at their eldest brother. To them he always knew everything.

'*Mamae* told me that *Papai* used to drink before they met, and it made him violent.'

'*Papai* violent?' echoed Pedro, incredulous.

'Alcohol changes people.' Solomon stared at the façade *Papai* had painted.

'Does it make him like *Tio* Mauricio?' Talita was aghast.

At two in the afternoon the three men staggered back in the stifling heat to the simmering fury of their wives. Ezio walked into his house, unrecognisable to any of his children.

'What's the matter?' he drawled, slurring his words and falling back against the door. 'Where's Bella?'

'She's pregnant!' announced Talita. 'You didn't know that, did you?' She was horrified at the appearance of her darling *Papai*.

Isabella appeared from her bedroom. She looked exhausted and unusually unkempt.

'Solomon,' she said quietly to her eldest son, 'please, *querido*, would you take the children out for me for a little while?'

Solomon hesitated. He hated to see his father in this state and it scared him to leave his mother alone with him.

'I'll be OK, go on!' She looked at him firmly.

Ezio collapsed into one of the armchairs. 'Come here, Bella, sit on my knee.' His eyes were heavy and bloodshot and his mouth sagged. 'Go on, kids, get lost, all of you!'

Aghast at his father's harsh tone, Solomon lifted Daniel from his chair and called to the others to follow him out.

He set off up the steep slope of the shanty town, through the twisting alleyways crowded on either side with dilapidated homes, bars and grocery shops. The twins followed behind. People sat on their doorsteps gossiping with neighbours, women hung their washing on lines, loud pop music blared from radios and cassette recorders. Teenagers wearing very little in the shimmering heat flirted with each other without embarrassment.

'Hey, slow down! Where are we going?' puffed Talita.

'Just follow me!' snapped Solomon over his shoulder, but he slowed down a little. Daniel was becoming heavy in his arms.

'It's dangerous at the top!' Talita continued concerned. 'That's where they shoot from!'

'Are we going to the very top?' asked Pedro breathlessly, suddenly charged with curiosity to go where they should not.

'Yes, but don't worry. I have friends up there. Just follow me!' Solomon replied sharply.

He had promised himself that he would not accept the invitation given to him yesterday afternoon by the foreigner with the palest eyes he had ever seen. However, in this new emergency, there was nowhere else he could think of to go with his family. At least his brothers and sister could be safely distracted from their current predicament for an hour or so. He would simply drop them off, excuse himself, and go and find Stephano, who was bound to be flying his kite on the ridge.

The little group stopped when they reached the summit to catch their breath and check their sense of direction.

'Wow!' cried Pedro. 'We're on top of the world!' He stared around and saw a dirt football pitch that was being played on by a noisy group of men, a large white church with a steeple and, beyond it all, the magnificent view of Rio de Janeiro which spread out way below the shanty town. 'It doesn't look very dangerous up here to me,' he said, spinning round and round with his arms outstretched.

'Look! There's the sea!' exclaimed Talita, pointing.

'And there's *Papai*'s factory! It looks tiny from up here.' Pedro pointed in the opposite direction.

'And there's our school over there!' cried Talita excitedly.

Daniel was thirsty and started to cry for his *Mamae*.

'Come on, the house must be that one over there.' Solomon indicated a white house built of brick. It was nearly hidden among a mass of tall plants on the other side of the dirt road that ran horizontally across the ridge, dividing the two shanty towns. As they approached the house they could hear children's voices singing. Pedro opened the small gate and ran up the two steps to the front door.

'Knock, Pedro!' said Solomon.

Madeleine came to the door. Pedro looked startled as he stared up at this woman who was so different from anyone he had ever seen before in his short life. He thought they had come to the wrong house and turned to Solomon for reassurance.

'Solomon. I'm so glad you came!' Her Portuguese was tinged with a foreign accent. 'And who have you brought with you?' She turned towards Daniel, who cried even more fervently. Solomon was only half attending. He had caught sight of a piano, not unlike his own, in the room behind her. It seemed like an eternity since he had last played, at the concert in the cathedral.

'These are my brothers and sister,' he responded dispassionately, 'but I'm not staying!'

'I'm Pedro,' said Pedro, feeling inexplicably drawn to this strange lady.

'And I'm Talita. We're twins!'

'And I'm Madeleine and it's a pleasure to meet you both!' She reached out with her long, slim arms and took the baby from Solomon. 'And who's this?'

'Daniel,' said Solomon, as he turned and walked back towards the gate.

'But you'll come back for tea, won't you, Solomon?' she called after him. 'I've made some ice cream!'

Madeleine closed the door behind her, just as Solomon shut the gate.

Stephano was not on the ridge, but Solomon decided he would pass away his time up there anyway. It was fun watching others fly their kites and soothing to be alone for a while. He found a can and two empty brown bottles on the ground amongst the litter and propped them up a few

feet in front of him. Gathering some loose stones, he practised his aim. As his confidence grew, so did the distance
between him and the three objects, and soon other boys were
attracted to the game by his accuracy and asked to join in.
More bottles and cans were found until they quickly created
amongst themselves a lively game that Solomon won every
time.

He soon forgot about the homemade ice cream and his
brothers and sister at the white bungalow on the top of the
hill, until suddenly the unmistakable crack of gunshots ripped
through the lazy afternoon from the direction of the lower left-
hand side of the shanty town. Solomon and the other boys
froze as a terrific drilling noise exploded into the sky from a
machine gun on the opposite lower right-hand side, shattering
the atmosphere. The staccato sound ricocheted around the
mountain.

'Run for cover!' shouted someone from below the ridge.
'It's a police raid and they're shooting at everything that moves!
They're looking for the gang members.'

Solomon jumped as a helicopter swooped in from nowhere
and hovered above them with a deafening noise. He squinted
up through the blinding sunlight and saw two armed policemen
standing at the open door of the flying metal bird, as if searching
for their prey.

What followed during the next few minutes seemed to
Solomon to unfold in slow motion. Blindly, he started to run
in the direction of Madeleine's house. He had to get to his
brothers and sister. But as he reached the top of the ridge, he
ran head on into four heavily armed gang members. In an
instant the blood rushed from his face, his heart pounded
harder and every breath he took sounded like thunder in his

ears. One of the *bandidos* grabbed him by the arm and pointed a gun at the back of his head. Solomon closed his eyes. The thug screamed like one possessed. 'Where are you going, you son-of-a-bitch?'

Solomon was pushed down into the hot dust, and a boot was stamped onto the back of his neck. He was convinced he was going to die at that moment and his only thoughts were for his *Mamae*. She would be frantically looking for her children and he had been responsible for their safety.

'Don't shoot!' Solomon begged between breaths, choking on a mouthful of dust. 'I have to get my brothers and sister!' The boot pushed down even harder, but he persisted. 'Madeleine's house . . . please don't shoot . . . please don't shoot . . . my brothers . . . my sister . . .'

'You liar!' The *bandido* pulled his head back violently by the hair. Solomon cried out in pain. There was a click and he knew the finger was on the trigger. Solomon closed his eyes and prayed to a God he did not know.

'Stop!' hollered another voice from somewhere behind them. 'I know this boy! He's a friend of Felipe. Let him go!'

The *bandido* regretfully fired his shot into the air, but gave Solomon's head a final kick with his boot. Solomon groaned as someone pulled him up roughly by his t-shirt and shouted in his ear. 'Get lost! Fast!'

Solomon squinted up into the face of Fernando, his head pounding from the blow. He forced his legs to carry him once again in the direction of the white bungalow.

Madeleine opened the door immediately and he fell forward into her arms, filthy and limp with terror. Without a word, she led him into her little kitchen.

'Sit down here.' She gave him some water. Solomon leaned

his aching head against the cool wall. His heart seemed about to burst from his chest.

He heard Talita's voice. 'What happened, Solomon?' She was relieved to see that her brother had not forgotten them after all. 'It's six o'clock!'

'You look terrible,' said Pedro, appearing behind her.

More shots rang out, closer now.

'Follow me quickly. We must get away from the windows.' Madeleine led them from the kitchen through a small back yard protected by a high wall and into a dark, windowless room. An elderly nun in a wimple appeared from nowhere with a sleeping Daniel in her arms. Madeleine closed the door and touched a switch. A single bulb feebly illuminated the scene. The walls were painted white to give an illusion of coolness. In keeping with the rest of the house, furnishing was at a bare minimum. Only a small crucifix decorated a side wall. Daniel was placed on the sofa, still sleeping, oblivious to their predicament. Solomon sat down next to him and briefly caressed the limp little form. Pedro and Talita settled themselves cross-legged on a crocheted rug. The shooting continued.

Madeleine handed Solomon more water and started to wipe the dirt and saliva from his grazed face with a damp cloth. Sister Ingrid, the elderly nun, produced a pile of picture books and jigsaw puzzles for Pedro and Talita and lowered herself onto the rug beside them.

'I hate this place!' Solomon suddenly grabbed the hand that was wiping his brow. '*You* don't have to live here! Why don't you go back to your own country, away from all this?' His eyes bored into hers, as tears welled up.

Madeleine looked down at the hand clasping her wrist, and he released her.

'Drink some more water.' She finished cleaning his face. He closed his eyes, and the tears did not fall.

'I have let Bete know you are here. Pedro told me what had happened at home today, and I thought they'd be concerned.'

Solomon was relieved, but he was not going to let on, not to the nun.

He decided to change the subject. 'Why don't you wear the habit?' He observed her pale blue skirt and cotton shirt and her fair hair which, free of any wimple, fell to her shoulders, framing a face that did not need the enhancement of make-up.

'I have permission to wear lighter clothes for my work.'

'But why did you want to become a nun in the first place?'

'You ask a lot of hard questions, *Senhor* Solomon.' She sat down on the only wooden chair beside the sofa.

There was shouting outside, followed by short sharp gunshots. Madeleine ignored them.

'Where shall I start? I was born in France in a little village near the border with Germany. We lived in a very old house with only two rooms and a kitchen in the middle. My mother became ill when I was six years old and she suffered for many years, completely bedridden. Three Catholic nuns would come to the village on their bicycles in sunshine, rain or snow to take care of the people who were ill. I would watch them as they washed my mother, gave her injections and fed her. They never took any money from us. My father told me they were doing it because they were serving God. So I thought to myself, to serve God I have to be a nun! But we were Protestants and I had never met any Protestant nuns. Then one year the pastor of our church invited a group of people from a Lutheran church in Germany to speak to us. Some of them were missionaries and came from other lands. So in my head I thought, to serve God I must become a nun *and* be a missionary.'

'How old were you then?'

'Thirteen years old.'

'But didn't you want to have a boyfriend or get married?'

'Oh, I had lots of boyfriends!' Madeleine laughed again. 'I was wild as a teenager. And one man in particular I did fall in love with. He was called Theo Panzon and he used to say that he fell more in love with me every Sunday when he saw me playing the organ. Of course in my village if a girl and boy kissed they were expected to marry. People there believed that you loved only once. Eventually we became engaged to be married, but after a while Theo said to me, "Madeleine, if you believe you are being called to do something, you must obey. Many haven't, and it doesn't always lead to happiness."'

'What happened to Theo?' asked Solomon.

'Well, he waited for me for a few years, then when he realised I really wasn't coming back from the convent he married my best friend, Laurence.' Madeleine paused. 'I was twenty-five when I took my vows. Three years later, I came to Brazil for the first time and knew immediately that this was where I was meant to be.'

'What were your vows?'

'They were poverty, chastity and obedience.'

Solomon felt stunned. 'That's impossible! Don't you even miss not having children?'

Madeleine smiled at his expression. 'Oh, I have been given many, many children to look after over the years, Solomon. More than I could ever have asked for.'

She stood and bent to pick up Daniel, who was just beginning to stir from his sleep.

Talita and Pedro helped Sister Ingrid pack up the jigsaw puzzles that had distracted them for the past half hour.

'The shooting seems to have stopped,' Madeleine said briskly. 'I will walk you home.'

Chapter 8

Cowboy Heaven

The tiny leaves of the aspen trees shimmered above them, making a gentle rustling sound, as the coffin was lowered into the grave. Liam cried uncontrollably, the pain of his loss more acute than ever. How could he continue? He had lost his very breath of life. But as Keira and Callum, standing close beside him, wrapped themselves around him, sobbing into his shirt, he looked down through blurred eyes and knew that he could not give up. She had left him with two precious children and they were part of her. Liam bent his head and held them close with all his might, as the grief racked his body.

Close to Liam and her two grandchildren stood Molly Cartwright, Katherine's mother. Her sturdy figure was smartly dressed in a dark suit, her hair neatly confined by a small, veiled hat. It was only Molly's second visit to Montana in the fifteen years that her daughter had lived here. But thankfully, during those years, the Kavanaghs had made trips to Europe with her grandchildren, and they had always finished their vacation with a visit to Sunderland. Katherine loved to be in the home where she had grown up, and spend time at the seaside showing her children how to brave the freezing waters of the North Sea, as she had as a child. Despite the long miles between them, a strong relationship had been forged between Keira and Callum and their English grandmother. Katherine had made sure of that;

with regular phone calls to share all the news, and constant references to her family and her childhood in north-east England.

It had taken a great deal of organising, leaving her bed and breakfast business and her younger daughter Jane, who had contracted polio at the age of twelve and was now confined to a wheelchair. But Clarice, her housekeeper, had insisted they could all manage without her. The journey from Sunderland had been a real ordeal, as she was fearful of flying. Liam had suggested that she take a taxi from King's Cross Station to Heathrow Airport, but she would not dream of putting him to such expense; the coach was fine.

Now, as she watched her beloved daughter's coffin disappear into the grave, Molly's iron reserve broke and her shoulders shook. She felt Keira's warm hand take hers, and as she leaned close to this much-loved granddaughter, her tears flowed unchecked. On her other side, Faye placed a supportive arm around her waist, as Uncle Jack, Bill, Jake and Max released the ropes. Aunt Gloria was the first to step forward to throw blue camas flowers and pink calypso into the grave, and many others followed, some picking wild flowers from amongst the long grass that grew at the edge of the lake.

Joanna stared in disbelief as her husband Bill and the other men picked up their spades to complete the burial. Two funerals. Two precious people dead in such a short time. Turning, she walked away from the scene to the end of the line of aspen trees where she knelt down by the grave of her own son, buried nine weeks earlier by the very same people. A new tombstone bore the words '"Teddy Blue" Ed Whitely 1970–1988. Beloved son of Bill and Joanna Whitely'. Joanna passed the palm of her hand over the carved letters and began to sob. After a few moments she became aware that there were many more flowers than usual on the grave, placed there today by friends who, like her, were attending their second funeral at Goodnight within weeks. She noticed a white envelope among them and reached over to pick it up. On it was written, 'To Ed – from one good old cowboy to another.' She drew out the sheet of paper inside the envelope and saw that an anonymous hand had written out a poem for her son. Joanna got to her feet and took a few steps to the nearest tree, where she sat down. River appeared beside her and nuzzled his head into her shoulder as she began to read. The poem was called 'Cowboy Heaven', and Joanna reflected that this truly represented what Ed's life had been. With no one else in earshot, she began to read it out loud, with the dog as her audience.

> I never did do it for the money,
> I guess you done figured that out.
> But eyes never broke, for long anyway
> Gettin' rich ain't what it's all about.
> Gettin' high on the smell of the sunrise,
> A horseback, a long way from camp,
> Over the sound of crickets competin'
> With a hassin' kerosene lamp,
> That's reason enough to be out here, that . . .
> And livin' my life nearly free,
> Cause I ain't punchin' cows for the payday,
> It means more than the money for me.
> If I could I would stay here for ever
> Without meaning or disrespect
> To those folks sellin' box seats and glory
> And passin' the plate to collect.

Somewhere inside me they say there's a soul
Just waitin' to fly when I croak,
And I'd sure be a bit disappointed
If heaven was only a joke.
And I'm ready to go, if I have to,
Though I plan on wearin' my hat,
But I hope it's as good as they claim it,
'Cause it's hard to beat where I'm at.
Some believers have reached a conclusion
That men get recycled like cans,
Then eventually end up in heaven
After wearin' numerous brands.
If that's true, then my soul probably lit here
By chance, on a wing and a prayer,
Which explains why it's so much like heaven,
'Cause maybe I'm already there.

Back at the graveside, the Reverend John Beard, their friend and minister, cleared his throat and read from the leather Bible he held in his large hands. His own emotions were clear to see.

'Where can I go from your Spirit? Where can I flee from your presence? If I go up to the heavens, you are there; if I make my bed in the depths, you are there . . .' He stopped briefly to compose himself. Living in a small town like Ovando meant you knew everyone personally. It made taking funerals all that much harder for the big man.

Keira turned and looked up towards Morrell Mountain. Two eagles circled overhead, their majestic wings outstretched. 'Ed,' she whispered, 'take care of Mom. I miss you both so much.'

* * *

When Katherine knew she was dying, she begged the doctors to let her stay at home. She refused the chemotherapy. What was the point? It might extend her life a little, but at least without it she would die with a full head of hair. And so, sedated and eased as far as was possible with all available medication, she was nursed by her family and held night after night in the haven of her husband's strong arms. Her room was filled with flowers and the sight of them brought a smile to her pale and sunken face now and again. The beautiful, familiar view from their four-poster bed of the breathtaking landscape around Goodnight, now burgeoning into its summer bloom, was a constant joy to her.

Keira could barely tear herself from her mother's side, terrified that she might die when she was not there.

'Mom,' she cried into Katherine's shoulder, 'you won't see me getting married. You won't be there to see my children and help me raise them.'

Katherine's eyes welled up. 'I know,' she said, a catch in her voice. 'I'm so sorry, pet lamb.' Her arms moved slowly to hold her trembling daughter close to her. 'There's so much we don't understand, sweetheart. It breaks my heart to think I have to leave you and Callum and Papa. But we all have to die sometime, and I guess my time is now.' Her daughter's sobs were heartbreaking to her. 'But darling, I shall always be with you in your heart and in your memories. No one can take that from you.'

'Who will call me "pet lamb", when you're gone?' whispered Keira.

'I will, of course, in your memories of me.'

Soon after Grandma Molly arrived from England, Katherine was sleeping for much of the day. Molly sat at her daughter's bedside hour after hour, speaking softly to her about her childhood in Whitburn Bay in Sunderland. Almost too weak now to speak, Katherine was aware that her mother was with her, and as she spoke of her family in England, of her late father, Harry Cartwright, and her sister, Jane, the hint of a smile flickered over the pale lips, and Molly felt a slight tremble of the thin fingers lying in her own warm, plump hand. When she reminisced about a childhood party, or a lost toy, Katherine's eyelids fluttered open and she smiled up at her mother.

Full-time nurses were employed at the homestead day and night, and every so often they would glide across the room to check the drip and feel Katherine's pulse. The faint breaths were becoming barely audible and, one morning, were so slight that Molly and Keira had not noticed that the breathing had stopped. Molly had been recalling the summer when they had found a nest of fledglings in Harry's ancient automobile, when the nurse's expression told her the worst. As Molly held her daughter's limp hand to her cheek and Keira flung herself onto the bed, Liam and Callum, who had been briefly out of the sickroom, rushed back to the bedside.

The nurse left the family alone to grieve for the woman they had all adored, in the room with the view she had treasured.

The mourners turned and walked back towards the homestead around the edge of the lake. Keira let go of her grandmother's hand and stopped to watch some Canada geese and their fluffy goslings enter the water from the bullrushes close by. She went closer and crouched down. The sight of new life somehow gave her hope.

'Keira!'

As she turned, the sun caught her long auburn hair. Mary was running towards her.

'I'm sorry I'm late, it took me over two hours to get here from Helena!'

Keira stood up and walked towards her friend. As Mary hugged her, the tears flowed anew.

'Come on, let's go back to the house for some tea.' Mary gently led her friend by the hand.

'You look good in black!' said Keira, squaring her shoulders and brushing away the tears.

'Thanks! I would have thought your dad would have expected you to wear black too.'

'This was Mom's favourite dress, all covered in flowers. Dad bought it for her.'

'It looks great on you.'

'Liar. It's not me at all, and you know it!'

Mary laughed and, as they entered the large hall, she turned and gave Keira a small cream envelope. 'By the way, this is for you.'

'Who's it from?' Keira did not recognise the handwriting.

Mary grimaced and disappeared into the kitchen.

Keira opened the envelope and took out a small card. Frowning, she turned it over and read the writing on the back. 'I am so sorry to hear about your mother.' It was signed 'Cass xxx'. Her cheeks flushed crimson and her heart raced madly. She looked at the front of the card. There was a picture of a beautiful white rose and underneath it were printed the words:

Love is as strong as death,
its jealousy unyielding as the grave.

She caught her breath, and fearing that someone would see her, she ran quickly through the hall and into the cloakroom, locking the door behind her. Over and over again she read Cass's message to her. Over and over again she looked at the picture of the rose and the inscription under it. Where had she seen those words before? She could not remember. Keira read his handwriting once again. 'Maybe he does love me?' she thought to herself, carefully putting the card back in its envelope. 'Why three kisses?'

Molly invited her grandchildren to spend the rest of the summer in England with her. She knew Keira and Callum both felt overwhelmed with the stark memories of their mother that Goodnight gave them. Keira felt torn between the desire to get away for a while and the need to be there for her father. However, Liam insisted that they both go to England. He could not bear to see his children so upset and believed that time away from the ranch, in their mother's childhood home that they knew so well, would be a time of healing for them. Keira was only persuaded to leave her father when Uncle Jack and Aunt Gloria offered to move in with Liam to give him company and support during the month of August until they returned. Cousins Max and Fin were on the ranch anyway, and with the help of a fax machine and an extra telephone line they could both work from the ranch or drive into Helena when it was absolutely necessary.

They flew to London via Seattle and New York in the last week of July. Once again, Liam insisted they take a taxi from Heathrow to King's Cross Station, and that they travel first class on the train. Callum smiled as he watched the waitress in the dining car balancing plates and trays of drinks while the train swayed unpredictably from side to side. Keira was not hungry and ate sparingly as she watched the English country-side flash past her, so different in colour, texture and scope from Montana. Molly was trying to read an Agatha Christie novel, her mind still misted from the loss of her daughter, but steadfastly resolved to help her young grandchildren through this tragedy. She smiled as she noticed the number of passing glances her granddaughter received from fellow passengers. There had been so many over the last forty-eight hours, she had lost count. This was going to be an interesting summer.

Chapter 9

The Loving Cup

*A*fter Molly had been left a young widow with two small daughters to support, she had wasted no time in transforming her home, The Olde House, into a successful bed and breakfast business.

The Olde House, situated on Whitburn Bay, was full of pink-lustre Sunderland pottery inherited from the family. There were jugs, wall plaques, mugs, tea sets, decorative plates and figurines with their famous biblical verses and rhymes spoken between lovers bidding farewell on the city's docks, as yet another ship set sail towards the perilous North Sea. Molly had no time for her inheritance; she had lived with the clutter of it all her life and would have been quite happy to get rid of the lot. But she realised that Sunderland pottery had become extremely collectable and it was this very feature of her bed and breakfast that the Tourist Board promoted in their guidebooks. Collectors from around the world came to the city all year round to spend time in the museum and the antique shops, and many stayed at The Olde House.

Molly had been hoping that the sun would be shining when she arrived home with her two grandchildren. It was midsummer, after all. But a stubborn grey cloud wrapped itself around the city of Sunderland and as the train pulled into the station the cloud released a heavy downpour of rain.

'Oh, this is all we need!' she exclaimed, as the porter deposited their suitcases at the taxi rank.

The taxi rank had no shelter, and there were no taxis waiting. They were getting wet, and Molly ushered her grandchildren back to the station waiting room and went into the red phonebox to call The Olde House.

Fifteen minutes later a green Corsair pulled up, and out stepped a skinny young man with round spectacles and no umbrella.

'Mrs Cartwright! Over here, Mrs Cartwright!' he called out to the bedraggled group huddled by their luggage. He ran towards them on long bandy legs. 'No cabs, then? You know what happens when it rains in this city. The cabs are all out when you need them! Let me help you with those suitcases.' He looked at Keira and flushed with embarrassment. He had not expected Mrs Cartwright's granddaughter to be quite so pretty. Callum helped the flustered young man fit the cases into the boot of his car.

'You're a pet, Brian,' said Molly gratefully, sinking into the front seat. 'Trust you to be there just when I needed you!'

Brian manoeuvred the car out of Athenaeum Street.

'My sympathies for your daughter, Mrs Cartwright,' he said in a low voice, turning towards her in the passenger seat. 'We're all right sorry about it at The Olde House.'

'Thank you, Brian. It's very sad, especially for the children,' replied Molly, her eyes filling with tears, 'but I'm so pleased that they've come back here with me for a few weeks. We shall do our best to comfort each other, I'm sure.'

'Good, that's good,' responded Brian, speeding up his windscreen wipers as the rain grew heavier.

Keira noticed he had a twitch in his left shoulder, which

jerked at odd intervals. She realised that he was looking at her furtively in the rear-view mirror, and edged her way along the back seat out of his view.

'Brian's been living at The Olde House for almost two months now,' Molly informed Keira and Callum over her shoulder. 'He comes from Newcastle and works for a big company here.' She always forgot the name of it.

After two miles they turned off the coast road into quaint Whitburn village and Keira sat up. Her demoralised expression brightened. 'Wow, I always remember this! All those cute old cottages and the cobbled road! And there's that pretty church over there! It must be ancient, Grandma.'

'Aye, have you seen the list of rectors inside? It dates from 1245!' put in Brian, who, with his photographic memory, had accumulated more knowledge about the history of the village in two months than Molly had in seventy years, much to her amusement.

'That's incredible!' Callum exclaimed.

Brian was in his element. 'Apparently, at the beginning of the century everything looked very much as it does today, apart from the railings which used to run along the front of the houses next to those narrow pavements. They were taken away so that the metal could be melted down for the war effort, and—'

Molly interrupted his flow. 'And here's The Olde House! We'll go into the coach house first.'

Aunt Jane was overjoyed to see them all. She manoeuvred her wheelchair with practised speed and precision and greeted her mother affectionately. The two of them were rarely separated. Molly hugged her, relieved to be back home. Keira and Callum stood awkwardly by the door. They were taken aback by Aunt Jane's resemblance to their mother.

'Children, come and give me a hug!' she cried, noticing their hesitation.

'Aunt Jane, you look so like Mother,' said Keira, almost in a whisper.

'You've got her eyes and her hair,' added Callum, staring at her, fighting the tears.

'Go on! I'm not nearly as pretty as your mother, although I could always beat her when we raced along the Roker promenade together!' Aunt Jane reached out to them for a hug.

There was a stir and a door burst open. It was Clarice, hurrying from the kitchen.

'Hello, hello, hello!' she cried. 'Goodness, look at you both, you've grown so tall!' She shuffled her feet, clad in well-worn burgundy slippers, as her bulk rolled from side to side.

'Yes, haven't they grown, Clarice dear?' Molly greeted her friend and housekeeper. 'But I'm sure they're tired and would like to rest a little in their room. Could you take them up, dear?'

Clarice ushered them through the door that led from the coach house into the main building. They could smell wax polish from the antique furniture as they followed her up the wide staircase to the first floor and across the sloping landing into one of the suites facing the village green. The familiar tick-tock of the grandfather clock accompanied them.

Clarice took them to the room where Keira usually slept. It had a high ceiling and windows draped with splendid gold curtains braided with tassels. There were two single beds with dark carved oak bedheads. Floral bedspreads picked out the gold of the curtains. As they entered, Keira ran her hand over the flocked wallpaper. She had always liked the feel of it. Clarice

156

shuffled to the window and closed one that had been opened to air the room.

'Here you are! Hope you two don't mind sharing this time? If you do, we can arrange for one of you to sleep back in the coach house, but it would be a bit of a squeeze. Unfortunately, our spare room where Callum usually sleeps is being used as a sewing room, and there's so much junk in there I couldn't face taking it out just for the summer.' She spoke in short wheezy breaths, her two large hands on her round hips.

Keira had forgotten how kind Clarice's face was.

'There are clean towels in the bathroom.' Clarice turned and shuffled back again. Her fine grey hair was escaping from her loose bun. 'Just join us in the coach house when you're ready.'

The heavy door shut and Callum flung himself on the nearest bed.

'I'm beat!' He turned to look at his sister. 'This is weird, sharing.'

Keira perched on the edge of the other bed and sighed. 'I don't want to be on my own.'

'I'll look after you.'

Keira raised her eyebrows. 'You sound like Papa.'

'We should call him.'

'What are we going to *do* here for the next four weeks?' Keira stood and went over to the window. 'I mean, look at the weather!' She sighed again.

'I dunno. They're all over sixty, apart from Brainy Brian who has a fit every time he looks at you!'

They both laughed.

'You want the first bath?' asked Keira.

'After you.'

'Since when have you been a gentleman?'

'Since a few seconds ago.'

There was a loud knock at the door. 'It's only me!' puffed Brian, from the other side of it. 'I've got your suitcases!'

The rain and drizzle did not stop for five days. Keira cried herself to sleep every night and Callum dreamed of Montana. They saw little of the other guests. The Smiths and their terrier were asked to leave after another bad night of barking, and the Dutch couple returned to Holland. The Tylers, who stayed at The Olde House every summer in order to spend time with their daughter who lived in Cleadon with her large family, were only ever seen at breakfast, as were the Crastons, who were in Sunderland for the second year running to research the history of the pottery industry, and spent their days poring through books in the library or visiting the museum. Hardly a word was exchanged when they all met at breakfast. What these people did all day long in Sunderland was a mystery to Keira and Callum. Brian kept himself to himself, nodding and twitching to them in the morning as he left for work. In the evenings, the guests who were in for dinner sat at their separate tables and disappeared into the library afterwards, where they remained, speaking in monotones, until the grandfather clock struck eleven.

Aunt Jane read and worked at her tapestry most of the day in her room on the ground floor of the coach house. Keira and Callum often sat with her, talking about their mother and listening eagerly to everything Aunt Jane could tell them about her childhood with her sister, their friends and their school days. It was always strange to think that their mother had actually lived here, had a life here, a life to which they could hardly relate. Molly Cartwright made sure that her grandchildren accompanied her when she set off each day running errands in town and stocking up in the supermarket with all the kitchen requirements that had been written on a long list by Clarice. In the evenings they were joined for dinner by their neighbour, George Cruikshank, a retired army officer in his early seventies, whose wife had died some years before. He was not very tall, but he held himself very straight and had a habit of twirling his moustache. Keira thought he looked like somebody out of a history book. More amusingly, his affection for her grandma was very clear.

After dinner, when they sat down to play a game of cards, George's stiffness would disappear as he joined in the laughter with the rest of them. One evening, during their first week, Keira excused herself from the game and went to bed early. Molly had noticed that her granddaughter had been particularly quiet that day, and she felt concerned. After helping Clarice clear the tables, she popped her head round the sitting room door and told the others to start without her. As she climbed the old staircase to the first floor and neared the bedroom door, she could hear Keira crying. She knocked gently.

'Keira, pet lamb, can I come in?'

The crying grew louder, so Molly let herself in. The lights were still on and Keira was lying face down on her bed, nearest the window.

'Oh my dear, dear child,' said Molly, lowering herself onto the mattress and placing her hands on Keira's trembling shoulders.

Keira turned, sat up and leaned against her grandmother. Molly held onto her with all her might, as the sobs of grief and shock at the past two months racked her slim body. After a while the sobs subsided and Keira looked up into her grandma's sympathetically weeping eyes.

'Why? Why did she have to leave me? I miss her so much. I was looking at a picture of her downstairs. Callum and I were standing with her. Poor Papa, do you think we did the right thing coming here and leaving him at Goodnight? I worry about him.' She burst into tears again. Molly gave her more tissues and wiped her own eyes. 'I miss Ed too, Grandma. It should have been me!'

'There, there now, my poor child. My poor little pet lamb.' She held Keira tightly once again, rocking her slightly.

'Mom called me "pet lamb".'

Molly kissed her granddaughter's forehead. 'There's so much pain for you at the moment, my darling. It's good to cry, good to mourn. It's all part of the healing.'

'Callum cries at night sometimes. I wake up and hear him.'

'It's hard for both of you.'

'And for you too, Grandma.'

'Yes, pet. It's very hard to lose your child, your daughter. I keep thinking that I wish it had been me instead, and not her.'

'Sometimes I wonder what this life is all about. I never thought about death before, and now suddenly I've lost two people who I loved so much and it just makes me think about it. It makes me think that during the short time I'm here, I want to get it right. For Ed. For Mom.'

'I'm sure you will make them both very proud, Keira,' said Molly smiling, her eyes still wet.

Keira lowered her head briefly and then looked up, a serious expression illuminating her face. 'Mom told me once that you used to tell her to search for the key to the song of life.'

Molly smiled and nodded. 'I'm impressed you've remembered that so well.'

'It means a lot to me.'

'A writer called Henry David Thoreau wrote that most men lead lives of quiet desperation and go to their graves with their song still inside them. But I feel sure that won't happen to you.'

'Mom found Papa. I also believe there's someone out there I was born to love for ever. And until I find that person, I won't give myself to anyone else.'

Molly put her finger under Keira's chin and lifted her head slightly. 'You have been blessed with beauty, Keira. But you will need to be wise with it. Love is a very powerful force. We're each compelled to find it. Yet human beings can be very fickle indeed.'

Keira smiled. 'You're so wise, Grandma.'

'Oh no, pet. I'm old, and therefore I've seen and read much.' She rose to her feet. 'You're tired and need to get some sleep. In the morning we have my dear French guests Theo and Laurence arriving. I'm sure you're going to get along very well together.' Molly bent to kiss Keira. 'Goodnight, pet.'

She closed the door gently behind her and went slowly down the staircase to speak to Callum.

Theo and Laurence Panzon arrived the following morning, and with them came change. Outside, the low cloud dispersed, revealing blue sky and allowing the sun's warmth to flood down on Whitburn Bay. The stuffy atmosphere at The Olde House lifted too, and with it a new energy seemed to enter into the old building. Keira and Callum were in their bedroom when sounds of an arrival pulled them to their window. Looking down, they saw a tall man lifting cases from his car, while a woman gathered coats and bags from the back seat and walked towards the door of The Olde House. They ran downstairs at once, and found Molly welcoming the couple in the front hall.

'Theo and Laurence, welcome my dears!' exclaimed Molly as they each took it in turns to kiss her on the cheek. 'May I introduce my grandchildren from America who are staying with me at the moment?'

Keira held out her hand politely, lifting her eyes up to the man's smile.

'*Enchanté*!' he said, with a little bow.

Keira noticed that his movements were direct and precise and that his dark hair was already flecked with grey. His wife was nearly as tall as he was, and she moved gracefully. She had high cheekbones and short dark hair, and looked elegant in her well-cut trousers, navy blue blazer and colourful silk scarf tied loosely around her neck. Keira liked the couple immediately. She decided they were probably a bit younger than her parents.

'Do you play football?' Theo was asking Callum as they all set off up the staircase.

'I play American football!' exclaimed Callum, turning to follow.

'Then tomorrow I will teach you to play soccer on the beach.'

'You will?'

'Of course, but there is one small problem.' Theo stopped and grinned down at the boy's eager face. 'Do you have a football?'

'No, I don't.' Callum looked concerned. 'Grandma! Do you have a football in the house?'

Molly was not listening. She had unlocked the door to the

suite next to theirs and was enjoying the view of the village green from the window with Laurence.

'Grandma!' Callum called more loudly, worried that this first sign of fun since he had arrived in Sunderland might elude him.

Theo put his finger up to his lips and bent down. 'Shhh. No need to shout. What is your name, American boy?'

'Callum.'

'This is a good name, a good name. Well, Callum, I never leave home without my football, so we are in luck.' He winked and walked on into his suite, leaving at the door a boy grinning from ear to ear for the first time in weeks.

That evening, the atmosphere at The Olde House was transformed. The French couple were already on friendly terms with most of the guests. There was a buzz of conversation and even some jokes between the tables of those who ate in that night. After dinner, Theo persuaded them all, including the Tylers and the Crastons, whom he prised out of the library, to join them in the sitting room where he proceeded to remove his jacket and tie and sit down at the piano. Song after song was sung in French and English. The music soon drew in Brian from his bedroom and Clarice from the kitchen. Caught up in the spirit of the moment, Molly produced a bottle of homemade sloe gin with a tray of little glasses. When the grandfather clock struck eleven, no one noticed. Mrs Craston was standing on the coffee table singing 'God Save The Queen' at the top of her voice, an empty glass in her hand, while everyone else covered their ears. Keira thought Aunt Jane might fall out of her wheel-chair, she was laughing so much.

The following day was Sunday and breakfast was later than usual in The Olde House. Theo arranged several tables so that everyone could sit together in one party, and George re-appeared unexpectedly from next door, unwilling to miss out on anything.

'I believe there is a circus by the beach today,' Theo remarked, 'and—'

'We've been longing to go!' interrupted Callum. 'I've never been to a circus in my whole life!'

Molly appeared with a fresh carafe of coffee.

'I don't know your plans, Molly,' Theo continued, holding out his empty cup, 'but everything in town is closed today, naturally, so why don't we all go to see the clowns and the horses and the acrobats? It will be very amusing.'

There was general enthusiasm for the idea.

'*Bien*! But first some football, eh, Callum?'

It was quite a large party that left The Olde House soon after breakfast to walk to Whitburn Bay. Brian walked beside Jane in her wheelchair. George and Molly followed close behind. Clarice walked slowly, next to Mr and Mrs Tyler, who were complimenting her on her shepherd's pie from the previous evening. Mrs Craston, with her husband in tow, kept as close as possible to Theo, who was explaining to Callum the rules of soccer. Keira and Laurence strolled together at the back of the group.

When they reached the promenade, they queued for ice creams at a van parked nearby, and Theo and Callum set off for the beach with the football.

'Would you like to walk on with me?' asked Laurence. 'The weather is so nice.'

'Sure,' answered Keira, finishing her ice cream.

For a while neither of them spoke, each enjoying the fresh salt air and the sun on their faces.

'You have a really neat husband,' remarked Keira eventually, her hands thrust into the pockets of her denim jacket.

'Yes, I do, don't I?' smiled Laurence. 'We have been together for seven years now, but we have known each other for ever. We grew up together in France. Actually,' Laurence said lightly, 'he nearly married my best friend. Theo waited for her for almost seventeen years.'

'Seventeen years?'

'She left him to become a nun.'

'A nun!'

'When he realised she really wasn't coming back, he asked me to marry him.' She smiled again.

'Wasn't that hard for you?'

'No. He loves me very much. Theo and I have always been very good friends, you see. In the village where we grew up there were only forty houses and less than two hundred people living there.'

'It sounds like Ovando, where I live.'

'Do you miss it, your home?'

'I miss my Mom.'

Laurence put her arm around Keira. '*Pauvre petite*. It is very hard for you all.'

Keira nodded. They both stopped to look back at the game of football. Laurence laughed as Callum successfully tackled Theo. They started walking again.

'Why did she become a nun?'

'She felt it was her vocation, her calling. Madeleine is the most compassionate person I have ever known. Today she is a missionary living in a very poor slum area of Rio de Janeiro and spends all her time trying to make life better for as many people as she can. She has been there for several years now.'

'But why would she want to give up her whole life? What a waste!'

'Ah, but Madeleine does not see it like that. I envy her in a way. She has found complete peace and contentment because she is doing exactly what she feels she should be doing, in exactly the right place for her.'

A breeze blew in suddenly from the sea. 'I suppose I'm searching for something like that.' Keira frowned as she swept her hair off her face and tucked it behind her ears. 'But for me I think that such peace and contentment would be found with the person I'm going to love and spend my life with. I long for that already.'

'Ah. But you are still very young.'

'I know that, and my friends think I'm old fashioned. Maybe I'll change my mind.'

'You are a very unusual girl,' said Laurence, turning to look at Keira's profile. 'I detect that you already know this special person. Am I right?'

Keira felt her cheeks flush and she smiled involuntarily.

'What is his name?'

'Cass Henderson. He sent me this when my mother died.' Keira carefully drew the small, creased card from her back pocket.

Laurence studied it. 'How strange,' she said slowly, reading the inscription. 'Tell me about this Cass.'

By noon they had all returned to The Olde House, carrying portions of fish and chips wrapped in paper bought from a stand by the beach. The circus performance would begin at three o'clock, so everyone returned to their rooms to rest for a while. As they reached the foot of the stairs, Laurence turned to Keira.

'There's something I would like to show you, before we leave for the circus.'

An hour later, Keira passed Theo on the landing as she left Callum in their room.

'I was just coming to persuade Callum to play a game of chess with me,' he said. 'Laurence is waiting for you, *cherie*. Go in, the door is not locked. I will see you later.'

Laurence was brushing her glossy dark hair at the dressing table in front of the mirror.

'Come and sit down, Keira.' She turned and patted the bed. 'I want to show you something I bought in a wonderful antique shop in town before we checked in here at The Olde House.'

Keira sat down.

'Just after we were married, we saw a piece of Sunderland pottery quite by chance in a shop in Brussels, where we both work. It was a pink lustre jug with a picture of two lovers standing by a ship at the docks with the iron bridge in the background, and we just had to have it. One of the verses on it seemed so wise. It said, "Be familiar with few, have communion with one, deal justly with all, speak evil of none." I have no idea how it got to be in that shop, but we fell in love with the pottery at that moment. You know, Keira, I don't think your grandmother realises how valuable her pottery pieces are,' added Laurence, raising her eyebrows slightly.

'Grandma doesn't really like them much,' laughed Keira. 'I think she got sick of them when she was a child.'

Laurence went over to the mahogany wardrobe and took out a box containing several parcels. 'Look at this,' she said, taking off the brown paper. 'Isn't it beautiful? It's a loving cup. See? There are two handles so both lovers can hold the cup and drink at the same time.'

'It's really pretty.'

'I bought it for Madeleine because of the inscription on it, but today I have decided I want to give it to you instead.' She handed the loving cup to Keira. 'It is over a hundred years old.'

The cup had an embossed border colour-washed in the familiar pink lustre, and on one side a delicate floral wreath formed an oval around the verse, with an angel blowing a trumpet at the top. Keira bent to read the text and caught her breath.

'That's incredible!' she gasped.

'What do you think of it?' inquired Laurence.

Keira raised her head, the colour of her cheeks now almost matching her auburn hair. 'I can't believe it!' She looked again at the jug and read out the words:

> Set me as a seal upon thine heart,
>   as a seal upon thine arm:
>   for love is strong as death;
>   jealousy is cruel as the grave.

Keira met Laurence's gaze.

'And the last two lines are similar to what is written on your card from Cass, are they not?'

'Yes,' Keira whispered, reading it again. 'Do you know where the words come from?' she looked up at Laurence hopefully.

'They are taken from the Song of Songs, a love poem written by King Solomon in the tenth century BC. I believe it celebrates the sensuous and the sensual with wonderful passion and gentleness.' She paused. 'Madeleine would interpret these words as an allegory of the love between Christ and herself.

But I think perhaps you, Keira, will read it as a statement of love between yourself and that special person in the future. Am I right?'

There was a knock at the door and Theo entered. 'The others have gone ahead of us.'

Laurence closed the wardrobe and put on her coat.

'One more thing, *cherie*. Perhaps you should keep an open mind about this Cass Henderson?'

'What makes you say that?'

'Just a feeling I have.' Laurence held out her hand to Keira and smiled. 'Shall we go?'

Chapter 10

The Streets of Silver Lining

*E*zio lost his job at Souza Cruz after only ten weeks' employment. There was no explanation, only a statement that they were making some cutbacks. As a last resort he sold his Chevy for next to nothing and when the money ran out he started to collect paper and used cardboard boxes from the street litterbins, dumps, back entrances to hotels and hospitals. Ezio borrowed some money from *Tio* Marcos, bought a wooden cart and six days a week trudged the sweltering city streets for kilometres, pulling it manually. On Saturdays Solomon and Pedro went with him. The crazy Rio traffic had little regard for the paper collectors at the best of times, and because of the size of the cart there was no option other than to walk the same tarmac as the city traffic.

A once-thriving sugar cane warehouse, now very run down, was used as a recycling centre where the carts were stored at night and where all the paper and cardboard boxes were accumulated and weighed in exchange for a pittance. It was filthy work and after five weeks the monotonous and humiliating grind began to take its toll. Ezio increasingly turned to drink for solace. The alcohol entered his blood like venom and reawakened his old addiction, as if the demons had only been in temporary hibernation. While this gave him a few hours of relief, his demeanour at home worsened. The aggression and lack of control manifested themselves once more. He stopped playing his *cavaquinho* and became more and more withdrawn when sober. Solomon watched his hero become someone wretched, even hateful.

While there would be days of regret and promises of a new beginning, Ezio's self-esteem had never been so low, his will as weak as a used elastic band. In the bars he started to meet members of the drug gangs, and the temptation of trafficking a bag of cocaine to a city client seemed somehow less perilous and sinful than before. Besides, the pay was $1,000 a week, or so they said. He quickly calculated that he could make more in a month than he would have made in a whole year working at Souza Cruz. Perhaps there was no harm in trafficking under-cover for a few months? In no time he could take his family out of the *favela* and buy them an apartment and a brand-new car. After all, he would not have to tell Bella and the children what he was doing.

But, as in most communities, gossip was rife and within two weeks Isabella heard that her husband was running drugs. That evening, when he rolled in drunk once again, everything suddenly became too much to bear. As the children watched, she confronted him with her anxiety. Suddenly, the man she loved so passionately became demented – something in him snapped, opened up and raged forth. Blindly charging at her from the door, Ezio grabbed his wife, shook her and threw her heavily pregnant body against the hard brick wall in the sitting room. Then, shouting and swearing, he stormed out of the house.

When the trickle of blood between her legs increased to a steady flow and the cramps in her stomach became unbear-able, Isabella's children turned to Joao Batista for help. Taking in the horrifying scene, Joao drove her to the hospital, accompanied by *Tia* Bete. Late that night, Isabella lost her baby.

Tio Marcos was racked with guilt. He felt it was his fault that Ezio had degenerated into a violent drunkard, and *Tia* Bete was not slow to harangue him, expressing her own strong feelings on the matter. He decided he was going to have to step in and help make amends. It seemed to him that the first thing he needed to do was to get Isabella and the children away from the *favela* as quickly as possible. He approached the orphanage, *A Esperanca*, that Sister Madeleine had recommended.

'We have a vacancy for a cook,' he was told over the phone by *Senhor* Alfredo, the orphanage's director. 'Isabella can come and stay with us, and when she's feeling better she can fill the post. However, we do not have room for all four children. We could only take in the baby and the little girl.'

'Solomon and Pedro will have to live with us then!' stated Bete to her husband later that night. 'They can keep their own rooms and I can look after them.'

'What can have become of Ezio?' wondered Marcos for the hundredth time.

'We will have to try to contact his family in Petropolis tomorrow. Doesn't their *Vovo* call them once a month?' inquired Bete.

'Solomon told me that his grandfather called him yesterday from Correas, and he had seen nothing of Ezio. The old man was concerned, although Solomon didn't tell him everything. Solomon's adamant that he and Pedro won't go back to live in the valley.'

The next morning Solomon and Pedro sat in silence as *Tio* Marcos drove his sister and her children to the orphanage on the other side of town. The boys clutched onto Daniel's dismantled cot, his chair and a few black binbags full of clothes that had been thrown into the back of the pickup with them. After driving through heavy traffic for an hour, the old colonial house, situated down a long tree-lined drive, came into view. As they approached the blue gate, a group of barefoot boys and girls playing on a mound of sand forgot their fun and followed behind, running and cheering until *Tio* Marcos pulled up by the main entrance. *Senhor* Alfredo appeared, looking much older and frailer than Marcos had imagined, and gently helped Isabella out of the truck and led her into the house to a bedroom that had been prepared for her behind the kitchen. The room was cramped but clean and had two single beds and a cupboard, and a large window that revealed a view of a vibrant vegetable garden. Isabella was helped onto one of the beds, propped up with pillows and covered with a white sheet.

'You must be Isabella!' cried a plump, elderly woman from the doorway. 'My poor girl!' *Senhora* Dora, the wife of Alfredo, walked quickly over to the bed and planted two loud kisses on the pale cheeks. Holding Isabella's hand, she turned and greeted Marcos. Talita stood holding Daniel's hand as close to her mother's bedside as possible, with a terrified expression on her face.

'Talita,' said *Senhora* Dora kindly, 'I think it would be a good idea if you shared this room with your *Mamae* for the moment, and then you can help us take care of her. Would you like that?'

Talita nodded, her eyes filling with tears.

'And what is the name of your little brother?' The *Senhora* bent and lifted Daniel, who was now hiding behind Solomon's leg. Daniel grabbed his big brother's hand and began to cry.

'Let's go and have a look at the rest of the house,' said *Senhora* Dora warmly, distracting her little visitors with experienced skill. 'You can meet some of the other children!'

Senhor Alfredo followed his wife, his arm around Talita's shoulders. *Tio* Marcos, looking relieved to have found such a warm, hospitable welcome in the midst of the nightmare they were living through, left Solomon and Pedro with their mother and went out to the truck to begin unloading their few belongings.

'Come here, my boys,' whispered Isabella, her thin arms outstretched towards her sons.

They each took one of her hands. Pedro sat on the edge of her bed and Solomon knelt down beside it.

'*Meus queridos*, I am so sorry that this has happened to us. It won't be long before *Papai* returns, I am sure, and then everything will be fine again. Be strong for me, my darlings, and look after each other. *Tia* Bete is a good lady and she will take care of you, I know. We will only be separated for a short while.'

Pedro lifted her hand to his cheek. Solomon watched his beloved *Mamae* as she spoke, his eyes remaining hard and dry. Isabella pulled her sons towards her one at a time and held them close.

'Solomon,' she whispered, 'when your *Papai* returns tell him where I am. Tell him that I love him and forgive him. Please tell him this for me.'

Solomon shook his head slowly from side to side, and wiped his *Mamae*'s tears with his fingers.

She looked at him steadily. 'Please tell him, Solomon.'

Pedro did not want to leave his mother's side. 'Pedro, darling, stick with your brother. Let him take care of you.'

As the van drove away, Solomon looked back. He had lost his home. Now he had lost his beautiful mother. Where was *Papaï*? He felt as though life was draining out of him. Everything that had been his security had gone. He forced to the back of his mind the memories of how their lives had been in the valley, only months earlier, before Dauro Vasconcellos had taken everything from them.

* * *

'Wake up, Solomon!' *Tia* Bete hissed urgently, as she shook her nephew's shoulder hard.

'What's the matter?' groaned Solomon, confused at the rude awakening. 'What's the time? Are we late for school?'

'No, it's only four in the morning. Come quickly, *filho*, something's happened!'

Solomon removed Pedro's arm from his chest without waking him. Since leaving the rest of his family at the orphanage three weeks earlier, Pedro had hardly left his side. Solomon felt an overwhelming urge to protect his younger brother. After all, they only had each other now.

He followed his *Tia* Bete through the unlit communal bathroom, up the narrow corridor and into the darkened sitting room at the front of the house. As they entered the room, a cold fear came over him and a shiver ran down his spine. His eyes gradually became accustomed to the gloom and he was able to make out the figures of Joao Batista, *Dona* Maria and *Tio* Marcos. They were leaning over someone who was lying on the dining table. *Tio* Marcos put his two hands on Solomon's shoulders. The boy walked forward, steadied by his uncle's hands, until he reached the head of the table. He stood silently, as he tried to take in what he was seeing.

'Get some more cloths, someone! Get anything that we can use to stop the bleeding!' ordered *Dona* Maria.

The bullet had entered Ezio's chest. He was barely breathing and moving in and out of consciousness.

'Solomon,' urged *Dona* Maria, 'tell your *Papai* that you are here. Talk to him, *filho*, we must keep him conscious if we can, until we can get him to the ambulance.'

Solomon looked down at the face he had loved all his life. He felt numb with disbelief. How had this happened to his father? Blood seemed to be everywhere.

'*Papai*,' he said quietly. '*Papai*, it's me, Solomon.'

There was no response.

'Speak louder, *filho*,' said *Dona* Maria urgently, pressing a towel into the seeping wound.

Solomon leaned forward. '*Papai*, it's me. *Papai*, speak to me!'

Ezio's eyes opened and wandered in the direction of his son's voice.

Solomon held his *Papai*'s strong fingers.

'Don't die, *Papai*!' he pleaded. '*Mamae* loves you!'

Ezio smiled weakly, his breath coming in short gasps. 'For-give m-e,' he whispered brokenly.

'We're going to have to get him into the truck, or we'll miss the ambulance!' shouted *Tio* Marcos from the doorway.

Dona Maria put up her hand. 'Wait one minute, Marcos, he's trying to say something to Solomon.'

'So-lo-mon, I'm go-ing to die.'

Solomon shook his head vigorously. 'No, *Papai*!' he said desperately. 'You're not going to die!'

'Pro-mise me some-thing, *filho*.' Ezio winced with pain, then continued doggedly. 'Don't for-get your g-ift . . . find peace in

y-our heart.' He stopped to gasp for breath. 'I found it . . . a-
and then I l-et it go. But you . . . m-ust do bet-ter than me.'
He closed his eyes.

Solomon nodded. 'I will, *Papai*! I will!'

Ezio tightened his grip on Solomon's hand, and then his
arm fell limp, as the last breath left his body.

Tia Bete's hands flew up to her mouth, smothering her
scream.

Solomon stepped back and stumbled out of the sitting room,
unnoticed, as the others crowded around his father's body. He
ran out of the house as the first sun lit the sky and started to
climb through the *favela*. All he knew was that he had to get
away. He had to get away from that scene. Driven by a desperate
surge of emotional energy, his legs carried him upwards with
unnatural strength through the silent alleyways, up past the little
dwellings that were just beginning to stir as their occupants
started a new day. Finally reaching the top of the mountain
where so many people clung to existence in their squalid homes
made of sticks and plastic bags, Solomon flung himself onto
his knees. Reaching his hands up to the sky, he cried out, '*Take
me! I want to die! Take me!*' Not knowing what he was doing,
he stood up and began to run in huge circles, shouting and
waving his arms in the air. 'Where are you, *bandidos*? Come
and kill me! Here I am, where are you? *You bastards*! You shot
my father, you bastards! Now come and shoot me!'

He fell to the ground and beat his fists on the bare earth.
As he vented his fury to the wide, empty sky, somewhere deep
inside him a dam of anger and self-control crumbled into an
explosion of anguished sobs which seemed to burst out with
such force that his fingers dug into the sandy earth as if to
anchor him to the ground. Solomon wept at last for all that

he had lost: his home in the valley, his dog, his *Vovo*, his music, *Senhora* Francisca, Ze, his *Mamae*, Talita and Daniel. Now his *Papai* was gone for ever. He mourned the loss of the chance to be able to get their relationship right again. He mourned those precious days of the past, fishing in the river pools in their mountains, in their valley, just man and boy, father and son. Those days that could never be given back to him.

As the morning sunlight flooded Rio de Janeiro, the boy remained prostrate and motionless on the mountain summit, lost in time and space. Gradually, in his deepest consciousness, Solomon thought he heard music, beautiful music, music he knew, with words sung as if by a choir of angels, that penetrated his soul.

Where was the music coming from? Solomon stood and started to walk. As he reached the gate of the white bungalow, the music stopped. But he noticed that the front door was ajar, and was compelled to enter. No one was in sight. He saw the piano and sat down on the small stool. How he ached to play. How long had it been? It seemed like an eternity. He closed his eyes and spread his hands over the ivory keys. As his voice broke into song, he was aware for the first time how much he needed to play, how for him to play was to reach down into the stillness of his soul, how to sing was to express all that he could not say in words. As the tears poured down his cheeks, he started to sing softly and then gradually louder and louder as his emotions soared.

Madeleine stood listening in the shadow of the doorway.

Solomon sensed that he was no longer alone. He stopped playing abruptly and swung round.

'That was beautiful,' she said softly, her face pale.

He stood and stared back at her, bereft of words.

'I've just heard about your *Papai*,' she said quietly. 'I'm so sorry, Solomon.'

'I don't believe in your God!' he said coldly. 'If he existed, why has this happened to us? We were a happy family. We were poor, but we were happy. Now everything has gone.'

He walked towards the door, empty of emotion. 'I don't believe in your God,' he said again. His green eyes glared into her pale grey ones that were now brimming with tears.

'He's crying with you, Solomon. He gave us free will to make our own choices. Through no fault of your own, choices have been made which have brought about this terrible situation.'

Solomon wanted her to move out of his way.

Madeleine stepped aside. 'I will do everything I can to be of help to you and Pedro.'

'Thank you, but we don't need your help!' Solomon walked out of the still-open door.

He reached the ridge and sat down, pulling his legs up into his chest and tucking his head between his knees. Then he heard Felipe's voice calling him. He looked up and saw the dark, lanky teenager running towards him with Pedro not far behind. His brother threw himself down beside him.

'Solomon! Where have you been? I was so frightened, I thought you'd left me too,' he sobbed, 'then I remembered you liked coming up here.'

Solomon held his brother close.

'I found Pedro looking for you,' croaked Felipe. 'Sorry, man, sorry about your father.'

Felipe turned to leave.

'Where are you going?' asked Solomon, seeing the rucksack on his back. 'To school?'

179

'No, man, I'm going to the streets to meet some friends.'

'Can we come too?'

'Sure! Follow me.'

The two brothers followed him down the mountain, their arms intertwined.

One of the first rules when living on the streets was to lose your identity. 'Self-protection,' the brothers were told. Within a week Solomon had cut off his long thick hair, changed his name to 'Rocco' and created a story about his background that was so elaborate that Pedro had to keep reminding him of the finer details every time he told it. Solomon wanted to escape reality; the pain was too unbearable. He could not afford to allow himself to dream about returning to his valley; that dream was dead, along with his father. Memories of that death, that morning, were forced down and buried deep in his subconscious mind. Pedro chose the name 'Penguin' for himself, and thankfully he did not have to bother making up a story because Solomon had done that for both of them.

Felipe's friends frequented no set place on the streets, preferring to keep on the run in order to avoid both police and gang confrontations as far as possible. However, their regular meeting place was behind the central train station. Here, a community of makeshift shacks had sprung up which prostitutes, drug-traffickers, alcoholics, bootleggers and runaways called home. Next to this heaving beehive of illicit busyness stood a once-magnificent mansion, now in ruins. Within its crumbling walls mounds of putrid litter from the city were dumped throughout the day by large belching trucks. As a result, everything and everyone who lived in the area was covered with a film of black soot that also found its way into nostrils and ears. This shadowy community had a hierarchical structure of its own and an overall leader known as Morreno. A huge bull of a man with a square head and a scarred face, Morreno was a legend amongst this low-life community for the crimes he had committed, for which he was never caught. Morreno had enough paid contacts in high places to keep himself out of prison. Members of the police were paid so little that bribes were often an irresistible supplement to their income.

Morreno was a small-time gangster who was feared and respected by all who worked for him, whether prostitutes or bootleggers. His son, whom he nicknamed 'Elvis Presley' after his favourite rock star, dealt with the couriers from the *favelas*, who funnelled supplies of the white powder to pushers in the rundown areas. Morreno's operation, though small, was profitable and while, realistically, he was never likely to free himself from the magnetic claws of the underworld, he dreamed of a time when he might do so.

Elvis Presley modelled himself on his father. He was just sixteen, and one of several children fathered by the chief. Elvis had been the nominal leader of a small gang of street kids for the past two years and, like his father, had developed an ability to manipulate and control others through threats and aggression. Second-in-command of the gang was his fifteen-year-old sister Silvana, who was strong and tough and could protect herself better than anyone else he knew. She was not pretty, but she was alluring, with her hair in a mass of braids that fell around her full, firm breasts. Silvana knew men looked at her body and she used it to her advantage, wearing tight tops and high-cropped shorts which skimmed her curving hips. She had perfected a feline walk like a cat on heat and watched under her eyelashes as smart businessmen cast furtive glances at her as they passed. She would ignore them at first, then, just when they thought she had not noticed, she would catch their eye and give them a knowing wink. But Silvana would never be a prostitute as long as her boyfriend Sergio was around. He would kill her if she slept with someone else, and to make sure it never happened he never let her out of his sight. Their mother had deserted Elvis and Silvana soon after she was born, and had never returned.

'Morreno!' cried Elvis Presley. He never referred to him as *Papai*. 'Felipe has brought us two new boys, Rocco and Penguin.'

Morreno was seated in a rundown bar behind the train station, surrounded by four large but bedraggled-looking men who sat staring nervously at their chief, waiting for his next instructions. He looked up with his one eye, nodded in their direction and took a drag from his cigar.

'Come here, boy!' he roared, looking across at Solomon.

All eyes turned his way. Solomon felt suddenly light-headed. Two weeks on the hard pavements covered only by cardboard and plastic sheeting had exhausted him, and the lack of proper nourishment did not help. But going back to the *favela* was out of the question. He had known that on the morning when he and Pedro followed Felipe into the city. He knew from the network of informers that surrounded Morreno's organisation that his uncle and several of their friends from the *favela* had come looking for him and Pedro within hours of their disappearance. Luciano, the friendly butcher, knew the streets and their gangs well and word quickly got around that two olive-skinned brothers called Solomon and Pedro were being searched for. Felipe and Elvis Presley were sworn to secrecy, and the boys decided they would never reveal their true identity to anyone.

Strangely, it had not occurred to either of them to concern themselves with the effect their disappearance might have on their family. Maybe it was the extreme shock of all that had happened to them, but it just never entered their heads. In fact, nothing much bothered them other than the need to survive in their new world. Like so many of their new street friends, they started sniffing glue. The numbing effect of the drug spread through their bodies, dulling painful memories and hunger pangs.

'Come here!' repeated Morreno impatiently.

'Yes sir,' said Solomon, walking over to the huge man.

'Are you looking for work?' he grunted with a sly grin. He could do with more couriers.

The boys exchanged glances and nodded. What did they have to lose?

'Good! Elvis will look after you. Stay out of trouble and do what he says, otherwise I'll have you sent back where you came from! Do you understand me?' Morreno squinted at them and wagged the stub of his cigar.

'Yes sir!' they said in unison.

Chapter 11

Candelaria

Silvana had her arm through Sergio's and was stroking his face. Sergio, who was about sixteen, had a fuzz of newly peroxided hair and the beginnings of a goatee. He was several inches shorter than Silvana, but this deficit was made up for by his strong frame and broad, muscular shoulders. Sergio never smiled, and guarded Silvana with the jealous eye of a territorial lion. He started to become watchful when the lean, handsome Solomon was around. The remainder of the gang were grouped around the fondling couple, awaiting the return of Elvis Presley. Telma, aged twelve, and her younger brother Adriano had lived on the streets behind the rubbish dump with their mother and flea-infested dog for as long as they could remember. One night about a year earlier their mother had vanished and never returned; not even Morreno's network could trace her whereabouts. The dog and the children were quickly adopted by Silvana, whose kind heart could all too easily relate to their pitiful predicament. Telma was shy, with long chestnut hair and fine bone structure. Her little brother had lighter skin and a face covered with sores. Adriano was the youngest of the group, but had the quickest hands and legs when it came to stealing wallets. Another boy, Fernando, and his brother Luis were cousins to Elvis Presley and Silvana.

Fernando had a quick temper and was always prepared to

stand up to his leaders. They were, after all, blood relations. When Solomon and Pedro first joined the gang, Fernando's hair had been covered in thick lumps of dried glue. One night Silvana shaved it all off and he now resembled a young Yul Brynner. As for Luis, he was everyone's friend, easy-going and obliging. His face wore a permanent smile. They had all grown up in Santo Cristo, a *favela* covering a low-lying mountain which loomed in the background of the rubbish dump and community of shacks.

'Let's go!' cried Elvis Presley as he approached the circle of scruffy urchins. He turned suddenly without further explanation and walked off briskly in the direction of the bus stop in front of the station, carrying two school rucksacks on his back and wearing his favourite dark sunglasses. They all jumped up and fell in behind him, jogging to keep up. Some were barefoot and others wore battered flip-flops. Elvis Presley always wore sneakers.

'Where the hell are we going?' shouted Silvana, angry that he had not consulted her first.

'Candelaria!' He tossed her one of the rucksacks.

They jumped onto the back of a slow-moving bus and filled up the back two rows. Two women sitting in front of them vacated their seats quickly and moved forward, clutching their handbags.

Solomon looked out of the window at the towering statue of Christ Redeemer, its mighty steel arms outstretched to the cloudless sky over the *cidade marvilhosa*.

'We'll grab something to eat in Candelaria and then split up,' ordered Elvis. 'Silvana and Sergio can deliver in the port area and Solomon and Pedro will come with me to Copacabana. The rest of you can wait for us to return.'

'What about Fernando?' Silvana hissed to her brother.

'He's doing too many drugs these days, I can't trust him with deliveries.'

Silvana looked doubtful. 'But he's used to working with you!'

'It's too risky. Leave Fernando to me. Right?'

Candelaria was an area by the port situated at the far end of Rua Primeiro de Marco. It had a large square with a statue in the middle of it and an ornate church. This busy main road ran long, straight and wide from the main train station and Morreno's headquarters. A colourful moving collage of buses, cars and pedestrians covered the sun-scorched tarmac, and grey concrete buildings stood high and tall above shops and cafés on either side. A rival gang was already gathering in the square behind the seven white marble columns that held up a tall office block in front of a windowless marble wall at right angles to the church. This was a favourite sleeping area for many street-dwellers. Grids in the pavements blew out warm air twenty-four hours a day. Charities dedicated to helping the homeless brought food and blankets regularly to this spot.

The gang jumped off the bus and jogged across the square to the charity minibus, where hot meals were already being distributed to hungry street kids.

'Who are your two new friends, Elvis?' said a voice from behind them as they sat on the kerb eagerly scooping rice and beans into their mouths with large plastic spoons.

Elvis Presley did not turn round. '*Oi*, Sergeant, *tudo bem*?' he replied through a mouthful.

The young uniformed policeman squatted down beside them. Solomon and Pedro stopped eating and looked at him curiously. They had heard many bad stories about certain notorious, corrupt policemen and security guards who were prepared to exterminate gangs of children for payment in order to 'clean up the streets'. Sensing their alarm, Elvis said, 'Don't worry, lads, this is Sergeant Paulo and he's cool.'

'Hi boys!' The young sergeant shook Elvis's hand and patted him on the back.

'These are two new friends of mine, Sergeant Paulo – Rocco and Penguin!'

'You know what I always say to you, Elvis.' The young sergeant extended his hand to Solomon and Pedro. 'If you decide to come off the streets, these kind people here handing out the food have shelters. Remember that, Rocco and Penguin!'

'They're fine with me, Sergeant, thanks,' Elvis growled.

'You watch your backs with him, boys!' jested the sergeant. 'You're both new on the streets, aren't you?'

'Go and bother someone else, Sergeant Paulo!'

'We're from another city,' interjected Pedro.

Solomon shot a warning look at his brother, which did not go unnoticed by the friendly sergeant. He stood up. 'You know the streets are no place to live, son. Why not go home?'

'We haven't got a home!' said Pedro flatly, ignoring Solomon's stare.

They watched the slim back of Sergeant Paulo as he walked over to the minibus, where he began talking to a couple of the women still handing out food. The three of them turned and looked in their direction.

'Now you've done it, Penguin!' hissed Solomon.

'Done what?' answered Pedro defensively.

'It's OK,' interrupted Elvis. 'Finish your food, we've got business to do and you both need some practical lessons in selling! But first we'll need to get some clean clothes and shoes for you both.'

The brothers looked down at their filthy feet.

* * *

'Can I ask where we're going today?' Solomon asked Elvis a few weeks later. He had noticed his slight nervousness on their now familiar bus journey, careering past long stretches of white sandy beaches covered in half-naked sun-worshippers, energetic volleyball players, roller-skaters and people walking their dogs.

'We're going to a hotel in Copacabana,' Elvis replied tersely, his fingers drumming on the rucksack on his lap.

The boys had once again changed out of their street rags into white trainers, jeans, t-shirts and baseball caps stolen from the flea market, in a toilet at the back of a rundown bar near Candelaria. Elvis again produced toothpaste, toothbrush, a nailbrush, a comb and a bottle of cheap aftershave to cover any bad odours. As the bus jolted along the beach front that afternoon, Solomon knew they no longer looked like street kids.

Pedro stood as if shell-shocked in the hall of the palatial hotel. He and Solomon gazed up at the huge, shimmering crystal chandeliers suspended from the vaulted ceiling, as Elvis Presley greeted a large black man in a suit and shades who had appeared from nowhere as they walked through the glass entrance doors. The man turned to Solomon and Pedro and kissed them as though they were his long-lost nephews – all a guise to allay the suspicions of the vigilant hotel staff.

Within minutes they were riding a gilded lift to the third floor, where they were ushered into the stranger's bedroom suite. The boys looked around them, incredulous at the opulence. A high-pitched voice with a strong Rio accent called from behind the closed bathroom door.

'Is that you, Mauro?'

'Yeah, boss, it's Morreno's boy!'

The toilet flushed and the door opened. As Solomon looked up, his blood ran cold. The man who walked towards them was the same man who had haunted his dreams since his family had been forced to leave the valley.

'What you got for me today, pop star?'

Elvis gritted his teeth and handed the man his rucksack.

Solomon was in a state of shock. Gone was the thick moustache, the smart city suit and shiny black shoes. But the voice was the same, and he would never forget those eyes with their hooded lids.

'Who you brought with you?' The beady gaze bored down on Solomon as the man unzipped the bag. A diamond ring glistened on his right hand. Solomon pulled the peak of his cap lower over his face and glanced away. His heart was pounding. His mind was in a tumult. He had dreamed of this moment. The urge to pin this man against the wall and punch the life out of him was almost overwhelming.

'You got a fucking name, or what?'

Solomon looked from under his cap. 'Rocco! My name's Rocco!' He spat the words out with such venom that Pedro did not recognise his own brother's voice.

'Have I seen you before, Rocco?'

'No,' answered Solomon coldly. 'I don't hang out in places like this!'

Dauro Vasconcellos grunted, and bent to examine the contents of the rucksack.

'You didn't bring much today, you son-of-a-bitch!' He threw the bags of white powder on the bed.

'It's what Morreno gave me. He wants cash up front, says you still owe him.'

Vasconcellos shot an uneasy look at Solomon and then at Pedro, through half-shut eyes. Something was bothering him.

Elvis Presley did not have a university degree, but the experience of his short life had made him intuitive and streetwise. He sensed that something of an unspoken dimension was going on in the room and that he needed to get Solomon and Pedro out of the hotel as quickly as possible.

'You got the cash, or what?' Elvis snapped with all the authority he could muster.

Vasconcellos opened the small drawer next to the bed, took out an envelope and tossed it at Elvis, who caught it, snatched the empty rucksack and headed for the door. Solomon and Pedro followed him. The door slammed behind them.

'OK,' said Elvis impatiently once they were on a bus. 'What's up? Give it to me straight, and don't bullshit with me because I haven't got time for it, OK?'

Solomon told him everything. Elvis listened without interrupting.

'I knew there was something going on in there!' Elvis paused. 'He works for Morreno and has done for years.'

Solomon glared back at him. 'You mean to tell me that it was *Morreno* who destroyed my family, and now I'm working for him?'

'Morreno isn't about to steal land from anyone! And what's more, he's not going to like it when I tell him that his own cousin is operating behind his back.'

'His cousin! That bastard's related to you?' Solomon jumped

to his feet and grabbed Pedro, who was sitting across the aisle. 'Come on, Penguin, we're getting out of here!'

'Sit down!' yelled Elvis, pulling Solomon back onto the seat. 'We may be in the underworld, but we operate within a set of rules. Morreno doesn't steal anyone's home and land from them, and nor do the people who work for him. *Droga*! You better be telling me the truth, or I'll have you beaten to a pulp!'

Solomon sat down again and put his head in his hands.

Later that night, Morreno exhaled smoke and listened intently as Solomon spoke. It was midnight now, and the shadowy community was buzzing with life. The night air was sticky. Pedro had fallen asleep curled up on a sofa in a corner of the shack behind the bar.

When he had finished, Morreno fired some questions at him and Solomon did his best to answer them clearly. It was difficult not to exaggerate when talking about the man who had destroyed his life.

'I need to know near enough the date your father and these other farmers signed those documents.'

'It was the end of February this year.'

'That son-of-a-bitch!' Morreno pushed his chair back and paced the small hovel. 'No one works deals behind my back, especially my own cousin!' he growled, stubbing his cigar out on the floor with his foot. He turned and barked at Elvis, 'Get me Eduardo and Daninho now!'

A clap of thunder cracked through the humidity, and lightning flashed across a sky now heavy with dark clouds ready to burst. Despite his exhaustion, the adrenaline was churning through Solomon's body like a stimulant. The two men arrived almost immediately, like spaniels called to their owner's heel.

Morreno snapped his fingers at them. 'Bring my cousin in, and bring him alive! No one does business behind my back and gets away with it!' he roared, as a second clap of thunder exploded over their heads and the tropical rain began to fall like hard pebbles.

He turned to Solomon. 'Rocco, get some sleep! I need you in good shape tomorrow. No fucking glue sniffing, you hear me?' He pointed a gnarled finger. 'Elvis, don't let him out of your sight!' He stormed out of the shack.

Chapter 12

'Jesu, Joy of Man's Desiring'

*I*t was three o'clock on a Saturday morning, and the city streets were empty around Candelaria. A line of makeshift beds had been contrived out of old newspapers and pieces of cardboard and plastic, which now cradled the forms of several sleeping children. Most were sharing the comfort of a blanket, which had been stuffed out of sight down a manhole during the day. The stench of urine, compounded by the paint thinner that many were still sniffing on bits of rag, stifled the air around them. Silvana was lying next to Solomon. She stretched and moved closer to him, snuggling her head into his shoulder. Solomon sat bolt upright.

'You want Sergio to put a bullet through my head?'

'He's in hospital, remember?'

Sergio had suffered a burst appendix two days earlier, and he had been admitted to the state hospital in an ambulance.

Silvana propped her head up with an arm and gazed up at him seductively.

'You're handsome, Solomon Itaborahy! It's been hard for me to resist you these last few months . . .'

'The name's Rocco!'

'Morreno says you sing and play the piano like a god. He says you don't belong here with the likes of us.'

'I owe Morreno.'

'For what?'

'For sorting out Dauro Vasconcellos. Morreno gave him his comeuppance. We won't be seeing him any more.'

Silvana reached up and placed her hand behind Solomon's neck. She gently drew his face to hers. 'I want you.' She kissed him.

Solomon liked the kiss, but then, for some inexplicable reason, he felt as if he were betraying someone else. He took hold of her restraining hand, and gently pulled away from her.

'And I like you,' he said tenderly.

'But what?'

'I don't know.'

'Come on, Sergio won't find out.'

'It's not that.'

'Then what is it?'

'I can't explain.'

All at once, shouting and heavy footsteps exploded out of nowhere.

'*Levanta*! Stand up!' yelled a man's voice from over to their left. 'All of you stand up! Up! Up! You scum!'

Solomon jumped to his feet and saw four masked men in dark uniforms bearing down on them. All carried guns.

'*Levanta, levanta, levanta*!' the men repeated in unison. Solomon noticed that a fifth man with his back to them was keeping a lookout down the square. One of the men kicked out at three children still lying asleep, drowsy from the effects of drugs. They screamed with pain and terror.

'Get up, you scum!' shouted one of the men. 'Legs apart and hands in the air!'

Solomon looked frantically around him. Where was Pedro?

'We're in trouble!' hissed Silvana. 'These are off-duty

policemen and security guards and they aren't here to be nice to us.'

'Where's Penguin?' asked Solomon urgently. 'Where's Penguin, Silvana?'

One of the men spun Solomon round and punched him in the stomach. 'Shut up!' he bellowed in his face.

'You crazy son-of-a-bitch!' screamed Silvana, grabbing the thug.

'Ah!' he said, laughing at her and pinning her arms behind her back. 'And *who* do we have here then? Nice tits! You a prostitute? Eh?'

Solomon wanted to hit out, but he was bent double on the ground.

'Get off me, you son-of-a-bitch!' whimpered Silvana.

'Hey, Jose, here's a lively one!' Silvana was dragged off kicking and screaming by two of the men. They disappeared into an alleyway.

Solomon forced himself upright. *I've got to find Pedro*, he thought, gasping for breath. He screamed Pedro's name over and over again, but his voice would not operate properly.

Another black-clad man seized Solomon by the shirt, threw him up against the wall and held a revolver to his temple. 'Stay here and shut up, or I'll shoot you sooner than I plan to,' he hissed into his ear. He left Solomon slumped by the marble wall. Luis was nearby. 'Penguin is on your left next to Elvis at the end of the line-up,' he whispered as the guard moved away.

At that moment, a siren could be heard in the distance. It grew louder and louder until a white police car screeched to a halt some yards from them.

'Shit!' screamed one of their tormentors.

'Need any help?' called a voice from the white car. It was Sergeant Paulo.

'No, we're covered!' shouted back one of the guards hastily. 'Drug raid!' he lied.

Sergeant Paulo and his colleague prepared to drive away.

Solomon knew he had to stop the sergeant from leaving. All at once he seemed to sense a voice in his mind saying, '*Turn and run to the car. Move! Now!*'

He whipped round and started to run, gasping out the words, 'Sergeant Paulo! Stop! They've got Silvana! They're going to kill us! Don't go!'

Behind him he heard Pedro cry out his name. He heard a gunshot, then everything was overtaken by darkness.

'Solomon!' Pedro was shaking him. 'Get up! Get up! We've got to get out of here!'

Solomon struggled to get to his feet, Pedro tugging urgently at his arms. He forced his legs to impel him forward, then put a hand to the pain on the side of his head. It felt wet and sticky, and he realised he was bleeding. Pedro was pulling at him, almost dragging him across the square and away from the chaos, the nightmare. Hand in hand they staggered on blindly, down back streets and little alleyways, until Solomon knew he could go no further.

'Stop!' he gasped, sinking down against the wooden gate of a rundown building in a narrow passageway. 'We've run far enough! I've got to stop and get my breath back. My chest is burning.' He felt his head swim. 'Where are the others?'

Pedro was removing his grubby t-shirt. 'I don't know. I'm going to wipe the blood away a bit, Solomon,' he said, gingerly stroking at the red stains on Solomon's neck and skull.

'The bullet passed on! I'm alive, Pedro!' He pressed on the part where the bullet had struck him. 'Am I cut badly?'

In reply Pedro burst into tears. He covered his face with the bloodstained shirt and sobbed. 'I want to go home, I've had enough. I want *Mamae*!'

The brothers clung together in the dark little alleyway.

'I know, Pedro, little brother.' They held each other close.

For the first time since the death of *Papai*, Solomon allowed himself to visualise them all: *Mamae*, little Daniel, Talita, *Vovo*, *Senhora* Francisca. What were they all doing? What were they all thinking?

'Let's stay in here for a bit.' Solomon pushed ajar one side of the padlocked gate as far as the chain would go, giving them the inches they needed to slip into the abandoned garage. 'I recognise this place.' It was dark inside, but he remembered there was a large old sink at the back end of the building with running water. He had to have a drink. He had to wash away the blood.

They both took their clothes off and washed the filth of the streets from their bodies. Solomon hung his hurting head under the running tap. The water felt cool and calming in the midst of the nightmare. Wringing out their t-shirts, Solomon hung them both over the edge of the sink to dry. Pedro found a large cardboard box amongst the pile of old papers in the corner under a small window that allowed a little bit of light to filter in. They had slept here once before with their gang, he could not remember when. Suddenly their months on the streets felt like years. Climbing into the box next to Pedro, Solomon covered them both with some newspaper. Despite his aching head and the hunger pains in his stomach, it felt good to be clean. The two boys huddled in each other's arms for warmth in that deserted, forgotten backwater of Rio de Janeiro. Exhausted and emotionally spent, they slept for thirteen hours.

'What's the time? Is it tomorrow? Why is it still dark?' asked Pedro.

'We must have slept all day!' Solomon winced from the pain in his head as he pulled himself out of the box and carefully put on his t-shirt, which was now dry.

'Let's go and find something to eat!'

They pushed open the gate and slipped through the gap under the chain. As they hesitated, unsure which way to go, Solomon gripped Pedro's arm.

'Can you hear that, Pedro?'

'What?'

'That music!'

'I can't hear anything.'

'It's the same music I heard on the mountain when *Papai* died! We've got to find out where it's coming from.'

'But I can't hear anything!'

Forgetting his hunger and the pain, Solomon set off at a jog in the direction of the music.

'Wait for me!' cried Pedro, confused.

The passageway which had been their shelter led into the wide main street of an affluent area of the city. On the opposite side of the street stood a large church.

Solomon stopped at the kerbside to allow Pedro to catch up with him. 'We're close,' he said.

'Close to what?'

'Look, it's coming from over there, from that big church.'

'I can hear it too, now!'

The boys crossed the street, where a great many expensive cars were parked. Several liveried drivers chatted together, smoking and sharing a joke or two. Without a second thought Solomon headed for the flight of marble steps that led to the huge oak doors now wide open at the top. A large, elegant canopy shaded the entrance, which was framed on either side by huge pedestals of fragrant white flowers. Unnoticed, the boys reached the red carpet and stood gazing, transfixed, at the magnificent scene before them. The vast interior of the church was lit by thousands of candles that sparkled everywhere, and by shimmering crystal chandeliers that hung from the vaulted ceiling. It was like a fairy tale, a vision of light and gold and movement and music, which now reached a crescendo as the organ rang out the notes so familiar to Solomon. 'It's Bach's "Jesu, Joy of Man's Desiring",' he whispered to Pedro. 'Come on, I'm going in.'

Inside the candlelit church thousands of roses and lilies lined the aisles, and seemed to pour themselves through the sanctuary like a cascading river, their scent filling the air. At the top end of the long red carpet stood the bride, dressed in white silk, her long veil drawn back to reveal a radiant face, as she looked up at the young man beside her, her bridegroom, whose hand she held. The congregation was full of beautiful, carefully coiffed women in exquisite clothes, whose jewellery glistened in the candlelight, and men in evening suits with white roses in their buttonholes. They saw a boy from the streets standing in their midst, tall, emaciated and shabby. He represented a world they recoiled from and feared.

As the music soared, Solomon was drawn up the red carpet as though sensing that whisper from his dream long ago: '*Come to me, Solomon, come to me.*' Pedro stayed by the door, rigid with fear. 'Stop!' he called out in vain to the retreating figure of his brother. Solomon walked on. He looked up into the chancel and saw, at the furthest and highest point of the building, the figure of that young man, nailed to a cross. *He suffered too*, he thought, *just like me*. He saw the face of the bride as she turned to look at him, calm but taken aback.

The street boy stopped and stood there in his shabby shorts and washed-out t-shirt. He opened his mouth and raised his voice, loud and clear, to the music of the beautiful anthem. His eyes, full of unshed tears, remained fixed on the man on the cross. There was a gasp as the entire congregation was thrilled by the beautiful sound. People from Rio de Janeiro's highest society shifted in their seats as they strained to see the source of this angelic sound.

The woman playing the organ knew this voice, and her fingers froze and missed a note. She had thought she would never hear it again. She wanted desperately to go to him, but there was a wedding service to finish and she was at the organ playing before more than one thousand guests.

As Solomon finished the song, the bride and her groom stood transfixed just a few feet away from him. They were moved beyond words. Who was this boy ? Where had he come from? But as they stood and wondered, the boy before them looked suddenly confused and embarrassed, and he turned and walked quickly away, out of the church and back into the dark streets.

Madeleine left through the side entrance of the church as soon as she was able. She stopped in the light of the doorway to search in her bag for her car keys, then hurried down the unlit street where she had left her car. She must get home and tell the family that she had seen Solomon. As she reached her car, she stopped and turned round quickly, sensing that she was being followed.

'Who's there?' she demanded, searching the darkness.

Two silhouettes emerged from a doorway a few yards away. Madeleine gasped in fright.

'Sister Madeleine, it's us, it's Solomon and Pedro!' The children stepped out of the shadows. 'We saw you in the doorway of the church when you came out.'

The priest had noticed two street children following her and came running up the street.

'Solomon! Pedro!' Madeleine clapped her hands to her mouth and then opened her arms to embrace them both. 'I'm so happy to see you! We had all given up hope of ever finding you again, until I heard your voice in the church just now. It was me playing the organ!' She turned to the anxious priest. 'Please don't worry, *Padre*, I know these boys well.'

The priest stopped in his tracks, dumbfounded. 'So this is the boy with that beautiful voice!' He leaned forward and placed his hands gently on Solomon's shoulders. 'The streets are no place for you both to live, son.'

Madeleine quickly unlocked her car and opened the door. 'Don't worry, *Padre*, they're coming home with me.'

PART II

Chapter 13

The Challenge

Missoula, Montana, USA 1994

'Come on, Mary! If you stop, you'll never make it to the top!' Keira sat down next to Fin and wiped the sweat off her face with the hem of her t-shirt. She took a long drink from the water bottle in her rucksack and handed it to her cousin. 'You should take your fiancée on more jogs, Fin!'

He gave a good-natured laugh and shook his head in defeat. 'You know Mary. She hates the very word "exercise"!'

They both looked down over the top of the university campus at the sleepy city of Missoula beyond. The weather was warm for early October and the valley, filled with poplar and maple trees, remained green. Mary, who had collapsed to the ground way below, staggered to her feet and broke into a pathetic jog as she continued to force herself up Mount Sentinel to the giant letter 'M' which had first been painted onto the side of the steep hill some eighty-seven years earlier.

Keira had thought of the idea the night before. It was the university's homecoming week, and traditionally students sang on the steps in front of the Main Hall, with the presentation of the Alumni Awards and the crowning of the Homecoming Royalty. The pep rally had featured football coach Will Murphy and his star players from the Grizzlies, the college football team, along with the cheerleaders and someone dressed up as Monte the Bear, the University of Montana's mascot. As the throng of students sang 'Old College Chums', hundreds of lights had lit up the white 'M' above the campus, and Keira had turned impulsively to her friend Mary with the idea of a picnic lunch the following day on the Mount before the game. Mary had found every excuse she could think of to avoid such an energetic outing, not least her Saturday date with Fin.

Since Fin's graduation from the University of California, he had been employed as a reporter with his father Hank on the *Missoula Independent*. As usual when an idea struck her, Keira had persisted stubbornly. Fin had taken no persuasion at all. The Grizzlies would be playing against the Cal State Northridge Matadors that afternoon, and from the picnic on Mount Sentinel, which hovered over the top of the Washington-Grizzly Stadium, it would not take long to get to the game.

Mary finally caught up with them and slumped down on the ground next to Fin. He put his arm around her and gave her a kiss. 'It's taken longer than I thought to get up here, honey, so we'll have to eat quick and go straight back down to the stadium!'

'*What*?' cried Mary, trying to get her breath.

'We can't miss it!' exclaimed Keira, taking a bite out of her tuna sandwich. 'Cass is playing.'

Mary raised her eyes. 'You're too good for Cass Henderson. When are you going to give up?'

Keira ignored her friend's comments, and threw her a sandwich instead.

Mary caught it, and gave her a half smile back. She felt a stab of irritation. She was sick of Cass Henderson. Her sister Alana had been roughly courted, used, and abruptly discarded. Clearly he saw no need to make a commitment when the world was his oyster and plenty of attractive girls were falling at his feet. She just wished Keira was not one of them.

Keira's feelings for Cass over the last seven years had never changed, despite her graduating from high school and blossoming into adulthood. She remained quite certain that one day a light would go on and Cass would realise that what he needed was her: she was prepared to wait. There had been many other young men who had dated her, but nothing could change what had been determined, she was certain.

Growing up as a teenager without her Mom had been so hard at times, and there had been precious moments alone at night in her bed when she would talk out loud to her mother about her fears and longings as though she were right there in the room with her.

Keira had corresponded with Laurence ever since they had first met in Sunderland that summer after her Mom's death. To her delight they had once managed to coincide their trips to England and had all stayed together at The Olde House with Grandma Molly. A couple of years later, after many invitations, the Panzons had finally made it to Montana. With Laurence, Keira felt she could discuss almost anything. She was so easy to talk to, yet the subject of her feelings for Cass was never mentioned, because she sensed that Laurence was uncomfortable about him.

During her two years at UM, Cass had given Keira just enough encouragement to keep her believing there was hope. Mary had reminded her again and again that he flirted with every pretty girl at the university, but Keira closed her ears every time. The memory of that close encounter all those years ago at Greenacres still haunted her as though it were yesterday. Again and again she remembered the details of that evening.

He had wanted her, she was sure. But her immaturity had ruined it and turned him away. She had only been fourteen, after all. As for the card he had sent her after her mother died, she had read and re-read it so many times that the words were etched on her brain. Mary had told her more than once that she was convinced Cass had taken the card from a drawer in his mother's desk, and that the wording on it had probably meant nothing to him.

'There's no getting away from it,' said Fin, sinking back into the grass and placing the beer can on his chest. 'Cass Henderson's a majestic player to watch.'

'Apparently the NFL scouts are after him,' commented Keira casually. Far below she could see that a few people were already taking their seats in the stadium.

'That's because he was voted second best college player in the country last year.' Fin sat up and started to eat his sandwich. 'They reckon he'll win the Heisman Trophy this year.'

'He was runner-up two years ago!' Keira snapped open her can.

'So what makes a great quarterback?' asked Mary, forcing an interest.

'What makes a great quarterback, sweetheart? He's got to know how to throw.'

'And he's got to be smart,' said Keira.

'Cass is "Mr Confidence" too, which helps.' Fin finished his beer. 'Confidence is catchy and his team-mates need to believe in their quarterback. A high-calibre quarterback can inspire his team-mates to raise their game.'

'Well, he certainly doesn't lack confidence,' Mary said evenly.

'That's no bad thing!' Keira was always defensive when it came to Cass.

Fin stood up. 'We'd better go, or we'll miss the start of the game.' He held out his hand to Mary. 'It will be quicker on the way down, I promise you, honey!'

She allowed herself to be pulled to her feet.

'I'll race you down!' cried Keira, throwing her rucksack over her shoulder.

The atmosphere in the stadium was electric. Only seven minutes into the game, and Cass had scored a touchdown. The exuberant home crowd had erupted; horns, pounding drums, chants and cheers exploded out from the arena. Fin and Keira were on their feet, along with the rest of the crowd.

'He's done it again,' sighed Mary, looking down at Cass as his six-foot-three athletic frame pounded the field in the Grizzlies' football strip with padding and silver helmet. She turned and watched Keira's profile, pride illuminating her face.

Cass Henderson was in his fifth year of an MBA in business administration. After graduating at the end of the academic year, he would be going on to law school. But his passion was the game, and he prided himself on his position as the quarterback 'superstar' of the University of Montana. As quarterback he was in charge, all the action went through him on the field, and he knew how to bark commands at his team with authority. This, coupled with his natural skill and superb fitness, made him the great player he was, and he knew it. There were more than five hundred plays to learn and thirty different defences to understand and Cass knew them all. He dreamed of playing as a professional, longed for it. He had already enjoyed a taste of the high pressure, high glamour and responsibility that the position brought, and he knew that he had the wherewithal to handle the heat. However, nothing was going to stand in the way of his father's ambition for a political career for his son, and Cass, still heavily under the influence of Jim Henderson, whether he wanted to admit it to himself or not, did not dare suggest to him that his own preferences might lie elsewhere.

Coach Murphy proved to be an unexpected ally for Jim. The Grizzlies had been top of the 1-AA division for four consecutive years, thanks to this talented quarterback, and it had done wonders for his reputation as coach. Retiring from the spotlight after years as a professional player for the Seahawks had not been easy. He missed the publicity and the glamour that went with it. So the huge success he had found in his new role with this college side, largely due to the talented young Henderson, had helped boost a flagging ego. Whenever a scout came sniffing too close for comfort, therefore, Will would point out to Cass that he did not need the money anyway, and that playing for a college was less demanding on his time.

At half time the Grizzlies were leading 28-11.

Fin was still considering Cass Henderson's game. 'Shame his character doesn't match his sporting attributes,' he remarked aloud. He was feeling the effects of the beer.

'And what's that supposed to mean?' Keira did not take her eyes off the field.

'Nothing,' Fin said hastily, regretting his slip immediately. He hated confrontations.

'I think you're jealous of Cass!' Keira fumed.

'Perhaps I am,' he said feebly.

But Keira knew that her cousin Fin rarely spoke ill of anyone, and his words bothered her, hanging in the air like an unwelcome black cloud.

'What's wrong with his character, then?' she persisted.

'I don't know him well enough to say . . . it's just things I've heard . . . from others.' Fin felt he was digging a hole for himself.

'Others? Who?' Keira was becoming annoyed.

'People in the bars . . . OK . . . my Dad.'

'Your Dad? Ha! Since when has Hank spent time in Cass Henderson's company?'

'It's a small city . . . rumours . . . forget it, Keira.' He willed the game to restart.

'What rumours, for Christ's sake? That he likes women? That's no secret. He just hasn't found the right one yet is all.'

Mary gave Fin a dig with her elbow. She chose to stay out of this conversation.

Keira turned away and as a slow autumn wind caught the thick auburn curtain of her hair, she shivered suddenly.

Fin decided he had nothing to lose. 'Just don't let your infatuation impair your judgement, Keira,' he remarked.

'What *are* you talking about?' she retorted, swinging round to face him.

'Dad knows a few things about Henderson Senior,' he ventured. 'He says Cass is like a puppet on a string. Everything Jim didn't achieve in politics for himself, he intends to achieve through his son, one way or another. There's a suspicion – just a suspicion, mind – that when Cass was voted in as president of the Association of Students last year, the other two candidates were bought off during the elections, clearing the way for Cass.'

Mary was horrified. 'Where did you hear that?'

Keira broke in. 'I don't believe it for a second! There are a lot of sad people in this community who have nothing better to do than make up malicious lies to destroy other people's credibility.'

'Well, maybe, but Dad says that both of those candidates had debts which suddenly disappeared a month after the elections. He knows someone in administration here on campus.'

Keira's fair complexion flushed to a shade which clashed with her blaze of hair.

But Fin had begun, and he decided to continue.

'Apparently Cass has just been named by the governor of Montana as student regent, making him a voting member of the board of regents, who are the governing body for the university system in the state. It's going to be announced next week. If he hadn't been president of the ASUM, this appointment wouldn't have been possible. Naturally Jim Henderson knew that, after all it's what he did all those years ago at this same university. Ask your Dad, Keira, if you don't believe me.'

Keira felt a shiver going up her spine. 'What happened between my father and his?' Her eyes narrowed.

'I don't know. But Jim is a staunch Republican and your father is a staunch Democrat. Liam Kavanagh ran as a candidate for president of the ASUM when he was here in 1969. He lost to Jim Henderson, didn't he?'

Keira's mind was racing.

Fin continued, 'Anyway, now Cass is student regent there's a sure bet he will be voted in as legislator for the House of Representatives in law school. After that who knows? Attorney general . . . senator . . . Washington . . . then the big one!'

Keira stared across at Fin's profile. *It can't be true*, she thought. *Reporters get things wrong, everyone knows that. Besides, Hank is a member of the Democratic Party too, like Dad. He's bound to dig up trash.*

Fin read her mind. 'Keira, listen,' he said gently. 'Dad is

convinced about this. Think about it: Jim supplies the money, the ruthlessness and the shrewd schemes; Cass supplies the looks, the charm and the talent. They're a team. What do they have in common? A weakness for power and control. People like that don't like to lose, it becomes an obsession.'

Suddenly Keira's mood changed. She did not want to hear any more of this, and her sense of fun came to the rescue. 'I feel like Juliet again!' she cried loudly, jumping up and taking up a theatrical stance with her hand on her breast. Last year she had auditioned for the part of the love-struck Juliet in the university's production of Shakespeare's *Romeo and Juliet*, but had only won the part as understudy. As luck would have it, however, the girl who took the role, Georgina Cole, was taken ill during the run of the play and Keira had stepped into the part. She had gained good reviews and her picture had appeared on the front of the campus newspaper, much to Georgina's fury. Now Keira started reciting loudly and dramatically to anyone within earshot,

> My only love, sprung from my only hate!
> Too early seen unknown, and known too late!
> Prodigious birth of love it is to me
> That I must love a loathed enemy.

There was a pause, then some of the other spectators around them applauded. Keira noticed, to her embarrassment, that they included Professor Hessler, her English professor, and his wife, who were sitting two rows behind them.

'Just my luck!' she hissed ruefully, while Fin and Mary laughed.

The horns were blowing loudly again, echoing around the

stadium. A line of blonde cheerleaders kicked shapely legs in skin-coloured tights as they frenetically waved pom-poms in the air. The second half of the game started, and the centre passed the ball to Cass. Cass quickly put his middle finger on the third lace and the inside of his little finger under the fifth lace. Pulling back his strong arm, he threw it with precision, his index finger the last to leave the ball, causing it to spin in a hard, straight spiral.

'Whoa, now that's accuracy!' Fin cried with enthusiasm.

Keira went home after the game and spent the next few hours getting herself ready for the post-match party. Her bed was strewn with discarded clothes and accessories when she finally achieved the look she wanted. Her tight black cocktail dress had a halter-neck that accentuated her beautiful shoulders and slender back. Cathy, her roommate, made up her face skilfully, enhancing her eyes and her high cheekbones. Her thick mane of auburn hair was twined, twisted and pinned on top of her head, showing off her slim neck. Earrings set with blue stones, which Laurence had given her last year, dangled from her ears. The effect was stunning.

'You look gorgeous, Keira!' raved her sorority friends, as she left the two-storey Tudor-style house on Gerard Street later that evening.

The letter from Laurence and Theo Panzon had arrived a week earlier, and immediately Keira had known what she should do. As luck would have it, Jed Buchanan had telephoned with an invitation to go with him to the post-match party at Cass's house, and all at once inspiration had come to her.

Like Keira, Jed was in his senior year, although she would be getting her English degree, with a minor in drama, in three years as opposed to his four. Jed was also one of the Grizzlies' defensive linemen, responsible for stopping the run and getting the ball to the quarterback. Five foot ten and built like an ox, Jed was a player highly rated by Cass. What he lacked in physical beauty he made up for with a good sense of humour. Jed had fallen in love with Keira the day he met her and had pursued her devotedly ever since. Keira liked him as a friend, but accepted his devotion and his offers of a date if it meant being in the same room as Cass for an evening. So far she had managed to keep him at arm's length without too much trouble, and 'Ox', as he was nicknamed, seemed resigned to this arrangement.

The party was heaving as they both walked through the front door of Cass's home on Grant Creek Road. Meat Loaf was playing loudly, 'I Would Do Anything For Love', through a babble of voices and laughter, clouds of cigarette smoke and the reek of beer. Extracting herself from Jed's encircling arm, Keira pushed her way into the sitting room in pursuit of her quest. She forced herself through the crowd of male and female bodies, standing on tiptoe every now and again, like the periscope of a hidden submarine breaking the surface of the sea. She searched the mass of faces for the two she intended to confront with her plan. But by the time she reached the far end of the room, a wave of claustrophobia had swept over her, making her feel faint, and she steadied herself by leaning up against the wall. From where she now stood she could see people squeezing past each other through a double doorway. Peering over their heads, she saw into a room that was evidently being used as the bar. Feeling flustered, she had started to retreat to the place where she had left Jed, when a shock of pain ran through her as someone pinched her bottom hard. She whipped round furiously to face the culprit.

'That hurt, you creep!' she shouted.

'Hey! Cool it, chick!' leered the face of Buck Fiennes, another Grizzly player. His eyes rolled as he took another gulp of beer. A girl Keira did not recognise put her arm around Buck's shoulders, as he continued to run his bloodshot eyes up and down her body. The sense of being mentally undressed infuriated her further.

'Don't call me "chick", Buck Fiennes! My name's Keira!' she retorted angrily, turning on her heel.

'Well, excuse me for living, Keira!' retorted Buck. 'Sounds like you need a good shag to cool you down!'

The girl on his arm laughed.

Keira turned back to face him. She was seething.

'Why, you arrogant son-of-a-bitch!' Her voice was now louder than Meat Loaf's. 'I would rather stay celibate for the rest of my life than spend five minutes with you, Mr Fiennes!' Her eyes blazed and Buck looked stunned. He opened his mouth to speak, but said nothing. The girl stopped laughing. People around them stopped talking. Everyone was staring. Keira's one thought was to escape this hateful crowd, but as she set off across the room she found her way blocked by two solid torsos. Looking up, she caught her breath.

'You have some temper on you there, lady!' said Coach Murphy in his deep drawl.

Beside him, Cass Henderson stared at her in surprise. Keira found herself confronting the very two people her mission had sent her to find.

'Perhaps you should teach your men some manners, Mr

Murphy!' she heard herself say, glancing quickly back in Buck's direction.

'Buck!' cried the coach to her tormentor. 'It would seem you owe Miss . . . ?'

'Kavanagh,' interjected Cass, continuing to look at Keira.

'It seems you owe Miss Kavanagh here an apology.'

Buck stepped to Will Murphy's side. 'Yes sir!' he saluted his coach. There were some sniggers, as he went down ungracefully on one knee. 'Forgive me, Miss Keira Kavanagh, I was out of order.'

Keira smiled in spite of herself and looked away. Buck staggered back onto his feet and hastily withdrew.

Cass remained standing before her, all ruffled blond hair, tight t-shirt and jeans. Keira returned his stare, then turned to the coach. She smiled gratefully. 'Thanks.'

'Who are you with?' demanded Cass, struck once again by the beauty of this girl he had sworn never to get involved with again.

'Jed Buchanan.'

'Well, the Ox ain't exactly looking after you, is he?'

'Can we get you anything, ma'am?' interrupted the coach. 'A drink?'

'Sure – anything but beer!' said Keira, laughing as both men led her out of the crowded room and into the relative calm of the kitchen.

'No bad-mannered Grizzly players in here!' grinned Cass, patting a high stool by the bar counter.

Keira glanced at his beautiful, aquiline profile, overwhelmed by the realisation that suddenly everything was going her way.

The kitchen was spacious, up to date and very white. Will Murphy pulled up a stool next to Keira while Cass poured her a glass of cold white wine from the fridge. Keira watched his muscles move under his clothes.

'How's this?' he asked, placing the glass before her.

'That'll do fine, thank you, Cass.' She smiled broadly at him, holding his gaze for a few seconds. Saying his name out loud to his face like that made her feel more confident. Everything was different now, she told herself. He was dealing with a twenty-one-year-old woman and not a vulnerable fourteen-year-old adolescent.

Cass sat down on the opposite side of the counter and watched her drink her wine. Will glared across at Cass. This one was off-limits, and not for his quarterback's devouring, he seemed to imply.

Keira took a deep breath. 'Mr Murphy, I have a proposal for you.' She put her glass down. The coach's face broke into a big smile and he raised his eyebrows. Cass's expression reflected surprise. 'Well, that was quick!' he quipped.

Keira ignored him. 'Mr Murphy, I think maybe your team needs something more than football and parties. I think they need a challenge!'

'I'm listening, Miss Kavanagh,' said the coach, intrigued by this stalwart girl.

Feeling reassured by his kindly face, she picked up her purse and took out the letter from Laurence.

'I'd like you to read this, Mr Murphy. It's from Laurence, a friend of mine from France. My brother and I met her a long time ago in England, just after my mother died. We've kept in touch over the years, and she and her husband Theo have stayed with us at Goodnight. She's always talked to me a lot about Madeleine, who works with very poor people in Rio de Janeiro in Brazil. Madeleine's a nun – a very different sort of nun,' she added hastily. 'She's been living in the middle of a shanty town for the past twenty years.'

'You mean a sort of Mother Teresa type?' interrupted the coach, looking down at the letter.

'Uh huh,' responded Keira eagerly. 'She does some amazing work. But now she's asking for help, practical help. She needs a team of volunteers to go out this Christmas to help build a crèche for a hundred kids in the shanty town where she lives.' Keira paused for a moment to allow her words to take effect. 'What I was thinking, Mr Murphy, is that maybe a group from your team might go out there?' The tone of her voice was now serious. She was astounded at her own audacity as she directly addressed the coach about this. She never once glanced over at Cass.

The door burst open and the noise of the party suddenly erupted into the kitchen, breaking the silence. Georgina Cole stood there, wearing a tight leopard-print catsuit with a large fur collar. 'I've been looking everywhere for you, babe!' she complained, directing a cool glance at Keira, as she minced over to Cass and draped a slim arm around his neck. 'What's this? A secret meeting?' She had been drinking and slurred her words. 'Come on, Cassie baby, Georgie's lonely without you!' She nuzzled into his neck.

Cass stood up reluctantly. He smiled awkwardly at them as Georgina dragged him out of the kitchen and back into the party.

Keira forced a smile, but her heart sank. What was he doing with Georgina Cole?

Will Murphy cleared his throat as he finished reading the letter and folded it back into its envelope. Handing it back to her, he said, 'OK, Miss Keira, let me ask you something. What are you doing next Wednesday evening?'

Keira looked at him alertly. 'Nothing!' she responded instantly.

'OK then. All twenty-two men in the squad will be meeting with me after team practice at the stadium. I'll give you ten minutes to convince them to take up this challenge. Be ready to answer their questions.' He smiled, winked and raised his beer can to her. 'It won't be easy.'

During the following days, Keira read everything she could about Brazil from books she found in the library. One was a large glossy hardback, full of attractive, colourful pictures, and as she flicked through them she saw half-naked girls with mahogany skin on Copacabana's white sandy beach; an orange sunset in Salvador behind an old colonial church somewhere in the city; the vast statue of Christ Redeemer, arms outstretched over the hazy, sun-drenched city of Rio de Janeiro; a yellow sun dawning over Brasilia; majestic hills covered in coffee trees laden with ripe beans; feathered men with tall, exaggerated headdresses, and naked women with tassels on their nipples dancing at a carnival. *I'll show them these pictures*, she thought, laughing to herself.

Another book she looked at was a small paperback and the author had a name she could not pronounce. She opened it and went straight to the centre pages, where she found a small selection of black-and-white pictures. They told her a different story, another side of Brazil: a litter-strewn back street lined with shacks constructed of sticks and plastic; two young children, a boy and a girl, staring back at her with distended stomachs and sunken faces; four boys with swollen, unshod feet asleep on the pavement under a shabby blanket; a small crowd gathered around the bullet-ridden remains of a young teenage girl lying in a gutter while a policeman looked on; a little girl no older than five years, dressed in rags, carrying a baby and begging in the middle of the city traffic. Keira felt her eyes fill with tears. Laurence had shown her pictures like this before, but until now it had all seemed so far away. Turning to the front of the book again, she pored over the photograph on the front cover. Then she began to study the text, unable to put it down.

At 6.55 p.m. on Wednesday evening, Keira walked down the long corridor beneath the stadium. The sound of her footsteps echoed on the stone floor and somewhere nearby she could hear the players' voices and laughter. The butterflies in her stomach intensified and she stopped walking. Suddenly, a voice she recognised called her name from behind. 'Miss Kavanagh!' Coach Murphy jogged up beside her dressed in a grey flannel tracksuit and trainers. He grabbed the small white towel from around his neck and wiped the beads of sweat from his clean-shaven face.

'Please call me Keira.'

'OK, Keira, are you ready to meet the Grizzlies?'

Her face reflected her nervousness.

'Don't let me down now! Where's that fire I saw in you the other night?'

Will Murphy entered the meeting room ahead of her, and his voice immediately became authoritative. 'Right! Where are you all? There's a lady here and I don't want any bad language, bad manners or disrespect. Is that clear?' he roared.

Keira entered hesitantly and followed the coach to the tiers of pine benches that flanked three sides of the room. She sat down carefully as the players drifted in, showered and dressed, after their training session. The smell of musky aftershave filled the air. Framed photographs of college football teams from over the years decorated the otherwise bare walls.

Keira tried not to look at Buck Fiennes, who had just walked into the room. Instead, her eyes fell on Cass, who was tying his shoelaces by the door. Jed smiled at her in surprise as he sat down nearby and lifted his hands as if to say, 'What are you doing here?'

Mary and Cathy had helped her choose her outfit. 'Nothing too sexy, too preppy, too casual *or* too serious,' Cathy had stated emphatically the night before. It had not been easy deciding and the giggles had eventually turned to moans, when she settled for what her friends had thought was far too casual. A pale pink jumper over a white cotton polo shirt, faded blue jeans over cowboy boots and a brown leather coat borrowed from Cathy.

All at once the room seemed full with the large young men strewn around it. Will stood up. 'Right, you guys, don't let's waste any more time! Are all the men here or not, Cass?' he drawled, placing the small towel back around his neck.

'Everyone except Jim,' replied Cass, the team's captain, leaning forward with his head in his hands. His wet hair was combed back off his face, now flushed from the exercise and the hot shower.

Keira swallowed, knowing her time was near.

'Well, men, our lovely visitor this evening is Miss Keira Kavanagh. Some of you may know her, or some of you may remember her as Juliet in the campus play, if you were fortunate.' Keira felt her cheeks redden. She smiled and lowered her head. 'I invited her here tonight,' the coach continued, 'because she has convinced me that you lot need a challenge!'

There was a cat-whistle and a babble of voices. Suddenly

Keira wished that the polished floor would open up at that very moment and devour her. Maybe this was all a big mistake.

'Keira, it's over to you!' Coach Murphy sat down. He felt like being entertained. How would this striking redhead handle twenty-one strapping football players in their own stadium?

She stood up. Sniggers and more cat-whistles greeted her.

'Shush!' 'Quiet!' 'Shut up!' A few voices cried out over the noise.

Keira cleared her throat and began to speak. 'I, um, um . . .'

'Speak up, *chick*, I can't hear ya!' jeered Buck, as he laughed and nudged the two players on either side of him.

Keira turned and glared at Buck, remembering the painful bruise he had inflicted on her so recently. Then she thought of those pictures, of children sleeping under their shabby blankets on the pavements, of the rubbish heaps being picked over by hungry teenagers, of Madeleine working tirelessly to help them. Drawing confidence from the righteous anger that was starting to rise within her, she stood up and looked steadfastly at all twenty-one faces around the room. The men fell silent.

Clearing her throat, she started to speak from her heart. 'I won't keep you long, I promise,' she began. 'But did you know that in many parts of this world there are children who long to have what we all take totally for granted every day? Daily food, a bed to sleep in, a family to care for you, an education, a future.' She opened up the file of enlarged photocopies she had made from the paperback book the day before and drew one out.

'This is a picture of a brother and sister in Brazil. They can't be older than nine or ten, but they're sleeping under cardboard and plastic sheets on the pavements. Here is another picture of a boy carrying his baby sister. They live next to the city dump and are looking for food amongst this mountain of putrid waste.' She held the picture high, turning so that everyone present could see it. Her whole face was full of expression and her eyes were alive with indignation. 'Did you know that *hundreds* of children like these were murdered by extermination squads last year in the city of Rio de Janeiro alone, and that the killers were paid for doing it?'

Keira knew that she held their undivided attention.

'Who are these squads?' interrupted Jed.

She turned to him. 'Apparently the squads are often made up of corrupt ex-policemen and private security guards. They see the slaughtering of these children as "cleaning up the streets", and I quote.'

'But who pays them?' questioned Buck. The leer was absent now.

'I understand that they're paid to do it by some local people who claim their businesses are affected by the presence of these street children.'

There was a gasp from the men, and a murmur of conversation.

Now Cass spoke up. 'And what are the Brazilian government doing about it?' he inquired.

Keira turned to him, her heart pounding. She had known that Cass would ask this very question. His political background was so ingrained. So she had done her homework.

'Apparently the government are trying to do something. Let me quote what it says in this document: "A national commission has been set up with equal numbers of representatives from government departments and non-government organisations, specifically dedicated to the defence of these children's rights. They recommend investigations of death-squad killing, a review of police recruitment and training, legal sanctions against police officers accused of using violence against children and greater control of security companies, especially those employing police officers and security guards who were shown to be members of death squads."'

'So why hasn't this commission been effective?' probed Cass, leaning back against the bench behind him.

'From my research,' responded Keira, 'it seems that the problem is with the police forces. They're not controlled by the federal government, but by each individual state within the country. Each state has a civilian as well as a military police force, and the recommendations of the federal government can be implemented or ignored as they feel inclined.'

Cass watched her face intently. He had seen this fire, this passion in her once before. It had stopped him from stealing her virginity all those years ago. But now here he was being challenged once again by the daughter of Liam Kavanagh, the man his father hated. That same attraction he had felt all that time ago at his ranch was stirring again, and it frightened him. He could not allow himself emotions that would mean losing control of his life.

Keira was answering another question. '. . . it's only about seven or eight years since Brazil emerged from years of military rule,' she was saying. 'Apparently, corruption is rife in high places. There's a population of more than one hundred and fifty million and yet seven out of ten Brazilians live in poverty.'

'So what's this, then, a history lesson?' It was Buck again. 'What's all this got to do with us, for Christ's sake?'

Keira turned on him. 'OK, here's the punch line, Buck. What are you doing this Christmas?'

'Eatin' turkey!' he laughed, and looked around for support. It did not come.

'Well, let me tell you what *I'm* doing,' retorted Keira. 'I'm going to Brazil! A woman called Madeleine, who's been working with very poor people in Rio de Janeiro for the past twenty years, is looking for a team of volunteers to build a crèche for a hundred poor kids in the shanty town where she lives. My challenge to all of you this evening is this: who'll come with me to do this for Madeleine and these children?'

For a few seconds there was a stunned silence. Then Will Murphy stood and walked over to Keira's side.

'Men, I've heard enough for tonight,' he said, putting his hands in his pockets. 'But before we leave the stadium I want you to know that I'm our first volunteer for that team. Think about it. The trip would involve just two and a half weeks of your lives. Sure, you'd have to give up your Christmas and New Year plans and pay your own way, but think of the rewards. I'd also like to suggest that we raise all the cash needed for the construction materials. Go away and think about what you've heard tonight, but if you decide to join me, you'd better let me know quick, 'cos I'll need to get onto the airlines. Goodnight, men.'

Keira parked her car outside the sorority house and let out a jubilant scream. '*Yes!*' She banged her hands on the steering wheel a few times and laughed out loud. 'You did it, girl!'

There was a beep as she opened the car door, reminding her that the lights were still on. Keira flicked the switch, locked the car door and started walking towards the back entrance of the house. She was oblivious to the red sports car that had followed her home and was now parking slowly on the opposite side of the street. As she reached the darkened doorway, she thought she heard a noise. 'Who's there?'

A light, cool breeze blew across her face, and a cat meowed behind her. She smiled and squinted into the dark night, searching for the animal. 'Here kitty, kitty!'

The ginger cat ran up to her and rubbed itself against her legs, purring. She crouched down to stroke it, then stood up abruptly.

'Who's there?' she said again.

The outline of a man came into view and she opened her mouth to scream.

'Shush! It's only me, Cass!'

Her heart lurched and she caught her breath. 'You frightened the living daylights out of me!'

He stepped into the beam of light that shone from an upstairs window. The collar of his black leather jacket was turned up, framing the face she had thought about for so many years.

'I'm sorry, I didn't mean to scare you.'

She did not know what to say.

'You were great tonight. I was impressed,' he said. 'I've come to tell you that I accept your challenge.'

She bit her lip and tried to subdue the joy that threatened to burst out of her. 'Good,' was all that she could say.

He moved closer and took hold of her arms gently, his face suddenly appearing vulnerable.

'What is it?' she whispered.

He shook his head. 'I don't know.'

Without a second thought, Keira placed her hand on his chest. Slowly he bent down and kissed her. As he did so, he drew her in closer, their bodies touching. She closed her eyes as they kissed again, for an exquisite, lingering moment.

'Wait!' she cried, breathing heavily.

He looked down intently at her, not wanting to let her go. 'Wait for what?' He blinked, searching her face for a clue.

'What about Georgina Cole?'

'It's over.'

'Since when?'

'Since Saturday night.'

'It didn't look over to me.'

'It is, I promise.'

'I'm not going to be another conquest for you to dispose of, Cass.'

'I know.'

'No, I don't think you do know.'

She wriggled to free herself. He let her go. The cat meowed and she bent down and picked it up and started for the door.

'Wait a minute, Keira!'

She glanced back over her shoulder.

'Would you like to go out for dinner? Have you plans for the rest of the evening?'

'Thanks, I'm busy.'

'What about lunch tomorrow after class?'

'Sorry, that won't work.'

'Dinner tomorrow night?'

'I'm busy.'

'OK, so tell me when you're free!' demanded Cass, beginning to feel exasperated. He was not accustomed to being turned down for a date.

She opened the door.

'I like you, Keira! I want to spend time with you, get to know you better.' He followed her to the door. 'I feel different—'

'Different?' she interrupted.

'Yes.'

'Different because our fathers happen to hate each other, for reasons I still can't understand and perhaps it's better that I don't anyway?'

'Different because I feel different. Give me a chance, Keira . . . please?'

'Are you begging?'

'I'm begging!'

'Call me tomorrow and I'll see when I can fit you into my schedule.' She smiled to herself and turned away. 'Night, Cass.'

'Night,' he replied to the closed door.

I've waited long enough for him, she thought to herself, leaning up against the door and letting the cat jump down onto the tiled floor in the empty hallway. *Now he can wait for me.*

Chapter 14

Feliz Natal

The dust-covered minibus roared up through the narrow streets of the *favela* and stopped with a grinding of gears in front of *Dona* Cecilia's bar in the *Praca*. In the comparative quiet that followed, Keira and Mary could hear the excited voices of the children who were soon swarming around their rented vehicle as they gathered their few belongings together and prepared to leave the bus. It was Christmas Eve, and the team from Montana had come to join in the celebrations arranged by Madeleine in their honour. They could hear the children calling their names.

Liam Kavanagh opened the sliding door and the children watched in awe as the strange white giants who had arrived in their midst five days ago once again erupted from the vehicle, which seemed to adjust itself gratefully in the moments following their departing weight.

'Merry Christmas!' called out Madeleine, appearing with a further group of children from an alleyway to their left. 'Welcome!'

Coach Murphy called a greeting back to Sister Madeleine. His face reflected the joy and enthusiasm that this trip had engendered in him.

'The little ones have a surprise for you!' She beckoned to the team over the sea of bobbing little black and brown heads, raising her voice above their chatter. 'Please! Follow me up to the sports court!'

Madeleine had mesmerised Coach Murphy from the moment he met her at the airport on the day of their arrival. His experience of women had not been a happy one. Two acrimonious and expensive divorces had left him bitter and determined to avoid further entanglement with the female race. But he had felt immediately drawn to this uniquely serene lady who had vowed away a worldly life. To make matters more confusing for him, Madeleine did not look like a nun. Her fair, shoulder-length hair was free of the severe wimple nuns usually wore. She wore a simple uniform of cotton shirt and skirt, which in his view only accentuated her charming appearance. Coach Murphy took every opportunity to be in her company. He was fascinated beyond words.

When Liam Kavanagh had heard about Keira's plan to persuade the university football team to go on a goodwill mission to Rio de Janeiro, he immediately asked if he could be part of it. Neither he nor Callum could imagine Christmas at Goodnight without Keira. The seven years since Katherine's death had done nothing to heal the pain of her absence; Liam continued to mourn her deeply. His solace was his arduous work on the ranch, and the presence whenever possible of his daughter and son.

Keira did not hesitate when her father tentatively broached the possibility of his joining the team in Brazil, and she had told him she could not possibly imagine leaving him and Callum behind. However, there was one member of the signed-up team who was less than enthusiastic when he heard of Liam Kavanagh's inclusion in the party: for Cass Henderson it was devastating news that threatened to undermine all his plans.

Never had a girl kept him at arm's length for so long. Never had he felt himself so little in control of his emotions. The trip to Brazil had seemed to offer limitless opportunities for getting Keira into bed at last. Now that father of hers, whom he had always known to be hostile to him, would get in the way.

'Does your father really have to come? You know he and I don't get along. He doesn't like me!'

'What do you mean? It's Christmas! I want him with me!'

'You know exactly what I mean, for Christ's sake!' Cass had retorted.

But Keira admitted to herself that she needed her father and brother with her on this trip. She needed their support on this big adventure, this audacious project to bring a high-profile group from her homeland to carry out a work of compassion in a place she had dreamed of since her first meeting with Theo and Laurence, seven years ago. And since she was being honest with herself, she also needed their presence as she struggled to maintain the upper hand in her relationship with Cass.

Cass considered dropping out of the project. He was surprised and annoyed that events had taken this turn. But there was no going back now. His father had been surprisingly enthusiastic when he had first discussed it on the telephone after signing up for the trip.

'Son, that's a great idea!' Jim had roared down the receiver. 'That'll help bring in the votes when you're on the campaign trail!' In Jim Henderson's mind, his son's portfolio could now be expanded to include evidence of a compassionate social conscience.

Keira and Mary stepped off the bus in the wake of most of the men. They laughed in delight as several little hands reached up to them, competing for hugs and attention. They were led eagerly across the busy square, with Fin following behind, stopping every now and again to take another picture with one of the cameras hanging weightily around his neck. The *Missoulian* newspaper had not hesitated to commission a photographic record of the famous footballers' trip to Rio de Janeiro. The title page had already been planned, with the headline 'THE GRIZZLIES BRING A MERRY CHRISTMAS TO THE POOR CHILDREN OF BRAZIL!' And the editor was expecting to feature the story in his New Year's Day edition, complete with personal interviews with individual players.

'*Sorria*!' Fin repeated again and again as he clicked away. He had taken no time in learning the Portuguese for 'smile'.

His newspaper had also generously offered to fly their reporter business class and place him in a somewhat more elegant hotel than the two-star hostelry in Saens Pena, not far from the *favela*, into which the Grizzlies party had been booked. But Fin had opted instead to fly at the back of the plane with the rest of the group, and to purchase a ticket for Mary with the extra cash. This was wonderful news for Keira, who had felt daunted by the prospect of being the only girl in the group. She could not have chosen a better person to share the experience.

Nine of the players had signed up for the trip within forty-eight hours of the meeting at the Washington Stadium. To Keira's consternation, these included Buck Fiennes and Jed Buchanan. But although Jed had felt sore with Cass for stealing 'his' girl, his big heart responded to the challenge of doing something to save some of the poor kids from those extermination squads. As for Buck, he saw an opportunity to stay on the right side of his coach.

The others who had volunteered to give up their Christmas

in Montana were brothers Mike and George Martz, both running backs, wide-receiver Charlie Gaubel, centre Joe Linderman, and the two defence linebackers Ted Lucas and Mark Lane. As these young men strode through the streets of the shanty town, they presented an impressive sight with their white teeth, gleaming hair, fancy clothes and Nike footwear. The whole community stood in awe of these gigantic young visitors, and by the end of the second day two of the armed *bandidos* from the *favela* had taken it upon themselves to become team bodyguards. Much to the Americans' relief, there had been a marked lull in gang warfare during the first few days of their visit – but Madeleine had informed Coach Murphy that the nights were worse, which was why he insisted they all return to their hotel by five o'clock each afternoon.

An excited group of children led Keira, Mary and Fin around the side of the little Pentecostal church and on up the winding lanes of the *favela*. Once again Keira's senses recoiled at the stench rising from the open sewer in the centre of the pathway, and the filth that was everywhere to be seen. On the corner of one alleyway she noticed some skinny chickens pecking at a huge mound of litter that included used food cartons and tins, rotting vegetables and excrement. Swarms of flies covered the pile and a few mangy dogs hovered nearby. Keira retched, but resolutely squared her shoulders and concentrated on Vivianne and her brother Tiago, who were leading her by the hand. Beside the dump, an iron gate on rusty hinges set between two corrugated iron hovels suddenly flew open. A woman Keira recognised stepped out and called to the little girl. 'Vivianne!' She held out a hairbrush and a pretty ribbon.

'It's *Tia* Bete, isn't it?' Keira whispered to Mary.

Bete had her hair in curlers, covered by an old pair of tights.

234

Vivianne ran over to her mother, who brushed her daughter's thick curly hair off her face and into a ponytail with practised speed.

'*Tia* Bete, *ola!*' said Keira and Mary, who knew that this competent woman was responsible for the trays of delicious lemonade and homemade pastries that appeared at regular intervals throughout the day.

Tia Bete spoke rapidly to her daughter.

'What did she say, Vivianne?' Mary asked, as they smiled and nodded at *Tia* Bete, before being hurried on by their little friends.

'Solomon coming here!' proclaimed Vivianne proudly.

'Who's Solomon? Oh *please* teach me some Portuguese, Vivianne!' pleaded Keira to the young girl, who was tugging at her hand with all her might.

The old sports court, positioned high above the square, was buzzing with activity, as news spread around the *favela* that something exciting was about to take place. Heat from the midday sun shimmered off the rough tarmac of the court, whose lines, marked out for football, volleyball and basketball, had almost disappeared after years of use. Most of the shabby, cracked concrete benches around its perimeter were already crammed with people. The children darted into the crowd, pushing and shoving until places for Mary, Keira and Fin were found.

Keira watched as Vivianne and Tiago skipped over to a clump of leafy acacia trees thriving triumphantly in this core of privation and dirt just behind their seats. Madeleine and Sister Sonia were there, preparing a crowd of children for the concert of songs they had been rehearsing for several days. Keira studied the nun's face, calm and smiling in the centre of all this chaos. She was just as Laurence had described her, and clearly commanded the love and respect of these people she had served for so many years.

Keira saw Coach Murphy in the shade of the acacia trees, filming the scene with the video camera he had purchased from the duty free shop at Seattle Airport on their way over. Beyond the acacias, she had a clear view down over the poorest area of the slum. She could see the site for the crèche, with its foundations prepared for the grey bricks now piled to one side. Around the site several shabby huts, many constructed from mud and sticks, clung crazily to the red earth. The people who lived here were the victims of an accident of birth, she reflected. It broke Keira's heart every time she looked into the smiling faces of these lovely children and thought about what the future might hold for them. They had not asked to be born here. She turned away from the milling crowd of children to say something to her friend beside her, but Mary was wrapped in Fin's arms, oblivious to Keira.

Where was Cass, she wondered? He had been ignoring her for the best part of the trip so far, and she felt a mixture of regret and irritation that he had allowed his annoyance at the presence of her family on this trip to affect his behaviour so demonstrably. Her heart ached suddenly, as her companions sat entwined beside her. Was that Cass, sitting over there? She squinted through the thin heat haze, and was sure she saw him on the far right-hand corner of the arena. He was surrounded by four scantily dressed teenage girls, each with silky mahogany skin and long, thick, shiny hair like the ones she had seen in that big glossy book back home. They were fluttering around him like butterflies, flirting and giggling, and Cass was enjoying every minute. A stab of anger shot through her, and at that precise minute his eyes met hers across the arena, catching her indignation. Cass smiled gleefully. Jumping to her feet, Keira began to make her way through the crowd towards him. Ignoring her was one thing; taunting her was quite another.

All at once a small boy with unkempt hair and a dirty vest stood before her, arms outstretched, barring her way. He seemed to be trying to tell her something important.

'Solomon! Solomon!' he cried. 'Solomon *chegou*!' He was jumping with excitement now, holding her arm and pointing urgently at the alleyway up which they had so recently climbed. A loud cheer rang out as more children rushed by her from all directions. She was completely distracted from her moment of irritation, and caught up in the rush of small bodies. Wanting to know what all the commotion was about, she joined the crowd as it moved towards the ridge.

Vivianne was suddenly beside her. She caught Keira's hand.

'What? Who is it?' asked Keira, allowing herself to be led forward.

A young man appeared on the ridge ahead. Keira watched him as he hugged one small child after another, and called each one by name. He was tall, compared to other Brazilian men, and she liked the way his thick, dark hair fell to his shoulders. He was laughing in the centre of the excited crowd who had clearly been awaiting his arrival, and she saw that his face was alive in a way that drew her to him. Keira watched as the children's shrill voices competed for his attention, their bodies hustling, pulling and pushing, in an effort to speed up his arrival in their midst.

Solomon felt the usual surge of joy as he was propelled along by these children he loved. He knew every one of them, their backgrounds and their circumstances. This place, which he had hated so much when he was first brought here, had over the years become the place where he most wanted to spend his spare time. He could identify with these people's inner pain, their needs, their daily struggle to survive in a world that had stolen their security, their fathers, their brothers, their childhood, their futures. He had been fortunate. God had sent Sister Madeleine to pluck him from the gutters, from the road to destruction down which he had ventured when his life had fallen apart. He had been spared. Now all he wanted to do was to dedicate himself to them as she had done.

Over the years of living with Sister Madeleine, the healing had finally come as he had begun to understand that forgiveness was a kind of letting go. This did not mean that the horrible times had not happened, but that he had to let go of the anger he carried against Dauro Vasconcellos who had taken his childhood from him, and against his father who had left them. He remembered kneeling beside Sister Madeleine in her prayer room in the apartment one morning, and feeling a great weight lift off his shoulders, and as it left him a peaceful presence seemed to flood his being. He had started to weep, not tears of sadness, but tears of joy and relief. Suddenly he had seen his father not as a hero who had let him down, but as a normal human being who had made mistakes. He knew that he wanted to redeem what his father had lost. It was not about revenge; it was about fulfilling God's purpose for his life and using the gifts he had been given. He recalled his father's dying words to him – to rediscover his musical gifts, and to find peace in his heart. His father had found both and then let them go, and Solomon was determined to do better.

He would become a priest to the poor, to the very people whose lives were etched into his. He was already two years into his training at a seminary. This was his vocation in life, he was sure.

Solomon felt someone pulling at his shirt. He crouched down so that his eyes were on the level of his little cousin's.

'Vivianne, Merry Christmas, *querida*!' he said gently.

But instead of walking into his arms, she took his hand and placed it into Keira's. Solomon stood quickly and turned to the young woman, and as he did so a terrifying sensation ripped through him. He was staring into a face so striking he could not imagine that she had not always been there, engraved on his mind. The girl was smiling up at him awkwardly, her forehead crinkling, her eyes narrowing. She removed her hand, embarrassed. Solomon continued to gaze at the beautiful face, more on a level with his own than most women he had known, and drew in his breath sharply as he absorbed the blue of her eyes, the clear, smooth skin, and the flame of dark red hair. Vivianne's voice broke into the tumult of his thoughts.

'*Isto e* Keira,' she said clearly.

'Kei-ra.' Solomon repeated the name slowly. 'I . . . have I met you before?' he said in English.

She looked at him. 'You . . . you can't have. I've only been in Brazil for a few days.'

'It's just that . . . I . . . I must be mistaken. You are with the team building the crèche for Madeleine?'

'Yes.' She gave a short laugh and was surprised to feel herself blushing from the impact of his presence. 'You speak English, what a relief!' she said hurriedly.

'I have to go,' he said over his shoulder as the children led him away.

Keira stood watching as he disappeared, like the Pied Piper, over the ridge towards the sports court.

The children were arranged in carefully organised rows, tallest behind, smallest in front. All eyes were on Madeleine, who stood before them with hands raised, guiding them expertly through their songs. A harmonica accompanied them, played from somewhere out of view. From her place in the crowd, Keira studied their small, happy faces. This was Brazil and these were Brazilians, she thought, reflecting on the varying shapes of their faces and the colour of their skin, which ranged from the blackest black, through chestnut brown to pale olive. Their hair, too, was equally diverse: some was tightly waving or coaxed into a pattern of plaits; some was thick, straight and glossy; some stood out in a thick, wild halo in shades of brown to blond. Here stood represented a racial mix of several different influences: the indigenous Indian tribes of South America, the descendants of slaves brought here from Africa, and the descendants of those who had brought them, the conquerors from the Old World who, hundreds of years before, had instigated this kaleidoscope of culture. Keira observed their worn clothing and bare feet, t-shirts too large and shorts and dresses too small, and felt humbled as she thought of the privilege and luxury that had been hers all her life, which she had accepted as being hers by right. A vision of tables prepared for Christmas Day back home flashed across her mind. Yet in this place of deprivation she sensed a strength, a richness. These were open, generous people, enduring life with opti-mism in the midst of their hardships.

The children had sung their final song, and were leaving the arena in an orderly file. Madeleine stood smiling at each child as he or she passed by. Then there was an explosion of applause, and Solomon walked into the centre of the court with a *cavaquinho* in his hand. To Keira's surprise, he was followed by Callum carrying a wooden stool, and by Buck Fiennes, who set up a microphone and two large battered speakers. Both Americans walked quickly away, and Solomon waited, head lowered, hands spread over the strings of the small guitar, as another young man manoeuvred his way to the centre of the stage in a wheelchair. He lifted a small silver harmonica to his lips and looked at Solomon with intense concentration, his dark face somehow illuminated. The crowd, which had grown in size as word got around the *favela* that Solomon had arrived, fell silent.

A beautiful sound then arose into that world of stark poverty and destitution. A magic was woven by the two friends with their small, precious instruments, which transported everyone in that arena to a place of grace. Then an unearthly tenor voice rang out, soaring over the winding alleyways of the *favela*. Keira felt the purity of its sound reach into the very core of her soul. Despite the heat, a shiver ran through her. She had never heard such a voice. As if hypnotised, she fixed her eyes on Solomon. His amazing face shone with the passion he was investing in the song he was singing. The emotion expressed in each word was evident even though the language was unknown to her. Glancing briefly around, she saw in the eyes of each person present that this voice was reaching inside them too – some mourning, perhaps, for that which would never come to them, some feeling the pain, the bitterness and the strife they endured daily slip away from their troubled lives for a few divine moments. Keira studied Solomon as his thick lashes lowered and his eyes closed briefly, then opened again, the green eyes widening, the dark hair falling forward across his face as he moved his head to the rhythm of his song. She felt herself inexplicably drawn to him.

Then she gasped as an arm slid around her waist and a voice breathed into the back of her neck, 'This is *our* song!'

She flinched and tried to pull away. The arm tightened.

'It must be a love song,' Cass hissed into her ear, nibbling at her earlobe. 'It's lovely, like you. I want you.'

Keira closed her eyes and relaxed into his embrace. But as she did so, she found herself wishing they were the arms of the young man she had just met.

Cass misread her lack of response and pulled her closer. 'Don't worry, your daddy can't see us. Relax!' He kissed her neck again.

A few feet away from them, Solomon raised his head as he sang the final words of the song his father had written for his mother. As he did so, his eyes fell on the exquisite red-haired girl, and he felt his spirits soar for an instant. Then a moment later he saw one of the Americans with his arms around her. Instantly he was gripped by feelings he had never experienced before. He felt a violent stab of envy ... then relief that she already belonged to someone else ... then envy again ... then anger at his own weakness. He was shocked at his own reaction.

Confused, and hating himself for the violence of his feelings, Solomon remained on his stool next to Stephano, oblivious to the applause and to the people who were rushing over towards him. First alongside him was Pedro. 'Are you all right, brother?' He had noticed the strain on Solomon's face.

'I'm fine!' he said shortly, pulling himself together. He swivelled round to face Stephano.

But the crowd were upon them, and Solomon was raised up by countless hands so that he rode high above the throng. He willed himself not to look in Keira's direction again, but as his friends carried him along, he glimpsed her and Cass walking off together, the young man's arm across her shoulders.

Voicelessly he prayed, a feeling, an extension of what lay all through him, fighting, fighting, banishing these disruptive emotions. He had taught himself to sublimate his human feelings almost perfectly, throwing himself into his music. *Lord, I am your servant. I will become a priest. Nothing, no one, will stand in my way …*

Chapter 15

Different Worlds

The white bungalow on the brow of the hill was a welcome, cool retreat for the heat-struck Grizzlies, who sank gratefully onto the ceramic floors after devouring their lunch. *Tia* Bete had produced a series of traditional dishes for them that included piles of garlic-flavoured rice and ladles of black beans.

Buck sat leaning his hot, sweaty back against the cool concrete wall and surveyed Jed, who was propped nearby with his head between his knees.

'You all right there, Ox?' he inquired, chewing on some gum.

Jed moaned, and the coach pulled up a chair beside him. 'You need to keep off them beans, boy!' Coach Murphy advised.

Buck laughed, and Jed staggered off in the direction of the bathroom, clutching his stomach.

'So what's the state of play 'til tonight, then, boss?' asked Mike Martz, running his large hands through his fine golden hair.

'Giving a hand here with what needs to be done for the Christmas Eve party, then a quick siesta back at the hotel before things kick off here again around ten tonight.' Coach Murphy leaned back in his chair, legs outstretched, and glanced over his shoulder towards the kitchen, where Madeleine was washing the dishes. Mary, Keira and Liam Kavanagh were helping her, and Fin was outside, conducting an interview with Mark Lane.

'Can't get my head around celebrating Christmas the day before,' yawned Charlie Gaubel, suddenly feeling homesick and longing for some snow.

'You'll get over it,' drawled Cass, pulling his baseball cap down over his tanned face. 'Don't make much difference so far as I can tell.' He wondered if he could escape back to the hotel with Keira.

'Where's Callum?' asked Joe Linderman, stretching out flat on his back and lifting his legs up against the wall.

'He hung back at the sports court with that cool Solomon guy and his brother,' countered Charlie.

'My new hero!' shouted Joe. 'What a voice! What a story!'

'Yup,' interrupted the coach, striding restlessly over to the window. 'It's the sort of stuff Hollywood films are made of.' He wanted to be in the kitchen helping Madeleine, and wished it had been he who had volunteered, instead of Liam. He looked out and noticed their two self-appointed bodyguards, smoking a joint. Maybe he should go outside and have a drag himself?

'Hell!' exclaimed Buck, still chewing loudly. 'I sure wish I could sing like that!'

'Watch your mouth, Buck! You're on holy ground here, remember?' said George Martz, nodding at Madeleine.

Cass peered out from under the peak of his cap and stared at George with a cynical eye.

Coach Murphy spoke again. 'I'm told Solomon's friend in the wheelchair is another of Madeleine's protégés.' He dragged his gaze from the two smokers outside. After all, drugs had nearly finished his career. 'He lives with his family in one of those brick houses at the entrance to the *favela*, near that big butcher's shop. And get this!' He moved unhurriedly back to his chair. 'They once lived at the top here, in a tin shack. His older brother was shot by other drug-traffickers, traffickers like our two friends out there.' He sat down heavily and sighed. 'Madeleine helped them move, and also rescued one of his younger brothers from the streets. She told me Stephano's just qualified as an accountant, and he's going to fulfil his lifelong ambition of moving his family right away from this place. Now *that's* what I call grit, men.'

'You sure are spending a lot of time talking to Sister Madeleine.' Cass spoke from behind his cap, not moving his head. 'You're not going religious on us, are you, Coach?'

Some sniggers followed this remark.

'Yeah, yeah, yeah. Well, you can just mind your own business there, college quarterback. You've got enough problems of your own!' Coach Murphy grinned.

Buck snorted.

And Cass wished once again that he had stayed at home in Montana.

There was silence in the room for a while, as they listened to the sounds of children playing outside, the distant barking of dogs and the muffled voices from the kitchen.

Suddenly, the front door burst open and Callum stood before them.

'Hey, you guys!' he panted, his square face flushed. 'Pedro has got up a team at the sports court and they're challenging the Grizzlies to a game!'

'Did you explain we don't play soccer?' Joe was still lying on the floor.

'Sure did, but Pedro said, and I quote, "We beat those Yanks even with kids in our side!"'

'Now there's a challenge!' roared Buck, jumping to his feet.

Coach Murphy stood. 'Come on, you lazy bunch, if you don't know how to play soccer, you soon will!'

There was the sound of men scrambling to their feet and shouts of 'Count me in!', 'And me!' and 'I'm in!'

'Didn't Pele get raised in a shanty town?' wondered Ted Lucas, tying a shoelace. 'I tell you, these guys will be dynamite with a round ball!'

Cass had not moved.

'Cass!' ordered Coach Murphy. 'You'll have to come to make up the numbers!'

'I'll be there in a minute.'

'We'll be waiting for you.' Coach Murphy strode to the door. 'Mark, you'll be in goal. Wrap up the interview, Fin, you'll want some shots of this, my boy.' He banged on the bathroom door as he passed. 'You still alive in there, Jed?'

There was a grunt from inside.

'Find yourself somewhere to sleep, son, and we'll catch you later.'

There were more groans.

Madeleine came to show Jed into a small dark room, which was bare but for a small bed, a table and a crucifix on the wall. She gave him two white pills and a glass of water.

'Sorry to cause you trouble, ma'am,' said Jed faintly. He looked at the bed and felt even more light-headed. The idea of lying on a nun's bed was appalling. Reading his mind, Madeleine smiled.

'Don't worry, no one sleeps in here any more. After Solomon and Pedro came to live with me, we moved to our small apartment two kilometres from the *favela* near Saens Pena train station. Sister Sonia keeps this room for emergencies, such as this.'

The door closed quietly, and Jed was alone. He lowered himself carefully onto the bed and lay still in the cool, simple room. He stared up at the small wooden cross and remembered his father, a devout man whose dogmatic views had eventually turned Jed away from church. He thought of his childhood home, and tears began to trickle down his cheeks.

Jed's thoughts and the peace of his surroundings were rudely shattered by the opening of the door. Cass entered, dragging Keira by the arm.

'Sorry, bro'!' hissed Cass behind his hand, and closed the door with a snap.

Jed turned to the wall and wiped his eyes. This was horrible.

'Cass, don't!' he heard Keira say. 'Don't ruin everything now! My father's not stupid, and I don't want to make him angry.'

'Shit, Keira, who's more important, then, your father or me?' He was breathing heavily, his handsome face taut, his eyes on fire. 'Him or me?' he repeated heatedly.

'Don't do this to me, Cass. You know you've always been important to me, but I don't want him upset on this trip.'

'Damn the trip! Why do you think I signed up to come?' demanded Cass, incensed.

A faint voice spoke from behind them. 'I'm here dying of food poisoning! Don't you guys have any compassion?'

'Jed, sorry, we're just going,' said Keira, meaning it.

Suddenly the door opened sharply, and Liam Kavanagh stood framed in the light.

'What the heck do you think you're up to, Keira? You OK?' his voice demanded.

'Dad, I'm fine! Ox is really sick, and Cass is just on his way to the football game. Do you want to go with him?'

She took a look at her father's face and saw he was nonplussed. Cass had no alternative but to move towards the door, and Liam Kavanagh stood aside as the quarterback, seething with rage, ambled towards the front door of the house and disappeared.

'Does Madeleine need any help right now?' continued Keira, closing the door on Jed and gliding past her father.

'Keira!' Liam did not move.

She stopped at the door to the kitchen, but could not look round. 'Yes, Daddy?' She closed her eyes.

'There's an old saying: "If you play with fire, you get burned."' Liam turned on his heel and walked off.

Cass slumped down on one of the concrete benches. The game was at full throttle and once again a large crowd had gathered, this time to shout and offer advice on how to beat these *Americanos*. Cass watched half-heartedly as the coach dribbled the soccer ball and passed it smartly to Buck, who raced on with Mike Martz calling to him that he was right there. Instead the ball was whipped away by a boy half his height, who snaked his way towards the opposite end, flicking the ball past Joe, Mike and George, before finding the net with a spectacular shot that Ted had no chance of stopping. A wild cheer went up from the crowd.

'*Gu gu! Gu gu! Gu gu!*'

Fin appeared behind the goalposts with his camera, clicking away as the youngster was jumped on by his jubilant team-mates. Cass groaned and buried his head in his hands. Could things get any worse?

A voice spoke from beside him. 'Your friends need some help!' The owner of the voice sat down next to him.

Cass responded without raising his head. 'Yup!'

'I'm Solomon,' the voice continued, and a hand was extended.

Unwillingly, Cass squared himself up and took the outstretched hand. 'Cass Henderson,' he said automatically. Solomon remained silent, so he added, 'You sing well!'

'Thank you.'

'You should get a recording deal.'

Solomon laughed at this.

Cass felt irritated. 'What's so funny?'

'I was offered one a while ago.'

Cass looked impressed, and turned to face his companion with a new respect. 'So, life will be changing for you, I imagine?'

'Not in the way you think.' The guy's English was excellent.

Cass looked puzzled.

'My life has already changed dramatically. You see, I am to become a priest.'

'A priest! What the hell for?' Cass was incredulous. This good-looking young man had talent and a big future. Why would he want to throw away the possibility of becoming rich and famous?

'We each have a path in our lives. This is mine.'

'A singing priest! That's something else!' Cass gave a short laugh and shook his head. 'You're a good-looking son-of-a-bitch, you've got an ace voice. What about women, love, sex?' His own exasperating problems with Keira paled into insignificance.

'I'm not that old, my friend, but I have seen a lot of things . . .'

Cass had lost all interest in the game and fixed his eyes on the young Brazilian as he spoke.

'. . . very sad things. Until seven years ago I lived with my family in our home in the mountains. Then we lost everything. My father was killed that same year, here in this *favela*. I hated it here.'

Solomon took a deep breath and exhaled slowly, looking around him. Cass followed his gaze, yet he sensed that Solomon's feelings for his surroundings had changed.

'I lived on the streets for a while, with my brother Pedro,' Solomon continued.

'You were one of those street kids?' frowned Cass.

The two of them focused for a few seconds on the game, just as Pedro was deftly robbing one of the Grizzlies of the ball.

'I was very nearly killed; but I survived, and I believe that was for some purpose.' Solomon smiled at Cass, his green eyes intense. 'Sometimes hardship is the greatest friend to the soul.'

Cass felt himself shudder as those words penetrated into his restless mind. He felt uncomfortable with the openness of this young Brazilian, and changed tack. 'Where did you learn to speak such good English?'

'Madeleine. She has always given me books to read in your language, and I love books. With books, you can be anywhere, escape to other, better places.' Solomon turned back to the game in time to see his brother score a goal. He was on his feet in an instant, whistling and cheering loudly.

The score was 3-0 to Brazil, and the crowd was going mad. '*Gooooaaaaalll*!'

Solomon sat down again, elated. 'The brother of your girlfriend has told me that you are a great American football player.'

'My girlfriend?'

'Callum had lunch with us.'

'Did he tell you Keira was my girlfriend?'

'No. But I saw you together this morning.' Solomon willed himself to stop this conversation, to walk away now and ask no more questions. But he could not move. He had to find out more about her.

Cass groaned and moved his Grizzlies cap on his head. It was almost four in the afternoon, but the sun was still hot. 'She's playing hard to get,' he said flatly. Solomon's frankness was infectious.

'Hard to get? What does this mean?' Solomon bent to gather some stones from the dust and began to juggle them in the air.

'I like women, Solomon, but unlike you I need to satisfy my desires. She's driving me crazy. Crazy! Her father and mine are enemies, have been for years, and what does she do when we sign up to come on this trip, but invite her dad to come with us! I believe she did it on purpose to annoy me.' Cass's voice became hoarse with indignation.

'Surely not?' exclaimed Solomon, turning to look at him in sympathy. He noticed that Cass had caught sight of something on the opposite side of the court. Following his gaze, Solomon saw two girls walking with swinging hips towards Fin, who was busy taking their photograph.

'Jeez, your Brazilian girls are gorgeous!' breathed Cass, entranced by their voluptuous sexuality. He sighed. 'I'm used to getting what I want, Solomon. Life for me is a challenge, it's all about conquering the unconquerable!'

Solomon repeated the words slowly. 'Conquering the unconquerable.' This was hard for him to pronounce.

'That's right. You've got it, man!'

Cass did not know why he was being so frank with this total stranger, whose plans and ideas seemed so different from his own. He felt a surge of irritation when he considered what this young man sitting next to him represented. He had sacrificed all that life could offer him for a faith in God, whom Cass did not believe existed.

'I'm very ambitious, Solomon,' he confided, 'extremely ambitious. I'm going to make a name for myself in politics. I was lucky enough to have been born rich. But you can never have enough of anything, ever. And women! I have known many, and intend to have many more. Keira, she won't hold out for ever, she'll give in eventually even if I have to marry her first. She'd be a good wife for a politician ... beautiful *and* rich! She's holding out for marriage, that's why she's playing her hard-to-get games.' His bravado wavered.

Solomon narrowed his eyes. 'I don't believe that happiness depends on what we have, but on what we are.' He looked Cass full in the face. 'If the heart is not full, even a rich and powerful man is poor.'

Cass clenched his teeth and looked down at his feet. Solomon's words had hit him like a blow.

'My heart is just fine, man!' he snapped.

Intuitively, Solomon changed tack. 'So the future president of the United States is here in Brazil to see how 48 per cent of the world's population lives? This is good, very good!'

Cass responded with a slight smile.

'But many people live far worse than this,' Solomon continued.

'You mean the people who live on the streets?'

'Yes.' His face grew serious again.

'Well, take me there! Show me what it's like!' Cass said impulsively. 'You're right, it would be educational for a future politician to see how the other half spends Christmas!'

'OK. I can be at your hotel around eleven o'clock tomorrow morning.'

'But won't you be with your family?'

'I am going to visit my mother and brothers and sister tonight. In Brazil, Christmas Eve is the time when our families come together and we go to Mass.'

'Fine then,' Cass said. His plans for a day off on the beach would have to wait.

'Maybe your friend from the newspaper could come too? The world should see the desperate cry of so many children,' Solomon added. Out of the corner of his eye he noticed the figure of Keira approaching. His heart gave a lurch and he spoke hurriedly. 'I can only take the two of you – you and your reporter. I will see you tomorrow.' He stood up hastily and walked away.

When she saw them together deep in conversation, Keira stood watching them for a while. What could they be talking about, two young men from different worlds, with totally different priorities? They were both striking to look at, she thought. But there the similarity ended. One was fair-haired, his skin tanned by the sun, self-confident to the point of arrogance. The other was dark-haired and olive-skinned, proud in a different way, so deeply assured in the strength of his gifts and his calling. They seemed indifferent to the clamour around them. Did they realise how many female eyes were on them? Feeling suddenly envious of Cass in his proximity to this magnetic young musician, Keira advanced towards them, charged with a deep curiosity and desire to get to know the Brazilian too. She saw that he had noticed her approach, and felt immediately hurt as he rose and walked quickly away. It seemed like a deliberate move on his part to avoid her company. Had she offended him somehow?

'Cass!' she called out.

He turned and saw her. 'Yes, Mrs Henderson?'

'What did you say?' She could not have heard right.

'Nothing.' He put his arm around her and drew her down on the bench beside him. 'What did your father say?'

'Nothing much.' She changed the subject. 'What were you talking about with Solomon?'

Cass was surprised at her interest. 'Why d'you wanna know?'

She turned away, afraid that her expression would reflect the troubled feelings that this young man had aroused in her, feelings that she had not had time to think through.

'No reason, just wondering,' she said as casually as she could.

'He's going to take me to see life on the streets tomorrow,' Cass told her, watching for her reaction. Keira looked back at him expectantly.

'Sorry,' Cass said slyly. 'He said he could only take two of us. He wants Fin to go along to make a report, take photos, etcetera.'

Keira looked crestfallen. Cass pulled her into his arms and kissed her on the lips. 'Don't worry, I'll tell you all about it when I get back.' He looked up as Liam Kavanagh appeared beside them.

Keira stood immediately. 'Dad, hi!'

'Let's go back to the hotel, Keira.'

'But the game's not over yet, Dad!'

'We can walk and the rest of the team can take the minibus when they're ready.'

Cass could no longer control his annoyance. He jumped to his feet. 'Mr Kavanagh – sir – this can't go on!' he exploded. 'You seem to be following us around the whole time! I'd really like to know, sir, and I believe you owe it to me to tell me, what it is about me that you don't like? Keira's a big girl now, she can make her own decisions, surely, about who she sees and who she likes?'

'Cass!' winced Keira. 'Don't!'

Her father interrupted sharply. 'OK, let's talk! Why don't you and I take a walk back to the hotel, right now, and we'll see you later, Keira.'

Angry and tense, the two men set off together down the alleyway towards the *Praca*. Keira watched them go, her heart in her mouth.

Liam Kavanagh leaned on the small round table in the bar next to the hotel. They were the only customers. Cass watched him, his mind confused, his thoughts hostile, wondering uneasily what he was about to hear. Liam had refused to answer his fire of questions as they had walked from the *favela* to Saens Pena, insisting that he would only discuss what he had to say when they were sitting down face to face. The empty bar seemed the perfect place. Both men took a long drink of cold beer, relieving their thirst and the tension of the moment. Then Liam leaned back in his chair and looked Cass full in the face.

'You're right, Cass, when you say your father and I don't like each other. The reasons are many and go way back. At university he nearly succeeded in ruining my reputation and having me kicked out of campus during the elections, when we were both candidates for the presidency of the ASUM. By highly devious means, he made damn sure he won.'

Cass banged his glass down on the table, his expression mutinous.

Liam continued. 'And that was just the beginning. I believe history repeated itself with you, Cass. Did you really win a straight fight when you were voted into the same office?'

Cass shifted angrily in his seat. 'What are you accusing me of, sir?'

'I think you know! The governor of Montana has voted you student regent, just as your daddy fixed up for himself all those years ago.' Liam held his stare.

Cass flushed scarlet, and pulled at his baseball cap. Liam Kavanagh had confronted him with what he had always succeeded in pushing to the back of his mind. It was not what he was expecting. He rallied himself, trying to seem calm and collected. 'What evidence do you have, Mr Kavanagh? Maybe you're just a bad loser?' He took a swig of beer, and smiled with a bravado he was far from feeling.

Liam ignored the taunt and came to the point. 'Does the name Amos Kidston mean anything to you?'

'Nope.'

'Then let me remind you. Amos Kidston worked for eight

years as foreman on your father's ranch near Wolfcreek. You must've known him, Cass. I don't believe you don't remember him.'

Cass held Liam's gaze. A trickle of sweat ran down the length of his spine under his shirt, but he did not speak a word.

'Amos Kidston's wife came to see me last month. She told me that her husband had recently died, and that he died a tormented man. He confessed something to her on his deathbed, something that all these years had bound him in fear for his life. He made her promise to find me and tell me about it. Seventy-two hours after she buried him, that's exactly what she did.'

The young man across the table did not move. Liam Kavanagh did not let up.

'As you may recall, in May 1988, one of my cowboys was killed by a grizzly during our branding weekend. It was all over the papers at the time. Keira was part of the team who'd ridden up to the high pastures to drive down the cattle grazing below the Bob Marshall Wilderness. When they reached the top they found the fencing had been vandalised and at least five elk carcasses were left as bait across the forest. Just as these vandals planned, some of my team ran into a six-foot grizzly. Ed Whitely, my foreman's seventeen-year-old son, died saving Keira's life. They planned murder, Cass, and murder is what they got!'

Despite the heat, Cass felt his blood run cold. He was suddenly back in his father's study that Saturday night, seven years earlier.

Liam sensed a change in Cass's body language. He went on. 'In all those years working on your father's ranch, Amos Kidston was a loyal and dependable foreman. But he made one big mistake: instead of asking for a loan, he helped himself to $350 from the petty cash box to pay off medical bills for his wife. It was discovered and Jim saw his chance. He wanted to take revenge on me in the worst way possible, so he used Amos to do some dirty work.'

Cass looked away. He remembered vividly now confronting his father about the vandalism up at the Goodnight ranch that had led to the death of the foreman's son.

'So Amos cut the fences and drove the herd way up into the wilderness, while other hands from your ranch laid the bait. Why? I believe your father gambled that whoever rode up there from my ranch in search of the cattle would meet a grizzly or two.'

The barman glanced over in their direction.

Liam returned to the point. 'Earlier that same year, your father had to give up his political ambitions when the Maureen Jacobsen scandal broke. He knew that Gloria and I were behind it, and he was looking for revenge. And I've often wondered what Jim must've felt when he heard my daughter was one of the herders up in the wilderness that morning. And I reckon he probably wished it'd been her, and not the foreman's son, who died.'

Cass's mind was spinning.

'It means you should watch your own back, Cass, even though you're his son. Your father is a very ruthless man. He's not happy with his menial job in Washington. I believe he's made up his mind that you're going to succeed politically where he has not. And I'm warning you, nothing will get in his way this time.'

Cass jumped up and his chair fell back onto the tiled floor with a crash. He had to get away from the bar. 'Mr Kavanagh, whatever you may tell me, he's my father. And I will stand by him!'

'And I will stand by my daughter!' countered Liam. 'Leave her alone!'

Cass pulled out some coins from his pocket and tossed them on the table.

Liam watched him leave.

Chapter 16

Copacabana

Solomon checked his watch as he approached the modest hotel situated over the other side of the borough of Saens Pena from his apartment block. It was a few minutes after eleven, and he reckoned that Cass and Fin should have had plenty of sleep, despite returning late from their party. It was Christmas Day, and the back streets were empty but for the litter, a family who had made their home out of boxes and plastic bags up against a wall at the back of the old cinema, and two stray dogs who were relieving themselves on the locked door of a shop whose multicoloured Christmas lights were now only flashing red. As he climbed the four marble steps and walked into the lobby of the hotel, Keira saw him first. If it had been the other way round, he would have surmised the situation in a flash and left.

'Solomon!'

He saw her jump up from a green sofa behind a long black table on which were spread several brochures advertising trips to Sugar Loaf Mountain beside a small silver Christmas tree. The receptionist was speaking on the telephone.

Solomon's face reflected his consternation at this unexpected turn of events.

'Hello, Keira. Where's Cass? I've come to meet him and the one with the camera.'

Keira felt awkward. She saw immediately that Solomon was not pleased to find her there, and felt the need to explain her presence. 'Cass and Fin have asked me to come in their place. Cass isn't feeling well, and Fin wants to spend Christmas Day with Mary.'

Solomon stared at her, his eyes troubled under the finely etched brows.

Keira walked over to him. 'I can do what Fin was going to do! I can take some photos and make notes for the newspaper story.'

Solomon said nothing.

She tried again. 'I've been really moved by what I've seen in Rio, and I want to do something to help the children. I intend to write a really good story about what I see today.'

Solomon lowered his eyes and shook his head. 'I'm sorry... I...' His voice tailed off.

She was staring at him, not understanding his torment. She was longing for him to reassure her that she would be as welcome as Cass and Fin. But he did not. To her dismay he murmured, 'Excuse me,' and turned on his heel, walking quickly through the open glass doors and down the steps. Keira stood dumbfounded, her heart tightening, as she watched him disappear down the street.

She sat back down on the sofa. *How rude of him!* she thought indignantly. What possible reason could there be for this extraordinary behaviour?

Then suddenly he was there again, standing before her.

'Forgive me, Keira,' he said formally, holding out a hand to her. 'I did not mean to be so rude.'

She took the hand and stood up immediately. She smiled shakily at him.

'Shall we go?' he said, releasing her hand.

This sudden metamorphosis stunned her, and she hurried down the marble steps after him before he could change his mind.

As the bus roared into the centre of the city and started to fill up with passengers, Keira broke the silence. From the zipped pouch clipped securely around her waist, she produced a small red Christmas cracker and holding one end firmly, offered the other end to Solomon.

'Merry Christmas!' she said, laughing at Solomon's puzzled expression as he surveyed the cracker.

'Merry Christmas!' she said again, gazing directly at him with her cornflower-blue eyes. 'It won't bite! Future priests can still pull crackers, can't they?'

There was a little 'crack' as it broke in two, leaving Keira with nothing but ripped paper. They both laughed as the people sitting around them turned and stared.

'You've won!' she cried. 'What've you got?' She leaned closer to him and peered down. 'Some cheap toy and a bad joke?'

Solomon tipped the ripped cracker and out dropped a little gold ring set with a glass stone, and a small piece of yellow paper.

'There it is!' she clapped her hands.

He picked up the ring.

'*Feliz Natal!*' He handed it to her, bowing his head in jest.

'Wow! Thanks, Solomon, a lot of thought must've gone into that!' She casually put it on her finger and held out her right hand. 'Perfect fit!'

They laughed again.

'So, read the bad joke!' She leaned in and he could feel her brush against his bare arm. He quickly adjusted his body, moving closer to the window, and handed her the yellow piece of paper. 'You read it!'

'It's a Chinese proverb. Far too serious for us, don't you think?'

He shrugged his shoulders. 'What does it say?'

'Fragrance always clings to the hand that gives you roses.' She screwed up her nose.

He grinned at her expression. 'Madeleine always says a soul is nourished when you are kind, but it is destroyed when you are cruel.'

She changed the subject. 'We missed you last night.'

'I was in Caxias visiting my mother and my younger sister and brother.'

'Caxias?'

'It's the other side of the city. My mother and sister work in an orphanage there. In return they have a bed and food.' He pointed over to their right. 'Look up there. It's the Christ Redeemer.'

Keira's eyes followed his gaze and saw the high and mighty statue towering dramatically above the white billowing clouds, arms outstretched over a city of extremes; the very rich and the very poor juxtaposed in a sprawling landscape.

'Have you been up there?' he asked her.

'Not yet. Will's organising a trip next week with the whole team, before we leave.'

'On a clear day, the view is magnificent.'

She looked at the astonishing face beside her, and wished more than anything that she could go up there with him.

The bus roared away spewing diesel fumes, and Solomon

led her towards the large entrance to the Central City Station with its huge domed roof.

'This morning you are going to see a way of life that you may find disturbing,' he had told her as they rode along on the bus, 'but don't worry, the people who live there know me well.'

As she followed behind him, she felt a pang of excitement tinged with fear. They emerged on the far side of the station and stepped into a different world, a twilight zone, whose almost tangible pulse-beat struck her like a body blow. As far as her eyes could see, row upon row of cardboard shacks ran on and on until they merged into the lower edges of yet another shanty town, which followed the contours of the flat-topped mountain that soared away above and beyond where they stood. Here existed hundreds, maybe thousands of victims of misery, all living well below the poverty line. Keira's heart missed a beat.

Solomon stopped walking and looked down at her. 'When Pedro and I lived here on these streets, these were the people who protected us and kept us alive.' He sensed her uncertainty. 'Don't worry, Keira, the family we are going to visit are my friends.'

Keira tried to look as if she were not shocked by what she saw, nor affected by the stench of smouldering litter and filth.

'Don't take any pictures. It makes them angry.'

The truth was that Keira had no wish to take photographs in this hub of human degradation. At that moment, more than anything, she wanted to clutch Solomon's arm for comfort. But a sense of respect for him restrained her.

As they crossed the narrow road that led away from the station, Keira saw a group of half-naked children with extended bellies, playing in the dirt in front of a makeshift bar. A skeletal woman, mere skin and bone, squatted in the gutter begging for money. Keira saw that she sat in a pool of her own urine. As they drew close to her, Solomon reached out and touched her head; she looked up into his face with deadened eyes, her spirit gone, leaving just a shell. He crouched down and spoke to her quietly, then stood and walked on through a small gap into a dim alleyway. Keira followed nervously, sickened to the pit of her stomach by the hopelessness of what she was seeing.

'That poor woman, she looks terrible!' she said to Solomon's retreating figure.

'Rose has AIDS' he replied tersely, over his shoulder.

'Why isn't she in hospital?' she gasped.

Solomon stopped abruptly and called to a skinny boy he apparently recognised. Some coins were handed over and instructions given, and the child ran off bright eyed to accomplish his task.

'What was that all about?' Keira wanted to know everything. She must try to remember all this, she reminded herself, to do justice to the article that she would write describing this day. People back home needed to know about the suffering lives of these people. Surely they could help in some way?

'I asked him to buy Rose something to eat,' he explained. 'She doesn't want to go to hospital. There's no money for medication. She knows she's dying, and she'd rather die here.'

Keira stopped walking and turned briefly to look back at

the wizened figure, now silhouetted at the end of the darkened passageway. *People like Rose needed taking care of*, she
thought with despair, as a fire of compassion seemed to burn
through her. People like Rose needed a home where they could
be nursed and cared for in the remaining days of their miserable lives on earth. People like Rose needed to know they were
loved . . .

At that moment a sultry voice called to Solomon from behind
them. Keira whipped around again and saw a young, plump,
sensuous woman, with wonderfully thick black hair and
mahogany breasts bulging from a brief bikini top. The woman
threw her arms around Solomon, planting noisy kisses on both
his cheeks. Her husky voice was entrancing.

Solomon laughed. 'Keira, this is my good friend Silvana!'

Silvana turned to regard her.

'*Tudo bem?*' tried Keira, approaching them.

Silvana kissed her too, but without as much warmth, and
eyed her quizzically. '*Bonita, muito bonita, Solomon!*' she said
in tones of exaggerated approval.

'She thinks you're beautiful,' he smiled awkwardly. 'Her
father, Morreno, has invited us to have lunch with them.
Morreno looked after me and Pedro when we lived here as
children.'

Keira suddenly felt frumpy in her baggy, knee-length shorts
and Grizzlies t-shirt, as they followed Silvana, whose body
oozed femininity, through the alleyways ahead of them. Clad
in a skin-tight denim mini-skirt, Silvana swayed her hips erot-
ically.

Morreno's house was a surprise to Keira. Although modest,
it was brick-built with a rendering of painted plaster, and the
windows boasted coloured glass. Beside the neighbouring

shacks, it appeared almost palatial. As they entered, she began to feel she was living through a dream – or was it a nightmare? A collage of strange faces surrounded her, all speaking a strange language, all speaking at the same time, all loudly welcoming to Solomon and blatantly curious about her. They exclaimed over her eyes, her slim figure, and above all her auburn hair.

A meal was produced, and somehow in the midst of it all Solomon managed to introduce her to his friends. Sergio, with spiky peroxided hair, was married to Silvana, he explained to Keira. Their two small children were Lara, four, and Ivan, two. Alicia was the current girlfriend of Silvana's brother, known as 'Elvis Presley', which Keira was able to relate to with a smile. Elvis himself was dressed in black from head to toe, and he had a jagged, very recent knife wound down his cheek, which she was told had seventeen stitches holding it together. Alicia was proudly displaying a swollen belly, which protruded like a smooth, brown football between her jeans and halter-neck top. Two girls aged about fourteen and twelve were, Solomon told her, the younger daughters of Morreno and his third wife, Fatima.

Morreno sat at the head of the table, large and intimidating, resembling a giant bulldog. He was banging his hand on the table, shouting something again and again. Keira was alarmed when Solomon told her that he was demanding that she sit by him. She suspected that he was already drunk, and thought he looked quite scary with several scars on his face. He continually looked at her, and as the meal progressed, Solomon watched anxiously as the old man flirted shamelessly with her.

Solomon had one of Silvana's children on his knee and was

feeding him rice and chicken. Ivan turned to his *Tio* between mouthfuls and surveyed him with huge brown eyes. Elvis Presley, sitting next to them, wanted to know more about Keira.

'You fancy her?' Elvis shot Solomon a knowing look.

Solomon flushed and busied himself with the child on his knee. 'She's not for me, my friend. You know what my destiny is. I have made my decision, and it's the right one for me, I am certain of it.'

'Solomon, it's OK! Really, I'm fine. It's all an amazing experience for me,' Keira insisted.

They were on another bus, and Solomon continued to apologise.

'No, I shouldn't have taken you to such a place.' He looked at her with concern.

Taken aback by the sudden softening in his attitude towards her, Keira put her hand out and touched his. 'Don't worry about me.'

A startling tenderness for her overwhelmed him. He fought against it.

Her voice spoke into his thoughts. 'Tell me about your life, Solomon. I mean, before you came to Rio. I don't understand how someone like you came to be living on the streets with – well – with people like Morreno?' She looked at his averted face in concern. 'Do you mind talking about it?'

'I never talk about it. I have tried to forget.' He still did not look at her.

'Tell me about your father,' she said softly.

'*Papai*?' He opened his eyes with a start, then narrowed them. 'I do not want to talk about my father.'

She scrutinised his face, and saw the pain. 'What happened?' she probed gently.

They left the bus at one end of Copacabana and began to walk slowly along the length of the famous beach. The sand was warm in the afternoon sun, and they took off their shoes and meandered between the sun-worshippers and the volley-ball games to the edge of the calmly lapping sea. He found himself telling her more about the loss of his idyllic child-hood than he had ever been able to admit to anyone, even Madeleine. He spoke of the degrading conditions in the *favela*, of how he used to talk to himself in the bathroom mirror, promising that one day he would get even with the phoney lawyer who had cheated them of everything that was good and innocent, and who, worst of all, had destroyed his father's spirit.

Sometimes they would stop in their tracks, as Solomon's story reached a point that could hardly be spoken of, and stood silently facing the sea, oblivious to everything and everyone around them. Finally, when they found themselves back at the place where they had begun, Solomon bought a coconut and they sat down in the sand drinking its cool milk through two straws. Keira reflected that he had spoken of leaving his home; he had told her of their rescue from the streets by Madeleine; of his music and voice lessons; of his decision to study for the priesthood. But he had told her nothing at all of his boyhood in the valley.

As the sun started to set near the horizon where the blue sea met the even bluer sky, Solomon got to his feet and brushed the sand from his jeans.

'I want to take you somewhere different now,' he said with a smile. 'I want to show you how the richer Brazilians enjoy themselves.' He offered her his hand. As she took it, and stood up before him, she gazed into his extraordinary eyes and knew she had taken a new path. Solomon did not move.

'You have the most beautiful face I have ever seen,' he breathed. He touched her cheek gently and moved away a strand of hair. 'Your eyes . . . did you know that the eyes are the mirror of the soul?'

Keira slowly shook her head, unwilling for the moment to pass.

'Do you belong to Cass?'

She looked away, frowning, as if the very name was an intrusion.

Time seemed to stand still and their very breath seemed to cease for an instant. Then Solomon stirred and, placing an arm about her, led her along the promenade to the Copacabana Palace Hotel.

The lush opulence of the five-star hotel overwhelmed Keira's senses. The contrast with the environment in which she had spent the morning, indeed in which she and the team had spent the past week, was extreme. It was like being transplanted back into the world she had left. The vast lobby was a shimmer of crystal chandeliers, rich red carpets and gilt furnishings. A huge Christmas tree dominated the scene. In the background, the *ting*, *ting* of the elevators rang out repetitively. Men in livery and white gloves ushered elegant guests from place to place. Uniformed reception staff busied themselves behind cream marble counters. Solomon headed for the Piano Bar, which overlooked the long blue swimming pool, now lit by spotlights that twinkled beneath the surrounding palm trees. It was Happy Hour, and as they approached, a middle-aged man in a dark suit clapped his hands and hurried towards them through the gathering crowd of guests who were enjoying complimentary glasses of champagne.

'Solomon! *Feliz Natal*!' The man shook Solomon's hand with enthusiasm, then turned to Keira, waiting politely to know who she was.

Solomon put a hand gently on her back. 'Keira, I would like you to meet my friend Guilherme, assistant manager of this hotel. I used to play the piano here in the evenings.'

Guilherme took Keira's hand. 'You speak Portuguese?' he asked.

'No, none at all,' she answered frankly, wishing for the second time that day that she did not feel so inappropriately dressed.

Guilherme clicked his fingers at a waiter bearing a tray of champagne flutes. 'One for you, *Senhorita*, and one for Solomon too! I know you don't drink, *amigo*, but tonight I think is special, yes?'

He showed them to a table, bowed to Keira and left them with their Moët Chandon.

'I am so glad that you have met my friend Guilherme,' said Solomon. 'He used to live in the same apartment block as Madeleine and was a great encouragement to me and Pedro in the early days, when once or twice the pull of life on the streets was a temptation. And then later, when I needed money to pay for my studies, he got me the job here in the hotel bar.' Solomon raised his glass to her. '*Salut*!'

Keira sipped her champagne. 'You really never drink?'

'Only today, with you.'

Looking into his eyes, Keira was sure she saw a tenderness which, combined with the champagne, made her feel light-headed. This was a mind, a spirit, from whose influence she did not think she would ever pull free.

After a while she asked, 'Will you take me to your mountains?'

He looked down at his hands and the barely touched glass. 'Perhaps, one day.'

Keira saw his pain. 'You never finished your story,' she said. 'You started at the end and didn't tell the beginning.'

'It has not ended.'

'What happened to your dog?'

Solomon leaned back in his chair, his elbows on the padded velvet armrests, his hands clasped together. 'No one knows. My grandfather kept him for a while, but he was very restless and one day he disappeared. When I think about him even after all these years, I still long for him . . . I will never stop longing for him.'

'You've been through so much.' She was silent for a while, then asked, 'Do you ever see your great friend, your cousin?'

'Ze? He hates big cities and will not come here even for me.' Solomon's hands moved automatically to the small wooden fish around his neck. 'He's an artist. He carves and paints figures out of wood and sells them to tourists in a pretty mining town called Ouro Preto in the state of Minas Gerais.'

'What about your grandfather?'

Solomon's face lit up. 'He is the most important person in my life. I don't see him enough, but we often speak on the phone. He has a special friendship with my old piano teacher, *Senhora* Francisca. It fascinates me. They don't live together, but every weekend they meet for dinner on Saturday night at her house in Petropolis. She plays the piano for him and they dance alone together to the music of the *cavaquinho*. Then he goes home.'

'That's so romantic. How old are they now?'

'*Senhora* Francisca must be over seventy years old. And *Vovo*? He's almost eighty.'

Keira's heart warmed to the idea of Solomon's grandfather finding happiness after the trauma of losing half his family to the city. She allowed herself to imagine for a few moments what it would be like if the Kavanaghs had to leave Goodnight. 'When did you last visit the valley?'

Solomon was silent for a while. He held her gaze. 'I prefer not to go back to my mountains. It is too painful still.'

Keira leaned forward and placed her hand over his.

Solomon did not move his hand away. 'Did you know that touch has a very great power because we live inside the world of skin?' he asked her.

Keira burst out laughing. His English was excellent, but some of the things he said were very unexpected, and made listening to him even more intriguing.

'Yes, our skin is alive.' He opened up each of her fingers one by one, then placed his larger hand with its long fingers over her palm. 'Touch communicates belonging and tenderness.' He reached over and tucked her hair behind her ear. 'Also, it is wonderful to have the gift of hearing. With it we can know music, one of the most beautiful gifts given to the world. Through great music, the ancient longing of the earth finds its voice. That is how music ministers to our souls.' Her eyes never left his face. He touched her mouth. 'Out of the mouth speaks the heart. The tongue is so small, but so powerful.' Their eyes met. She waited. 'Ah, the eye! There are so many ways of seeing: there is the greedy eye, the judging eye, the resentful eye. But best of all is the loving eye . . . the loving eye is bright, everything is hopeful and real.'

'Do you believe in fate?' Keira whispered.

'No, not fate.'

She drew away her hand. 'Then why have we met? Do you really believe it was just chance?'

'I cannot say.'

'But we have met, Solomon. And you felt you already knew me, you said that! And I feel . . . I feel . . . just complete, completely comfortable with you . . .' Her voice faltered.

'Keira, I don't know why we have met. I do not believe I can say it is "fate", because I know I have the power to make choices in my life.'

'Then choose not to become a priest!'

There was an electric silence.

Solomon looked down for a moment, then shook his head slightly, and smiled across at her.

'I believe this is God's plan for me, and—'

'God? Who is God?' she interrupted. 'He took my mother from me!' She leaned back in her chair, challenging him. 'My mother did nobody any harm. She was a beautiful person in every way. She died of cancer.'

Solomon's eyes reflected his compassion for her. 'There are many things we do not understand. I cannot explain why a beautiful person like your mother should die so young. Sickness is a terrible thing. When my father was killed, I blamed God too. But then I came to understand that what happened to him was in a way the result of his choice to join a dangerous way of life. To me this could not be fate.'

'Maybe not,' Keira reflected, her tone softening. She paused and took a sip of champagne. 'Can I share something with you that means a lot to me? Not long before Mom died, she told me that she believed our lives are like a song, and each one of us has to search for the key to unlock it. For me I think that key is a person, a soulmate.'

Solomon recalled his father's dying words as he replied, 'For you that key might be a person; for me it could be the priesthood, or the gift of music, or my family in the *favela*. Our lives are full of good things. I think it is when we learn to be thankful for all these things that we find peace – even if sometimes we have to let go of those things or those people . . .'

The assistant manager was approaching their table. Solomon straightened his shoulders and smiled at his old friend.

'Excuse me, *Senhorita*! I need to borrow Solomon for a while.' Guilherme helped her move her chair back. 'Come this way. It is a long time since we heard Solomon play. He has a great, great talent!'

Keira sat on a stool at the end of the piano. She remembered her camera; it flashed just as Solomon stood and bowed his appreciation to the cheering crowd. He spoke briefly and then sat again, and began to play some samba-jazz *bossa nova* music by Tom Jobim. She watched his face as he played, and felt transported to a different place – worlds away from everything that had formerly felt like reality. How could she be feeling so completely at one with a man from a different world, a man she had only just met? As the melody drew to its close, an eruption of claps and cheers started to break out. Once again, Solomon's compelling voice had drawn his audience into a new dimension of experience. The uproar continued, and Solomon was persuaded to sing again.

He turned to Keira. '*This song is for you,*' he mouthed. 'It's called "*Meu Amor*".'

She felt all eyes upon her.

Solomon sang the song his father had sung to his mother, when their lives had been untouched by disaster and everything was certain. But tonight he was singing for the girl who seemed so familiar to him but who could not be allowed into his heart.

As he finished, Solomon smiled and stood up, acknowledging the enthusiastic response. Then he resolutely closed the lid of the piano. He saw the tears on Keira's cheeks. 'Come,' he said, taking her hand.

They walked slowly along the promenade, arm in arm in the warm air, and looked up at the magnificent night sky.

'When were you born?' Solomon asked her abruptly.

'I was born on 31 December 1973.'

Solomon stopped walking and laughed out loud. 'Then we share the same birthday!'

'No way! I can't believe it! Do you know the exact time you were born?' she asked him.

'On each of my birthdays – until we left the mountains, that is – my father would take me fishing. At midday, when the sun was high above our heads, he would say, "*Agora*! This is the time you came into the world!"'

'Then I'm older than you!' laughed Keira. 'I was born at seven in the morning, in an ambulance which had got stuck in the snow on the way to the hospital. I beat you into the world!'

'Ah, but what about the time difference?' responded Solomon, laughing too.

Her mind raced. 'Montana is five hours behind Rio!' She

turned to him incredulously. 'What other coincidences do you need, Solomon? We were born on the same day, in the same year, at exactly the same time! We were destined to meet!'

Solomon smiled, but said nothing. Instead he hailed a taxi and they rode back in silence, each lost in their own thoughts. At the team hotel he paid the driver, and they walked up the steps.

Leaning against the glass entrance door stood Cass. 'It's late!' he said angrily. 'Where have you been?'

It ended so suddenly, so unexpectedly, the brilliance of the day fading, growing grey, then gone. It already seemed like a dream.

Solomon stood between Cass and Keira. The atmosphere was hostile. 'I hope you're feeling better now, Cass? Sorry if we're late.'

Cass ignored him and continued to glare at Keira.

Solomon turned awkwardly to her. 'Good night, Keira,' he said softly. Then he backed away down the steps and started along the street.

Keira wanted to run after him, to find again the assurance and happiness his company had brought her. But instead she turned to face Cass, and as she did so it was as if a veil closed around her heart.

Solomon could not sleep. Eventually, he left the bedroom he shared with Pedro and climbed into the hammock slung across the narrow balcony, which stretched along the rooms of their apartment. He listened to the sound of Pedro's breathing for a while, then jumped as he heard Madeleine softly call his name. He turned his head and saw her emerge from the door of the small living room. She was wrapped in her long, pale blue dressing gown.

'Did I wake you?' he asked her anxiously.

'No, I just felt something was wrong.' She stood by the open glazed doors.

Solomon swung his legs over the side of the hammock.

'Madeleine, I have to get away from here. I'm going to return to the seminary.'

'So early? But perhaps you can visit me again, perhaps when the team has left here?'

He was surprised, but then she never missed anything.

'She is very beautiful.' Madeleine watched his face as she sat down in the lone chair on the balcony.

Solomon stared ahead without comment.

'Have you read the Song of Songs?'

'Yes.'

'Then you will know that it is a love poem,' she said quietly. 'For many it is a mystery that it was allowed into the canon of scripture. For me there is no mystery. Yes, it is a great spiritual treasure, showing the intimacy of God's love for his people, but I can also read it as I believe it was written – as a hymn to human love, a love song written by your namesake, King Solomon.' She sighed. 'Don't you understand, my son? It is a gift of God to man. It is not forbidden fruit.'

He was silent.

'When I made my vows, Solomon, it was not a struggle for me inside myself. There was no doubt, ever, that this way was the way for me. You must be sure, my dear young friend, that the priesthood is your calling, your vocation.'

'Stop!' he shouted, jumping to his feet. 'Don't say any more, please.' The empty hammock swung to and fro as he strode heavily from the balcony and into his bedroom.

A few minutes later Madeleine heard the front door open.

She rose from the chair and went after him calling his name. He stood by the door, not meeting her eyes.

'Call me, won't you?' she said.

He nodded and went out. He was carrying a small suitcase.

Chapter 17

The Wedding Day

The day had been perfect, with a warm sun shining down from the vast arch of the azure Montana sky to bless the ceremony, which took place beside the lake. The big Reverend John Beard pronounced them man and wife before more than a hundred friends and family, beneath a simple white canopy filled with flowers picked from the mountainside: pink calypso orchids, lilac pasqueflowers, blue camas, white sego lilies, yellow arnicas. Caterers produced an impressive buffet lunch that was eaten at long tables set up in the dining room and great hall of the house. A group of volunteers from Ovando, including the sisters from the post office, Linda and Beryl, helped Faye with the serving and clearing. Beryl had married Buckskin Joe the previous year and was now an inhabitant of Goodnight. Joe and the other cowboys dispensed the drinks from a bar set up in front of the house.

'Catch!' Mary called from the staircase at Goodnight, as she threw her bouquet over her shoulder in the direction of her best friend. For as long as she could remember, she had wanted to have her wedding at the Goodnight ranch. Liam had agreed wholeheartedly when Fin had approached his uncle, soon after their engagement, requesting the possibility. Today Mary's dream had come true. She watched her bouquet as it rose in an arc towards the huge crystal chandelier in the great hall, then began to descend towards the hoard of chattering, laughing guests, whose outstretched arms reached up to grasp it. It fell directly into Keira's waiting hands. There was a loud cheer as she caught it and shot a startled look back at the bride. Mary laughed out loud and blew a kiss at her best friend and maid of honour. Fin stood waiting at the foot of the staircase for the girl he had known and loved for so many years. He took her by the arm, and to the shouts and cheers of their wedding guests, led her through the panelled hall to the big oak doors and out to the waiting limousine. Mary's mother and father embraced their daughter. Fin kissed Gloria and shook Jack's hand, who in turn grabbed his stepson with his free arm and hugged him. Fin's father Hank opened the passenger door of the limousine, his proud face breaking into a wide smile, as the bride and groom climbed in.

Keira stood on the steps of the house in her elegant cream silk suit, waving until the couple had finally disappeared from view. A sudden loneliness gripped her in the strange new quiet that now fell on the wedding party. Although she could not be happier for Mary and Fin, she knew that in their new lives as Mr and Mrs Jefferson, something of them was lost to her for ever.

As the guests began to filter out past her through the front door and down the steps, heading for their cars, Keira lifted the bouquet of lilies to her face, searching for their scent. Suddenly she felt she needed to be alone for a while. She ran into the house and up the staircase, past portraits of Kavanagh ancestors, along the carpeted landing to her bedroom, where she quietly closed the door and walked over to the window to look out at the view her mother had loved so much. In the stillness of the room, she wept uncontrollably. She missed her mother so much now, more than ever. Who could she talk to? Who would understand?

Wiping her eyes, she carefully placed the bouquet on her dressing table, took off her jacket and began to remove the clips from her hair that had held the white flowers in place all day. She shook her head, glad to let her hair fall free at last. Then, walking over to her bed, she sank down on the soft covers and closed her eyes.

'Why did you leave me? Why?' she said angrily as the tears flowed. 'I miss you, Mom, I miss you so much. What have I done that the people I love don't stay with me?' She buried her face in the pillows.

The shattering news had reached her a few days after her graduation party, in a long-awaited letter from Madeleine. Over the previous five months, since their time together, she had written to Solomon several times, but had never received a reply. Finally, in despair, she had written to Madeleine. She had been hoping against hope that Solomon might not continue his studies for the priesthood. After their extraordinary time together on Christmas Day, perhaps he had changed his mind? She had felt so strongly that they were destined for each other. Every fibre of her body told her that he had felt the same strong feelings for her; that their attraction had been mutual. She was sure she had not imagined it.

Madeleine's letter had been kind in its choice of words, but firm in its message: Solomon was adamant that he could never see Keira again. She felt devastated. And yet, had she not known from the beginning that he belonged to God and not to her? How could fate be so cruel? Teasing her with what could never be. What a fool she had been to convince herself that it could be otherwise.

Someone was knocking at the door. She chose not to hear it. After a moment, the door handle turned and someone came quietly into the room. Although she was facing away, Keira knew who it was and why he had come and what he wanted. Over the last few months he had pursued her relentlessly, and with the same determination she had rejected him. Keira felt him looking down at her, and then the mattress sank under his weight as he sat down on the bed, running his heavy hand across her bare shoulders. She shuddered. Moving her head, she looked up into his intense eyes. For so long she had believed that he was the one person in the world whom she was born to love for ever. Why could she not believe that now? Where had that conviction gone? If only she had not met Solomon. By comparison, Cass now seemed shallow, both in mind and soul. But Solomon was as good as dead to her! Dead for ever to the love and affections of a woman, in the pursuit of a higher vocation that demanded this sacrifice.

Cass put his hand inside his white jacket pocket. Pulling out a square black box, he placed it on the pillow in front of her eyes. This was his trump card and he was sure she would not be able to resist. Not after today. He wanted her and he was going to get her, even if he had to marry her and face his father to do so. No other man had a right to her after all this time.

'Keira, marry me!'

She sat up at once, leaning on her elbow and sweeping her long hair back off her face.

'Open it!' Cass watched her. Although pale and drawn, her beauty remained unflawed.

Mechanically, Keira picked up the small leather box and lifted the lid. Her blue eyes, still wet with tears, lit up momentarily at the shimmering stone. 'It's beautiful,' she whispered.

'At the end of the day, your father will want what you want. It's your life!' His fingers touched her face. 'I'll speak to my father tomorrow.'

'He won't like it any more than Daddy will.'

'They'll have no choice.'

Cass leaned forward and kissed her cheek, then pulled back to search her face for a response. He saw his opportunity as her eyes showed a hint of resignation. He leaned over again and kissed her mouth this time, and as he did so he pulled his legs up onto the bed and lay down next to her. Taking hold of her hand, he slipped the diamond onto her finger.

'What about the other women in your life?'

Cass feigned a bewildered look.

'Don't look like that! How can I ever trust you?'

He put his hand under her head, locking her hair in his fingers so tightly that she could not move, his wide-open mouth urgently pressed up against hers, his tongue probing. Keira began to struggle to be free, and he released her.

'I haven't said "yes" yet!' she gasped, trying to push him away.

He stared at her, breathing hard, his eyes dancing, his handsome face twisting with desire. 'I swear I won't touch another woman after today if you say "yes"!'

She narrowed her eyes at him.

'I promise.'

She looked away.

Cass shrugged off his jacket and began removing his gold cufflinks. Keira watched him take off his shirt. She noticed his dark chest hair that dived down his taut stomach in a long thin line. He gave a brief smile of triumph as he unzipped her dress and pulled it down over her hips. He began to kiss her breasts, and she felt herself tingle unexpectedly. Then his movements became more urgent as he pushed down her pants and laid his beautifully toned body on top of hers, pinning her down to the bed. His mouth was now on hers again, and she could feel his tongue probing, making it almost impossible for her to breathe. Lifting his hips, he unzipped his trousers, hurting her with the weight of his chest. Now he was prising open her long slender legs with his knees and blowing in her ear through short, sharp breaths.

She wanted to scream out for him to stop. This was horrible. He was hurting her. She felt paralysed under his weight, and could feel him prodding more vigorously. Her body was not responding, and as his frustration grew, so did her fear.

'What's *wrong* with you?' He looked down at her angrily.

All at once there was a loud knock at the door. 'Keira!' It was her father.

'Shit!' hissed Cass into her ear between clenched teeth. 'Answer him!'

'Yes, Daddy?' she managed to say. Her voice sounded small and weak.

'You all right?'

'Uh-huh.'

'Can you come down? Everyone's leaving.'

'I'll come now.'

They listened to the pad of his retreating footsteps through the thumping beats of their hearts.

'Shit!' Cass swore again, rolling off her. He grabbed his clothes and stormed into her en suite bathroom.

Keira lay motionless in her nakedness for a few seconds, and then felt an overwhelming sense of relief. Quickly finding her clothes, she climbed into her dress and struggled to zip it all the way up as she slipped her feet into her stilettos. Grabbing the suit jacket, she opened the door slightly and checked to see if it was all clear. Then she ran along the carpeted landing to another bathroom, where she splashed her face with cold water and tried to pull her tumultuous thoughts together.

As she came out, Cass was standing there on the landing. Keira froze.

'I'm sorry,' he tried to reach out to her.

'Not now!' She pushed past him and ran down the staircase into the hall, where her heels clattered against the stone floor.

Cass smiled to himself. The engagement ring was still on her finger. He was almost there.

Later that evening, Keira walked into her father's study and closed the door. Picking up the phone, she called England.

'Grandma?'

'Keira, pet. How was the wedding?'

'Beautiful.'

'Your day will come.'

'I've got engaged.'

'Engaged!'

'To Cass Henderson.'

There was silence.

'Grandma?'

'Keira, my dear. Are you listening to your heart?'

'I'm trying to.'

'Is he really the key to your song?'

'There is no key, Grandma. No song. That was all fantasy.'

'Are you quite sure, pet?'

'Yes. This is reality. I'm engaged to Cass Henderson.'

'Do you love him?'

'What is love, Grandma? Lust? Desire? I've always wanted Cass.'

'What about Solomon?'

The words came as a shock. His very name stirred her.

'What about him, Grandma? He's going to be a priest!'

'My sweet Keira.'

'Aren't you going to congratulate me?'

'If you can tell me you love Cass.'

The door opened and her father walked in.

'I have to go, Grandma. I'll call you soon.'

'Over my dead body!' roared Jim Henderson, crashing his fist down onto his desk and jumping to his feet. 'Are you out of your mind?' He ripped his reading glasses off his flushed face and pounded heavily across the red Persian rug in the direction of his son. 'Do you know what this Kavanagh family have done to us? Huh? Do you have *any* idea? They're still tryin' to destroy me!' Beads of sweat broke out across his forehead and upper lip. He jabbed his glasses in Cass's direction. 'Have you lost your mind?' He pulled away, his body language expressing implacable opposition to his son's intentions, and strode back across the rug towards the window.

Jim swung round, narrowing his eyes and lowering his voice to a controlled, venomous twang. 'I will not have it! I was cooped up on my own in DC for almost two years, thanks to that son-of-a-bitch, until the lawyers cleared my name with the Justice Department.'

'On your own, Dad?' Cass held his ground. 'Or with your mistress?'

'You watch your tongue there, boy!' Jim stormed back to his desk, furious.

'Anyway, what are you complaining about?' Cass interrupted, walking up to the desk and feeling more confident. 'You're back now, aren't you?'

Jim was looking away, shaking his head. He had never heard his son speaking to him this way before. 'This is preposterous! Outrageous! I'm not hearing any of this! And I'm certainly not having you marry a Kavanagh!'

'Christ, Dad, you wanted me to sleep with her when she was only fourteen!'

'That was different!' He jabbed his finger in the air. 'It would have given me great pleasure thinking of my own son using and exploiting Liam Kavanagh's precious daughter at such a tender age. But as for falling in love with her! Shit!' He banged the desk once again with his fist. 'And as if that ain't enough! You walk into my study on a Sunday morning and tell me you wanna *marry* her! Is this your way of thanking me for all I've done for you, Cass? Is it? Why, if it wasn't for me, you wouldn't have been voted in as student regent, and you know it! Your career in politics has just started, for Christ's sake!' He was yelling louder now. 'Hell, Cass, you marry her and I'll have you cut off from everything I have, just like James! Is that clear?'

Cass was not expecting this.

Patty walked into the study. 'What's going on?' Despite the perfection of her hair and her beautiful clothes, she looked terribly thin, her face sunken and pained.

'Tell her, Cass! Tell your mother what you've just told me!' Jim leaned his weight on the desk.

Cass looked down at his frail, worn mother. 'I want to marry Keira Kavanagh.'

The very sound of her name catapulted Jim to his feet again.

'I won't allow it, Patty!' he shouted. 'It's not going to happen, or Cass will lose everything – everything, just like James. Do you hear me? The money, the house, his career in politics . . . everything, he'll lose the lot!'

The phone started ringing down the hall and Patty gratefully left the study to answer it.

Cass waited for his father to calm down. 'You don't get it, do you, Dad?' he said quietly, eyeing his father. He thought he would try a different tack.

Jim breathed heavily, his mouth taut.

'Don't you see that if I marry Keira, it's like poking Liam Kavanagh in the eye?'

Jim sank down in his chair and squinted at his son.

'She's the apple of his eye,' continued Cass, placing both hands on the desk and leaning towards his father. 'He'll never stop her from marrying me, if that's what she really wants to do. And once I'm her husband, I'll have access to what is his through her.'

'I don't buy it. He'll give everything to his son, if she marries you.'

'No he won't. I'll make sure she gets what is rightfully hers.'

Jim shook his head and closed his eyes for several seconds. Then he looked his son in the eye. 'I'll strike you a deal, son.' He reached forward and took a cigar from the wooden box. 'You stick a diamond ring on her finger if that makes you happy. But you won't marry her until you graduate from law school!'

'Graduate from law school! Dad, that's too long!'

'It's that or nothin'!'

Cass clenched his fists. His father had beaten him once again. Reason told him that three years was too long. Keira had already graduated from university and would not be returning to Missoula where he could see her every day. But he knew that he had no choice. He was not about to throw away his vast inheritance or his future career in politics, and he needed his father for both. Incensed, he turned to leave.

'Oh, and Cass.' Jim lit a cigar. 'I've got to go to DC tomorrow. I want you to come with me.'

Cass nodded and left without looking back.

Jim picked up the phone and called his old friend Bill Bridger in Washington. He needed to get Cass out of Montana and away from that girl for the rest of the summer. A part-time job in the Justice Department for three months would do nicely.

Chapter 18

Restlessness

*M*onsignor Andre Cavalcanti, small and sinewy and clad in austere black robes, welcomed Madeleine warmly as she entered the cool, dark colonial building from the heat and brightness of the day outside.

'Ah, how is my Lutheran Sister today?' He walked towards the large doors, his hand extended.

Madeleine smiled. '*Monsignor*, I am well, thank you.' She took his slim hand.

His angular face broke into a grin, his head bowed slightly. 'And how can I be of service to you, today, Madeleine?' A few strands of white hair stuck out around his skullcap. 'I imagine this visit has everything to do with that young man of ours?'

'He tells me you inspire him greatly with your wisdom, *Monsignor*.'

'But you are too wise to believe everything you hear, Sister.' He smiled again and peered over her shoulder, pointing with an arthritic finger. 'I believe Solomon is rehearsing in the chapel, which you will find . . .'

'Yes, yes, thank you, I have been here before!'

'Solomon continues to bless us with his music.'

'He was born with a remarkable gift.'

The *Monsignor* nodded. 'It is a pity that he has such a fight going on in his heart.'

292

Madeleine's eyes searched his.

'He has said nothing to me, but I can see it in his eyes.'

Madeleine gave a bleak smile. This gracious man had great discernment.

'I hope to see you before you leave us.' He bowed and smiled at her. '*Bom dia*, Sister Madeleine.'

'*Bom dia*, *Monsignor* Andre.' She watched the slender black figure walk stiffly away.

Madeleine's footsteps echoed on the polished wooden floors. Music from the organ gallery grew louder in the corridor as she neared the chapel. All at once the voice she knew so well rose above all the other sounds. Pushing open one of the heavy entrance doors, she slipped inside. At the altar a novice was lighting candles, and to one side sat a priest reading from a prayer book. She slid quietly into the nearest pew and allowed the sense of peace in that place to settle in her. She looked up at the ornately decorated ceiling, as Solomon's voice filled her consciousness. He was singing Mozart's *Ave Verum*, rehearsing for the Holy Communion service.

Seeing her as she entered the chapel, he soon fell silent. The organ quietened.

Solomon came down from the organ loft and approached her with a warm smile. She watched him, scanning his face for clues. Her heart instantly felt that same stab of love for him as a mother feels for her son. He was not hers, but God had given him to her to care for, to nurture, to love, and for that she would always be grateful.

Madeleine took his arm and they left the chapel together. They strolled across to the small tropical garden at the back of the old building, where they sat down on a stone bench.

'I didn't mean to interrupt you, Solomon.'

'I'm glad you did.' His handsome face broke into a warm smile. 'I am always happy to see you.'

He loved Madeleine as he loved his own mother. He suddenly remembered that first night when she had taken him and Pedro to live in her home after months of living on the streets. Unlike Pedro, he had not been able to sleep and Madeleine had held him as he cried for most of the night.

'You haven't visited us for a while. We all miss you. Pedro sends his love.' She paused and examined him. 'You've cut your hair. It suits you.'

He pulled a face, and she laughed.

They sat in silence for a while enjoying the beautiful garden.

'I've just seen the *Monsignor*.' Madeleine spoke first.

'Sometimes I get the feeling he can see right down into my soul,' he said. 'It unsettles me.'

Madeleine did not reply. Instead she asked, 'Has your mother been to visit you recently?'

'I saw her last week.'

'She is very proud of you.'

'I think she is.'

She searched his face. 'Are you feeling any regrets?'

He turned and looked at her, his green eyes troubled. 'Only that I will never be able to buy her a house of her own.'

'Well, there's always Pedro!' said Madeleine, attempting to cheer him. 'Although I'm not sure teaching will be all that lucrative . . . Talita tells me she wants to be a nurse. I can see her caring for all the sick babies in this world!'

'She has compassion like our *Mamae*. And Daniel . . . Daniel reminds me of our father. He would be happier living away from the city.'

They both watched the fountain trickle water into a pond.

Madeleine bent and lifted her familiar bag onto her knees. She looked inside it and took out a parcel. 'This is for you, Solomon, although it arrived addressed to me. So I opened it.'

He took the parcel from her, surprised. He turned it over in his hands and then he noticed the stamps. 'It's from America.'

'Yes.'

'I cannot receive it, Madeleine, any more than I could open any of her letters.'

'I think you should open this.'

'You know why I can't.'

'She's engaged to be married, Solomon.'

Her unexpected words hit him like a thunderbolt. The desperate weariness he had felt for weeks seemed suddenly overwhelming.

'She's engaged to Cass Henderson.'

He shut his eyes.

'I thought this news would help you to let go.'

There was a pause.

'A man like that will never make her happy,' Solomon said slowly.

'No. I think not.'

Solomon had nothing to lose now. He withdrew the piece of Sunderland pottery from its wrapping. 'What is this, Madeleine?'

She stared at his profile. 'It's a loving cup. See? It has two handles, one for each of the lovers, I assume. Keira says in her letter that she wants you to have this as a gift from her. She believes the inscription on it is relevant to your vocation. Apparently, it's an antique piece of pottery from the city in England where her grandmother lives. It's a miracle it didn't break in the post!'

He carefully turned it over in his hands and read the inscription.

'What does it say?'

Solomon read it out loud. '"Set me as a seal upon thine heart, as a seal upon thine arm; for love is strong as death; jealousy is cruel as the grave." This is from the Song of Songs,' he reflected quietly. Then he stood. 'I have to go back to the chapel, Madeleine. Forgive me.' He still held the loving cup.

'I understand.' She stood and kissed him on both cheeks. 'I'll stay here for a few minutes on my own and enjoy the stillness of this exquisite garden. I can find my own way out.'

'Are you sure?'

'Go on!' She shooed him away with her hands. 'Come and visit us soon!'

Madeleine sat down again on the bench and carefully folded the discarded brown wrapping paper.

Keira treasured her summer on Goodnight as never before. It was a relief to know that Cass was away in DC for nearly three months. She needed time on her own to think over what had happened after Mary's wedding. At Goodnight it was easy to throw all her energy into what came as second nature to her. Her father and brother, and the men, welcomed her presence on the ranch. Keira's sunny personality, sense of humour and no-nonsense attitude always injected a refreshing enthusiasm and joy into life on the ranch.

Liam wisely chose not to make a scene about her engagement to Cass Henderson, and he firmly requested that the rest of the inhabitants of Goodnight do the same. He knew that Jim Henderson would rather die than see his son married to Keira, and therefore rested in the belief that, diamond ring or no diamond ring, this was a wedding that could never be. He would let time take its course.

June was the time for irrigating and spraying the acres of arable farmland in preparation for July and August when the barley, brome, orchard, timothy and alfalfa grasses were cut and baled. Keira knew how to work the machinery and she helped Callum, Jake and Pete drive the tractors, which pulled the swathers and the balers. Bill, Joe, Tom and Jim drove the other machinery, stacking the tons of hay bales, each five feet in diameter and weighing fifteen hundred pounds, into the barns for the winter. The physical work was arduous but exhilarating, and as the sky turned fiery red in the evenings they relaxed together, drinking cold beers around makeshift barbecues by the lake, where stories, jokes and the events of the day were shared for hours on end, until the stars of the northern hemisphere filled the night sky.

At the end of July the bulls were pulled from the pastures of pregnant cows and put into separate pastures situated at the opposite end of the ranch with electric fencing. The cows were driven up into the summer pastures to graze until the first week of September. One disastrous year, bulls from a neighbouring ranch had found their way into Goodnight, and nine months later two hundred black Angus cows produced grey calves. It was an expensive accident and one Liam was not about to let happen again. Fencing had to be checked regularly, and Keira gladly volunteered.

It felt good riding out in that wide-open country where the horizons offered no limits. River could still keep up with her, despite his thirteen years, and was always careful to keep clear of her horse's heels. It was on days like these that she missed Ed most, his memory becoming ever more vivid. Seeing the blessings around her with a fresh eye and a renewed appreciation, Keira started to consider the daunting possibility that perhaps Ed had been right all along. Perhaps *this* was all she needed to still her restlessness? Not wealth, or fame, or a man with good looks and status in society, but the simplicity of living at one with nature, far away from the madding crowd.

There were evenings when she would escape, unseen, and walk over to the aspen trees and sit by the graves. She would talk to Ed and her mother about what had been happening that day. Being able to share her feelings, her doubts and her fears out loud in the stillness of that place seemed to bring a new healing to the wounds caused by their sudden deaths. They had been the two people who understood her best.

One night at the end of August, while Keira sat leaning up against the bark of a tree alongside Ed's grave, a strong breeze blew in from the lake to her right, disturbing the tranquillity of the warm, still atmosphere and causing the leaves above her to shiver and shake, rustling fiercely. The shrill, eerie sound they produced seemed to wrap itself around her, stirring her from the drowsiness of her thoughts. She sat up. The wind whistled and seemed to say, '*Go . . . don't be afraid . . . go to her . . .*' They were not spoken by a human voice, but soft, gentle words spoken around her, into her mind and into her heart, convincing her to do what she had been thinking about doing for the last few days. Getting to her feet, Keira set off resolutely towards the little cottage on the far side of the lake. But as she turned, she drew in her breath sharply, for coming towards her was a figure lit white by the glow of the evening sky. She stopped and moved back a little, shrinking into the shadow of the trees.

Joanna Whitely knelt silently by her son's grave, unaware that she was not alone. She shivered and rubbed her arms. The thin cotton wrap did little to protect her from the cooling evening breeze. Suddenly she turned her head, sensing the presence of someone else. Keira stepped out from behind the shadows and Joanna let out a short, sharp scream.

'It's me, Keira!'

Leaping to her feet, her heart pounding, Joanna wrapped her arms around herself.

'I'm sorry I frightened you,' said Keira. 'I've been here for hours. I was on my way to find you, when suddenly I saw—'

'I couldn't sleep,' interrupted Joanna, 'and I needed to come here . . . sometimes I do at night when everything is quiet.'

Keira held her gaze. 'Joanna, forgive me. Please forgive me. Ed died saving me. He loved me so much, he gave his life for me. Don't hate me for not loving him back the same way. I was young, a child. I would do anything to have him back, anything. I miss him so much.'

The tears rolled down Joanna's face and the two women clung together, their bodies trembling.

Then Joanna stepped back and searched the younger woman's face. 'I've always loved you, Keira.'

Keira bit her lip, her eyes swollen.

'You're different since you returned from Brazil.'

'I know.'

'Whatever you found there, don't let it go.'

'I already have let it go.'

'I can see that whatever it is has taken root in your heart and you'll never be the same again. Why don't you write about it, about your experiences there?'

Keira gave a short laugh and wiped her face with her hands.

'Uncle Hank keeps reminding me of an article I still owe him for his newspaper.'

Joanna took hold of her hands. 'Keira, you must write this article!'

'Yes, you're right. For some reason, I haven't been able to do it until now. Thank you for coming here tonight, Joanna. It must be past midnight and you're cold. I'll walk you home.'

Chapter 19

The Seal Over My Heart

*T*here was a light knock on the door and *Monsignor* Andre Cavalcanti glanced up from his desk where a letter and a magazine article were spread out in front of him.

'Come in!'

The wide panelled door creaked open and Solomon peered round it. 'You called for me, *Monsignor*?'

'*Sim, sim*, come and sit down.' He waved his hand, indicating one of the armchairs on the opposite side of his beautiful inlaid desk.

The spacious room with its vaulted ceiling was starkly furnished. The desk and chairs were positioned in the centre, and against the far wall stood a large armoire set between the two tall windows whose giant shutters were wide open, giving a full view of the tropical garden with all its bright colours and scents. Rays of sunshine beamed in at a sharp angle, giving the whole room an unearthly feel.

Solomon sat down uneasily.

The *Monsignor* lowered his large dark eyes to the letter in his hands. 'Each of us has something to do here on earth that can be done by no one else.' He raised his head and held Solomon's puzzled gaze. 'If someone else could fulfil your calling, then they would be in your place. Do you agree?'

Solomon frowned, his green eyes narrowing as his mind searched for the meaning behind the *Monsignor*'s words.

'I want to ask you something, Solomon,' continued the old man. 'When you read the Song of Songs, what is your interpretation?' He paused. 'Are you the beloved expressing your passion for your lover? Or are you the believer expressing your love for your Lord?'

Solomon flushed in surprise at the unexpected question. Why was he continually being confronted with the image of this book?

The *Monsignor* gave a brief smile, rose from his hard chair and walked stiffly over to the window. The shaft of sunlight struck the top of his skullcap, turning it into a shining white halo. His presence seemed all at once mystical.

Solomon shifted in his seat, dreading what this unexpected meeting might be leading to.

The old man spoke without turning round. 'Sometimes I look out of this window at the sunshine and the flowers and I am convinced that nature looks as if it wants to dance. For me it is the most intimate reflection of God's sense of beauty.' The old man watched a tiny, fluttering hummingbird dart amongst crimson bougainvillea, and then shuffled back to his desk. Edging himself down into his chair with some effort, he looked directly across at Solomon. His eyes grew serious. 'Religion has often represented the body as a vessel of evil, lust and seduction,' he sighed. 'Of course, the body deserves to be respected, to be cared for and understood in its spiritual nature. Scripture tells us that the body is the temple of the Holy Spirit.' He cleared his throat. 'So perhaps, therefore, this very theological insight shows us that the sensuous is sacred in the deepest sense. What do you think?' He raised his white eyebrows.

Solomon nodded hesitantly, his eyes wide, but he could not reply.

'Do you believe that sex and sexuality are dangerous to your eternal salvation, Solomon?'

Solomon's strong face twisted. 'I believe I have been called, like you were, *Monsignor*, to rise above my human desires. Of course, I am a man and I have all a man's weaknesses. But I am still a virgin, and when the time comes I will be prepared to take my vows.'

The *Monsignor* folded his hands together on the desk and looked at the young man over the top of his spectacles. 'But there is a struggle, Solomon, is there not?' he said gently. 'If you feel you can tell me about it, I believe I can help you.'

Solomon sat back, shocked. 'There is nothing to discuss, *Senhor*.'

'There is nothing you can tell me which will make me think less of you. You have been given physical beauty and grace. Your sufferings in childhood have enabled you to become a man of insight and wisdom way beyond that of many men twice your age. But during these past months I have known that you are wrestling in your heart, fighting against something which has almost overpowered you.' He paused again, and all that could be heard was the sound of tropical birds. 'Is it the love of a woman?'

Solomon shook his head emphatically. '*No!*' His voice sounded strangled as he tried with all his strength to subdue the volcano of emotions the *Monsignor*'s words had ignited. It was as though a sword had pierced his heart, and with one flick had cut open the padlock sealing a forbidden door.

'I fear for you, my son. I fear because I believe I can detect in you a pride. It could be that you are in love with an idea, the idea of being a priest perhaps?' He paused again.

Solomon did not move.

The old man continued gently. 'Perhaps in Sister Madeleine, who has meant so much to you in your life, you have admired an exclusiveness which you now yearn to have for yourself?'

There was silence. At last Solomon spoke.

'I respect your words, *Monsignor*, and I have to agree with you that Madeleine does mean everything to me. But I have been so sure, from the time my life was spared when I lived on the streets, that God had singled me out so that I could dedicate myself to Him as Madeleine has.' Solomon took a deep breath and looked at the sunlight that slanted across the stone floor. 'Everything was going so well, until I met a girl, an American girl, when I went back last Christmas to the *favela*. She was with a team who were building a crèche for Madeleine. When I first saw her, I cannot put into words how I felt. It was as though I already knew her, her face, her eyes . . . she seemed to capture every part of me and draw me in. I tried to avoid being with her, but it was impossible . . .' Solomon stopped and faced the *Monsignor*.

'We spent a day together. It was not what I planned. One of the team members, her boyfriend, had asked if I would show him what life was like for the people living on the streets. But he felt ill on the day and she took his place, insisting that she wanted to take pictures and write an article for her cousin's newspaper back in the United States. During the hours I was with her, I felt as if my whole world turned upside down. I took her to meet Morreno's family. It was a mistake. I must have been crazy!' He paused. 'But she amazed me, as I watched her – despite the language barrier, the culture barrier, she seemed to take it all in her stride. I should have taken her back to her hotel sooner, but I couldn't let her go. I wanted just a few more hours with her. We went to Copacabana and walked and talked until I lost all sense of time or where we were. I was able to talk to this girl I hardly knew with an openness I find hard even with my own family. I confess, I wanted to hold her, to kiss her, but I fought it . . . I fought it!' He paused again.

'I eventually took her back to her hotel and her boyfriend was waiting for her. I had to leave them as quickly as possible. It was one of the hardest things I have ever had to do. I could tell in her eyes that her life had changed through our meeting, as mine had.' Solomon shook his head slowly. 'But it's over. Over! I am committed to the priesthood. This was my last sacrifice. She has sent me many letters over these months, but I cannot open any of them.' Solomon gave a short laugh. 'One thing I did open was a parcel she sent me. Madeleine brought it here. It was a loving cup. She'd sent it all the way from Montana in the mail!' He shook his head and smiled to himself.

The *Monsignor* had not moved at all as Solomon spoke. Now he remained absolutely still, except for an eyebrow which he raised inquiringly.

Solomon continued. 'Strange, there were words from the Song of Songs printed on the cup – that's why she sent it to me.'

'What were the words, *filho*?'

Solomon spoke out the verse.

'Ah, yes, the beloved to the lover . . . this goes back to what I said earlier—'

Solomon interrupted him. '*Monsignor*, for some reason my life was spared, and in gratitude I want to serve the people who, like me, have known the sting of poverty and despair.'

'But there are other ways of serving them, my son,' said the old man quietly. 'You do not have to be a priest to help those people you love so much. You have been given a very remarkable gift of music, for example.'

'How can my music change their misfortunes?'

'Because your music is anointed, it reaches down into people's hearts. I know more about you than you realise. I have heard how these people flock to hear your music. Do you not realise how powerful a gift you have? Solomon, when you were born you were not consulted on the major issues which have shaped your life. Your identity was not offered for your choosing – where you would be born, or to whom you would be born. But you were given freedom and creativity to carry you beyond what was given and to find and fulfil that calling.'

Solomon looked down at his hands. 'My father spoke to me as he was dying. He said something to me about finding peace and not letting go. I believe that the priesthood is my vocation and I will not let it go.'

'Then I have a suggestion that perhaps will help you know for sure if you have indeed found your vocation, your calling, or if you have yet to find it. It will settle this battle in your heart once and for all.'

Solomon looked up.

The *Monsignor* picked up a letter on his desk. 'A Miss Keira Kavanagh has written to me.'

Solomon's eyes widened, and he felt the blood drain from his face. 'She's written to *you*!' he gasped.

'Indeed. It would appear that you are famous, Solomon.'

'Famous?'

Across the desk, the *Monsignor* handed him a copy of the

New York Times magazine, open at one of the inner pages. 'This *is* you, isn't it?'

'I don't understand!' Solomon was incredulous as he stared down at a photograph of himself.

'It appears that Miss Keira wrote an article for a local newspaper in Montana, where she lives, and it caught the attention of the national media.'

The colour picture of himself, playing the grand piano at the Copacabana Palace Hotel all those months ago, stared him in the face, transporting him back to that evening he had struggled in vain to forget. In his mind's eye he could still see her face as he played his father's song for her. Taking the magazine from the *Monsignor*, he read the article Keira had written. Then he looked at the other pictures which showed street children huddled together in the gutter, their small feet sticking out from under a tattered blanket.

The *Monsignor* leaned back in his chair, his kindly face tranquil, his hands folded together on his lap.

'In her letter, Miss Keira explains to me that a lot of journalists have contacted her, wanting to interview you. However, she writes that there is one national television programme in particular that wants to fly you over to America to take part in their show. She believes it is a good opportunity for you to talk about the plight of the poor in our country. She has explained to them that you are studying to become a priest, and has written to me to see if there would be a possibility of releasing you for a few days. I have taken the liberty of speaking to her on the telephone, and I have told her that I would discuss it with you.'

'*Monsignor!*' breathed Solomon. 'You have spoken to Keira on the telephone?' He was astounded.

'I have.'

'Well, what are you suggesting I do? The whole idea is impossible!'

'Nothing can be deemed impossible until it has been properly considered.'

Solomon shifted his weight awkwardly in the chair. 'You're not saying you approve of this idea, are you?'

'I not only approve of it, I have taken the liberty of telling Miss Keira that I think you should go.'

'Without asking me?'

'You would have said "no".'

'I still say "no"!' Solomon stood up, scraping his chair on the stone floor. 'Excuse me, *Senhor*. May I have your permission to leave?'

The *Monsignor*'s calm demeanour did not falter. 'I want you to go, my son. It is only for a few days. When you return, your battle will have been settled for ever. Trust me.'

Solomon slumped down again, speechless, and stared squarely at the old man. After a while he said quietly, 'When am I to go?'

'Today is Monday. They would like you to appear on the show this Friday. I am not an experienced international flyer, you understand, but I am told there is a flight from Rio de Janeiro to New York. You would have to leave on Thursday night to be there on Friday. You can fly back the following day if you can't stand to be away from us any longer! What are three days out of your life, Solomon?' The *Monsignor* rose to his feet, indicating that the meeting was over. 'There is enough time to get your passport and visa. But if you really do not wish to go, let me know after Mass this evening.'

'Very well, *Senhor*.' Solomon bowed his head in the habitual gesture of respect, and left the room.

*   *   *

Keira fixed a nervous gaze out of the window of the yellow cab and gripped the safety strap above the door as it snaked through the heavy traffic, sounding its horn every few metres. They were on 37th Street, heading uptown for Madison Avenue. Her journey had seemed like a slow nightmare from the moment her flight was delayed in Seattle. When she finally arrived at John F. Kennedy Airport, she found that the car that had been sent to meet her had left without her. Tony, the researcher from the show, had not sounded happy when she had reached him by phone from a telephone booth by the taxi rank, where an extended line of people queued with piles of luggage. He had spoken curtly to her.

'Your Brazilian friend is also running late! Right now it's 2.25 p.m. and we start recordin' with the studio audience at 5.30 p.m. There's no way the producer is going to agree to this Solomon guy playing his song on the show before they hear him rehearse. If he's not here at the theatre within the hour, your slot will have to be filled by another feature.'

Her heart sank. 'Do you know where Solomon is?'

'Lady, your guess is as good as mine. I've phoned the hotel: they say he checked in this morning.'

Keira groaned. 'Well, what should I do?'

'Grab a cab. We'll reimburse you. You'd better get prayin', though. You can't do the interview on your own!'

'Am *I* being interviewed?'

'Sure, he wants the two of you together. So hurry up and get here!'

The line went dead.

When she finally managed to secure a cab for herself, the traffic was appalling.

'Have we far to go?' Keira urged the driver for the tenth time.

In reply he glanced at the reflection of the anxious young woman in his rear-view mirror, as the mascots hanging from it swung with every jerk of the cab, and said nothing.

Keira scowled back at him and ran her hands fretfully through her hair. She looked at her watch. It said 4.04 p.m. Oh boy, she was late, really late! She tugged at the hem of her slim-cut black skirt, but it made little difference to the length. Perhaps it was too short? Her plan to check into the hotel and take a long shower before the show would have to be abandoned. Crossing her long legs, Keira seethed at the traffic. 'How can anyone stand driving in this day after day?'

'Welcome to New York, ma'am!' The driver finally spoke in a monotone as he swung the cab to a stop.

Keira leaped out, grabbing her overnight bag, and shoved some dollar bills into his hand without waiting for a receipt. The audience for the show was already forming a long line outside the entrance doors and Keira excused herself as she pushed her way to the front of it and banged on the big doors. It was opened almost immediately by a page. 'Stay in line, lady! We'll be lettin' you in soon to go to the bathrooms. At 5 p.m. you'll be going into the theatre.'

Keira felt desperate. 'But I'm on the show! And I'm running real late.'

'What's your name?'

'Keira Kavanagh. I've been speaking to Tony. Tony knows all about me.'

The page, who introduced herself as Jackie, let Keira in and shut the door on the noise of Manhattan. 'Follow me!'

Keira followed Jackie through the lobby and into the back of the audience area. The studio felt cool, but a rush of adrenaline hit her at the sight of the familiar set, which appeared smaller in real life. It consisted of a desk behind which the host of the show would soon be sitting, three armchairs for his guests and, over to the left, the position for the band. Behind hung a backdrop depicting New York at night. As she was taking it all in, a short dark man with a floppy fringe and round glasses perched on a long Roman nose appeared behind the desk.

'Better late than never!' he called to her over the rows of empty seats as she walked towards the stage. His voice sounded rather kinder than he had intended. 'Thanks, Jackie,' he said to the page, 'I'll take over from here.' He shook Keira's hand, impressed by her good looks. This was quite unexpected. 'Can I take your bag?'

'Thank you. Has Solomon arrived?' She felt her heart beating. She could hardly bear to ask the question.

'He has.'

She almost sobbed with relief. 'Was he in time to rehearse his song?'

'And record it. I can tell you, we were blown away by his talent! His English is awesome and the guy's never been out of Brazil! Awesome. Great story all round.'

Keira could not contain her elation.

Having thought his neck was for the noose, Tony was now feeling quite pleased with himself. When the magazine article had been thrown his way by the producer two weeks ago, he had felt a little offended. His speciality was booking the very famous and he made it his business to dine regularly with all the top agents in the city in order to keep abreast with what was going on and who was making news in the industry. To make matters worse, a new researcher had booked Tom Hanks and had managed to get him to appear tonight. However, Tony's eight years' experience in television had already told him that his two unexpectedly charismatic interviewees were in fact going to give the other guests a run for their money – even if they were Tom Hanks and David Hyde Pierce.

Keira followed Tony down a corridor past the prop room, the control room, the sound room and the Green Room, where guests waited to be called. People clasping clipboards, crackling radios and earphones, all with a strong sense of their own importance, dashed about in all directions. Tony placed a hot hand between her shoulder blades and urged her forward. 'You're gonna have to step on it, darlin'! You've just got time to have your make-up done and then I'll have you taken to your seat in the audience. Solomon is in his dressing room upstairs, so you won't be seeing him 'til the show. No time.'

Made nervous by the familiarity of his touch, Keira shook herself free of it, but he quickly placed his hand on her waist instead and steered her into the make-up room. As she entered, Tom Hanks stood in front of the mirror, his make-up session completed. Keira watched in awe as he politely thanked Jan, the make-up artist.

'Tom!' cried Tony. 'How you doing? Good to see ya again! This is Keira Kavanagh. She's just flown in from Montana.'

Keira felt her cheeks flush scarlet, as she found herself shaking the famous Hollywood actor's hand. She was instantly star-struck.

'Beautiful place, Montana.'

She smiled back shyly as he turned to leave the room, and sat down on the warm black leather seat as Tony introduced her to Jan. A long mirror surrounded by bright yellow lightbulbs made her blink. The platinum-blonde make-up artist got to work wordlessly, expertly selecting her tools from the vast display of brushes, foundations, powders, lipsticks, eye-shadows, eye-liners and mascaras on the red formica shelf below the long mirror.

Tony was still fussing at her side. 'He's gonna call you up from the audience once he's introduced Solomon. You'll be sitting in the front row facing his desk.' Tony moved behind Jan and put his hands on her hips. 'We've got ten minutes, darling.'

'No problem, Tone.'

'You must be Keira Kavanagh from Ovando!' bellowed an instantly recognisable voice from the doorway.

Jan was painting her right eye, but she managed to open her left one and reached out a hand that was firmly grasped and shaken by the famous TV host.

'You know what they say about the weather in Montana, don't you, Jan?' he jibed. 'If you don't like it, wait five minutes!' Jan gave a deep, rasping smoker's laugh.

'Well, Keira, you sure found a great talent there! What a waste! Bet you're sorry he's set on becoming a priest? Most of the production team are!' he laughed, slapping Tony on the back. He winked at Jan and left the room in the direction of the studio, still laughing loudly.

Tony rolled his eyes in the mirror for Jan's benefit, and pursed his lips.

As Keira was shown to her leather seat in the front row, the charged-up audience were being entertained by a stand-up comic who was giving them instruction in the art of cheering. The noise was deafening. Once he was satisfied with the volume level, he introduced the band members as, one by one, they picked up their instruments and joined in the theme tune. Towards the end of the song, the comic reappeared and whipped up loud cheers.

'Hi everybody, thanks for coming out here tonight!' He glanced over at the floor manager. 'Corky! How much time?'

'A minute fifteen.'

'A minute fifty? Good.'

'No, a minute fifteen.'

'Fifteen?'

'Yes, fifteen, well actually, one minute now!'

Keira hugged herself and wished the butterflies in her stomach would go away.

The show began.

Keira was finding it hard to concentrate. If only she and Solomon could have met and talked before the show. Suppose he was angry with her for what she had done? Here she was, about to be interviewed on national television with the man she had fallen in love with nine months ago and had not seen since. What *was* she doing? Suddenly the whole scenario seemed completely surreal.

The interview with David Hyde Pierce passed in a complete blur, apart from the moment when he spoke directly into Camera Three, which was positioned right in front of her, to reassure his dog that he would be home soon. That made her laugh.

'You're on next,' hissed Corky to Keira.

'I don't think I can do this,' her voice quavered, but Corky did not hear her and Jan appeared from nowhere to touch up her nose with a long powdery brush. The people sitting next to her stared with new interest, and wondered who she was.

If the last interview had been a blur, what happened next might as well have been happening to someone else. All at once the sound of his voice, that incredible voice she had first heard in the *favela* in Rio de Janeiro, was filling the theatre.

His face, that remarkable face, with the translucent green eyes, appeared on every screen. Keira felt a shiver going up her spine. She knew without turning that every person in that place was captivated. Surely a star had been born? In five hours' time this would be broadcast into homes across the whole of North America, and all because she had written that article.

Then he was on the set, sitting so near, dressed in a beige linen suit and white shirt. She thought his hair suited him shorter. He answered questions about his journey, about the Brazilian football team, the Grand Prix, and Brazil's latest president.

They talked briefly about his life as a boy in the mountains, and the discovery of his musical talent. 'And what a talent, eh?' There was applause and many people cheered in agreement. They talked about the sudden loss of his home, the dramatic move to the *favela* and the death of his father at the hands of the drug barons. What was life like in those *favelas* and on the streets? How many children suffered around the world like Solomon, victims of cruel circumstances out of their control? Gone was the interviewer's jaggedly sarcastic grin and assured, quick-witted jibes for quick laughs, struck out by the raw image of humanity portrayed in the testimony of this talented young man beside him. Why was Solomon becoming a priest? He did not look the type …

Keira is sitting riveted in her chair. Suddenly Camera Three swings round and focuses on her. She is up out of her seat and walking onto the stage. Is this a dream? Solomon turns, half stands up, and smiles at her. Her legs shake uncontrollably. She sits down in the chair next to him, trying desperately to compose herself, and tucks the long flame of hair behind her right ear. She glances at him, her heart flooding with emotion.

She answers questions about the weather in Montana. The host wants to make his studio audience laugh. Lighten things up a bit. If he wins them over, he will win the folks over at home. The astringent twinkle is back in his eye and he wants her to tell him how she persuaded the Grizzlies to go with her to Brazil. The startling colour photographs taken by Fin as they worked in the *favela* are flashed up on the screens. The audience recognise superstar college quarterback Cass Henderson right away. But Keira does not want to talk about Cass, and with determination steers the conversation back to Solomon and why she wrote the article in the first place. People in the West need to be aware of the perilous conditions for children living on the streets in developing countries, and do something to help! She looks across at Solomon and he is already looking at her. He smiles that special smile again, and their eyes meet and lock. The chat show host is aware that Keira has made an appeal, but he lets her get away with it. After all, he agrees with her heartfelt cry to the land of plenty on behalf of people in need – but more importantly he admires a spirited and beautiful woman. As he brings the interview to a close, he looks at the two of them and says, 'Hey, you two make a hell of a good team!'

It all seemed to be over as quickly as it began. There was another commercial break and everything and everyone was running against the clock. Corky was at her side again, ready to scoop them off stage. The audience and the band rose to their feet spontaneously, and applauded them as they left. Tony appeared from the corner of the set with Tom Hanks, who was next on. The actor gracefully congratulated them both and said he would like to buy the CD of Solomon's song once it was released.

Tony looped his arm through Keira's. 'You were wonderful, darling! The phones are already ringing with people wanting to make donations to that work in Brazil . . .' He swung round to Solomon. 'And as for *you*! Oh my!' He gesticulated with his free hand. 'A star has been born, no doubt about that. I've been in the industry long enough to know when I see one. And to think it all started on this show! How about a drink? A snack?'

'No thank you,' said Solomon firmly, 'I think I will go to the hotel.'

The researcher was clearly disappointed. 'Jeez, stay 'til the end of the show!' Tony did not want to let his new star go, but Solomon was adamant. 'OK, let me order you a car.'

'No thanks. We can walk.'

'What about your bags?'

'Mine is at the hotel. And yours, Keira?'

'It's small, I can carry it.'

Solomon shrugged on his overcoat and took Keira's overnight bag from Tony, who reluctantly showed them out of the theatre, insisting that they treat themselves to dinner. 'And don't forget to watch the show! It goes out at 11.30 tonight!'

It was already getting dark, and the yellow and orange city lights were dazzling. Taxi horns honked as Manhattan buzzed with the signs of early nightlife. They stood together outside the theatre.

'I've missed you,' Keira whispered, searching his face, wanting to touch him, wanting to be held.

Solomon stared back at her, unable to speak.

'When you sang in there, who were you singing for?'

He shook his head slowly. 'Keira, what have you done?'

The city continued to whirl around them.

'Do you know the way back to the hotel they've put us in?' Keira asked, breaking the silence.

'Yes.' He took her hand and navigated the crowded side-walk.

They walked past City Music Hall, the Rockefeller Center, St Patrick's Cathedral and Saks Fifth Avenue without Keira noticing them. All that mattered, all that she was aware of, was the warmth and intimacy of her hand in his. She wished they could walk on for ever.

'That's the hotel, over there, opposite the cathedral.'

Keira stopped suddenly, her blue eyes wide. 'Wow!'

'You think I made a mistake?'

'I imagined something smaller.'

The hotel was almost overpowering in its splendour as they entered the gated courtyard that led into the elegant lobby with majestic arches and a sweeping marble staircase. They checked Keira in at the desk and a uniformed bellboy fussed around them, taking her small overnight bag and wheeling it on a large trolley towards the elevator.

Moments later they were standing outside her room on the twenty-second floor.

Solomon turned to her, his voice strained. 'I'm sure you're tired, Keira.' He looked at his watch. 'Why don't you take a shower, and I'll order dinner for the two of us in my room. The view of the city is magnificent from there.'

Her mouth curved into a smile and she nodded in agreement, her head pounding, her mouth dry. 'That sounds wonderful.'

Solomon watched as the waiter placed a crisp white cloth on the dining table in his suite and carefully laid out the gleaming cutlery and a small arrangement of flowers. He checked his watch. She would surely be here soon. He paced across the cream carpet to the window and back again.

'Shall I leave the dishes in the heated trolley, sir, or put them on the table?' inquired the waiter.

'Um, no, no, that is fine. Just leave everything like that.'

The waiter hovered, and instinct told Solomon that a gratuity was expected.

'Oh, I'm sorry.' He thrust his hands in his empty pockets and looked at the waiter apologetically. 'One minute, please.' He walked through the sitting room into the bedroom and after a search found some dollar bills and retraced his steps.

'Thank you,' he said, seeing the waiter out of the door.

Keira was standing outside in the corridor about to knock. She had showered and changed into well-fitting jeans and a pretty organza top. Her hair was still damp after her shower and was tied up in a ponytail, enhancing her slender neckline and striking profile.

'Hi!' The sudden glow on her face as she saw him gave Solomon a rush of pleasure.

'Oh my, will you look at this!' she exclaimed as she walked across the spacious sitting room and looked out over New York City, now aglow with millions of tiny lights below.

He leaned his weight against the door and closed it. 'We have a saying in Brazil. I think the translation is, "I feel like a fish out of water"?'

She turned towards him and laughed. 'I know what you mean. We say that here also.'

'How's your room?'

'It's fine, but nothing like this.'

I'm in love, she thought to herself. *I love this man.*

'You must be hungry. Would you like to follow me into our personal restaurant?'

She followed him into the dining area with its white uphol-stered chairs that looked as though they had never been sat on. She wanted to wrap her arms around him, to press her head between his shoulder blades and never let him go. Instead she sat down on the chair he pulled out for her.

'I hope you will be happy with what I have ordered for you. I asked for some water, but they have sent up some cham-pagne!'

He picked up the bottle and popped open the cork. He poured it slowly into the two flutes.

Keira grinned. 'I thought you didn't drink?'

'It seems with you I do!' He smiled back at her. 'What is it you say here?'

'Cheers.'

'Cheers!'

Their glasses clinked together.

'Keira, I have to ask you something. I heard you were engaged to marry Cass. But you're not wearing a ring.'

Keira flushed. 'No, I'm not. I thought for so many years that Cass was the man I was supposed to love. But I was blind. While he was away in Washington this summer, I knew that it was over between us and I think Cass did too.'

Solomon began to take the dishes from the trolley, removing their silver covers, releasing the trapped steam and a delicious aroma.

'I ordered trout, because it reminds me of the mountain streams in the valley.'

'I love trout!' In spite of everything, she suddenly felt hungry.

They ate for a while in an awkward silence. Then Solomon

put down his knife and fork. He looked at her across the table and reached out a hand. She immediately put down her fork and put her hand in his.

She wanted to go to him, but was almost afraid to move in case it broke the moment. Her mind was racing, her heart pounding.

'Do you remember our day in Rio, when you told me how your friend died for you to save your life?' he asked her.

'I will never forget our day in Rio,' she whispered.

'Well, I want to tell you that I would die for you too. You are the seal over my heart, a gift I cannot let go, Keira.'

She felt as though she could not breathe.

They looked at each other for a long moment, as the impact of his words enveloped them.

Chapter 20

The Valley

*N*othing that Solomon had told her about the valley could have prepared Keira for its breathtaking beauty. It was summertime in Brazil, and the countryside was lush with green foliage and tropical flowers. Through the open windows of the car, Keira exulted in the freshness of the cool mountain air. She closed her eyes as a sudden shaft of sun broke through the leaves of the tall trees lining the narrow road. She wondered if this feeling of belonging was what Ed described to her all those years ago. Perhaps he could see her now in this beautiful place beside the man she loved. *Ed would have liked Solomon*, she thought, looking over at his strong face.

It was a year on from their first meeting when Keira flew to Rio de Janeiro again, and since Solomon had met her at the international airport two days earlier, journalists and photographers had followed them wherever they had gone. But early this morning they had managed to leave the apartment by the rear exit and head out of the city, completely unnoticed.

As they drove through the town of Correas, Solomon slowed down and stopped outside the *Escola Catolica Padre Correa*. 'This was my school. My father drove us here every morning in his Chevy. I used to sit in the back with Duke. It was a race to arrive before Sister Marilyn closed the gates.' He smiled to himself as he remembered those times. 'We were all terrified of her, except for Ze, of course.'

'I'm looking forward to meeting Ze, after all I've heard about him.'

Keira admired what she could see of the gracious white colonial house with its faded blue shutters.

'My great-great-grandfather used to live here many, many years ago before it became a school. Some of the *padre*'s servants found him in a cave in these mountains when he was a baby. The rest of his Indian tribe had been massacred by a group of armed settlers. *Padre* Correa took the child into his home, and the cook brought him up. Eventually he married one of the Portuguese estate workers.'

She felt fascinated. 'So your family's been part of this land for many centuries?'

'It's part of me.'

At a sharp bend, further on, the cobbled road became a bumpy dirt track which ran up through the small village of Bonfims. A sudden sound of rushing water made Keira gasp, and she caught her first glimpse of the magnificent Paraiso river. Children were swimming in its pools, and women knelt on its banks washing their clothes and laying them out to dry on the large boulders which lined the river. On the other side of the track, flimsy shacks and little shops and bars proclaimed the poverty of the area.

They were silent as the bumpy road wound steeply up beside the descending river for another two kilometres. Ahead of them, as far as the eye could see, stretched the massive mountain range. Solomon pulled over and stopped the car again. He switched off the engine. All they could hear now was the roar of the river and the song of a thousand birds.

323

'These are my mountains, Keira.'

She looked around her in wonder.

'Behind that hill is the place where I grew up, the place I never wanted to leave, the place of happiness. When I remember my father I remember him here, not in that *favela* in Rio.'

She touched his face gently and kissed him.

'I'm afraid it's not going to be the same place I left. I'm afraid to discover the memories have lied to me. Perhaps we should turn around. Perhaps I'm better never going back, for then my memories can remain unspoiled. They're all I have.'

'I believe nothing can steal your memories, Solomon, however much a place or the people around you change. They happened, they were real, then. Today's a new day for you. Your family, your grandfather, even your uncle, are waiting for you.'

Solomon leaned his head into her shoulder.

'I'm with you,' she whispered.

Solomon sat back in his seat and took a deep breath. He started the engine.

As they came round the hill, the valley opened out before them, and Keira saw that every inch of the undulating land was cultivated with vegetables, row upon row, field after field creating a rich pattern of patchwork.

'Can you see the pink cottage up ahead? That's where Mauricio's family and *Vovo* live. But first I want to show you where I lived.'

Several cars were parked outside the pink cottage, but nobody saw them as they drove on towards the narrow bridge which led over the river and up to his father's land.

Solomon stopped the car and got out. Keira followed him

and went to his side, as he gazed in despair over the land he had known so well. Where once hundreds of sprinklers had watered the meticulously worked acres of vegetation and sunflowers had gleamed in their thousands, there now spread out a mass of unruly, untended scrubland. She put her hand in his and he led her up the weed-filled track to the ruins of what had once been his home.

'Look, Keira, look at what that evil man has done with our land! He stole it from us, and he stole the life out of it. You cannot know what it used to be like. It was the best garden in the valley. Now it's a graveyard.'

Someone had begun a job of demolition, and half the roof was missing. There was little evidence that the house had once been painted white. A few of the old green shutters still hung from their hinges. Several planks were missing from the veranda and the remains of the mosquito door swung forlornly in the mountain breeze. Solomon thought of Duke, and suddenly he was overcome with grief. He knelt down on the overgrown driveway in front of his childhood home and wept. Keira crouched down and put her arm around him, as the unshed tears of long years found their release.

After a while he stood up and took her hand. Looking out over the land of his ancestors, the land that he knew so well, he called up into the vast blue sky, 'Father! If you can hear me, today I make you a promise! I will rebuild our home! I will replant your land! I promise you this. With God's help, I will do it. From this day on, what the locusts have eaten will be restored!'

They drove back down the hill in silence to the pink cottage.

'Solomon!' cried his grandfather, hurrying down the steps from the veranda, his arms outstretched.

They stood together for a long while, each drawing strength from the embrace. Eventually *Vovo* stepped back and looked up at his beloved grandson. 'Welcome home!' Tears ran unchecked down his face. 'Welcome home!' Then he looked around him. 'Where is she? Where is she, then?'

Keira stood hesitantly by the car in her cool white linen dress, her hair falling around her shoulders. *Vovo* stepped forward and held out a hand to the beautiful girl before him.

'*Bemvinda, minha querida. Bemvinda!*'

She took his hand and said slowly one of the few phrases she had learned in Portuguese. '*Prazer te-conhecer* – it is a pleasure to meet you.' She smiled into a face she knew she would grow to love.

He kissed her on both cheeks, then looked back smiling at the young man by her side. 'Only God could have found you such a woman, Solomon!' He put an arm around each of them.

At that moment an elderly lady dressed in a brightly coloured suit and a mass of costume jewellery came out onto the veranda. *Senhora* Francisca could not contain herself at the sight of her favourite pupil and rushed towards him down the few steps that separated them. She threw her arms around his neck. 'And this must be Keira?' She took the girl by the hand. 'You are welcome here!' *Senhora* Francisca said in her best English, kissing her loudly on both cheeks, 'Solomon loves you, so *I* love you!'

Keira smiled back at the warm, wrinkly face that was so liberally coated with make-up, and reflected that Solomon's description of his music teacher had been perfect.

'You must be proud of your pupil!' Keira spoke as slowly and as clearly as she could, and took Solomon's hand.

'Very proud! Very proud!' *Senhora* Francisca was thrilled

to practise her English, and even more delighted with herself for being able to talk to this exquisite girl from overseas. After all, she had made it her business to become a woman of culture. 'Come! You are hungry? Yes?'

Solomon recognised Pedro's blue estate car, in which he would have driven their mother, Talita and Daniel from the new apartment he had bought for them on Ipanema Beach. He felt elated that his family were a family again, living under the same roof, in a home more comfortable than they could ever have imagined. After his trip to New York, he had spent many hours with *Monsignor* Cavalcanti. As the wise old *padre* had predicted, it had become clear to him that his calling was not to the priesthood. He had come to see that he did not have to sacrifice his peace of mind in order to please God.

Vovo led the way in through the door of the house, and stood aside as Solomon and Keira walked in. Solomon's mind flashed back to his fourteenth birthday in his father's house, as the room full of people he loved set up a cheer to welcome him back to the valley. But this time he was no longer a boy. He was a man, a man who had been forced to leave childhood behind him too early, who had known great tragedy and the deprivation of life in the gutters of Rio de Janeiro. He knew what it felt like to be looked down upon by society. But now, by some extraordinary change of circumstances, he had been catapulted to the other end of the spectrum. Already he had tasted fame. The song '*Meu Amor*' had soared to number one in the US charts and in Brazil and was beginning to get airplay in Europe. Yet he knew as he stood there among his people, with the woman he loved by his side, that no amount of wealth, no amount of fame, could ever give him what he would find here back home in the beauty and simplicity of life in the valley. This was where he belonged, and would always belong.

Ze was the first to approach him, and the two old friends embraced. Ze was simply dressed in a white t-shirt and blue shorts, with several beaded necklaces and bracelets. 'At l-l-least one of us is a s-s-success!' Ze smiled, ruffling his wild hair.

'I've heard you're not doing too badly yourself! We'll have to come and visit your shop soon in Ouro Preto.'

Ze's suntanned face broke into a wide smile. 'You guys st-st-staying the night here?' Ze looked over at Keira, who was being warmly greeted by his mother, *Tia* Ana, while Talita stood close. *Senhora* Francisca acted as interpreter.

'I believe so.' Solomon smiled at Ze.

'You w-w-want to go fishing as the sun rises?'

'I don't fish any more, Ze!' Solomon grinned at Ze's sudden forlorn expression, but stopped his teasing. 'Do birds fly?' he laughed and slapped his cousin on the back.

Ze looked cheerful again.

Solomon saw that *Tio* Mauricio was standing uncertainly in the background. He left Ze and walked over to him with his hand extended. '*Tio*, I'm glad to see you again!'

Mauricio stared at his feet for a few seconds, and then raised his head and looked into his nephew's eyes. 'I'm not proud of many things I've done, Solomon. I will regret for the rest of my life not speaking to your father before he died. I miss him more than you will ever know.' Mauricio's eyes were glazed with tears. 'I've not touched drink from the day your father died.'

Solomon embraced his uncle. 'My father always loved you, *Tio*, and he knew he should have listened to you. We should all have listened to you.'

Tio Mauricio wiped his face and put his arm around *Tia* Ana, who had come to his side.

'Solomon,' said *Tia* Ana, 'today's the happiest day of my life because you've returned to us.'

'Where are Felipe and Joao Carlos?' asked Solomon, noticing their absence.

'The last we heard from Felipe, he was in Sao Paulo, and that was almost three months ago. But Joao Carlos is still with us, still not married, but as loyal as ever to Mauricio.'

Then, as Pedro clapped his hands loudly over the other side of the room, Joao Carlos entered the house from the fields, now a grown man, his hair still blond and his dark blue eyes still reluctant to make contact. He timidly greeted them, as Pedro began his speech of welcome.

Pedro was speaking loudly, his arm around his mother, whose fitted floral dress made her look younger than her years.

'. . . I would also like to welcome Keira to this family,' he continued. 'Today is a new beginning for us all. We're back together again in the valley we love, with the people who matter most to us. But before we eat, I know *Vovo* has one request . . .'

There came a familiar sound of something heavy being pushed from the old man's bedroom, and as the piano came into view, manoeuvred by Joao Carlos and *Tio* Mauricio, Solomon closed his eyes and lowered his head.

'Solomon,' said *Vovo*, 'I have kept your piano for you as I promised I would. It is still in tune, I have also made sure of that. And it has been waiting too for this day, when you would return. Play for us now, *filho*. Today would not be complete for me, unless you play for us. I am so proud of you, of what you have achieved.'

Solomon smiled at the old man he loved with all his heart. 'I thank God every day for your life, *Vovo*. And I thank you for your pride in me. I am grateful that the sales of this song have given me enough money to buy the apartment for my mother and to buy back *Papai*'s farm. But I want you to know that when I signed the recording contract, it wasn't fame or riches that I was looking for, but the opportunity to use my musical gifts to help the children in the *favelas*. Keira and I have decided to open a music school so that they can have the opportunities that my *Papai* gave me. We want to give them hope and a future.'

He sat down at the piano and as he started to play he looked over at Keira, and spoke to her in English. 'I also thank God every day for you, Keira. I love you.'

Then he turned and looked back at his mother. '*Mamae*, come and sing with me,' he said to her gently. '*Papai* isn't here with us physically, but he is here with us through this song. He wrote it for you, *Mamae*. This song that is now so famous, he wrote it for you, a love song. I believe, today, he knows we are here together again, in his valley, and he is happy. He is happy. Come and sing with me, *Mamae*, like you used to sing with *Papai*.'

As they sang Ezio's song, it was not Solomon that Isabella thought of. It was not Solomon she could see before her, but Ezio. And as she sang there were tears in that room. Not tears of sadness, but tears of forgiveness and reconciliation. They were tears of joy. They were the tears that bind families together again.

Solomon and Keira walked arm in arm down the dusty pathway which meandered through green fields, where sprinklers brought the life-giving water from the river, and passed the old ruins of the grand home that once was the summer home of the Oliveira family. Solomon wanted to take Keira to see the small white chapel up on the hill, from where they could sit and watch the sun set.

'Ed used to tell me that the reason he felt so peaceful in Montana was because he knew that he truly belonged there,' she said, as he led her up the hill. 'I can see that you feel the same way about this valley.'

When they reached the steps of the little white chapel, Keira looked around her and knew suddenly that she belonged there too.

'I always thought Ovando was the most beautiful place on earth, but this really is heaven on earth.'

Solomon turned and took her in his arms. 'That's what my mother always says.'

'Then I must be right!' She kissed him.

For a few moments they just stood there looking into each other's eyes, feeling their own heartbeats, sensing that completeness of being with the one they were born to love, standing alone, on top of the world, with the beauty of creation as their footstool.

'Will you marry me?'

Keira caught her breath, and bit her lip.

He waited, never taking his eyes from hers.

'Yes,' she said simply.

'In the Song of Songs,' said Solomon, 'the lover says to his beloved, "Like a lily among thorns is my darling among the maidens."'

'And,' whispered Keira, 'she says, "My lover is mine and I am his."'

'"I have come into my garden, my sister, my bride."' Solomon took her face in his hands.

'"Place me like a seal over your heart,"' Keira said, under her breath, '"like a seal on your arm, for love is as strong as death, its jealousy unyielding as the grave."'

'"How beautiful you are, my darling!"' Solomon smiled. Then he kissed her, and she responded, and as they kissed it seemed that something happened, something spiritual, as their two souls became one.

Solomon took her by the hand as they went into the tiny chapel. It felt cool inside. They sat down on one of its old wooden pews. There was a small altar at the front and a round, stained-glass window that lit the interior with a blaze of colour.

'I spoke to your father yesterday,' said Solomon gently.

She looked surprised.

'I thought I should speak to him before I asked you to marry me.'

'What did he say?'

'He gave me his permission, and said he was very happy for us.'

Keira's face lit up. 'Did he say anything else?'

'Well, he did say that if your answer was "yes", he and Callum would take the next flight to Rio!'

In the moments that followed, they both had the same thought.

Solomon spoke first. 'Marry me on 31 December?'

'We could marry here in this chapel!'

'I don't think I can wait any longer,' he smiled.

'Neither can I.' She kissed him, then pulled back. 'But do you think we can organise a wedding so quickly?'

'Anything in Brazil can be organised quickly, it's part of our culture. Everything's very relaxed. The wedding ceremony can be small, just our families. Perhaps we could have the party you've always dreamed about at Goodnight for all your friends over there in the New Year? Maybe your grandmother from England could fly over for that?'

'I would love her to know you. What about a party for all *your* friends, Solomon?'

'Maybe we could have a party in the city before the wedding.' He took her hand. 'Come on, the sun's setting, let's go back outside.'

They sat down on the steps and watched creation display its glory, as the blazing sun disappeared behind the horizon, turning the sky red, then orange, then black, until a million stars shone down around them like a crown of celebration over the darkened earth.

Epilogue

Shifting Sands

A full moon shone its bright light over the valley, preventing the night from dominating the earth with its darkness. Solomon was unable to sleep and walked out onto the veranda through one of the many French doors which stood open in the heat of the summer. He sank into a hammock and pushed his foot against the outside wall of the house. The hammock rocked in response. Shifting his weight a little, he leaned his head back and looked up in wonder at the glorious night sky where a multitude of stars seemed to move with the motion of the swing. Giant crickets cried out to each other across the gorge. As the hammock stilled, he left it and whistled to his three dogs. Descending the veranda steps, Solomon strolled across the well-tended lawns to the edge of his garden, and his eyes followed the contours of the mountainous horizon, illuminated so dramatically by the light of the moon. The sight seemed to feed his soul. He lifted his head upwards and spoke silent words of thanks.

One of the dogs whined at his feet, and he smiled down and stroked the animal's smooth black head. Straightening up, Solomon paused briefly, looking with pleasure at the long low outline of his home, built on the site where his father's house had once stood. He and Keira loved their weekends in the valley, he reflected, where the air was always cooler than the humidity of the city. Calling the dogs, he returned to the veranda and bid them goodnight.

He walked through the mosquito door and paused again. From where he now stood, Solomon could see his piano in the sitting room across the long hall. A sudden impulse drew him to it and he sat down on its stool. His eyes moved to the photographs of his family arranged in several silver frames on the shiny surface, lit up by the moon which shone through the tall windows. He stared at the picture of his two-year-old son, Eduardo Ezio, sitting on his mother's lap laughing at the camera. The little boy, known as Ed, was the image of her, he thought once again. In another picture he and Keira stood under a canopy at their wedding party on the Goodnight ranch. Keira's grandmother Molly, her friend George Cruikshank, Laurence and Theo and Aunt Jane were all there. Aunt Jane was raising her glass of champagne to the camera. In another, Madeleine, Keira, Coach Murphy and Cass Henderson, and some of the children with their musical instruments, were standing at the entrance of one of their new music schools on the brow of the *favela*, each pointing at a cheque held by Cass, who was now a street lawyer in Washington.

Solomon felt a rush of emotion as he thought about his charity and the schools he and Keira had set up over the last three years, giving opportunities to many children to study music as he once had at the Santa Cecilia School. He felt excitement at the thought of getting back to the city to work on their latest project. Solomon took a closer look at Cass in the photograph. He remembered a report he had seen recently on CNN about his father, the old attorney general Jim Henderson, who still refused to admit to the charges that had convicted him. The light was catching another picture now, and he moved it slightly until the glare softened. It showed his mother and father on their wedding day, Ezio and Isabella Itaborahy. They were happy in that picture, in love. But they were always in love until their world turned upside down, he reflected. They had been victims of greed and corruption, victims of a fallen world, where the fine line between good and evil seemed almost indistinguishable in places. He searched his father's face.

Then, quietly, Solomon started to play. It seemed to him that life was like shifting sands, a constant motion in man's search, in man's drive, for the meaning of existence. *Perhaps Madeleine is right*, he thought. *Perhaps it is through suffering that we change. Perhaps tears are the telescopes through which we can see into heaven.*

Then she was there with him. Keira, his love, his joy, God's precious gift. Her long auburn hair spread over her shoulders and breasts, the light accentuating her firm body, her long legs, her hips, her narrow waist, the small bump of their next child. As she moved towards him, drawn in by the love affair of the music he was making, she swept back her hair and placed her hands gently on his shoulders, bending to place her lips against his neck. The sensation sent a pulse down to the core of his body, as he was swept by a longing to be one with her again. He turned, his arm reaching up to pull her to him.

Keira lay on the rug next to the piano, her mind lost in the beauty of the music he had made; her beloved, her friend, her lover. Solomon ran his hand tenderly over the swell of her stomach and bent to caress it with his lips, closing his eyes as he felt the firm, stretched smoothness of her skin. She ran her fingers through his thick hair and pulled him to her so she could see the love in his eyes. There it was. That look, that powerful look of love exclusively for her, his eyes penetrating hers. They were so close, souls touching, bodies connecting, to give and receive so completely the love they had for one another. They rested once again in the grasp of each other's arms, drawing in the familiar smell and sensation of their skin and the sound of their breathing.

* * *

Solomon was stirred from the depths of his sleep by the sound of someone pushing a note through the shutters next to his bed. He glanced at Keira, who did not move. He lifted himself up onto his elbow and kissed her hip tenderly, then pulled the white cotton sheet up to her shoulders. He swung his legs over the edge of the bed and took the note. He knew who it was from.

As he reached the pools below the waterfall, an orange sun was rising in the valley below and everything seemed tinged with shades of pink and gold. Solomon looked out across the moving river to Ze, who was fishing with his bare hands.

'Hey! No rod today?'

'Solomon!' Ze yelled back above the noise of the waterfall. 'Get the net! Today's the day!'

Solomon ordered his dogs to stay put on the bank, kicked off his sandals, threw down his tackle, grabbed the net and ran with perfect precision from rock to rock. All at once Ze stood, triumphant, spun around and with all his strength threw the fish high into the air while crying out at the top of his lungs. The two friends laughed, their heads thrown back, as time shut down into slow-moving frames and the flying fish, swinging its large head and tail in opposite directions, flung hundreds of thousands of drops of water like stars into the atmosphere.

Acknowledgements

*M*y gratitude to my readers Julie Jarman, Diana More and Janette Davidson, who each pored over the manuscript and helped to make it a better read. I also thank Cida Mattar, Dominic Coleman, Carol Salter, David Aikman, Fenella Briscoe, Susan Philips, Andrea Smith and my children Lucas, Daniel and Jessica for their encouragement, prayers and good advice.

I thank those of you who helped me with my research in Montana, Rio de Janeiro and Sunderland – you know who you are! I had such fun in Helena with Dana McCoy, Nick Jacques and Jacquie Bennett, and I loved riding out on the scenic ranches in Ovando with real cowboys. Thank you to my Brazilian friends Luiz Flavio and Silvia Guimaraes, for first taking me to those beautiful mountains above Petropolis in Rio de Janeiro – it was on that visit that the initial seeds of this story were sown. Thank you, Mum, for your great company in Sunderland and for your incredible encouragement, advice and input from the very beginning.

Many thanks also to my editor Elspeth Taylor, for really understanding this project and for your keen eye and editorial gifting. And a very big thank you to my publisher, Hodder & Stoughton.

Finally, I am so grateful to all those precious children I have had the privilege of knowing through my years working in Brazil with Happy Child – like Solomon, victims of circumstances out of their control. Their courage and ability to overcome adversity are an inspiration.

www.happychild.org
www.180degreesalliance.org

Sarah de Carvalho

In 1991 Sarah de Carvalho left her well-paid media career in London to live and work among the street children in the slums of Rio de Janeiro. Sarah went on to found Happy Child Mission which is dedicated to providing physical, educational and spiritual care for street children. Today, Happy Child runs nine homes in two major cities in Brazil and has rescued, rehabilitated and reintegrated over 8500 children. She is also on the steering committee of 180° Alliance – united global action with street children – which was founded in 2005. She is married with three children and lives in Surrey.

Questions for Book Clubs

1. *'You have to search for the key to the song of your life, and when you find it, don't let it go.'* How does this metaphor apply to the lives of both Solomon and Keira? Can you identify with the expression yourself – what is the key to your song?

2. Keira sees romantic love as the 'key to the song of her life'. What is it about Solomon that is so different from Cass, and why can't Cass be her 'key'?

3. Solomon's grandfather says that Solomon's musical gift carries responsibility with it. How do people respond to his music and how does he use his gift at different stages of his life?

4. Occasionally Solomon has a sense of a guardian angel protecting him, or a voice speaking to him. How much does a sense of a 'higher being' impact his life?

5. The 'Song of Songs', from the Old Testament, is referred to and quoted at various key moments in the novel. What point is the author making about love and intimacy through these references?

6. After so much turmoil, what elements do you think are most important in helping Solomon and Keira find a sense of peace in their lives by the end of the book?

7. In the book Madeleine has chosen the street children over the prospect of marriage. Do you think such self-sacrifice is admirable or foolish?